CHANCEY FAMILY LIES

2

CHANCEY FAMILY LIES

2

KAY DEW SHOSTAK

August South
PUBLISHING

ISBN: 978-0-9962430-2-5

Library of Congress Control Number: 2015912983

SOUTHERN FICTION: Women's Fiction / Small Town / Railroad / Bed & Breakfast / Mountains / Georgia / Family

Text Layout and Cover Design by Roseanna White Designs
Cover Images from www.Shutterstock.com

Published by August South Publishing. You may contact the publisher at:
AugustSouthPublisher@gmail.com

To Mama and Daddy
The happiest couple I know

And

To Rev. Peggy Little
For Thankful Sunday

Chapter 1

"No. Ricky cannot stay with us. He *is* still your boyfriend, right?"

"You don't care if you ruin my Thanksgiving, do you?" Savannah accuses me with one eyebrow shooting for the ceiling and a hand planted on her costume-covered hip, a costume I'd just finished pinning up the hem on.

That's why I'm kneeling on the floor at her feet, not because the pink, taffeta princess dress has moved me to express my undying loyalty to my sixteen-year-old daughter. I'm determined to do the whole stay-at-home-mom-best-holiday-ever thing. But, the month since quitting my job at the library has been a blur.

How is it possible to give up a full-time job and have life get busier? Not to mention, more confusing? We've lived here since summer, and still no one tells me what's going on in our tiny piece of small-town heaven. Like why there's a princess in the Thanksgiving show or whatever it is?

Yes, I am trying to listen more and not be so sarcastic. But it's not working.

My shoulders drop, and I blink several times at the chaotic kitchen around me. A raw, still-frozen, turkey, bags of stale bread cubes, a bushel basket of sweet potatoes (yes, a full bushel basket), pins and needles for tailoring, and Ricky's motorcycle helmet.

I stand up. "You're right. I don't care. I don't care so much that you can hem your own costume, clean up this mess and fix Thanksgiving dinner for your father, brothers, and grandparents." With my mouth tightening, I go to the refrigerator and fling open the door. There has to be something in here that will make me feel better. I grab a Diet Coke and hear mumbling behind me, so I turn. "What did you say?"

Innocence blooms in her sky-blue eyes, "Nothing."

My glare shows I don't believe her as I close the refrigerator and stomp into the living room where a bowl of candy corn wants to be my friend. I plop onto the couch, throw a few of the yellow, white, and orange triangles in my mouth and chase them with a swig of Diet Coke. The combination results in a mouthful of not exactly pleasant fizz, but it's different and something one only experiences this time of year. Everyone knows tradition squeezes all the calories out, right?

Savannah joins me in the living room and also grabs a handful of candy corn. She sits in the chair next to the window. She lifts up a piece of candy and examines it. "I only like the yellow part of the candy corn."

"Oh, so that's you leaving nubs of half-eaten kernels around the house. I thought we had a deranged mouse." I try thinking if I've ever eaten *part* of a piece of candy corn. Shoot, I don't think I've ever eaten just one. "Where's Ricky?"

"Out back with Bryan."

"You pushed your boyfriend off on your little brother while you asked if he could stay here?"

She pulls her long, dark hair back and smiles. "I told him it would be best."

"So you knew I'd say no." I bite off the tip of a piece of candy corn to see if it tastes different.

"I figured it wouldn't help to have him standing right here."

"So what's going on at his house that he can't stay there?"

"His mom is coming for Thanksgiving to meet Ronnie's girlfriend/fiancé/whatever and his mom's staying there." Savannah sighs and lies back in her seat, placing her fistful of candy on her stomach to sort through. "Ricky says when his mom comes, either she and his dad fight the whole time, or well..."

Forget trying to discern a different taste. I eat the rest of the candy corn in my hand and then have to fight the urge to reach over and eat the pile of orange and white pieces she's leaving. What is it about wanting to clean up my kid's leftovers? I realize she's looking at me like I know the rest of the story about Ricky's parents. "What? They fight or they what?"

She purses her lips and stares at me, eyes wide with meaning.

"What? I don't get what you're saying."

"Well, they, well, they *were* married, you know."

"Savannah, I don't know what you're trying to say, and I've got too much to do to sit here playing guessing games." I stand and pick up the various pieces of newspaper strewn around the room.

Yes, I promised to try and listen to my kids more, but it's just so much work.

Work on top of the work needed to keep this place going. Housecleaning has never been my strong suit, and now I have to clean for strangers? People pay money for one of the three train-themed rooms, mostly because they want to see the steady stream of trains on the bridge outside, but they kind of like clean sheets, shiny bathrooms, and floors they won't ruin their socks on just by walking on them.

"You are to clean the B&B bathroom. And clean it good. With sponges and cleaning stuff. Do it right."

"Okay."

She's not moved so I stop, arms loaded with papers, and try again. "So his mom and dad's fighting still really affects him? How long have they been divorced?"

"Mom, the fighting is bad but not as bad as when they get along. When they get along reeeeaaaallllyyy well." She pierces me with her eyes as her head bobs lightly.

"Oh." I blink. "Oh. No way." My knees fold and ease me onto the couch.

"Yes, way. Drives him crazy because he never knows how it's going to be. If they get along, his dad gets all moony and love-sick. He starts talking about her coming back and them being a family, but..."

I grimace. "But it never works out that way."

"Nope. So Ricky said he's going to clear out. He figured if he stayed here, there'd be fewer questions from his mom than if he stays at either of his aunt's houses."

"Why would there be fewer questions if he stays at his girlfriend's house?" I stand back up. "Never mind. I don't want to know that. He'll just have to figure out something else. For crying out loud, he's the town's quarterback. Lots of folks would want to have him stay with them. I have enough to deal with expecting your grandparents, your brother Will, and whomever he drags along. I can't handle Ricky's problems, too. Especially if it means getting in the middle of his family fights. Remember, his aunts are my friends and business partners."

Savannah dumps her sugary discards on the arm of the chair, stands up, and stretches. "Do I really have to hem my costume by myself?"

I just look at her. She couldn't thread a needle, much less stitch a hem. "Of course not. When you take the dress off, leave it on my bed." I throw all the papers on a stack by the front door. "And don't leave those chewed up pieces of candy laying there."

"When are Grandma and Grandpa getting here?"

"Sometime tomorrow. They'll be here in time for your show. You can try explaining to them why there's a princess in the community Thanksgiving celebration thing."

"Sure, after someone explains it to me. Mrs. Shields just gave me the dress and told me to show up for rehearsal tonight. Well, I'll get changed and then go tell Ricky he'll have to suffer with his mom and dad this weekend." She lifts the skirt of the taffeta dress high and ascends the stairs. The puff sleeves are droopy, and she's wearing flip flops, but she carries herself like royalty.

I tilt my head to get a better look and see her face. It's animated in pantomimed conversation and then, at the top step, she reaches forth her hand as if Prince Charming has asked to escort her to her chambers.

My smile stretches wide, and I turn into the kitchen. Almost a woman, still such a little girl. I sigh when I get a look at the mess in the kitchen. That's right. She gets Prince Charming; I get Tom Turkey.

The phone is crammed between my hunched shoulder and ear as I lean over the sink peeling bright orange sweet potatoes. I hit the first number saved in my phone, which is Laney Shaw. She's first in the list because she set the list up when she was here one day doing B&B stuff while I was at my library job. She's good for a lot of things like wearing crowns, sharing her hometown gossip, and she's actually better at technology than anyone else I know over the age of thirty. That's why she handles the computer and phone issues here at the B&B. Her sister, Susan, is a whirlwind and always on the go, so Laney and I let Susan do all the errands and shopping for the B&B. Which leaves cleaning to me. Yea, me. "Hey Laney, you want some sweet potatoes?"

"Depends. Are they the ones with the little marshmallows on top or with the brown sugar and nut topping? Mama makes the pecan ones for Thanksgiving, and Susan always brings just plain old baked sweet potatoes. Like what's the point of plain sweet potatoes. So, I could do with some topped with those little marshmallows. What kind are yours?"

They're the kind that's hard, lumpy, and unpeeled. Why would I be offering you an already made dish?"

"Because you love me and know I adore sweet potatoes?"

I laugh but then realize she's serious. Beauty queen is as the beauty queen does. "Why did I even call you? I should've have known you don't handle raw vegetables."

"Now, Carolina Jessup, I've placed many a cucumber slice on my eyes. They do wonders for looking bright. Why don't you come over and help me decide what to wear tomorrow night?"

"Yeah, right. I have all kinds of company descending on me tomorrow. I want to cook our Thanksgiving meal from scratch, and…wait. Tomorrow night? What's tomorrow night?"

Through the phone, I practically hear Laney rolling her big, *purply* blue eyes at me. "Honey, the town always puts on our Thanksgiving Festival on Thanksgiving Eve. Big dress rehearsal is tonight. So, you've not heard anything about it at all? No one's told you anything?

"About the community thing?"

"Yeah. I'm sure they've asked Savannah to be in it. And Bryan too, right?"

"Why would Bryan be in it?"

"Peter has him and Grant and a bunch of the junior high boys doing the scenery, using all this junk from the museum. At least, that's what Susan says, and she should know. She's been down there every spare minute this week and right now, Tuesday afternoon, is the worst."

"Yoo hoo! Remember we're new here? We don't just *know* this stuff. Shocking as it is, up 'til now my night before Thanksgiving tradition was fighting over pies at the grocery store bakery window because I forgot to place an order. But, hey, someone's beeping in and if it's Jackson I need to talk to him. I'll talk to you later."

Grime from the potatoes covers the phone as my fingers search for the right button. "Hello?"

"Hey there." Jackson comes in clear. "You left a message for me to call you?"

"Yes, you need to go to the store on your way home."

"Uh, that might be a problem."

"Why?"

"They're not going to get done tonight. I won't be home until tomorrow some time."

"No, you've got to come home tonight. You know what my mom will do when she sees this house in such a mess, and I can't get all this stuff ready for dinner and clean."

Yes, I'm whining. The reason I'm whining is because I don't think breaking down and sobbing will work. Whining probably won't work either, but I've got to do something besides panic. Nothing is going as planned. One side of the sink is lined with peels, the other side full of potatoes. I've only gotten three peeled. They are so hard and the peels don't come off in long strips, it's more like I'm chipping the skins off.

"I told you I might get stuck out here."

"But I ignored that. I distinctly remember ignoring that." I swallow the pouts and whines because I know he'd rather be here than there. Even if he has to clean. "Okay, it'll be okay. Has to, right? By the time they all get here tomorrow, things will be okay. Savannah is helping and when Will gets here, he'll help. He'll probably get here earlier than Mom and Dad."

"Honey, I really am sorry. Just can't be helped. You can't make concrete harden with wishes."

"I know. I know. I just wanted some time here with you before it got crazy. Oh, and the stupid turkey is hard as a rock. What if it doesn't defrost in time?"

He laughs. "It will. It will."

Travel is part of his job now, and every time I think I'm

13

getting used to it, I have a day like this where I want him here. Not there, wherever he is. "Where are you? The reception is great."

"Other side of Chattanooga. The bridge supports are taking longer than planned and trying to keep the railroad and highway guys from killing each other is a job. I hate when we're all trying to work in the same space."

"Honey, I've gotta go. Someone just rang the doorbell. I'd let Savannah get the door, but that's just so beneath Her Majesty. Love you. Bye." I drop the phone on the counter as I hear him say he loves me and will call later. I push on the water and wash the potato dirt and orange coloring off.

Making my way to the front door, I wipe wet hands on my sweat pants, which are stuck to my sweaty legs. I step over a case of water, around full grocery bags, and Bryan's school bag just to get out of the kitchen. Suddenly, my feet are surrounded by two mops. Barking mops, or maybe really yapping. I look up to find my parents standing in the doorway.

"Sweetie! Door was open so we thought we'd just let ourselves in when you didn't answer." My mother is petite, but her smile is always huge. Her turquoise shirt is open at the neck where she has a scarf of gold and white tied. Her lipstick and hair are perfect.

Now I'm really sweating. "I thought y'all were coming tomorrow?"

Mom comes toward me with open arms. "But we couldn't wait to see you. And look how excited the twins are." She kneels down and lifts a mop under each arm.

"The twins?"

My father is tall and reminds me of Michael Caine, except his accent is pure Tennessee hillbilly. I know. It's always messed with my mind, too. "Darlin', meet the twins, Pitty Pat and Prissy."

"Where did they come from?" I'm not an animal person. No

one is shocked, right?

We bought them in Maryland on our way home. Since," Mother hesitates then leans toward me whispering, "Since Melanie passed on, Ashley's been lonely." We all look down and there, still stationed by the door is Ashley. Mom and Dad's Boston terrier.

"Hi, Ashley." I bend down, and he stately walks to my outstretched hand for a greeting. I see suffering in his sad, black eyes. The mops are still yapping, and I can't help but think he envies Melanie. Poor dog, his new playmates are psychotic dust collectors.

"Oh look," Savannah exclaims from the top of the stairs. "They're adorable." She bounds down the steps and wraps her arms around Grandmother and dogs.

"Goldie, our granddaughter thinks we're adorable." Dad says as he leans in to kiss Savannah's cheek.

"Of course you're adorable, but these girls are, too?"

The twins scramble into her arms. Tiny pink tongues dart all over her face, and she laughs as she collapses on the couch with her new friends.

Ashley and I exchange looks of disgust.

"So. You're here early. I'm afraid…" I open my hands toward the mess. "I'm afraid I wasn't quite ready for you."

"Now, don't you worry." My father comes over and squeezes me in a one-arm hug. "We're not company. This place looks great, and I bet your view is something else. You got any coffee on?"

My parents have consumed regular coffee all day and evening long my whole life. Maybe that's why they always look so good and are so happy, permanent caffeine high. They never stop drinking it, so they never come down.

"I'll put on a pot right now. Won't take a minute. I'll holler for Bryan and let him know you're here."

With the coffee brewing, I step out onto the back deck. Bryan and Ricky are down at the edge of the woods messing with an old row boat Bryan and his friend Grant found at the river and dragged halfway up the hill. Our house is an old, three-story home on a hill overlooking the river to the back. At the front, we sit next to a double-line railroad track. The railroad bridge crossing the river is fairly new, and the old one has been turned into a walking bridge. The two bridges make this a sort of Mecca for railroad buffs. And now they also come to stay at our B&B.

Since a train is coming across the bridge, I know I'll have to wait for it to cross before the boys will be able to hear me. At the deck-railing leaning and watching the train, I can only shake my head at all my plans for today and tomorrow. How the house would look when my parents got here. Our perfect first Thanksgiving in our new home, our new town. Oh, well, why should my plans start mattering now?

"Bryan, your grandparents are here. C'mon in. You too, Ricky." The boys lope up the hill. Ricky pauses to wipe his face with his shirttail and then jogs to keep up with the thirteen-year-old Bryan, who dashes past me and into the living room. I wait for Ricky.

"I was planning on at least being clean when I met them, Mrs. Jessup."

"Yeah, me, too." I say with a raised eyebrow as I wave him on inside then follow. My hair feels stringy, my face oily, and my clothes sticky.

Bryan, my Mom, Savannah and the twins are all piled on the couch. Dad is watching them from the chair by the front window. When we enter the room, he stands. "Ah, Ricky, good to finally meet you. That film from the Douglasville game was something else, young man. You have some arm on you." As Dad shakes that arm, he pulls in closer. "Make any decision on those college offers, yet?"

I sit on the arm of the couch, "What offers?"

Mom pipes up, "You know, Ricky, Valdosta has a great

reputation for doing well in their division."

Turning, I stare at the woman sitting with my children, obviously not my mother. "Valdosta?"

Savannah talks at one of the mops in a baby voice, "But at Georgia State the program is new, so he'll get lots of playing time."

Mom laughs. "You're just saying that because you're interested in the theater program at Georgia State."

"And Bryan, the museum looks wonderful. I can't wait to get a guided tour." Dad sits back down. "Peter's done a great job. I brought those books I told him about. We're going to get together to talk about them."

I feel like a stranger who has walked in uninvited to a party I planned.

Ricky kneels in front of Savannah and plays with the dog she holds, "So is this Pitty Pat or Prissy?"

"Okay, that's enough." I stand up and cross my arms. "No one else says anything until you all explain how you know all this about each other."

"Facebook." More than one says.

"You're on Facebook?"

Mom nods and her smile brightens. "It's wonderful for keeping up with the kids. Why aren't you on it?"

I know my mouth is hanging open, but closing it would require something in my brain to work and it's not. It's frozen. My parents are on Facebook?

"I'm, uh, I'm going to take a shower." I walk through the room, up the stairs, and into my bedroom. I close the door, get undressed, and step into the shower.

This day began with me feeling I would eventually get ahead of everything. Now I know that's crazy. I'm so far behind, in so many ways, I must be walking backward.

Chapter 2

Shower helped. Hair blown dry and sweat-free clothes on, I feel better. Hands buried deep in the pockets of my jean skirt, I venture down the stairs and once again into the living room. They are all still seated much like before, but there are bags of chips and apple cores lying around the room.

Dad sits back in the chair by the window. His long legs crossed. In front of him, a bowl of peeled sweet potatoes resides on a kitchen chair. "There she is. I peeled those potatoes you had in the sink. I didn't know if you wanted the ones in the basket done, or if they're for later."

"Thanks. No, I'm trying to get someone to take the rest of them off my hands. I see we've had snacks."

"We ate all the chip dip," Bryan offers. "And we couldn't find anymore."

"Looks like y'all wore the twins out." I point to the two piles of white on either side of Ashley. Ashley lays near the center of the room with his back legs splayed out and his black eyes still wondering what horrible thing he's done to be subjected to this.

Ricky pulls himself off the couch and then pulls at his short hair, which is already spiked. "I gotta go. Nice to meet you." He nods at Mom and Dad and scoots around the end of the couch opposite where I stand.

"Honey?" At my mother's voice, Ricky's shoulders drop, and he stops his progress to the door. I expect to see Mom's face turned toward him, but she's addressing me.

"Yes?" I answer but watch Ricky. He stands there without turning back toward us, like he's waiting for something.

"Honey, we told Ricky we'd love to have him stay here this weekend. I hope that's okay with you."

"Mother, it's not okay."

Her blue eyes flicker at me, and I'm reminded of Savannah, who has quietly sunk into the couch next to her grandmother.

"I told Savannah that earlier. She must've forgotten to mention it."

Mother stands, and her pink lipstick is as perfect as it was when she first got here. She lays her hand on my arm and leans close. "Yes, she did tell us, but we'd love the opportunity to get to know Ricky better. She grins at me and winks. "Your father and I promise to chaperone. Don't we, Jack?"

"Oh, like these two need chaperones. You've got two responsible young people here, Carolina. Won't it be fun? Like an old-fashioned house party."

I groan. "Don't say it, Dad."

He says it. "Like the barbeque at Twelve Oaks. Did you know Ricky's never seen *Gone with the Wind*?"

Mother's eyes shine like Scarlett's eyeing the curtains for dress material. "We're all going to watch it tonight. Isn't it marvelous we got here early?" She lifts her clutched hands to her chin. "Popcorn and lemonade. Bryan you can invite your friends also."

The boy/man sprawled in the middle of the floor rolls over and looks at me. "Do I have to? Sounds kinda lame."

"Lame? Son, you know better than that." Dad leans forward. "You loved watching it with Grandma and me when you came in the summers."

"I never saw it. I always fall asleep when that girl is sitting on the porch talking to those wimps."

"Oh, Bryan." Mom waves her hand at her grandson. "That's just because you were so young. You'll love it tonight. I'm sure."

I hear the front door creak as Ricky tries to slowly pull it open.

"Ricky, do you honestly feel the need to stay here this weekend?"

He turns around and shoves his fists into his jean pockets. "Well, Mrs. Jessup, I don't guess I *need* to stay here, but…well I sure don't like how things are looking at my house."

"You don't think your parents will want you there?"

"Honestly? I don't think they'll know if I'm there or not. Savannah says she told you how it is with them?"

I sigh and catch my Dad's stare and his nod.

"Sure." My additional sigh lets everyone know this is against my better judgment. "Okay, you can stay in the Chessie room."

The solid-built quarterback releases a big breath. "Really? I appreciate it. I really do."

Savannah leans back and lays her hand out toward him over the back of the couch. He reaches forward and holds it for a minute. She offers me a smile. "Mom, I have rehearsal tonight, so we're not going to start the movie until I get back."

"You kids have school tomorrow. I know it's only a half-day, but you still have to get up."

Ricky opens the door. "And I have a paper due tomorrow, so I've got to go. Thanks again, Mrs. Jessup." He waves and steps onto the porch. The screen door slams behind him.

"I know. We'll have a movie marathon." Mother moves to sit on the arm of Dad's chair. "We'll watch it an hour at a time over the week and weekend. Oh, that's even better."

"Whatever, but I've got things to do first and so do the kids." I kick at Bryan's feet. You have vacuuming to do and, Savannah? The bathroom?"

Savannah leaps up. "Yep. I'm going right now." She brushes

past me and pats my arm. "Thanks. It really means a lot to him."

"You two just better behave. You hear me?"

She nods and heads toward the wing off the kitchen where the three B&B rooms and their bathroom are.

"Ricky moved our stuff into the Orange Blossom room. Hope that's okay?" Dad asks as he stands up.

"Sure. Mom had said on the phone that was the one she wanted to stay in first."

"Honey, it's just as you said, so bright and cheery with the white cotton curtains and comforter. And that quilt is so kitschy! Looks just like a map they might've handed out to all those rich northerners who rode the Orange Blossom Special in the 1920s. The room is like being bathed in sunshine, and Savannah turned on the CD player. How ingenious of the kids to find all those different versions of that song."

Dad puts his arms around Mother, who is still perched on the chair arm. "Of course, course I prefer the Southern Crescent room. Much more manly." He pulls his bride of fifty- two years to him and nuzzles her neck. "We might have to just check out each room before we leave, right, sweetie?"

"Shhh!" Mother laughs and lays her hand on his thigh. "You behave yourself, or you'll be sleeping out in the motor home."

Bryan rolls his eyes at me and pushes up off of the floor. Yet, behind his rolling eyes is a smile. I match it and swat at him as I turn to the kitchen and the disaster there. One thing about my parents already being here is that now I can't get everything ready for them. They've seen the mess.

"Here's the potatoes." Dad follows me into the kitchen. He searches for a clear place to sit the bowl but doesn't find one.

I take the bowl and set it down in the sink. "I have to wash them off anyway."

"You want me to cut them up? They're easier to cook that way."

"Sure. I didn't know a bushel was so many. I was at a roadside stand yesterday and when they asked if I wanted a bushel, I said yes because I thought that was one of those little baskets sitting on the table.

"They'll keep a long time. Just put them down in the basement where it's cool and dark."

"Really?"

"Sure, we used to buy a bushel from your Uncle R.C. when we'd go to North Carolina. Don't you remember?"

I try to remember, but nothing comes to me. I load my arms with boxes and bags from the table and begin filling the cupboards.

"Sorry we got here a day early, but we just couldn't wait to see this new venture of yours and Jackson's."

"I guess if I'd thought about it I would've realized you'd be here early. How was Maine? I haven't really talked to y'all since before you left."

"Oh, the fall colors were amazing. We loved the Fryeburg Fair." He stopped cutting to look at me. "That's the big fair in Maine we were talking about last summer. There are thirty-thousand camping sites. The crowds were huge, but we loved it." He turns back to the sink and his chore. "We met up with Bob and Libby Parks. They were up there visiting his son and daughter-in-law. It was fun to travel a bit with them, but they can get old quick. You remember them, right?"

I nod and stretch to wedge a box of macaroni in place in the shelves above the oven. "Oh, yeah. They were the story that summer before they got married. Everyone was so panicked about the two divorcees shacking up on his boat out at the marina."

"Now how come you remember that, but you don't remember the sweet potatoes?"

We laugh, and I lay a hand on his shoulder. "The women never held whispered, all-night chat sessions on the dock about sweet potatoes, but Bob and Libby starred in many of those talkfests. And I can't help that my bunk window opened dockside."

"And here we thought you were too busy reading to hear anything. So the kids said Jackson should get home tonight?"

"Naw. He called a little earlier, and they won't get done until tomorrow."

"He's liking it, though?"

"Yeah, he does. Neither of us are crazy about all the travel he does, but if he's happier." A shrug ends my sentence.

Dad rinses off his hands and picks up a kitchen towel lying by the sink to dry his hands. "And you're not at the library anymore?"

"Nope, we're going to make a go of the B&B. We already have a lot of bookings for next year."

"Well, the setting here at the railroad bridge makes for great scenery. I don't understand the fascination with trains, but then a lot of folks wouldn't want to travel around in an RV." He lays the towel down. "Let me go see what your mother is up to. She went out to bring in a few things when I came in here. And you're sure it's okay we stay in one of the rooms instead of the motor home?"

"I'm sure it's fine. Ricky's going to be in the Chessie room. Will's claimed the spare room next to Bryan's bedroom on the second floor, so, even with everyone here, the Southern Crescent room is still empty."

"We'll get the tour when we're settled." He leaves the kitchen and crosses the living room.

Where I'll put all the groceries surrounding me is worrisome. Full cabinets block my every attempt at squeezing one more box onto the shelves. Maybe when I get better at cooking I'll not have to buy all new ingredients for every recipe. One calls for all-purpose flour; another wants self-rising. Powdered sugar, white sugar, light brown sugar, dark-brown sugar all made the cut. Cool whip and whipping cream and heavy cream; corn oil, vegetable oil, and olive oil; pecans, walnuts, and almonds—surely some of this is interchangeable? My logical, librarian mind pulls up a flashing red alert every time I consider messing with a recipe's directions laid out in beautiful black and white. "If there was an appropriate substitute, you'd have been informed," is what the warning says.

A quick knock on ol' Tom Turkey says he's not ready to come out and play.

"No one answered your knock, did they?" Dad laughs and nods at my knuckles still tapping the plastic stretched around the frozen bird. He's carrying a large suitcase and a hanging garment bag.

"How long will it take to thaw this thing out?"

"Just put it in the refrigerator. You still got tonight and all day tomorrow and tomorrow night."

"I don't have any room in there. It's packed. But it's frozen. Why does it need to be in the refrigerator?"

Dad stops and tilts his head at me. "Uh, that's a little long to leave it setting out. Don't want to give everyone salmonella. How big is that thing, anyway?"

"Who knew all that would be left this week are huge ones? And there is no other store. It's like twenty-two pounds." My squeaking voice tells me panic is my next stop.

"Whew, that's a big one. But you can't leave it out. It's getting into the high sixties tomorrow. You got a friend with an extra fridge?"

"Yes. That's it!" I whirl around looking for my purse and keys. If I've seen one, I've seen a dozen extra refrigerators sitting in garages and on carports in Chancey. Now, just to remember where they are and to find one with extra room.

Chapter 3

My friends can't be found. Neither Susan nor Laney are at home, and Missus is a last resort. Luckily, Missus is out raining on someone's turkey parade and FM answers my knock on their back door. And even luckier? He has room in their extra refrigerator which sits in their back room off the kitchen.

"Back door's not usually locked, but here's a key just in case. Come on in and get it when you need it." FM pulls out on his suspenders and rocks to and fro. "From the size of that turkey looks like you're planning on a crowd for dinner Thursday."

With the germs beat and Tom safely deposited in the Bedwell's refrigerator on their screened porch, I take a deep breath. "Yeah, shaping up that way. You all staying in town?"

"Shoot, we're still fighting that one out. Missus plum wants to go all the way on the other side of Atlanta. Her sister's daughter is having everyone over there to her McMansion. I can't stand the thought of being in that vulgar Taj Mahal squeezed into that pitiful neighborhood of little ranch homes. I sure wouldn't be in no thankful frame of mind. And they always have something weird, like steak or spaghetti." He shakes his head. "Ain't goin'."

"You want to stay here?" my arms shake from carrying

around that frozen lump. I fold them across my chest and perch against the back porch railing.

"Heck no. Me and Peter are pulling for going over to my aunt's in Cartersville. Food will be incredible, and we can watch football all day. But Missus, well she don't like my aunt's tradition of inviting all her ex-husbands and their families to dinner."

"How many exes does she have?"

The gleam in Mister's eye matches his grin. "Five and she had kids with every one of 'em and they'll all be there, too. Sometimes you forget to watch football 'cause the sparring at the dinner table is so good."

"Five! And they all come for dinner? What do their new wives say about that?"

"None of 'em every remarried. Aunt Pru makes other women pale in comparison. Right this minute any one of them men, and probably a dozen more in town, would marry her tomorrow. It's like a never-ending Dating Game with her, and she's sixty-one. She's real religious, so she's a big believer in marriage. For a while she had a problem with divorce, but then she decided if God can love the sinner and hate the sin, she'd choose the sin of divorce. She says it's just like being addicted to alcohol, drugs, or food."

"Is she married now?"

"Yep, she and Josiah got married on her forty-ninth birthday. They had twins on her fiftieth birthday and her last baby was born the next year."

"No way."

"Yep. All her kids and grandkids will be there and their fathers. It's a blast. Missus just doesn't get it. What more could you want for a family holiday?"

"I can't imagine." With a wave of the key clutched in my hand, I walk down the porch steps slowly, looking back toward him. "Thanks again. You really saved me. I'll come get the turkey Thursday morning." My brain clicks on something he said. "Hey, wait a minute. She's your aunt but she's only sixty one?" my forward progress halts.

"Yep." Mister leans against a white porch post trimmed in salmon and gray. Even in the back, their big antebellum house is perfectly maintained. "Momma had fourteen of us, and I'm one of the youngest. My older siblings were having kids before I was even born."

"Fourteen?"

"Momma and Daddy got married when she was only thirteen. Can you believe that? There was one set of twins, but we're stretched out over twenty six years. The six girls were born first and then the last four of us were boys."

"Your poor mother."

"Naw, she loved it. She honestly did 'cause she never grew up herself. It was always like a party at home." His voice trailed off and his head dropped. His sigh was loud and long.

"FM? You okay?"

"Sure. I just sometimes feel bad for Peter. We should've had more kids. Shermy just, well, never mind. You just be sure and enjoy that full house you have up there, okay?"

My walk to my van continues, but slower. He sounds like my dad. Daddy always wanted a houseful of kids, but like Peter Bedwell, I'm an only child. Leaves crunch beneath my feet on the old brick path. Brown flower heads bob in the breeze. Zinnias splashed color down this path all summer, but now their colorful petals are gone and all that's left is the seeds, which will fall and make new flowers next year. More flowers, more life. That's what it's all about, right?

FM didn't know the half of it.

Bouncing across the railroad track in front of my full house, I see on the front lawn at least four people I don't know and another half dozen that look familiar, but none of them were here earlier. Late afternoon sunshine warming the porch reflects in the windows and a halo of light pushes into the front yard.

"Hey look, there's Carolina!" Laney waves from the rocker on the far end of the porch. "Come on and join the party!"

Our driveway is full, so I park out front, halfway in the ditch, and have to climb up and out of the tilted car. Balmy air brings the smell of the river to me. It's too warm for November, but as soon as the sun falls below the trees, the temperatures will plummet. If Thanksgiving Day is like this, we can eat dinner outside on the deck.

Loping off the porch, our first born meets me in the front yard. He's tall and blond like his dad. These days he reminds me so much of when Jackson and I met at the University of Tennessee. We meet with open arms, but in the hug he turns me around so I'm facing the tracks, then swivels back leaving one arm lying on my shoulders.

"Awesome. I've been home only ten minutes and already a train." His eyes focus on the train bridge to our right.

So greeting me wasn't his only objective. Across the river, endless blue sky meets the gray hills of bare trees. Tall, Georgia pines provide dark green splotches on the hills sloping down to meet the glassy river winding past our home. Two bridges cross the river. One bears the weight of a multi-engine freight train, details of which my husband and sons would gladly provide. Just ask. The other bridge is much older and instead of rails, has a bed of cement. Chancey officials convinced the railroad to turn the old bridge into a walkway instead of tearing it down. With wrought iron fencing and old fashioned lampposts, it's a popular place for town folk and rail fans. Yep, rail fans are just what they sound like.

Not able to talk, since the engines blow by us only thirty feet away, I relax and let my hand rest on his waist. Will is twenty-one and a senior at the University of Georgia. We turn to follow the end of the train as far as we can see it, but instead of continuing around toward the porch, Will pulls me back around so our backs again face the house.

"So, Mom. Things are good?"

Uh oh. I know this tone. Something's wrong. "What's up?"

"Nothing, just that…well, I kind of brought some friends home."

"Will, why? Who? For how long?" I try to turn and face him, but his arm holds me in place beside him.

"Must be something about y'all opening the B&B makes everyone want to come. And the guys that were here, you know back in the fall, they keep talking about the ghost and the trains and all. I guess that's it."

"You couldn't say no?"

Then he dips his head to look at me. "You don't think it will be fun?"

Oh no. His looking so much like his father has kept me from seeing *my* father peering out of those brown eyes. He can't mask his glee with fake concern. I walk out from under his arm and face him. "No, I don't think it will be fun. I think it will be a lot of work. So how many and for how long?"

"There's eight of us. Three girls and five of us guys. I explained they couldn't do their laundry here so we shouldn't be that much more work, right?"

Eight college students? My mouth falls open, and my eyes start counting the crowded porch. "Why is Laney here?"

Will tilts his head and frowns as we look at Laney. "I'm not sure. Something about the community thing tonight." He laughs. "Hey, she looks just like that woman in the movie, you know, that movie Grandpa and Grandma like so much."

My dad is even sitting on the steps like one of the Tarlington twins gazing up at Scarlett O'Hara. Mother is seated on the rocking chair next to Laney and also surrounded by the admiring hoards. And they do look like hoards. Savannah and her friends line the porch railing nearest the driveway. Bryan along with Susan's son Grant and several other junior high boys are playing football in the small front yard. Music floats out of one of the open cars at the top of the drive. This is my father's fantasy come to life.

Dad stands up as we near him. "Hey honey, so you found a home for the turkey?"

The front door swings open, "Carolina, where have you been? Your folks are delightful." Susan Lyles holds a tray of cookies and right behind her is a young man I don't know. He's carrying my iced tea pitcher and a stack of disposable red cups. Isn't Susan supposed to be too busy to think, much less be entertaining my parents? And my kids?

"I've been to my friends' houses looking for a place to stash a thawing turkey, but of course they're not at home. They're all at my house."

"Aw, quit whining and have a cookie. Your blood sugar's probably just low." Laney leans forward reaching for the plate her sister holds. "Did you put it in my fridge?"

"No, you weren't home." Laney's cleavage is on display in her burnt orange sweater's low V-neck. It would never occur to me to wear that sweater without a turtle neck or blouse. Her jeans fit perfect and are more effective in displaying curves right where they should be than Scarlett's mammy-tightened corset.

"Carolina, you know you can just go on in anytime. Door's never locked. You might've had to move some stuff around, but it should've fit."

"It wouldn't have fit in mine. Either of them." Susan may be Laney's sister, but she missed out on the curve allotment. She's thin, has flat brown hair, which she usually wears in a ponytail, and is permanently tan from working in her garden year-round. "From now until after the new year there's not a spare inch anywhere in my kitchen."

"I finally found FM at home and they have an extra refrigerator in their back entryway." Following Laney's advice, I grab a cookie before they're all gone and lean against the front railing. "So what's up with the party here?"

Mother smiles and lifts her hands, "It just happened. Will arrived with his friends and the next thing we knew it was a party."

"Yeah, Mom, you remember Arthur, right?" Will shakes his wheat-colored hair in the direction of a tall, muscular young man with short, black hair who is seated next to Laney's daughter, Jenna. Jenna's pressed against him.

Arthur waves at me. "Hey, Mrs. J. My dad said to tell you thanks for letting me come here for Thanksgiving. Plane ticket home to LA just isn't in the budget since I'll be flying home for Christmas."

"No problem. Glad to have you. How's tennis going?" Arthur plays on the tennis team at University of Georgia. He and Will became friends their freshman year.

"Team's doing great. Me? Not so good."

"Honey, you're always great," Jenna says with her eyes slanted upward toward him. She lifts a piece of her blond hair lying on her shoulder and puts it in her mouth. She is so obviously Laney's daughter. Her hooded jacket is short and doesn't quite meet her low cut jeans. The jacket's front zipper is only half pulled up and underneath it she's wearing a lacy, hot pink cami that looks like lingerie. Arthur installed himself around her little finger when he was here last month.

Will clears his throat, "And the guy helping out Miss Susan is Randy. He's just here for tonight." He points to our left. "That's Amir, Katherine, and Sidney beside Grandma.

The boy and girls wave. They remind me of a recruiting poster for any major college. Amir is very cool and middle-eastern. Katherine's bright smile jumps out of her dark face. She's dressed to the teeth, and her jewelry is better than anything I own. Then Sidney is the mid-western, corn-fed dumpling with red cheeks, short white-blond hair, and bright, blue eyes.

Sidney adds to her wave, "We sure do appreciate you inviting us, Mrs. Jessup."

"Oh, anytime." I invited them?

"Then there's T.J. who was here last time." Will nods toward his sister's group on our right sitting on the porch railing.

T.J. stands up to shake my hand. "Good to see you again."

He quickly reclaims his seat beside Savannah. On the other side of my daughter is Ricky, her boyfriend. T.J. and Ricky don't get along to well. Wonder why?

"Where's Anna?" Will ask.

"She took a walk down to the river," Katherine offers.

My mother reaches out to pat Sidney's hand lying on the rocking chair arm next to her. "Aren't they just the sweetest things? And we've got the sleeping arrangements all figured out. The boys are going to sleep in the motor home! Isn't that a grand idea?"

"She's talking about Will's friends." Ricky makes clear his position in the house.

"Anna is staying in the Southern Crescent room," Dad adds. "Sidney and Katherine can share the room Will was going to stay in up on the second floor." He frowns. "We thought about putting all three girls in that room, but then that would leave the Southern Crescent room empty."

Oh no, an empty room? Heaven forbid! "Sounds like you all have been busy. What are we planning for dinner? Let's see, there are eight college kids, mom, dad, me, Savannah, and Bryan. That makes thirteen." Despite my best efforts, sarcasm darts in and out of my words. Maybe if I smile really big?

"Thirteen? Why I see more like twenty here." Laney's purply blue eyes are stretched wide. "What are the rest of us supposed to do for dinner?"

"Go home?" This smiling thing is harder than it sounds.

"No, don't go home." Daddy stands up and pulls out his wallet. "How about pizza?" He lifts out several bills. "Need someone to get the pizza and someone to go to the store for drinks."

Susan holds her hand up. "Don't count me in. The kids can stay, if they're invited, but I've wasted too much time already." However, I notice she doesn't actually get out of her chair.

"Oh, I need to go to the store," Mother says. "Can I go along?"

"If Grandpa's paying, me and T.J. will go get the pizzas," Will volunteers.

Katherine raises her hand and looks at my mom, "I have my car. Mrs. Uh…"

"Miss Goldie, hun."

"Okay, Miss Goldie, me and Sidney can drive you to the store."

"Grandma, get popcorn for the movie tonight. Remember?"

"Oh yes," My mother's eyes are shining. "Savannah, honey, get me a pad of paper and a pen. We need to make a list." Mother squeezes Sidney's knee. "Don't you just love having a list?"

Sidney giggles. "Will, I love your family."

Katherine stands and smoothes down her wrinkled madras skirt and her Kelly green sweater. She looks down at Sidney, "Let's go get my purse, and I want to change. I'm so wrinkled from the car ride."

Sidney stands, as does Amir. The two girls head upstairs.

Amir speaks up and his rich, fluid accent floats, "Pardon me, but Will can we do a fire like you talked about?"

"Me." Ricky actually jumps. "I can do that. I'll get the fire going, and we can eat out back. C'mon, Amir, you can help me get the wood."

Susan's, Laney's, and my eyes meet and I try to suppress

a chuckle at their nephew's pronunciation of Amir's name. Ricky is a good ol' boy from the North Georgia Mountains. Instead of short and regal sounding, Amir gained a couple more syllables and some up and down inflections. It sounded more like *Aaameeer*. But Amir doesn't seem to mind, he leaps down the steps following Ricky around back. Bryan and Grant and the other two junior high boys follow them, yelling, "We want to help do the fire."

Savannah comes out the door with writing supplies for her grandmother and then goes back to lean on the porch railing with Susan's middle child, Susie Mae, and Laney's other daughter, Angie. Angie and Jenna are twins, but couldn't be more different. Angie has dyed black hair, kohl rimmed eyes, piercings in her eyebrows and several other places on her thin body. Jenna is the reigning Miss Whitten County, blond hair, boobs and all. Angie, Jenna, and Savannah are all sixteen and juniors at Chancey High.

"Grandpa, you want to go with me and T.J.? Mom, where's the pizza menu?" Will asks as he weaves through the porch to the front door, Daddy and T.J. following him.

"It's hanging on the fridge. Savannah, don't forget you have practice tonight."

"You, too." Laney says.

"You, too, who?" I ask.

"You. That's what I came to ask you about."

"Don't waste your breath. No. Whatever it is, no."

"Oh, Carolina, it's perfect for you. I'm so proud of you." Mother clasps her hands under her chin. "Just wait until you hear."

My mother has always carried around delusional thoughts about my stardom. She sought the spotlight for me through ballet, piano, swimming, tap dance, scouts, softball, basketball, bowling, and even Bible drills at Vacation Bible School. I buried myself in books. Reading is not something people pay to see you do. I'm in fifth grade again. "No."

Susan swats Laney. "I thought you said you asked her."

"I lied. Don't worry. She's going to do it."

Stomping up the front steps, my feet beat out my rhythm. "No. I. Won't."

When Savannah giggles, I turn on her. "Did you get the bathrooms clean?"

"Sure did. They sparkle. Grandma even checked." She gestures to the girls seated around her. "Let's go upstairs. Jenna, get off Arthur and come up to the tower."

Savannah has the third floor space for a room. The slanting ceilings and tiny windows make it like a room atop a castle. Since we call her princess behind her back, we took to calling her bedroom, the tower. Silly us. She feels living in a tower is her due, not a joke.

Laney laughs as the girls troop inside and Arthur exits for the backyard. "Law, I love how that girl calls out Jenna. Angie, even though she's her sister, couldn't say half of what Savannah says and gets away with."

"Hard to believe they were mortal enemies just a few weeks ago," Susan observes. "Since the pageant, I guess they've made up." She sighs. "And everything with Susie Mae bonded our girls."

Mother glances around and then leans toward Susan. "Since the children are gone, I want to say how well I think you handled everything. I know it was hard, but how are things now? I hope I'm not being nosy, but I guess I am."

However, the concern in Mother's eyes makes it clear she cares.

"We're doing pretty good. My husband, Griffin, is working on forgiving me. Laney and Carolina didn't take too long, but I didn't lie to them about their daughter." She takes a deep breath. "Honestly, I think our marriage will be stronger, eventually. Susie Mae loves her counselor, but she's still boy crazy, and I worry constantly about her. You know, once you've had sex, it's so much easier to cross that line again, and she's only fifteen."

Mother lays her hands in her lap and becomes still. Her voice is low, "Susan, honey, just because a girl has sex early doesn't mean her life can't turn out just wonderful. I know I'm an old grandma now, but I was one wild teenager. My first boyfriend talked me into it, and I was only thirteen. I don't know why I didn't worry about getting pregnant." Her eyes open wide and she flings open her arms. "Just wasn't thinking, I guess. Now I know it's difficult for me to conceive. Carolina knows how much her father and I wanted more children. I hated the idea of her being an only child."

"Wait," croaks out my mouth. "What do you mean you were wild?"

"Oh, honey. I was with every boy I could get my hands on in our little town. I loved the boys and being with them, and there wasn't anything else to do. When your Daddy came home from the army, he was so handsome and strong. I just had to have him. But he wouldn't have nothing to do with me. Then one day he showed up at my door with a huge bouquet of store bought flowers and a ring. He said he'd loved me since I was just a kid. Shoot, I was still a kid. He said if I'd promise to be faithful to him, he wanted to get married. So we did. Ran off to South Carolina that minute."

"I knew you eloped, but—but…"

Mother's eyes crinkle up, "But you thought we were above all that sex stuff?"

"No, no. I just never thought you could've been like that."

"Of course not. That's why I wanted to tell Susan my story. You grow up and things change. Giving Susie Mae someone to help her understand what's going on is good. You're doing the right thing, her being in counseling. Jack helped me understand I wasn't trash. Plus, the sex has always been great with him. So everything turned out fine." Mother beams at me, Susan, and Laney.

Laney laughs. "Well, Mrs. Butler, you sure are surprising. For the life of me, I don't know what to say."

Susan steps behind my mother and reaches down to hug her. "Well, I know what to say. Thank you."

Okay. *This* conversation never happened. "I need to see about things inside," I say, pulling open the front door.

"So, Carolina, practice is at seven tonight. You'll be there?" Laney speaks up.

"Of course. Seven." My mind isn't really working and besides, if I stay here, Mother might start talking again.

CHAPTER 4

"You caught me at a weak moment. I'm not going." I put my purse down with a thud on the back-deck table as I speak up. Maybe it was the bounce in my blood sugar from the pizza, but something gave me the courage to tell Laney no.

However, she just grins. Then she flutters manicured fingers at me. "Have to. Everyone's expecting you.

"Mom, I need to leave right now. Just come on." Savannah has the pink dress slung over her shoulder.

Laney smiles and leans back in her lawn chair. "Just go. The kids will clean all this up, right?"

Immediately the kids start gathering empty soda cans and pizza boxes. They're glad to do anything to ease the tension. Mother and Daddy are studying their coffee cups, well aware of my stubborn streak. I try to not think about their looks of joy and amazement when I pick up my purse and put it over my shoulder, then follow Savannah around the house.

Bryan, Grant, Susan, and the other high school teens left a half hour ago to get the scenery in place or to dart home for their costumes. Costumes? What if I have to wear a costume? "Savannah, go without me." I turn towards the front porch. "I'm not going."

"Okay, I don't care." She opens her car door and shoves the dress and its miles of skirts into the backseat. "But it might've been fun."

"Why do you think it could be fun? I can't think of anything less fun."

"Forget it."

Regret? Is that what crossed her face? Maybe she wants me there? No way. I shake my head and put my hand on the railing. But what if..? "Okay, I'll go."

Walking to the car, I study her face but don't see anything other than annoyance. My bad, and now it's too late.

Once in the high school auditorium, I slide into a seat. In the back. In the dark.

Missus and a tall, stout woman throw up their hands when they see Savannah.

"There you are," Missus exclaims. "You're not dressed? Get dressed, and hurry!" She shoos Savannah off to the side stage. "Through those doors. You'll see where." Missus then steps to the front of the stage. "Carolina? Is that you hiding back there?"

"I'm not hiding. Just sitting."

She stares at me, taps her foot and waits.

"Okay," I grumble and push up out of my seat. She gets me every time. White gloves, sharp tongue, and now, tapping foot. They all work on me, apparently.

The stout woman leans her head back and stares at me down her bumpy nose, then actually sniffs. "I knew Laney Troutman would get out of this. Just wasn't sure how she'd manage it. Just like Laney's luck to have a new woman move to town."

Missus shakes her head, "Laney does have the world's best

luck, doesn't she?"

"Y'all are really making me nervous. What's the deal?" My stomach is doing spins and the double pepperoni pizza feels like it was a bad choice.

Missus lowers herself to sit on the edge of the stage. Her white hair and wrinkles tell the truth about her age, but the way she moves puts most forty-year-olds to shame. "It's not that bad. Some women, like Laney, have made it a real chore, but it's not that bad."

"You're not making me feel better. What is it? Wait, first, Savannah's costume—why is there a princess in your Thanksgiving pageant?"

The woman on the stage bends down and pushes her hand toward me. "Hello, Mrs. Jessup. I'm Mrs. Oliphant, Savannah's English teacher and head of the drama department here."

"Oh, nice to meet you. Savannah really likes your class and is so excited about the spring play."

The woman nods. "I'm excited to have her, and she's not a princess in the pageant. She's Lady Bountiful."

"But I've never heard of a Lady Bountiful in a Thanksgiving pageant."

Missus nods. "It's a tradition in Chancey. Back about fifty years ago the mayor wanted a role for his daughter in the pageant, but she insisted she get to wear a ball gown. So they decided she'd play Lady Bountiful, the rich, charity-loving, beautiful society lady. She'd espouse the joy in giving to the less fortunate and it would all get tied into Thanksgiving. See?"

Both women look at me and wait. "Okay. Sounds fine. That's it?"

"Of course, that means we need to show the less fortunate, and no one ever wants to play the less fortunate, because in the early years the mayor would get a prisoner out of the county jail to play the part."

My eyes pop, "A real prisoner?"

Disgust prompts a grunt from Mrs. Oliphant. "Can you imagine?" Then her eyes take on a shine. "But it added such drama. I was ten years old the last time a prisoner was used, and the tension it added was dramatic. The mayor would get the grungiest, most depraved looking reprobate he could find. And then there would be the armed deputy standing at the edge of the stage." The teacher shudders. "My love of drama began right there."

Missus shrugs. "But when a new mayor was elected he stopped us from getting a prisoner. And no one would sign up, so the women's club has to elect the person to play the part of the less fortunate. We draw slips of paper out of a box."

A chuckle slips out. "Let me guess. Laney drew it this year."

Missus and Mrs. Oliphant nod.

"But now I get the honor?"

They nod again.

"Okay, that's not a problem. I can play a poor, down-on-my-luck soul. I don't have any lines, do I?"

Missus shakes her head and then scoots off the stage to stand beside me. "No lines, but the makeup and costume can get a little over done."

The concern on her face makes my stomach want to flip again. Suddenly the door behind us, through which Savannah disappeared earlier, flies open.

"Where is she? I don't have all night." Ida Faye Newbern bursts through the doors and stomps toward us. "So, Carolina, I hear you're my canvas."

"Oh, Ida Faye." My stomach quit flipping and plunged to my feet. Through some maneuvering and out-and-out hiding I'd managed to not see my old boss since the day I'd quit.

Wearing a velour turquoise jogging suit, she advances on me like a tank running down an unarmed man. "Your tangle of hair will mat into a perfect birds nest, I'm sure. However, I don't remember it ever looking cared for, so we'll have to really work on making it look worse than usual."

Did I mention I didn't give a two-week notice?

"We won't have to use much foundation since your pasty coloring looks kind of like prison pallor, anyway. We'll just rub on some mud."

Did I mention I said some rather unflattering things in my departure announcement?

"Oh, and you can wear that ugly brown jumper you wear so often, but I don't think this old burlap smells too bad for you to use as a shawl."

She shoves the brown mass toward my face, and I get a whiff of mold and rotten potatoes.

Her thick eyebrows shoot up, and Ida Faye leans toward me. "So good to be working with you again, Carolina."

Did I mention I might've used the words *small-minded* and *arrogant* when I left? And maybe even *hateful*?

Chapter 5

"There's not one reason to have done the whole getup tonight, except to multiply my humiliation at the hands of Ida Faye, Costume Dominatrix of greater Chancey." I use the one stop light in town, which always turns red when it sees me, to switch my cell phone to my other ear. "Jackson? I'm getting ready to turn up the hill, so I'll probably lose you. Wait, someone from the house is beeping in. I'll let you go, okay? See you tomorrow. Love you."

I press the green button and Savannah wails in my ear. "Mom, where are you?"

"What? I'm on my way home, but…" Before I can tell her I'll probably lose her on the hill, I lose her. "Oh, well, I'll be there in a minute." She and Bryan got a ride home from Susan since they were ready to leave when I was still smeared in mud and wrapped in rotting burlap.

With a quick toss, my phone falls into my purse. There were enough reasons to be worrying about what I'd find at home, without Savannah's call. At the top of the hill, the crescent moon smiles at me. It is the perfect Cheshire cat grin from Alice in Wonderland. The reflection in the river wavers through almost bare tree limbs. The leaves are brown, but they've not all fallen off. It's been a mild fall, with little rainfall or wind to tear the stubborn ones away. As the road slopes downward, I turn left onto our road. In the summer the weeds towered on each side, now they lay in brown heaps, right up to the railroad right-of-way. I turn my head to each side and, with the way clear, focus on our house. With three stories, and lights shining on every floor, it welcomes me. My eyes still search the long front porch, looking for our ghost. It's only been a few weeks since we discovered our ghost was Missus' and FM's son, Peter. A PR stunt gone too far. Way too far.

Parked to the side is the motor home, and there are lights on and people are moving around inside. The last space left anywhere near the driveway, right in front of the motor home, is where I leave the car. The closing of my car door is echoed by the slamming of the front door.

"Mom, where have you been?" Savannah strides down the front steps toward me.

"Did you see all that mud Ida Faye rubbed on me? Why?"

"Grandpa is ruining everything. He thinks he's some kind of general or something. You've got to make him stop. He just told Ricky ship up or shape out." She crosses her arms and leans against the hood of Will's car.

"Don't you mean, "shape up or ship out?""

"Yeah, whatever." She flits her hand in my direction. "You've got to make him stop."

"Honey…" I lean on the car beside her and shake my head. "Wait, what was Ricky doing?"

Her blue eyes widen, "Nothing, just, nothing." She tosses her hair and stands straight. "I'm going back inside." Her jeans are tight, and she has a brown bandana woven in the belt loops. Her cream stretch top with lace trimming stands out in the moonlight and as she walks away from me, her black hair swings down her back. I fight it, but a smile bubbles up as I watch the way she is marching up the sidewalk. Daddy might have finally met his match.

Inside the house, there's no evidence of a showdown. I follow voices to the kitchen and find every bowl I own waiting on the table. The back door is open and the deck lights are on.

"Oh, there you are." Mother leans up from peering into the microwave. "We're having a kind of early intermission. So I'm making popcorn. You didn't miss much."

"Believe me, I know the movie by heart. I didn't miss anything."

When Daddy's voice carries in from the deck, it catches my attention. Mother purses her lips and nods. "Your father is trying to explain how distracting the children's comments are during the movie."

"Children? Most of them are adults. Besides, they'll decide if they want to watch it or not."

Mother's pale blond eyebrows straighten and her eyes squint. "We made watching it mandatory for those staying here this weekend. Most of them had never seen it."

"You can't do that." At her look of confusion, I sigh and change my words. "Why would you do that?"

The microwave dings. "Popcorn's ready," she says loudly. "Dear, are we ready to resume?"

Daddy walks into the kitchen. "We're ready, if you are. Carolina, you're back. We have some things to discuss later."

My neck begins prickling, and I know my chest is turning red, but a quick nod is my only voluntary response.

Daddy accepts the nod with one of his own. "Goldie, the children understand and things should go much better now. You say the popcorn is ready? Ricky, go tell the young men in the motor home we're ready to start…again."

Behind him the giggles and rolling eyes show that Daddy is being taken very lightly.

"Mom, you didn't meet Anna this afternoon." Will steps toward me after he lets his grandmother pass with her bags of popcorn. "Anna, this is my mom."

A small girl with sandy blonde hair sidles up behind Will. "Nice to meet you, Mrs. Jessup."

She reaches around Will and holds out her hand. I'm struck by how tiny it is. Her eyes never lift to meet mine, so I'm left to talk to the top of her head. "We're glad you could come." The words are barely out of my mouth before she's disappeared behind my son again.

Mother looks over her shoulder and our questioning eyes meet.

Will reaches out to take a newly filled bowl of popcorn. "Intermission is over. Back to the *Greatest Movie of All Time*. And remember our just concluded lecture on cinematic viewing etiquette. Lead on, Grandpa."

Daddy beams and moves into the living room. He either ignores or doesn't hear the sarcasm.

With the kitchen empty, I begin unloading the dishwasher. My list of things to do has grown exponentially with each additional visitor and my involuntary involvement in that disgusting pageant.

Savannah appears at my shoulder. "Grandpa says you are to come watch the movie."

"There's too much to do. Tell him I'll be in there soon."

"He said, '"No excuses."'"

"Okay, I'll be right there." I straighten up, and Savannah places her hands on her hips.

"I'm glad Grandma and Grandpa are here, but if he thinks he's going to boss me around all month, he's got another think coming!"

"If you're so bold, why are you whispering?"

She tightens her lips and spins around. My first laugh of the night eases my face and relieves my tension. After drying my hands on a dish towel and clicking off the kitchen light, I step into the dark living room. Scarlett has just let fly the breakable figurine above the settee where Rhett is hidden. Good, one of my favorite scenes.

Wait. Did Savannah just say all month?

CHAPTER 6

When the kids were little, I liked having them at school the day before Thanksgiving. That gave me a chance to go to the grocery store and finish cleaning the house. Now, I could use them this morning to run errands and do chores. They sense this and are a merry group going out the front door. Plus, they know they won't do any real work at school since it's a half-day before the four day weekend. Ricky, Savannah and Bryan leave quiet behind them. The college folk won't be seen for a while and my parents haven't made an appearance yet.

The mops, Prissy and Pitty Pat, flounced down the hall earlier and went outside with Bryan. When they came back in, Bryan let them into his grandparents' room, and Ashley came out. After a trip outside to do his business, he lay down on the rug beside the back door. "Poor thing. You just want to go home, don't you? Do you know how long you're staying? You can tell me. Come on." Ashley's lifts his face and sad black eyes gaze at me. Then he sighs and drops his head back on my red braided rug.

Between the movie, the crowded room, and the panic of possibly having my parents stay a month, you'd think my eyes couldn't have drifted close. But they did. When the lights came on around eleven o'clock last night, I'd stumbled upstairs to bed. However, first ding of the alarm clock this morning, and it all came back.

Part of me wants to march down the hall and ask how long they plan on staying. Another part of me is afraid to know. Maybe muffins would be good for when everyone starts waking up. Yeah, Ruby's. That's a great idea.

Now I'm afraid someone is going to wake up and stop me before the house is in my rearview mirror.

Remembering Ida Faye's comments about my hair last night, I try smoothing it as I get out of my car and walk down the sidewalk to the gazebo. The tired summer flowers have been dug up and replaced by pansies and lots of pine straw. Last week the women's club had a work day in the park, which I managed to avoid. Some limits have to be set, because these people want to own me. However, they did a great job, and the mild weather has the pansies looking confident and sassy, bobbing their colorful faces in the breeze. I didn't even grab a coat. My jeans and loose black turtle-neck are warm enough. At the gazebo, I follow the gravel path around it to my right and turn toward the stores lining Main Street.

The park borders the street on this side and faces a line of two-story buildings of weathered, dark- red brick. At each end are old houses, which have seen better days. The stores include a florist, a couple of non-descript offices, a store with lots of little signs on the door about political things, and in the middle is Ruby's Café.

Ruby serves muffins for breakfast and anything else you want to ask for and she has available. There aren't menus, just the knowledge that her muffins are all fantastic. At lunch time you can get an assortment of soups and sandwiches – again what kind depends on what she has on hand and feels like making. Pies are a specialty item and appear for certain occasions. Being new to town, I don't know what the occasions are as they are not advertised. There are just some nights when Ruby is open and everyone goes for pie and coffee. When I asked one time for a calendar of her nights open, she looked at me like a kid who's just been told his summer vacation was cancelled. She never answered, just shook her head and backed away.

Four tables, just like the one my grandmother had in her kitchen, with white, glitter-sprinkled tops and rimmed in shiny chrome fill up the middle of the floor. The sides of the room are lined with booths. Not tall, private booths, but booths with short backs so everyone in the place can be seen. Turquoise vinyl covers the seats. The chrome-rimmed chairs around the tables have seats and backs in either red or yellow. Along the back is a counter with padded stools in front of it, also in red or yellow and rimmed in three-inch chrome. It would be very kitschy and stylish, except it isn't planned. It just is what's always been in Ruby's.

I push open the door and smell pie. Ohhh, pecan, pumpkin, chocolate. The air is heavenly.

"What do you want?"

Ruby's rough yell causes me to stop with one hand on the door and my nose still drawing in my surroundings.

"Libby! Why didn't you lock that door?" Ruby yells again, and Libby scurries from the back and around the front counter.

"Oh, Carolina. We're not open. I forgot to lock the door when I went over to Missus'". Libby's brown, pageboy hair is tucked up in a net and she has an apron over her old black pants and sleeveless shirt. She's in her fifties and usually this time of the morning she's serving coffee and muffins.

"But I need some muffins."

"Then you shouldn't have ordered so many pies. I had to close this morning," Ruby yells as she plants her fists on her hips.

"Pies? I didn't order pies."

"You, your dad. Whatever. They won't be ready until this afternoon. Come back then." She turns and disappears behind a swinging door.

"Libby, I don't know what she's talking about." I back up because Libby had taken control of the door and is trying to close it.

"Me either. I just know I got here to wait tables as usual, and Ruby told me to go get some list from Missus and then make sure to lock the door 'cause we weren't opening." She tilts her soft, lined face, and her voice is apologetic. "But I've got to go. I need to see if the pumpkin pies are set."

"Okay," is all I say before the door separates me from the café and I'm left talking to my reflection, and it's clueless as well. However, what I did hear is that Daddy and Missus are in cahoots and it involves pies. Lots of pies.

Assorted strips of Danish in flimsy aluminum pans and chip dip are the only things in my grocery cart, which I push into Angie's aisle.

"Hey, Mrs. Jessup. Can't believe you had to come back today."

"Yeah, me either. But there's a houseful to feed. How come you're not at school?"

"Today's my DECA day. I get out early since I take the distributive education class. And they're not doing anything at school today, but the store will be busy. Your dad was just in here."

"My dad?"

"Yeah, tonight sounds fun."

"Okay, Angie. Are you actually making fun of Ida Faye getting to humiliate me in this pageant thing?"

The rings in her eyebrows lift. "Oh, I don't mean that. I meant the after party at the B&B. I get to come because I'm helping with the scenery. Your dad, Mr. Jack, said so."

There you go, the missing ingredient. Pies, Daddy, Missus, and my house. Of course.

"Thanks." All that's left is for me to nod, take my bags, and head up the hill.

CHAPTER 7

Danish is not that easy to eat while driving. There's that whole sticky thing, and then they tend to bend and droop. As I bounce across the railroad crossing in front of the house, I lick my fingers and brush crumbs off the front of my navy sweater. My eyes flick to the clock on the dash, only 9:30. Wonder why the door to the motor home is open? The college guys can't be awake.

Then the answer juts his head out of the motor home. Daddy. He waves at me and hollers, "Hey! Good morning. Just getting the crew up and moving."

Eyeing the aluminum pan of Danish, I consider cramming in just one more bite, but there's no time. Mother calls me from the front porch. "Honey, the phone's for you." She's holding my phone in one hand and the broom in the other."

After ridding myself of the bags by dumping them on the kitchen table, I take the phone.

"Hello?"

"Mrs. Jessup?"

"Yes."

"This is in regards to your water testing. We've not received the results despite repeated requests."

"Excuse me?"

"The tests of your private well for the licensing of your bed and breakfast? You've received two warning letters, but we've yet to get anything from you. Your temporary license is set to expire."

"Oh, um, one of my partners is dealing with that. Let me talk to her and get back to you. Can I get your name and number? I'll call you right back."

"I'm only going to be here until eleven thirty, and first thing Monday morning, I'm going to have to turn you down. So you must call me right back, okay? I'm Jennifer Allsbury and my number is 678-555-9210. Remember, eleven thirty."

"No problem. Thank you so much."

"There's danish in those bags," I say to Mom. "I've got to call Laney." Out on the deck, I wait for Laney to answer but have to leave a message. "It's Carolina. Call me. The county wants the results of a water test for the B&B?" After leaving the same message on her cell phone, I call Susan.

She picks up on the first ring. "Hey, I can't talk right now. We've got a little crisis with the scenery. What's up? If it's quick."

"It's quick and important. The county wants some water tests results for the B&B. The lady said they've sent letters, but I've given everything like that to Laney. She's supposed to be handling all this, right?"

"Sure. I'm sure it's all fine. She's used to handling stuff like that since she does it all for Chancey, as treasurer. But she's unavailable this morning, 'cause she's having a spa day over at Barnsley Gardens."

"Well, of course she is."

"I've got to go. Just call the county back and tell them your business manager is out of town, and you'll have to call them back on Monday. Seriously, it's no big deal, I'm sure. Bye."

Susan's probably right. I hold the phone in my hand and look at it. There really is no way to get in touch of Laney. The spa at Barnsley Gardens is famous for its luxury treatments and as much as they cost, there's no way Laney's going to interrupt hers with a phone call. I could run over there, but it's a good hour and half from here. I went there once when my boss back in Marietta asked me to pick up a spa certificate she'd bought for her daughter-in-law. Okay, I really don't have a choice.

"Ms. Allsbury? This is Carolina Jessup. We talked a few minutes ago?"

"Yes, I remember. So, your test results?"

"That's a problem. My, I mean, our business manager is unavailable today, and she takes care of everything like that."

"Unavailable? What does that mean? Surely, she has a cell phone."

My mouth hangs for a moment, caught up in the attitude I'm getting. "Well, of course she does. But, well, she's—she's unavailable."

"This sounds like stalling, and I don't have time for this today. You've ignored the warning letters, and this call was just a courtesy. Your application will be denied on Monday."

"But, wait, she's unavailable because she's in the spa at Barnsley Gardens."

"Really?" the phone goes quiet, and for a minute, I think she's hung up. "Well, I guess I wouldn't answer the phone either. Do you promise to call me Monday morning?"

"Absolutely, Ms. Allsbury. I promise. First thing."

"Okay, but I'm putting your paper work right on top. Maybe I'll sign up to do your inspection for the license, because it sounds like your B&B is something else."

A smile accompanies my sigh of relief. "Oh, you've heard nice things about it?"

"No. I just figure if your business manager can afford a spa day at Barnsley Gardens, then y'all must have tons of money to put into the B&B. Are y'all going to do spa treatments there?"

"Um, no, we're more the rustic sort."

"Oh. Well. So you'll call Monday, right?"

"Right. Have a great Thanksgiving."

We hang up, and a laugh escapes when I think of a spa here. We're more the pizza from cardboard boxes around a campfire B&B. So one crisis avoided, now what else was I thinking about? Oh, yeah. The after party.

"But I have to get ready for tomorrow's dinner, remember? Turkey and all that."

"We'll all help. For crying out loud, it's just some pie and coffee." Daddy pours another cup of coffee for him and Mother. "You want some more?"

I shake my head as he extends the pot toward me. "No, I'm good. Pie and coffee for several dozen, I'm sure."

"Then we have work to do!" Mother stands and pushes the sleeves of her cream sweater up. She wraps her arms around my father and beams at me. "Honey, we are just so glad we can be here to help you with your little party."

"It's not my party. It's Daddy and Missus' party."

They both laugh and Daddy winks at me. "Now, you can say that all you want, but Missus has kept us up to date on all the parties you've thrown since you moved here. You've become quite the Society Queen of Chancey, according to her."

And the dawning begins. "Let me guess. Missus is on Facebook."

"Why, of course, honey. Now, what do you want us to do to help?"

CHAPTER 8

"And there's some under your arm. There above your elbow," Jackson says as he points, but doesn't actually touch my arm.

"That woman smeared that gunk all over me, and I know she knew how impossible it would be to get off." Jackson doesn't say anything so I turn to look at him. His face is turning purple trying to keep another burst of laughter from slipping out.

"I'm serious. If you start laughing again, I'm going to slap you. And then I'm leaving, and you can cook your own Thanksgiving meal tomorrow."

"No," he clears his throat and wipes his eyes, which are still wet from his last outburst. "But you've got to admit, she got you good."

"Yeah, and now I've got a houseful of people, and I'm up here with twigs still in my hair. She tied them in there. I know she did. And then she plastered them in with handfuls of mud." I lean against our bathroom vanity. "There really was a bucket of mud." I catch the reflection of Jackson leaning in toward me and sniffing.

"Do I still smell? Even after my shower?"

"Ahh, not really."

"You're lying, aren't you? "

"Maybe it's because we're in this little space. I'm sure with some fresh air, some circulation…"

"Ida Faye called it, Ode de Bum. Yeah, she had a name for it. She said it was cheap cologne, vinegar, and that stinky sports liniment rub." A shudder flies down my back, and I choke back a gag. "You go on down. I'll be there in a minute."

Jackson asks if I'm sure, but the whole time he's headed for the door.

The buzz from downstairs filters in when he opens the bedroom door. One more look in the mirror says I'm presentable enough. Besides, those people down there are the ones that did this to me. Laney, my supposedly good friend, owes *me* a day at the spa for this. And the look on Lady Bountiful's face as I crawled, yes crawled, up to her for a handout. I didn't know Savannah's nose could wrinkle that much. Oh, and the wide berth my proud parents gave me when I finally made their dreams of stardom for their only child come true. If it's good advice to keep you enemies close, then I'm as good as gold.

My black stretch cords, loafers, and gold sweater present an acceptable tableau. My damp hair—and twigs—are tied back in a scarf. I step into the hall. And if just one person laughs…

Passing Bryan's room, I see movement in front of the window, so I step back to look. Someone is sitting on the edge of the bed, light from outside shines on blond hair.

"Anna?"

The small girl sniffs and lifts her head.

"Are you okay?" Closer, I can see she's crying. "What's wrong?" The bed creaks a little when I sit down beside her.

"I don't like parties."

"Really? Honestly, they're not my favorite, either."

"Is it okay if I just stay up here?"

"Of course, but you're upset. It's more than just the party, isn't it?"

Her head barely nods.

"Is it one of the boys?"

"No, oh no." She looks up at me, and she looks so sad. "It's something else, but I can't tell you."

"Okay, but…"

Brightness blinds us as the light is snapped on. "There you are, Carolina."

"Missus. What is it?"

"I want you to quit moping up here and get downstairs. Who's your friend?" Missus crosses the room and sticks her hand at Anna.

"This is Anna, uh, Anna…" I look toward the girl. "I don't know your last…"

Anna's face is frozen in horror. She's staring at Missus with her eyes wide and her mouth twisted shut tight. She's leaning back as if Missus' hand hides a rattlesnake.

Missus jerks her offered hand away. "Oh, forgive me for intruding." She whirls for the door and gives me a look of disgust. "Carolina, you have more than one guest. And the rest are not so rude as to hide in upstairs bedrooms." She extends her look of disgust to Anna before leaving the room.

"What was that about?"

Anna shakes her head. "I don't know, I mean…I mean…I can't. But I'm fine, just go downstairs. I'll be down in a minute."

"Okay. Come down and have some pie. It's delicious." At the light switch, I turn back to Anna. "Light on or off?"

"Off, please. Thanks."

Leaving the girl in the dark feels sad, but I don't really know her, and she doesn't want to talk. Maybe one of her friends from Athens will come up and sit with her when I tell them where she is.

Slowly, my eyes scan the living room as I walk down the stairs. I meet Peter's eyes and he begins to clap. He's joined by others and my cheeks get hot. Peter has proven to be a better friend as a human. As a ghost, he was okay, but limited. Now we meet regularly for coffee and I've even helped with the displays in the museum. My librarian skills come in handy with the old files. He meets me at the bottom of the stairs with a gentlemanly bow.

With a deep breath, I smile and relax my shoulders. "Thanks, applause beats laughter every time."

"Carolina, what are we going to do with you? You've got to stop letting these people treat you like this. If you don't grow a backbone, you're going to be playing Scrooge in the Christmas Carol, Pilate at the Easter Service, and King George in the Fourth of July parade." His tanned face crinkles above his dark brown beard.

"You're right, but they get me every time. Like this." I wave my hands, and he steps back to look.

"It's a great party. But let me guess. Not your idea?"

"Of course not. Your mother and my father are a force of nature. They could run Atlanta, but they've chosen to run me."

"Did you get any pie?"

"No, and the pie is the only good thing about this night. That's where I'm going right now." Peter steps back to let me in front of him, and I get to the kitchen without meeting anyone's eyes. There's a steady stream of people heading toward the door, so the evening is almost over.

"Coffee?" Peter asks. When I nod, he splits off toward the coffee urn. One good thing is, these Chancey people know I don't have any of the supplies for something like this, and they bring it all. Forty cup coffeemaker, cream pitchers, sugar bowls, even the cups, plates, and forks. I'm their little "My Fair Lady" project. However, instead of teaching me how to pronounce vowels, they're trying to instruct me on being a gracious Southern hostess. Good luck with that.

There's a piece of chocolate pie left, so I grab it and a fork. Across the table, I see the young people out on the deck. Squeezing around the other end of the table, I head in that direction. Sidney and Katherine see me and open the door.

"Hey, girls."

"Mrs. Jessup, you poor thing. How did you ever get all that mud and gunk off?" Sidney's sweet face reflects her concern, and her white-blonde hair swings around her face as she shakes her head. Katherine, however, has an eyebrow, a shoulder and a hip–all cocked. Her royal blue silk dress and gold jewelry set off her dark skin. "I almost came up there, took you off that stage, and brought you home. How dare they treat a nice woman like you that way."

"Thanks, Katherine, but it was just a part. And I did say I'd do it."

"Under duress. I was here and heard it all."

Sidney rolls her big, soft blue eyes. "Can you tell she wants to be a lawyer?"

"I just can't stand to see someone railroaded like that." Then one side of her mouth crinkles up. "But it was funny."

"Well, enough about that. Anna is upstairs, and I think she's upset. Do either of you know what that's about?"

Both girls shrug.

Sidney answers, "I don't know her. Never met her until after we got here."

"She's not friends with y'all at school?"

"No," Katherine added. "I've never even heard of her. She seems awfully young, don't you think? Maybe she's one of those high school kids that get into college early because they're so smart."

"Could be. I'll ask Will later. Right now, I want to find my cup of coffee to go with this pie. You girls have everything you need in your room?"

They nod as I wave and walk back into the kitchen. Cleaning up has started and the chatter level is high. Peter motions me toward him. He's standing just inside the living room and he has two cups of coffee.

"Thanks, I just needed a word with the girls."

"Take a bite first. I'll hold your coffee. Lots of folks have left, but there's still nowhere to sit down."

"So how many were here tonight, you think?"

"Close to sixty, I'd say." He ends with a chuckle, which causes me to question him with raised eyebrows.

"Just thinking how much more fun these parties are on the inside. Many a night, I sat on the edge of the woods watching folks walk back and forth in here."

"Stop. That creeps me out when you talk about it. I got used to a ghost, but if I'd known a real person was out there…" I shiver, lay my fork on my plate, and reach for my coffee. "Who's that man talking to Savannah?"

Peter follows my glance at the couch. "Oh, I know you've heard of him. It's Cathy Stone's ex-husband, Stephen Cross. He teaches at the high school and helps with the drama club. This is his first year teaching after graduating from Southern in May. He helped me with the scenery."

"Is his fiancé here? Aren't they supposed to get married soon?"

Peter shrugs, "Guess so. He had Forrest with him last weekend and brought him to the museum to help us paint. Cute kid, but Stephen doesn't have a clue how to handle him. Wonder how his new bride will like Chancey?"

I roll my eyes. "Getting used to Chancey is hard enough without your fiancé's ex-head-cheerleader-wife whom he married and divorced inside a year and their son, whom he's seen only a couple times, living here."

Peter grins and leans against my shoulder, "Listen to you! Aren't you a font of Chancey gossip?"

"Shut up. It's not gossip if it's true and if everyone knows it. Think I'll go introduce myself."

Chapter 9

Another good thing about Chancey folk is that they clean up after themselves. My kitchen hasn't been this clean since we moved in. They even shooed me upstairs last night after the party before they were done. I got caught with a bobbing head trying to follow the conversation about Ricky's football future.

My thick robe feels good in the early morning chill. Very early morning, as the sun won't be up for a couple more hours. Extra-strong coffee will help, but mostly I'm spurred by nerves over cooking Thanksgiving dinner for all these people. In the past, I made use of the many, many options in the Atlanta suburbs. Reservations at nice restaurants for dinner with all the extras. Or ordering the entire meal from a local grocer. Or finagling invitations from those Martha Stewart wannabes who dream of hosting a meal like they've seen on TV. However, most of them only do it once so no repeat invites, plus I didn't really run in those circles.

This year, though, is different. We own and operate a Bed & Breakfast in the North Georgia Mountains and certain expectations should be met. I should be able to cook Thanksgiving Dinner for my family and friends. Right? I've got the menu planned, recipes printed out, ingredients bought and I'm up before the sun.

While the coffee brews, I put sweet potato chunks in a pot of water to boil and stir up three boxes of Jiffy cornbread mix for a pan of cornbread for dressing. Daddy cut up onions and celery yesterday, so I dump that into a pan of melted butter to sauté. Mother and Daddy went through the menu and wrote down the steps to help me out today. They promise, though, to let me do it myself. And, of course, I'm planning on them breaking that promise.

With a cup of coffee, I move to the living room clutching my sheets of directions. The heat kicks on, and I wonder what the temperature is outside. Last night was another abnormally warm evening. Humid, too. Through the front window, I watch crows meander at the crossing. With a squawk, they lift as one and head for the top of the pine trees across the road. I sit down in the easy chair and lay my head back to be able to see them. The sky behind them is beginning to lighten as the sun still lies behind the mountains across the river. Except for the crows settling on their perches, nothing moves and, even from inside, the air looks still and heavy. And so are my eyelids.

Then a screech descends upon the entire house. I snap to attention and look for the possible danger. Smoke floats from the kitchen. Doors bang in all directions.

"It's in the kitchen," Daddy yells.

By the time I get there, he's got pot holders around my pan of onions and celery. "Open the back door," he says.

I throw open the door and he rushes out with the smoking pan leading the way.

"Carolina? Are you okay?" Jackson dashes into the kitchen in an undershirt and boxers.

"Yeah, it's fine. I…I must've dozed off."

He steps back into the living room and looks up the stairs at the sudden audience. "You all can go back to bed. It was just a pan left on the burner." Smoky haze fills the area between us.

Daddy comes back inside. "I set it out there until it quits

smoking. Let me guess, that was the onions and celery?"

"Yeah, I guess I dozed off. Sorry you all woke up." At the stove, I see that the sweet potatoes about boiled out of water, and a check of the cornbread shows it's only a little overdone.

"It's okay, just glad that's all it was." Daddy pours himself a cup of coffee. "I was getting dressed, and I smelled the smoke right before the alarm went off. That's why I was here so quick. You got more celery and onion? I'll cut you up some when I finish this cup."

"Well, I'm going to go lay back down and see if I can get my heart to stop pounding." Jackson rubs his hands down his face and turns away. "Night, all."

And it is still night. Though the sky is a little lighter and pinker, the sun is still not in sight.

"One cup of coffee and see what happened? I'm already behind schedule." I throw down the towel I've been twisting in my hands.

"We'll get you back on schedule." Daddy grins and reaches out to hug me. "Don't worry."

"See, a little set back doesn't ruin everything. That was fantastic!" Jackson leans back and pats his stomach.

"Yeah, Mom. Best ever," Will yells from out on the deck. The college kids are seated outside, and we've got the doors open so it's somewhat like we're in the same room. Around the inside table sits Jackson, me, Mother, Daddy, Savannah, and Bryan. Outside are Will, Arthur, T.J., Amir, Anna, Katherine, and Sidney. Randy left this morning, heading home to Arkansas.

My very bones are tired, and while the food looks and smells delicious, there's something about having cooked it all that makes it not as appealing. I'm tired of it. Tired of thinking about it, fixing it, watching it, serving it. But when Bryan takes another scoop of sweet potatoes and Will comes in and says they need more dressing outside and Daddy winks at Savannah and asks her to sneak him "one more deviled egg," a strange warmth slides over me. My entire body loses its tension, my breaths deepen, and I'm sure my smile must reflect pure contentment. In the center of the table is an arrangement of crimson and rust mums. Sidney and Katherine's moms sent it to thank us for having their daughters for the holiday. The girls are from the Chicago area and since the weather there didn't look good for weekend travel, everyone thought it best they not go home. Of course, Will offered them shelter and sustenance.

"Miss Carolina?" Sidney says loudly. "We're going to clean this all up for you. So, you just go put your feet up."

"Yeah, the girls are feeling guilty," T.J. offers.

"The boys are, too. And that's not all they'll be feeling if they think they're bailing out on cleaning up," Katherine threatens. When the boys start groaning about missing the football game, she cocks that eyebrow again. "Good. That means you'll work faster."

"How about a walk out on the bridge? Sounds like things here are in good hands." Jackson rubs my back and leans his head to look at me.

"I'm so tired, but tell you what, let's start that direction and see how far we get."

"Deal. Anyone else want to join us? Mom? Dad?"

Daddy frowns. "Not me. I think these young folks need a little supervision to get this put away right."

"Oh, Jack, they're fine. Quit bossing them around."

"Now, Goldie, I'm not bossing." His eyes twinkle, "Just advising."

Mother waves a hand at him. "Whatever. You never think you're bossing. I'm going to walk down and take a look at this boat Bryan and Grant have found, if Bryan's up for it?"

Bryan nods and then slumps back in his chair, "Gran, I don't know if I can make it or not. I'm stuffed with those sweet potatoes. But for you, I'll try."

"Ricky wants to know if I can come to his Aunt Susan's for dessert later. Is that okay?" Savannah asks.

Jackson and I shrug at each other, "Sure."

"But don't stay long, and bring Ricky back with you," Daddy adds. "We want to get another hour or two of *Gone with the Wind* tonight."

Once Katherine and Sidney carry the first load of dishes in from the deck, everyone starts moving. Jackson hands me my jacket from the hooks by the door, and we slip out the front. The porch has leaves scattered on it and the sun is peeking through the trees across the tracks. Out on the bridge, we should be in the sunshine and lose the chill from the shadows.

Jackson looks off to the northwest. "There's a chance we'll get some snow tomorrow they're saying. Midwest is getting hit pretty hard from what I saw on Weather Channel this morning."

"Good thing Katherine and Sidney didn't try to make it home. I hope Randy is okay getting to Arkansas."

"He should be if the storm stays on the course they think it will take."

I tuck my arms in his. "So dinner was good?"

"Good? Honey, it was more than good. Thank you for doing all that. Wasn't Bryan funny with the sweet potatoes? And Savannah matching her Grandpa on the deviled eggs."

"My favorite was watching Mother and Daddy looking around at the kids. It was fun. Makes me wish I'd done it in the past. I always dreaded the holidays. There always seemed to be no time to make things special. And then lots of guilt because things weren't special. I didn't want to go to my folks or your folks, and I sure didn't want to have them to our house." Leaves crunch beneath our feet. The maples lining the driveway are mostly bare now and the yard is carpeted in gold and orange.

My warm feeling rises up again. "What if we invite your family here for Christmas?" A quick look up at Jackson shows a scowl.

"Now, let's not get crazy. Let's just get through this holiday before you start working on the next one, okay?"

"Okay, but think about it."

Halfway out, we stop to lean on the railing and look down at the river.

And smooch.

Leftover pie, a chocolate cake, and a pumpkin cheesecake from an Athen's bakery, which Amir and TJ brought, sit arrayed around the flowers from Katherine and Sidney's families.

"Coffee's done. Who can I bring a cup?" Jackson asks from the kitchen.

"Me. I'll get it," I say as I come down the stairs just as the phone rings.

"Carolina? Did you invite us for dessert?" Missus demands when I say, "Hello."

"Yes. Why?"

"So Mister didn't make up an invitation? I won't be inviting myself to barge in."

Laughter and disbelief clog my throat for a moment. "No, he's not making it up. Please come by...okay, see you soon."

"Who's coming?" Mother asks.

"Missus, Mister, and Peter. I invited Mister this morning when I went down to get the turkey out of their refrigerator. And, of course you know Missus wouldn't want to barge in anywhere." I chuckle as I take my cup of coffee from Jackson.

"Of course she barges in any other time. She must adhere to a different set of standards on holidays."

"Well, when you were upstairs, Savannah texted me that she and Ricky are headed here and may bring his mom and dad. I told her that was fine."

"Sure. I can't wait to meet this woman. Just glad we have all that pie left from last night."

CHAPTER 10

Chill wind pushes into the house when I open the door for Missus, FM, and Peter.

"When did it get so cold?" I exclaim.

FM pushes Missus ahead of him. "Not a one of us even took our coat to Aunt Pru's and now it's colder than a…"

"FM," Missus admonishes with a jerk of her chin. "Just because we've spent the day with your hillbilly cousins, doesn't mean I'll stand for any of their trashy talk."

Jackson comes in from the kitchen carrying a chair. "Hillbilly cousins? Why, FM, we might be related. There's a hillbilly branch or two on my family tree. Here ya go, Peter."

"Looks like you're expecting a crowd with all these chairs." Peter says as he motions his mother to the padded rocker between the door and window.

I lean toward him. "Crowd is already here," I whisper. "They're taking a tour of the B&B rooms."

Peter and I look up as we hear the tour group coming down the hall.

Missus tunes her antennae and then glares at Peter. "Speaking of hillbillies and trash, do I hear Abby Sue Troutman?"

"Yeah, Ricky and Savannah brought his folks back for dessert. They're taking a look at the B&B rooms."

In her best white gloved voice, Missus snaps, "How sensible of you to send chaperones along. Not that having an audience would particularly dissuade Abby Sue."

"Mother, behave." Peter lifts a chair from against the wall and places it up against his mother's chair. "Think I'll sit right here where I can help you keep a hold on your tongue."

"Abby Sue! Welcome home, you sweet thing." FM greets the petite blonde when she enters the living room. His effusiveness hides the disapproving sniff from Missus.

Abby Sue is a knockout. Except for being short, her measurements match those of a Barbie doll. Her ash-blond hair curves to her shoulders and lays on her black sweater in a bouncy, stylish cut. Her black wool skirt meets the top of leather, high-heeled boots. She exudes class and breeding until she opens her mouth. Then she's all country. I've never seen such a disconnect between a person's look and their mouth. Her usage of slang, backwoods terms, and off-color language is truly a masterpiece. And she's loud. How can anything that crude and noisy come out of something so pretty?

"FM, you old buzzard. Come give me some sugar, and I don't mean a pink pack of Sweet-n-Low. I want the real thing. You know I *always* want the real thing." Abby Sue plants a big kiss right on FM's mouth.

Thank goodness his mouth was closed, but it was the only one closed in the room.

Peter is right behind his father, but he holds Abby Sue at arms' length when she whirls away from FM and toward his son.

"Peter, Lord have mercy, you are the best looking thing in Chancey. Come here."

Scott has worked his way past Savannah and Ricky and reaches between his ex-wife and Peter to grab Peter's hand. "Hey, man. Good to have you back in town. Hear things are going great at the museum." He drops Peter's hand and then wraps his arm around Abby Sue's waist. And I do mean all the way around, like he's her seatbelt.

My mouth is working again. "Everyone sit down. I have another pot of coffee going, so when it's done we'll have some dessert."

Scott sits down in the easy chair and pushes it back to recline. He then reaches out and plants his hands on Abby Sue's hips and pulls her into his lap. She laughs, twists to face him, and they start kissing. Savannah is behind them, and she rolls her eyes at me and Missus. Ricky's face is turned to the floor, but its redness can't be hidden.

"We stacked up the wood in the basement." Will, his college friends, and Bryan pile into the living room, brushing dirt from their clothes. "We're ready for dessert. Second game should be starting soon. First one wasn't worth finishing." Will greets people until he gets to the scene in the easy chair.

"I'm going to cut those leftover pies. Y'all introduce everyone," I instruct as I step into the kitchen. At the counter I stare at the cabinets and try to keep from bursting out in laughter. Suddenly the space around me is filled with chattering girls.

"Oh my, did you see that?"

"They're like making out."

"He has his hand up the back of her sweater."

Savannah's voice cuts through, "Mom, you've got to make them go home."

I turn on her. "You brought them here. *You* make them go home."

"They didn't ride with us." She grins. "Ricky even tried to lose them, but how lost can someone get in Chancey?" Then she leans in. "Did you see Missus' face?"

"What about *my* face?"

Giggles gag the girls, and the circle takes a step back for you know who.

Missus ignores the girls and points a long finger. "Carolina, you have to get rid of them."

"Why me? I'm just serving coffee. Maybe if they have dessert and coffee in their hands they'll have to behave."

Katherine shakes her head. "If my parents acted like that, I'd have them committed." She apparently tries picturing her attorney parents in a lustful pile on display for her friends, because a shudder runs over her whole body.

Sidney giggles and puts out a hand toward Missus. "You're Missus, right? I didn't get to meet you earlier."

"Yes, that is me." Missus holds out her hand, but her nose flares and her chin lifts. "Whatever are you giggling about?"

Blue eyes shine in Sidney's pale, round face. "Just nothing. Just everything." Her Nordic sweater adds to the jolliness of her demeanor.

Katherine, wearing a cashmere turtleneck and dark wool slacks, scowls at her friend, "She's just silly."

Sidney swats at her friend and frowns. "And you're too serious." The two square off but are interrupted by Anna darting into the kitchen.

"Miss Carolina, all those books in the basement are yours?"

"Yes, you're welcome to read them, if you want."

"Really, oh, wow. I started looking while they were stacking wood and you have so many. It's like your own personal library. Oh, you…"

Anna's twinkle dies as she spots Missus. She blinks rapidly and mumbles incoherently for a moment.

Missus looks to heaven for help with the imbeciles she's forced to abide and then dismisses Anna with a wave of her hand. "You are a rude and obtuse girl." Missus turns her back on Anna. "Carolina, I want to know what you're going to do about those two in there." The hand she waved, stiffens into a finger pointed at the living room. "Either they leave or I am."

"Mother, enough." Peter pushes into the center of the room.

"This kitchen is too full for me to cut the pies. The sooner we have dessert, the sooner *everyone* can go home." My growl causes Sidney, Katherine, and Savannah to scoot into the living room.

Peter turns and notices Anna plastered against the refrigerator staring at him and his mother. "I don't think I've met you. I'm Peter Bedwell."

Anna stares at his offered hand, but then her eyes dart to Missus who is glaring at her. The girl peels away from the fridge and slides around the corner into the living room.

"Odd, odd child," Missus pronounces.

Peter stretches his fingers on his unshaken hand. "Who is she?"

"A friend Will brought from Athens, but that's all I know. How old do you think she is? Sixteen?"

Missus sniffs. "Who cares? She has no manners and acts as if she's got mental problems."

"Mother, you are just being ugly today."

"I suppose you're right, but it's been a horrible day. Help Carolina cut those pies so we can go home. My headache is only getting worse here. I'll sit and keep you company now that all the children are gone." She settles in the one chair left at the table. "Between that debacle of marriage mockery at your Aunt Prudence's house and the hormones swamping Carolina's easy chair, my nerves and manners are shot. And then that waif, Anna, sets my teeth on edge."

"She seems fine until you're around," I point out. "Maybe you scare her."

Jackson walks into the kitchen, "Want me to pour coffee? We've got to do something to break up that action in the easy chair. Can you believe them? No wonder Ricky is so glad he's staying here."

"What?" Missus erupts. "Carolina and Jackson, you are *not* letting Savannah's boyfriend stay here overnight, are you? Have you no sense of propriety at all? Do you not care about her reputation? I mean, look at what she's associated with already."

"Oh, they're fine," Daddy interjects as he enters the room. "Goldie and I are chaperoning them, the kids, not those two in the easy chair. You gotta send them home."

"Jack, you see from that display in the living room what the boy comes from. You and Goldie are no match for *his* hormones."

"Dessert is served," I say weaving between Daddy and Jackson. At the entrance to the living room I repeat, "Dessert is served." My gaze is drawn, against my will, to Scott and Abby Sue. Her hair hides their faces, but one of his hands is actually down the top of her boot, massaging her calf and the other hand is up the back of her sweater. Plus, her skirt is going to have little rolled up balls and snags on it from being rubbed against his jeans zipper like that.

Everyone is full again. Dessert plates and cups fill the dishwasher and I punch the buttons for heavy wash. The lights blink and the water starts running but stops just as quickly. "Did I blow a breaker? Jackson?"

In the living room, the only light comes from the fireplace as everyone looks at each other.

"No, I think the electric is out."

"Mom, your TV went off." Bryan calls from upstairs where he was watching a movie.

"Shoot and there's only five minutes left in the game." Ricky, Will, and the other guys lament.

Peter pulls open the front door and when he pushes the storm door open, frigid wind blows in. "Uh oh. We have a problem."

We crowd around him and look out on a shiny, gray world. There's just enough light left in the sky for us to see the steady rain. But the shine isn't from just wetness. It's ice. Peter steps onto the porch but near the edge he stops. "Everything is coated in ice." He grasps the porch rail and puts his foot down onto the top step. "Solid ice."

"Wires, too. Look." FM points up to the lines heading into the house. Icicles hang from them. "Probably what happened to the electricity. Only so much ice can build up before they snap."

"Then let's get back inside and close this door to keep in as much heat as possible," Jackson says.

I follow the crowd. "I guess the party's over. Everyone needs to get on the roads before things get worse."

Will laughs, "Mom, the party's just beginning. No one can leave. You can't walk down the sidewalk, much less drive."

Savannah, Missus, and me all shake our heads and at the same time look at Scott and Abby Sue, entwined and looking out the window. We're stuck with them?

I sigh and turn toward the stairs. Maybe I can escape upstairs, and in the dark, no one will miss me. However, on the first step above the landing, Anna is huddled. Her gray blue eyes are huge and tear-filled. She's hugging her knees with tense arms and she's staring across the room. I follow her eyes. Missus whispering to FM and Peter has her attention. When I get a chance, I've got to ask Will what's up with this girl, but right now, I need some ibuprofen.

CHAPTER 11

It's dark and cold. No charging light on the electric toothbrush or phone. Alarm clock face is solid black. Drat! Still no electricity. After downing three ibuprofen, I lay down, pulled the covers over me, and fell asleep. Jackson's not beside me. Wonder what time it is?

Freezing air hits me when the covers are thrown back. In the dark, my memory guides me to my thick robe, where I threw it this morning. Still wearing my clothes from earlier, but also wrapped in my robe and with another pair of thick socks in hand, I open my bedroom door. Orange light from the fireplace and voices beckon me toward the stairs. Looks like everyone is still here. Will, Savannah, and Bryan are where my eyes settle first for that obligatory check on my kids. And there's Jackson, okay.

"There she is," Peter says when I step onto the landing.

Jackson stands and meets me at the bottom of the stairs. "Hey, how was your nap? I came up to check on you and you were out."

I snuggle into his hug for a moment. "I feel better, but it's so cold."

With his arm around me, we walk to the couch, where Ricky has gotten up to give me a place to sit. Familiar comforters and blankets take on the light from the fireplace.

"We raided every closet and bed, as you can see," Savannah explains. Checking around the room I notice some folks are missing.

Jackson leans toward my ear on his side. "Abby Sue and Scott decided to keep the covers on the bed in the Chessie room and try and stay warm in there. FM, Missus, and your mom and dad have commandeered the motor home because they have the generator."

"You should've seen them, Mom." Bryan says from inside his sleeping bag on the floor at Jackson's feet. Only his face is visible in the little unzipped gap. "We laid towels on the steps and sidewalk so they could walk out there and then us guys walked with Grandma and Missus to make sure they didn't fall. Dad said we should take up the towels so they can't come back until the ice thaws."

"I did not," Jackson says.

Peter laughs. "Yes you did, and I seconded it. This may be a big house, but it's not big enough for all of us and those four."

A knock on the door, causes several to say, "Oh no" and one "They're baaack," but when Jackson opens the door, there's Griffin and Susan Liles and their thirteen-year-old son, Grant.

"Come in. Come in."

I scoot over on the couch and Savannah joins Ricky on the floor. He lifts the quilt Jackson's grandmother made, and she slides in next to him. Need to keep my eyes on that.

Susan sits next to me while Griffin stands in front of the fire and Grant sits on the hearth.

"We tried and tried calling your cell, Carolina, but you never answered. We decided to take a walk over and check on y'all."

Griffin rubs his hands on his cheeks, "Plus that house full of in-laws and out-laws made a walk in the freezing rain sound plum fantastic!"

"We've got ours shut up out in the motor home," Will offers.

Susan laughs. "Thought it might be something like that. We

knocked and waved. Told them not to open the door or their heat would escape."

"Savannah, hand me my cell phone, please. It's in my purse." One way to break up that dynamic duo under the quilt.

Savannah's voice snaps out of the darkness, "Bryan, get mom's cell."

The fact that he jumps up and does it before I can stop him shows how bored he is. He hands it to me. "Can me and Grant go outside and look around?"

"I'm not sure it's safe. It's awfully slippery."

"Hey, let's go. C'mon guys." Will pokes and kicks at his buddies. "I'm tired of just sitting here. We'll watch out for Bryan and Grant."

Griffin nods. "I think it will be okay. The only place there's ice is on the steps, sidewalks, and paved streets. And, of course, the electric wires."

With some prodding, all the young people decide to go outside for a while. Soon it's only Jackson, me, and Susan on the couch. Griffin in the easy chair and Peter in the rocking chair.

Susan lifts her backpack up. "Carolina, go get us some cups, and we'll have adult happy hour. I've got a thermos here full of hot chocolate with butterscotch schnapps."

Sipping on her full cup of rich, creamy, "special" hot chocolate, Susan finally asks. "Okay, where are they?"

"Who?"

"Scott and Abby Sue. Last we heard they were headed here for dessert."

Peter and Jackson both shut their mouths and look wide-eyed at me. So I get to tattle. "Okay, they're in one of the B&B rooms. Better than the easy chair, which is where they performed most of the afternoon."

Griffin wrinkles his nose and looks at his chair. "Why'd you have to tell me that?"

"Carolina, you missed it when you were napping." Peter

chuckles in the dim light. "Mama got caught telling some of Abby Sue's more adventuresome outings to the college girls. Abby Sue jumped all over Mama and then, well, she said something about Mama having secrets, and you'd of thought Abby Sue had something on her, because Mama started apologizing and backing down like nothing I've ever seen."

"What if she does know something about your Mama?" The question comes from a dark corner beside the fireplace.

"Anna? Is that you?" I ask.

"Yes, ma'am."

"I didn't know you were still in here."

"There's some light for me to read by if I lay here in this corner. I didn't want to go outside."

With raised eyebrows I look at Jackson. "Well, that's okay. But you should've let us know you were there."

"Don't worry. You didn't say anything I shouldn't hear." Anna stretches, stands up, and then walks over to sit in front of the fire.

"Anna, this is Susan and Griffin Lyles. Did you meet Susan the other day when you got here?"

"No," Susan says. "Anna was down at the river. Hi. You did meet Susie Mae. She's our daughter. I think you two are about the same age, right?"

Anna just shrugs. Then she turns toward Peter. "What if there is something about your mama you don't know? Something she doesn't want anyone to know."

Peter strokes his beard and studies the small girl huddled in the puddle of fire light. "That would be her business. However, she was born and raised in the house we live in now. Hard to have secrets when you've never left town and been pretty much the center of attention your entire life."

Anna nods and then reaches for her book. "Okay. Just wondering." Within seconds of looking at the page she opens to, she's lost in the book.

Her concentration and shutting down reminds me of myself. How I can block out the entire world with black letters on white pages. Around the room, we make questioning eye contact, but nothing more is said. We drink our hot cocoa and watch the fire.

CHAPTER 12

"Would you look at that? Not a cloud in the sky." FM leans past me to open the French doors onto the back deck. Both jumpy, noisy mops bound past us and down the few deck steps. Ashley, like the gentleman he is, waits for me to exit the house. He then descends the steps but heads in the opposite direction of his mentally-challenged step-siblings.

"They say the storm just clipped North Georgia long enough to dump all that ice, but the rest of the weekend should be sunny." Testing the footing, I follow FM to the edge of the deck. "Electricity came back on around six this morning. The heat and the lights kicking on woke me up." Sparkles shoot back at us from the slushy wetness on the grass, bushes, and trees. Everything is wet and shiny, but no solid patches of ice remain.

"Motor home was toasty warm. Slept like the dead." Taking in a lung-full of chilly, fresh air, he studies the sky. "Sure like your folks, Carolina, and they seem to like me and Missus. It's good for both of us to be around some outsiders. We've lived here in Chancey so long we don't know what it's like to get to know people. Share your history, learn theirs. Law, I don't know the last time I made a new friend." He sticks his tongue into his jaw and shakes his head then jerks toward me. "Well, now, you're a new friend, aren't you? But not like someone my own age."

The question on my mind but needing to be asked out of Missus' earshot leaps up. "How did things go at your aunt's house yesterday?"

FM grins and we turn back toward the kitchen. "It was a sight, like always. However, Peter being there was a new spin. Two of Aunt Pru's oldest girls are twins and they ain't married. They flirted something awful with Peter, which he took in stride, but 'bout near gave Missus a stroke."

"Where is the oldest living horror queen?"

The question startles us as we step into the kitchen. Abby Sue is standing at the counter, stirring her cup of coffee. "FM, I swear on Hank Williams, Jr.'s life, I don't know how you put up with that woman. Never mind. I guess the how isn't too hard to figure. She came with a house and money. But why? You didn't need her house and money and goodness knows, you didn't need a sack of self-righteous bones to sleep with. I bet you looked a lot like Peter in your heyday, didn't you?"

Abby Sue stares at FM for a moment and nods like he agreed with her. "Yep, you could've had any woman in three counties." She lifts her cup and takes a sip, all the time shaking her head and sighing. "Poor, poor man."

"Now, uh, now, that's not nice," I sputter.

FM steps toward Abby Sue and looks her up and down.

Abby Sue lights up like a puppy at the shelter about to be taken home.

His voice is hard, but low. "No poor FM. At least I don't have to settle for sex once a year when my wife—oops, ex-wife comes snooping back around. Why don't you quit messing with Scott and let him find a real woman."

Oh, no. This needs to be broken up, so my feet start shuffling toward them. Then Abby Sue breaks into sobs and throws herself onto FM's chest.

What?

"I know, little girl, I know." FM comforts Abby Sue and leads her to the living room. He places her on the couch and then comes back to the kitchen where I'm waiting with crossed arms.

He makes his way to the coffeepot. "So, you say it's supposed to be sunny the rest of the weekend?" He pours a cup of coffee.

"No, don't try talking about the weather. What's up with Abby Sue?"

"She's just a kid. She's got troubles—always has."

"Kid? She's got grown sons."

"Aw, that don't make no never mind. Some people just always stay kids." With the slam of the front door and Missus snapping his name, FM tilts his head. "And some never were kids."

"I want to go home now. I don't want to wait for you to finish your coffee. I want to leave now." Missus' arms are folded across her heavy, oatmeal-colored sweater. "Now that the roads are clear you know this place will get even more crowded. Carolina, I've never seen a place that acts like a people magnet more than this place. When will you get some backbone and not let everyone in a four-state radius turn you into a welcome mat?" She purses her lips and the crease between her eyes deepens. "And all these young people. I like that Katherine, but that giggly, blonde girl and wimpy, rude one should not be allowed back. Will must make better choices. I have such hope for him."

"I thought you wanted to leave?" FM interrupts her tirade. "Any other insults you need to leave with Carolina, or can we go now?"

"Carolina knows I'm not insulting her. She knows I'm just speaking the truth."

"The truth?" Abby Sue shouts from the living room. "Old woman, you and the truth ain't met in a long time."

My head drops. There will be fireworks now. But when I

raise my eyes to look at Missus I see, uh, I see fear not fire. FM looks at me and shrugs then follows his wife out of the kitchen. They leave without another word, from them or me.

All in all, an extremely successful exit.

Chapter 13

"Griffin says everyone comes on Thankful Sunday. Even more folks than Easter Sunday, and I can believe it looking at this parking lot." Jackson leans forward to make sure he's not going to clip the car next to us.

"Sounds interesting, but I still don't understand it. I know *I'm* not standing up and talking."

"And you don't have to, Mom." Savannah sighs. "What do you not understand? People put stuff on and around the altar before the service and then when the pastor lifts up that thing, that person stands up and tells why they are thankful for it."

I catch her eyes in my visor's mirror. "Did you bring anything?"

"Not telling. You'll have to wait and find out." She opens the sliding door and climbs out, followed by Ricky. Friday and Saturday turned into a holiday weekend you'd see in a Lifetime movie (well, up until the husband's mistress and illegitimate kids show up or someone gets killed. Both Lifetime staples.) However, ours was only the good stuff. Leftovers, games, football on the lawn, a bonfire and watching *Gone with the Wind*. Since the summer setting up the B&B rooms, I've learned to enjoy teenagers and those barely out of their teens. My good mood even got me to agree to go to church. But now that we're here, my good mood is quickly fading.

Jackson meets me at the back of the van. His smile annoys me. Church is not my thing. Sleeping in on Sunday is my thing. You'd think with all his traveling and early mornings, sleeping in would also be my husband's thing. But more and more I'm finding myself sleeping in alone on Sundays. The fact that he does this church thing while smiling is not a good sign. So, his smile annoys me. "I bet I know why it's so crowded for this Thankful thing. Without a sermon it will be short."

Jackson puts his keys in his pocket and reaches out to hold my arm as we head toward the front doors. "Could be."

A little crinkling noise lets me know he smiled again. Now just hearing his smile annoys me, but I manage to hide my annoyance. I was raised in the South, you know. My smile grows more genuine as we greet our friends, but once inside the sanctuary my heart and smile drop. The altar area is overflowing with junk. Seriously, junk. Quilts, pictures, stuffed animals, boxes, books. Forget this Thankful Sunday bologna, hold a garage sale during the service, and get the budget back in the black, because that's exactly what it looks like—a garage sale. A big one. We're never getting out of here. I should've eaten breakfast.

And then, like it's not already going to take forever, we sing songs and they read scripture. Finally, we get to the Thankful Sunday part. Wouldn't you know it? The pastor starts reading some more scripture and has to talk a few minutes. My sighs get louder. I know because Savannah keeps stabbing me with her eyes, and Jackson keeps clearing his throat. Well, if they'd let me stay home…

About the third item that the pastor lifts up apparently belongs to a little man seated in the row behind us because he says, "That's mine, Preacher." The old picture is one of those photos, into which yellow and brown have seeped. The woman in it leans over the back of a chair and her string of pearls hang away from her chest. Her hair is pulled back on the sides and her dress looks like it was made for dancing. Her laugh comes out of the frame.

The little man pulls himself up with aid of the pew in front of him. He's only a few feet from me, and I shift to see him more easily. His hands are visibly whitened by the force with which he holds himself upright, but he straightens and clears his throat. His old man voice quivers, but his accent is round and deep like the Georgia valleys he's apparently spent his life in.

"That there is my wife, Lucille. She can't make it to church no more you know, Preacher, not since she went to the home. They're real good to her, and they have a little service on Sunday night we sometimes can go to. But she can't make it here no more." He pauses and swallows. "That picture was taken on our honeymoon, and you can see she's a beauty. Still is." He swallows again. "I'm thankful for her, you know, but even more this morning I realize I'm thankful for all the Sunday's we shared sitting in this here pew." He chokes up and bends his head, but when he looks back toward the pastor, he's smiling. "Sure wouldn't know that I fought it for years, would you?" Laughter and tears mix in the congregation. "Now, there's no Lucille at home to get ready with on Sunday mornings. No one to drive here with and no one to hold hands with when the choir sings a song I like. But, preacher, I'm right thankful for all those years there were."

The old man lowers himself into his pew. Our eyes meet, and he winks at me. How could he know? He can't, right? It was just an old man wink. I turn around to watch what item the pastor picks up next. With a quick swipe, my hand takes care of the tears on my face. Then as I start to lay my hand in my lap, Jackson claims it.

Medicine bottles, wedding rings, baby blankets all have stories to tell. We're wrapped in memories and thankfulness, and I see why there's a crowd. In a plastic, agenda-filled and agenda-driven world, this is genuine. This feels good and right. I could stay here all day! Then the pastor lifts a set of keys up, shows them to the congregation, and waits to see who claims it. Like everyone else I stretch my neck, look behind me and in front. At the end of our pew a tall man stands up, but his accent isn't from Georgia. It's from Tennessee.

"Y'all don't know me, but I'm Jack Butler. Our daughter, Carolina, and son-in-law, Jackson moved here to Chancey this past summer, and I thought I'd use this opportunity to say we're thankful for our motor home. Those are the keys to it the minister is holding. Me and Goldie here, are thankful because our home on wheels allows us to stay here with you folks plum through Christmas!" He leans forward and waves at me and Jackson.

The quick applause hides a few audible gasps. Was that me gasping? Daddy waves to the rest of his audience then sits down finally, and the pastor moves onto another item from the altar.

Oh, yeah. Completely slipped my mind to find out when my folks were leaving. Oh, yeah.

Hey, Jackson really needs to loosen up his grip. My hand's going numb.

CHAPTER 14

"Were you surprised?" Daddy leans toward me and squeezes my shoulders with his arm on our way out of the church. "When Savannah explained what was going on at church today, I knew it was the perfect opportunity to let y'all know."

Mother and Daddy's delight is hard to take but not as hard as all the looks of sympathy we're getting from complete strangers. Our friends nod to us with raised eyebrows and stiff grins. There are only two people in this parking lot who think this is a good idea, no three. Bryan's happy. But he's got youth to explain his ignorance. In my pocket, I stretch my fingers which were only released from Jackson's death grip when we stood up to leave the service. Jackson hasn't said anything to me. We look like those political couples who've just realized they lost and have to go on TV and say how happy they are about it.

"Hey, Mr. and Mrs. Butler. Carolina." Laney prances toward us in a tweed suit. The prancing is due to the four inch heels on her ankle boots. The leather of the boots looks as smooth and supple as melted caramel for dunking apples. Her gloves are made from the same leather, and when she hugs me I can literally smell the spa treatments in her hair and on her skin.

The spa makes me think of something. What is it? "Oh, Laney. The state called about our water testing. I almost forgot with the ice storm and everything."

"They're always calling about something." She wrinkles her nose at me. "It's the holidays now, there's nothing that can't wait until January. And speaking of the holidays, Mr. and Mrs. Butler, you're staying until Christmas? Oh my, what will you do with yourselves in this dinky town? Y'all being used to traveling and entertaining and all."

Mother strokes Laney's glove as she cradles the younger woman's hand. "We're going to help Carolina and Jackson. The house needs ever so much work, as you must know. And for them to try and get ready for Christmas at the same time, well, we just don't see that we have any other choice." Mother's turquoise-colored eyes light up as she sees Laney's boots. "Dear, are your boots as soft as these gloves?"

"Absolutely. Aren't they divine? My shopper at Saks always knows what I like. Mrs. Butler, we must simply make time for a trip down to Lenox since you'll be staying with us. I can see you are a woman who loves beautiful things. I could hardly pay attention to the preacher today for wanting to see your dress close up. It's stunning, truly. Such workmanship."

"Please, call me Goldie." Mother leans into Laney and whispers, "Maybe we could show Carolina a thing or two about designers this month. Don't you think?"

The creases between both sets of eyes express their doubt.

"Me and designers? I'll stick to the ones at Target." I push out my foot and turn my black, fake suede flat for them to examine. "See these were only $19.99. Now, that was at least three years ago, so they're probably worth at least $24.99."

My laugh falls flat as they sigh and shake their heads.

"Mom, do we have to eat more leftovers?" Bryan rushes toward me, yelling his questions on his approach. "Can we go out?"

Daddy follows his grandson, only a little slower. "I'll treat, okay?"

"Trotman's will all be out at our place today," Laney says. "Chili is one of three dishes I make, so the Sunday after Thanksgiving, it's tradition to have chili out at the farm. I guess I better get going."

"Wait, Laney, the water people want an answer tomorrow morning, or they're going to deny our license. Tomorrow."

Laney flips a mass of black curls my direction and lifts a gloved hand in the air. "Fiddle de dee, I'll think about that tomorrow."

Mother glows. Daddy swoons. Just imagine, a whole month in a town where Scarlett O'Hara has come back to life.

At the van, Susan and Griffin, walk past on the way to their car but turn back toward us.

"Have you all seen the gazebo?" Griffin asks.

We shake our heads. "No, why?"

"Huge branch from one of the oaks in the park fell during the ice storm. Demolished it. Knocked the roof completely off its supports and leveled one side to the ground." Griffin shrugs. "We'd thought we might could salvage the roof, but Dean Smiltson, who's a carpenter, was just telling me he looked at it yesterday afternoon and all the supports are splintered."

"What about insurance?"

Susan smiles. "No one is sure. Mayor tried looking around at the files yesterday, but couldn't make heads or tails out of Laney's filing system."

"Us on the council know we pay some kind of insurance premiums, we're just not sure what all it covers." Griffin rubs his chin. "Guess we'll find out now."

"Doesn't Laney know?" I ask.

"She was down at the mall all day yesterday, and today she's got the chili dinner on her mind. Says she'll look into it tomorrow."

"She didn't add a 'fiddle-de-dee' when she said it, did she?" Couldn't resist.

We all laugh and Mother and Daddy's car pulls up. "How does O'Charlie's out at the highway sound? Oh, and Bryan's riding with us."

At Daddy's window, I nod. "Sure, sounds good. Where's Savannah?"

Mother leans over. "She's riding with Missus and FM. They're coming, too."

"Okay, see you there."

Their car pulls off, and we wave to Susan and Griffin as they head toward their car.

Jackson is in the driver's seat when I come up to his open door and lean in. "Hey, good lookin', there's a big old empty house up a hill right out of town. Lots of leftovers and working heat." I lean one hip against him and smile, "How about you let me show you a good time."

He reaches out and places his hand on my waist then leans toward me as he sighs. "The college kids are all there."

My eyes blink with the sudden shift of my thinking. How did I forget them? I shake my head as if I can make things fall in place. "My mind must be fried. First, I forget my folks are staying until Christmas and now I forget about a half dozen house guests."

The temperature drops, along with Jackson's hand from my waist. "You *knew* your parents were staying? When did you know that?"

"I didn't really know, know it. Maybe, just more like an idea."

"And you told them it was okay?"

"Not much. I kinda forgot to mention it."

"Well, it's a disaster, unmitigated disaster."

"They have the motor home. It will work out, it…"

"Remember you wanting to ask my folks here for Christmas?"

With a step back, I lift my shoulders and frown. "Yes, but, well, we can have them next year."

"No, we're having them this year." Jackson turns the car on

and reaches out to shut the door.

"Are you just trying to prove a point? You're the one that balked at inviting them."

He looks at me then agrees. "Yeah, it was me, so I decided I needed to get over it."

"Well, good. They can come another time. We better get on the way." As I turn and start around the van, Jackson calls my name.

"Yes?"

"They're coming. I called them."

"Oh. Okay." My breathing starts getting heavy, and my chest hurts by the time I get to the other side and in my seat.

"They'll be in Florida for a conference, so they'll get here December tenth."

"What? And they'll stay through Christmas?"

"Yeah. That's pretty much it."

The way his eyes won't meet mine makes me think there's more to this. "Pretty much it? What's *all* of it?"

"Shelby's going to be with them."

"Shelby? Your ex-wife, Shelby?"

With a quick nod, he puts the car in reverse. We back out and I try to remember: Is there a bridge we can drive off on the way to O'Charlie's?

Chapter 15

My head keeps falling forward and waking me up. We barely left the restaurant parking lot before the dozing started. Half asleep, half awake, but there's so much to discuss.

Jackson laughs. "Quit trying to talk. You're just mumbling. We're almost home."

When the car comes to a stop and Jackson opens his door, the rush of cold air startles me.

"We're home, Sleeping Beauty and looks like the caravan to Athens is preparing to get underway."

That wakes me up. "But I thought they weren't leaving until later. I wouldn't have gone to eat if I'd known they weren't all still asleep up here." I tumble out my door and into a driveway full of open car doors, comforters, pillows, and bags and young people in pajama pants. Even the guys have on flannel baggy pants emblazoned with cartoon characters or team logos. "Will, I didn't know you were leaving this early."

"Minute, Mom." He throws the bags in his hands in his trunk and meets me halfway. We've all got finals coming up, as Katherine…" He tips his head toward the tall, stately girl—the only one not wearing pajama pants. "…reminded us over and over this morning. Besides, I'll be home in a couple weeks for Christmas break."

We walk down the sidewalk toward the porch. "But I hate I didn't get to fix y'all breakfast. I figured you'd be sleeping in late, and I could make you something this afternoon."

"Aw, we're good." He holds the door open for me. "We raided the kitchen. 'Fraid we left it a mess. Mom, I do need to ask you a favor."

"You want food for the apartment? Okay, let's see what kind of mess you left." We enter the kitchen but stop short. The kitchen is spotless, no, better than spotless. It's shining.

"Oh, wow," Will approves. "Anna said she'd clean up. Looks great, doesn't it?"

"Sure does. That girl is my new favorite." I dump my purse and coat onto a kitchen chair and turn to open the refrigerator. "So, what leftovers do you want to take?"

"Anything's good, but that's not what I wanted to ask you. Can Anna stay?"

"What?" Another conversation that never happened. I was supposed to ask Will about Anna.

And the kitchen fills with people suddenly.

"Thanks so much, Mrs. Jessup."

"It was great, the food and everything."

"My folks are so happy we stayed here and weren't stuck in the snow."

Hugs and good-byes wash through, and Will tries to get swept away in the flood.

"Oh, no." I grab my oldest child's sleeve and pull him out of the undertow of coats and hats. "What is up with Anna? Where is she?"

Will swings his blond head back and forth as if he might be able to spot the tiny girl around any corner. "I think she's in her room."

"And?"

He sits down at the table. "She's only seventeen. She works, well, worked on campus in the cafeteria, and I met her there.

She lost her job a couple weeks ago, and she said she needed a ride to Chancey."

"You aren't dating her, are you?"

"Mom, really? She's a kid."

"Okay, good." One problem down, so I also take a seat. "Why did she want to come to Chancey?"

Will sighs and drops his shoulders, "I don't know. Things were crazy, and she just kind of came with us. And then we got here, and she didn't have anywhere to go." He frowns. "I kept meaning to talk to her, but…"

Okay, I might know where he got that trait. "Why isn't she going back with you?"

"Great, so she can stay?"

"Answer me first."

Relief loosens Will's face. "She lost her job, like I said, and for some reason she wants to stay in Chancey. She says she'll clean for you in exchange for a room and food, and she says she has some extra money so she won't be a burden."

"But, honey, she's only seventeen. Where are her parents?"

Will lifts his hands and then drops them. "Mom, all I know is if she goes back she says she'll have to live at a shelter. She says her folks can't help her."

Sidney pops her creamy, round face into the kitchen. "Sorry Will, but are you going to be much longer? Katherine won't let anyone get out of the cars, and it's getting ugly out there."

Will jumps up. "I'm coming."

He grabs me and practically pulls me out of my chair. "Bye, Mom. Thanks for everything."

I follow him through the living room. "Will, I'm just not sure about this thing with Anna…"

"It'll be okay. She's really sweet. Talk to you soon."

He runs down the steps and sidewalk and jumps into the driver's seat of his car. The cars back out and honk as they cross over the tracks.

Okay, Thanksgiving is officially over. Maybe my mind will stop spinning and can focus on the next month. And my folks. And Jackson's folks. And Anna. And—something else. Something big. That's right. Jackson's ex-wife, Shelby.

Horrible laughter swells up and escapes my mouth. Talk about conversations that should've happened. We never remembered to actually tell the kids about Daddy's first marriage.

Now, how could *that* have escaped our minds?

CHAPTER 16

"Anna, if you're going to stay with us you have to answer some questions for me." My gaze find hers over the boxes stacked between us. We're in the basement looking for the boxes of Christmas decorations. Heart-to-heart conversations over tea sound lovely, but they work better if there's something to keep busy with. "Here, stack the ones that say *ornaments* in this corner."

"Mrs. Jessup, you just ask and I'll answer. Promise."

After spending a couple hours this afternoon on the couch watching pro football with my eyes closed, I feel ready to have some of the conversations that keep getting forgotten. So here goes. "First, what about school? This semester is almost over, but I guess we need to go down to the high school and enroll you tomorrow?"

Dust falls from where Anna moves a box off the top of another one. She sneezes and shakes her head. "No, I finished high school. My mother homeschooled me, and then I took the GED, um, back in May and passed it."

"What about your mother now?"

"She died." Anna clears her throat as we both stop working. "She died last May, that's why I took the GED. It made her happy to know I had finished."

"Can I ask how she died?" My voice has dropped and my heart hurts.

Anna nods. "She, well, Mom had some problems when she was younger with drugs. They left her heart weak. She got pneumonia last winter, and it was too hard on her heart. She just couldn't get better."

"I'm so sorry."

"Yeah, but the last couple months she worked so hard to just breathe, every minute. That was really tough to watch."

"You weren't by yourself, were you? Do you have other family?"

"Some friends, but no family. It was always just me and Mom. Her parents were older, and she was also an only child. They died when she was in college. That was when she got into trouble with drugs and stuff. And got pregnant with me. I don't know anything about my dad." She sighs then mumbles, "I'm not sure she knew anything about him."

Anna looks up at me and shrugs before moving another box onto the ornament stack and continuing. "So, no family. But she was a good mother. She got out of the drugs by the time I remember anything, and we had a lot of friends at our church. That's how I got the job at the university cafeteria. One of my mom's friends worked there, and she thought I might get the chance to take some classes."

"That does sound like a good plan. But, Will said your job ended."

"Yeah, they cut back. And our friend, well, her daughter's husband left her so she went to live with her daughter and grandkids up in Kentucky. That was right before Thanksgiving, and when I heard Will inviting everyone here, I thought it sounded like a way to start over again."

I waited until I turned and could watch her before asking my next question. "So, no special reason for wanting to come to Chancey?"

Anna curls a brown curl around her finger. "I was working the tables that day at lunch, wiping down the table behind Will and his friends. They'd always been nice to me. Some people don't even see folks working in a cafeteria. I heard Will make an open invitation to the hotel his folks were opening."

My eyes narrow. "I knew it wasn't all in innocence how he always shows up with a crowd."

She grins and her blue-gray eyes crinkle up. "No, he promotes this place pretty loudly. Anyway, all that morning, after I found out they were cutting my position, I'd been praying about needing a second chance. Even as I wiped tables and eavesdropped on their conversation, the words were in my head, "Second chance, second chance." Then someone asked Will where his folks lived and he said, 'Chancey.' I immediately thought of a second chance in Chancey."

"I see. Makes sense."

"Only thing is, I thought with there being a hotel here it would be a bigger town and I could find a job. Then we got here, and I realized I might've made a mistake." She looks down and then turns away from me. Shame causes her shoulders to fold in.

"Anna, it doesn't have to be a mistake. It would be nice to have some help around here, and there's a junior college not too far away. Maybe you could start taking some classes next semester. You're obviously smart, and with no parents I'm sure you can qualify for financial aid."

The little girl doesn't turn around, but I hear a muddled, "Thank you." Figuring she needed a few minutes to herself, I move toward the stairs.

"I'm going to find Jackson and Bryan so they can help move these boxes upstairs. I'll be right back." As I climb up the open wooden stairs, certainty grows that she hasn't told me the whole story. But what I heard, I believed.

At bedtime, when Jackson opens the bathroom door after his shower, I sit waiting on the foot of the bed. The problem of Anna is fairly squared away. Now for Shelby.

"So, what do we do about Shelby?"

Jackson finishes putting toothpaste on his toothbrush and then sticks it in his mouth. He watches himself in the mirror for a minute then turns to me. In his plaid flannel pants from last Christmas and his white undershirt, he looks more like Will than ever., "I don't know," he garbles before he spits.

"You do remember we never told the kids." I smooth my hands down my gray jersey nightgown and then pick up a pillow and shelter it in my lap.

After rinsing, he nods and yanks the olive green hand towel off the circular holder. "Of course, I remember." He sits down beside me, still drying his hands on the towel. "I remember someone talking me out of telling them. Someone who might be my current wife."

Oh, crud. He does remember. How can he forget what I told him this morning, but on this he has total recall." I fall back on the bed. "It just seemed like such a hassle at the time, so unnecessary."

He folds the towel and lays it on his knee. "It wasn't just you. I went along with it. How do you think they'll react?"

"Will will be fine. Savannah will look for angles to use it against us, and Bryan will…" He's the one I don't know about."

"Yeah, he's so good natured." My troubled husband unfolds the towel and spreads it out across his knees. "But, well, he…"

I rise up and then lean against Jackson. I lay my hand on top of his, which is resting on the damp towel. "But he thinks you hung the moon. I know."

He lifts the towel and buries his face in it. "Why did I ever marry her? Why?"

"Because you were a nice boy who felt sorry for her. And besides, it was the storybook ending for everyone in your town. Well, everyone but you."

He wads up the towel in his hands and rests his chin on his fists, elbows planted on his thighs. "My parents even tried to talk me out of it. They knew it wouldn't work. And they told me that if I married her and made her part of the family, it would change things forever."

I tilt my head and press my lips tight then nod. "They were right about that. Of course, their moving her into a trailer next door to them after the divorce sure didn't help things fade away. Why is she traveling with them?"

"Dad apparently now needs a secretary. He was the keynote speaker for this senior citizen convention in Florida."

"I still can't believe your dad actually makes money on these books."

"Sounds like the sky's the limit for Hillbilly Hank. Every senior citizen group from here to Virginia wants him to speak every time he cranks out a new book. Latest one is *Hillbilly Hank Goes Hunting*. He's got this self-publishing thing down."

"Hey," hope creeps into my voice. "Maybe we can just say she's Pawpaw's secretary and leave it at that."

Jackson cuts his eyes at me, stands, and takes the towel back to the bathroom. "That's right. You've never been around my folks and Shelby. They don't act like she's the help. More like one of the family. I've always thought how we've managed to never go to Paint Rock when Shelby was home was a God thing."

"God doesn't get all the credit. Your Aunt Vel always letting us know when Shelby would be gone, or her actually getting rid of Shelby when we were coming gets most of the thanks." Off the bed, I walk into the bathroom where he's hung up the towel but is still playing with it. "Honey, I say we just don't worry about it. If it comes out we just act like it's no big deal. And it's not a big deal. I bet it won't even come up." I wrap my arms around him and pull him toward the bedroom. "Now, quit worrying and turn off the light. Thanksgiving weekend is almost over, and I haven't shown you how very thankful I am that you came to your senses and married me."

Chapter 17

"Carolina Butler Jessup, you are not to say one word. Not one word to Laney or to Susan. Are you agreed?"

"What?" My eyes won't quite open and there's no need for them to this early, except for some idiot calling at 6:30 a.m. Did I say idiot? I meant Missus.

"Do you agree to not tell Laney or Susan?" Even more urgent, Missus insists. "Do you?"

"I don't know what you're talking about."

"My word, Carolina, do you have to be difficult about everything? We will see you at 8:00 a.m. at Ruby's. For now, will you just not tell anyone, especially Laney and Susan—oh, Savannah, too, that we're meeting?"

"At Ruby's at eight, right?"

"That is what I said. Bye."

The cordless phone drops with a small bounce onto the carpet beside the bed. Jackson left at 5:00 a.m., so I didn't get up with him. A glance at the clock says it's set to go off in ten minutes. Instead of going back to sleep, I try to wake up.

From the next floor, I hear Savannah's shower going. Good, I don't have to go up her stairs to wake her. Wait, why would Missus include Savannah in her warning? Like Savannah would care. I could tell her I was going to have tea with the Queen of

England and she'd just shrug and say, "Whatever."

Now, Laney *is* on my list of people to talk to today. She has to check on the license for the B&B, whether she thinks it's important or not. Maybe I can text her and not actually talk to her until after coffee with Missus. Savannah's shower stops running, and I jump up. I don't know Anna's schedule, but I'm betting there's still hot water if I hurry.

Gray skies don't show even a hint of the sun and the chill is deep-seated. My short drive to Ruby's doesn't allow the car to warm up at all. And, because we don't have a garage here, I had to scrape the windshield, so my fingers are still icicles. Of course, I only made a little hole which allows limited, at best, visibility. Coming off the hill, I turn left toward Main Street at the stop light.

Train tracks run on one side of me. Along the other side, little houses huddle together against the cold. With a quick left, I park in the spaces facing the tracks. My eyes focus on the gazebo. Yesterday, Jackson and I were so caught up in Shelby coming to Chancey, we forgot to look at the damage. My heart sinks at the huge limb lying on top of and inside the white structure. Yellow warning streamers and orange traffic cones block off all access to most of the park. Within the orange and yellow boundaries stands the sad Christmas tree. Bare of ornaments, it awaits the grand decorating scheduled for Saturday and the lighting at Christmas on the Square, Saturday night. A shiver reminds me to move along. Bundled against the cold, I hustle across Main Street toward Ruby's Café.

Warm light from Ruby's provides a beacon in the gray morning. None of the other shops have opened, two of them

I still am not sure *ever* open. Chancey Florist's hours start at nine and the Christmas display in the window looks fun for checking out later.

Ruby's promised warmth is made reality when I pull open the door. Cinnamon and coffee waft on a sturdy, underlying aroma of baking muffins. Bright light from the white bowl light fixtures hanging over the center tables is matched by multiple strands of colored mini-Christmas tree lights adorning the walls. Old fashion bulbs, bigger, and in the standard primary colors, line the back counter and decorate the tree stationed on top of the counter. Carols pulsate from a CD boom box on the floor next to the front door. Full, frontal assault of Christmas spirit. I'm not really surprised. Subtlety to Ruby is like chitlin's to a vegan. Or a cross to a vampire. You get it, right?

The four tables and chairs in the middle of the room are full of kids and parents. Middle school begins at eight thirty, so there's a lot of activity with parents prodding and kids resisting. The booths along the side walls mostly feature the senior citizens who wait every morning for Ruby to open. Anchored on the aqua-colored seats, they wait out those darting in for takeout, the stream of parents and kids, and the workers stopping for a quick coffee and muffin. They hunker down, nursing coffee and bran muffins until the place becomes theirs, finally, around eight fifteen. Then the chatter flows over the low backed seats, and Ruby entices them with bacon studded muffins and whipped cream cheese. Us stay-at-home moms are given a grudging acceptance but mostly because we jump up and down getting them refills.

Over the exodus happening in the middle of the room, Missus waves at me from the back of the café where she is standing beside a table, making a mother redoing her daughter's braids nervous.

"Don't sit down in the booth," Missus tells me. "We're going to *eventually* move these two tables together."

"Oh, sorry, Missus. I should probably do this in the car," the woman says as she removes the rubber band from between her lips.

"I appreciate it, Joyce. We do have important business to conduct."

The woman looks at me like she's surprised Missus didn't apologize for standing over her. I look away as she loudly prods her kids to move faster. If she thinks she's going to shame Missus, she's got another think coming.

In the hustle, the people Missus had been sitting with escaped my notice. Now, as she begins ordering them on how to set the tables, the makeup of this group confuses me: the mayor, Jed Taylor; Cathy Stone Cross, who is a young single mother who lives with her parents; two older sisters of whom all I know are their names, Flora and Fauna; and a young man who looks familiar.

What is this meeting?

The young man in the sweater vest bounces up to me. "Hi, Mrs. Jessup? Carolina? I'm Timothy Leake?"

His bobbing head like a puppy eager to please and the way all his statements end in question marks makes me want to slap him on the back and tell him to "grow a pair." Maybe I've been hanging out with Laney too much.

I settle for holding out my hand. "Hi, Timothy." But that's all I get to say before I'm summoned.

"Carolina, get the muffins from the counter. I already ordered for everyone, so we can get to work." Missus gives me my orders then turns her attention to the rest of the group.

At the counter, Ruby, meets me with one of her large baskets, a dozen muffins nestle in the folds of a red and green plaid cloth. "Here ya go. So what's this meeting about?"

"Got me. I'm planning on eating my muffin, drinking some coffee, and getting excused." My eyes roam the basket trying to make my selection.

Ruby half laughs, half snorts. "Girl, you can't see Missus is in high form? There will be no excusing yourself from this. If you have a heart attack at that table, Missus will thump you a couple times on the chest and tell you to sit up and stop making a fool of yourself."

"Well, then I'm eating two muffins. That'll show her."

Ruby tucks her chin back and raises her dyed blond eyebrows. "Oh, yeah. That'll do it."

"Carolina? Are you joining us or not? Sit down."

I place the basket on the table and grab a cinnamon-cranberry one. The top is encrusted in sparkling sugar, and I know the insides will be spicy and tart.

As everyone else makes their picks and we begin passing the cream cheese, honey butter, and whipped butter in colorful ceramic ramekins, Missus leans forward and clears her throat.

"We have a problem with Christmas. I'm sure you've seen the damage to the gazebo. Well, the state it is in currently is the state it will remain in indefinitely."

Jed shakes his big head and red hair jumps to and fro. "Now, you don't know that."

"You going to shake down Laney Connor for it?" She pierces the mayor with her words and her eyes. It's a look I've backed down in front of many a time.

Jed's face settles into his double-chins, and he concentrates on buttering his chocolate-chocolate chip muffin.

Missus' nostrils flare a tad at the dismissal of the mayor. "That's what I thought. Until Laney Connor is brought to justice, things in the park must remain as they are."

The spicy tartness of my muffin is turning bitter. I dart looks around the table, but everyone focuses their eyes on the food in front of them. Finally my words come out in a whisper, "What did you say about Laney?"

Raised eyes around the table meet mine and most troubling? There are twinkles in those eyes.

"There's no funds," Timothy squeaks. "None at all in the town treasury and, well, Laney is the treasurer."

"What?" I question. "You don't think Laney stole...no... why would she do that? She and Shaw have plenty of money. Plenty..."

Cathy looks around as if to see if she's speaking out of turn. Obviously it's her first time to sit at the adult table. "Isn't that the problem?" The brightness of her eyes says she finds this all rather like living in the pages of the National Enquirer. "Where *do* they get all that money?"

The mayor swallows hard and then coughs. "Nothing is proven. Nothing. We'll get to the bottom of everything, eventually." His carefully styled red hair bounces with his assurances. He shifts his large body in his chair and licks his lips.

All the furious nodding around the table reminds me of baby birds being fed. So agreeable, so hmmmm, *manipulated.*

Missus is smiling sadly and sitting quietly. She gives a deep sigh and tilts her head in my direction. "And Carolina, what about the bed and breakfast? How are the books there?"

I hate the fear that flashes through my heart, but now that I'm thinking...

"Oh, no." Cathy moans.

Flora looks faint, and Fauna closes her eyes and fans herself.

The table is one mass of worry. How did this particular group come to be? Why am I here?

"Why am I here?" I ask.

Innocence blooms on Missus' white, pinched face. "The Christmas committee. You signed up for it..." she looks down at her notes "...last August.

Last August, when Christmas was so far off, and by which time I hoped to no longer live in Chancey. So I do the only thing left to do. Reach for a bacon-cheddar muffin.

The opening of the café door brings a bit of a chill.

"Mother, you didn't tell me the committee was meeting this

morning." Peter says as he comes barreling in our direction. "I told you I wanted to help with Christmas on the Square this year." In only a few strides, he crosses the floor, the tail of his tweed jacket flapping behind him and his thick brown hair bouncing on his shoulders. Usually he pulls it back in a low ponytail, but today, he looks like he's in too big of a hurry. His gray turtle neck matches his eyes and he makes a point to look at each occupant of the table and give a slight nod in greeting as he makes his way to us.

He grabs a chair from another table, whirls it around and sits down. The energy level of the table jumps like a rocket out of a Coke bottle. Relief, admiration, and desire surround the table. Relief from Jed, admiration from Timothy, and desire from Flora, Fauna and Cathy. Missus is just plain ol' disgusted.

"You cannot just *join* a committee because you *want* to."

"Yes, I can." Peter tips his head to me and winks. "So where are we? Mother libeled Laney yet?"

Next to him, Cathy lays her tiny hand on his tweed sleeve. "But what are we going to do?"

He swivels to look at Cathy sitting next to him. "Do? Uh, yeah, um. Well, we'll think of something."

I'm not sure, but I think her big brown eyes of melted chocolate, along with a tiny bite of her bottom lip, caused Peter's stuttering.

Tsking from the nature girls at the other end of the table, telegraphs their opinions, loud and clear. I start to giggle, but a glance at Timothy's ashen face stops me. "Timothy, you okay?" With his innocent eyes and shock of blond hair falling into his eyes, he looks like a little boy who just found out the lost puppy he found belongs to someone else.

"Sure, sure." He jumps and pulls his gaze away from Cathy. "So, at the Christmas thing what kind of songs do you want?"

Oh, that's who he is. The new music director at church. I knew I'd seen him somewhere.

Missus reclaims center stage with a stiff back and raised voice. "What Christmas thing? It's ruined, absolutely ruined and all because of Laney Troutman Connor. Perhaps it's time to return to the way Christmas use to be celebrated in Chancey. The leading citizens are invited to partake in a tasteful gathering at the mayor's home." Her chin jerks up and her nostrils flare again. "Not like that gaggle of riffraff which shows up for the lighting of the tree and to drink watered-down, barely warm apple juice."

"Oh, now I don't think—" Jed interrupts.

"Of course, Jed." Missus pats his hand. "You and Betty and all those darling children don't have the room to entertain properly. But as my father was mayor for so long, FM and I would be pleased to host."

Cathy, with newly licked lips, coos, "And we'll be able to bring dates? Being on the committee means we get to come, right?"

Flora and Fauna exchange pleased looks with each other and then grant cool approval with slight bending of their heads toward Missus. Timothy and I exchange looks and shrugs and are sufficiently convinced.

"No, that's not what we're doing. Mother, if you want to have a party, have a party, for crying out loud. But we are not uninviting the entire town. I called the police station, and the gazebo will be cleared away by Thursday, plenty of time for Christmas in the Square on Saturday."

"And where are they getting the money to clean it up?" Missus' eyes flash and her jaw tightens.

"Don't worry about it. So what else do we have to decide? I've talked enough. I need some coffee and a fresh muffin." He stands and walks to the counter.

"Let me see if I can get a pot of coffee for the table," I say. By time I get to the counter, Peter is sipping on a steaming cup.

He sighs and shakes his head. "That woman is like a bulldog.

I knew something was up when there was a full breakfast laid out for me at the house this morning. I was half through before I put two and two together."

"But all that about Laney? What of it is true?"

Peter's shoulders drop. "Don't know. She's pulling her Scarlett act and flitting around like it just doesn't concern her."

"She does spend a lot of money, Peter. Do you know what Shaw does?"

"I'm looking into it. That stinks, but this town wants answers. Honestly, they deserve answers."

He turns, put his hand on my upper arm, and squeezes. "Caro, your friend might really be in trouble." His eyes show concern and cause tears to well up in mine.

CHAPTER 18

Three messages await me on my arrival home. Daddy is sitting at the table drinking coffee, and he points out the light of the answering machine. "You got calls this morning, but we didn't answer them. We did listen to the messages to see if there was anything we should call you and tell you about." He shifts in his seat, folds his arms on the table, and looks at me from under a scrunched forehead. "Nothing of an emergency sort, but you might want to take a listen pretty soon."

First one is from the high school with a number to call back. Probably, they just want me to buy some concert tickets, right? Lord, I hope so, but a call from your kids' school is never a good thing.

Second one is from Jackson, and he wants me to call him. News of more travel, I bet.

Third is from the lady at the county. "Mrs. Jessup? Everything's been taken care of the license for your B&B, Trackside Delight, is in the mail."

"What did she say?" I ask as my fingers search for the replay button.

Daddy nods at me. "Yep, she said what you think she said. I've listened to it about a dozen times."

"I'm going to kill Laney Connor," is all I can say as I dial her cell.

"Hey there. I took care of the water thing at the county. It's all good." Laney says when she answers.

"Was the name Trackside Delight your idea?"

"Absolutely! See, that's what we used to call going up to park near the tracks. It's kind of an inside joke."

"There's nothing inside about it! It sounds like bordello in a railroad town."

Laney giggles. "Well, I heard about Scott and Abby Sue up there on Thanksgiving so maybe it's not too far off."

"It's awful, Laney. Change it."

"Oh, don't be so uptight. I'm sure you can call it whatever you want to call it. The county never has to know."

"Like Chancey never has to know how you're doing the books? Speaking of which, how are the books for the B&B, oh excuse me. I meant the books for Trackside Delight!" As soon as the words were out of my mouth, I regret them. However, nothing follows them to fix what I'd said, so I just wait.

My grip on the phone tightens instead of easing when I realized Laney is laughing. Hysterically laughing. "Don't let Missus and her minions get your panties in a wad. Everything is fine. But hey, I've got to go. The cleaners are here, and I haven't unlocked the door yet. Talk to you later."

She's crazy. All that hairspray has invaded her brain. And why does she get to have cleaners? No one else in Chancey has cleaners. *I* don't have cleaners. And just how does she pay for her cleaners?

"Can I freshen up your coffee?" I ask Daddy as I pour a cup for me.

"Sure." He holds out his cup. "Don't forget your other messages."

"In a minute." I sit down across from him and fill him in on the Christmas committee meeting. Mother comes in as I'm telling him about Peter's arrival.

"Peter Bedwell? That man turns my head. He's that perfect age, around forty-five, when a man is just fully ripe. Don't you think so?" she asks me with her wide blue eyes aglow as she picks up Daddy's cup to take a sip.

Daddy is grinning and pats his knee for Mother to perch there. Mother has always made comments like that, but now that I know of her wild past, they horrify me. Before, they just embarrassed me—however, that *is* a mother's job. Surely she'd never...nope, not going there.

"So what does Peter think?" Daddy continues.

"He said she could be in real trouble, but you just heard our conversation. She doesn't have a care in the world. You've met her. Could she be embezzling from the town? From us?"

Mother pours her own cup full and takes the chair at the end of the table. Her dark green sweater is topped with a Black watch tartan scarf. Her nails are perfect French manicures and tasteful jewelry provides a rich sparkle. "Well, I can tell you she has expensive tastes. Exquisite, but expensive. Those boots she had on Sunday are Louboutin and cost $1,500, at least."

"For one pair of boots?" My mind won't even accept that. "Heck, I should've at least touched them. Fifteen hundred dollars?"

"And that suit was designer. Armani, I suspect. That would be close to another $2,000."

Daddy whistles and nods at me. "So her outfit cost about as much as your van is worth."

"Thanks, Dad." I stand up. "I have to go return those calls. What I'll do after that is anyone's guess. Maybe Peter will find out Shaw is some oil tycoon and everything will be explained."

Walking through the living room toward the stairs, every stain, every sag, every scratch on our old furniture stands out. The dust in the corners and on the tops of the curtains points out the lack of cleaners. The worn carpet on the stairs came with the house, but Lord only knows, when we can afford to replace it. My brown shoes look like they came from Lands End to me, but to experts like Mother and Laney, they scream Wal-Mart.

Up until now, living in Chancey meant less well-to-do folks to compare ourselves with. The suburbs are a constant game of better cars, better schools, better lawn services, better toys. Just one of the things I tried to hide from when we lived there. Why is there always someone better off everywhere you go?

There's always someone.

Coming back down the stairs my furniture looks lovely in the noontime sun. Dust no longer serves as an embellishment worth noting, and the carpet presents no worries.

Jackson answered immediately when I returned his call. He wanted to ask me about disappearing with him this weekend up to the Lodge at Blue Mountain. Luxurious, no kids, no dogs, and no cost. His boss had to cancel out of a conference dinner for some kind of railroad gathering, and he asked Jackson to fill in. Since my parents are here, I'm free to go.

The other call I returned also didn't live up to my prediction of doom. Stephen Cross, the new teacher and drama coach wants to talk to me about "a part he wants me to play." Do adults get asked to be in high school productions? Was I that good in the Thanksgiving show? Maybe Savannah gets her acting ability from me. Maybe it's just my excitement about the night away at the Lodge, but I can't find a negative spin on meeting with Mr. Cross.

While I dig for my keys and cell phone, Anna comes into the room.

Wow, I completely forgot about her.

"Hey there. Have you had a good morning?"

She pulls the broom out of the pantry. "Sure. I played with the twins some and then went on a walk with Ashley out on the bridge. The room the girls were using upstairs, I vacuumed and straightened." She pushes the broom under the kitchen table, but then stands abruptly. "Oh, I didn't mean they left a mess or anything."

"Of course they left a mess. They're college kids who leave a mess even when they clean up after themselves."

Anna's agrees, "Like how they leave the tables in the cafeteria." She just shakes her head and continues sweeping while I look for my keys.

"Okay, I had them in my hand…" I mutter and search.

"Your keys? I hung them up on the key hook by the door there." Anna points past me.

"Of course, where they belong. That's why I couldn't find them."

"Sorry. I just have this thing about putting stuff away. Makes me feel better when everything is neat. Weird, isn't it?"

"Are you kidding? That's exactly what I need around here. I'm off to the high school for a meeting. What are you doing this afternoon? Do you want a ride anywhere?"

"To town? No," Anna says quickly as she begins moving the broom along the floor in front of the sink. "But can I use your computer to look at the college you mentioned the other day? Appalachian Tech's the name, right?"

"Right and of course. Help yourself. It's all set up there in that little office off the kitchen. I'm sure you can figure it out." I pull on my coat. "See you later.

This day just keeps getting better, cause I hate sweeping.

CHAPTER 19

Sitting on a bench at the entrance to the high school library, the thought of just how ridiculous life in a small town can be strikes me. This morning I had a meeting with Cathy and only a couple hours later I'm meeting with her ex-husband. And Cathy volunteers here at the high school with the cheerleaders, so Savannah will see them both in her afterschool activities. I can't believe Stephen's fiancé is okay with living here.

Wait, what am I talking about? My husband's ex-wife is coming to stay at my house for several weeks. Maybe I fit in better in Chancey than I thought.

"Mrs. Jessup." Stephen crosses the library entrance and holds out his hand. "Thanks for coming over so quickly." He motions down the aisle to my right. "There's a table back here where we can sit. I don't have a classroom assigned to me yet, but I found a table out of the way and claim it during my planning period."

My coat and scarf were already off, so I laid them across a wooden chair and then sat in the one next to it. "Probably is a little rough being the new teacher and low in the pecking order."

Dimples form in his cheeks and a shot of gleaming teeth causes me to flush. Wow, if his good looks do that to me, these high school girls don't stand a chance. Stephen drops into his seat and leans forward. He has the quarterback physique, which carried him through Whitten County High School four years ago. And curly black hair, which is cut short, but left a little longer in the back. In my romance books, the kind of hair which entangles young women's stroking fingers. Okay, cut it out.

"No, I understand. I'm just thrilled to find a full-time teaching position since I graduated mid-year."

"Is it hard being back home?"

His full grin this time includes a wink. A wink? I didn't know young men winked. "Being back home? Now, that *is* interesting."

"Are you living with your parents?"

"Yes, and, well, that's actually something I wanted to talk to you about. Have you met my folks?"

I shake my head. "Not that I know of."

"They're great people. Really super. Dad works with a carpet company up in Dalton and Mom is the world's best gardener. They live in Mom's family home way out near the highway."

"Sounds nice. How great for you to have a place to move right into."

Stephen frowns and his dimples make another appearance, however this time they are caused by the downward turning of his face. "Yes, that's true. But the problem is Patricia, my fiancé." He pauses and puts his hands on the table. "But that's for later. Right now I want to ask you about helping with the theater program."

Surely, I should be feeling apprehensive, but his warm smile and youthful enthusiasm disarms my usually alert volunteer-seeking-warning system. "Yes, how can I help? We are delighted in Savannah's interest in the theater."

Stephen leans forward, "We'd be so honored if your B&B would serve as our official sponsor. Now, I know, usually that means putting up money. But what we want most is a business to stand alongside us to occasionally provide us a place for a pizza party or a picnic. And after being at your home for the party after the Thanksgiving pageant, I feel you and your B&B would add a dimension of culture that is, honestly, missing in most of Chancey."

"Really?" Maybe it was the heady warmness of the library or the smell of several hundred books, but a feeling of well-being melted over me. "That's really what you thought at our house. Parties just seem to happen at our house here."

"That's exactly what I'm talking about." His wide gray eyes blink at me. "Exactly. Many people have the ability to follow direction or take care of detail. What we need is someone to set the mood, enhance our image, provide the setting a quality theater department needs."

"And you think that's me, or I mean, my—well our B&B?"

"Yes. Yes, I do."

I swear a thrill ran up my spine just like I was sitting in my high school library in Lenoir City, Tennessee, being asked to the prom by the quarterback. His name was C.J., and he did have dark hair now that I think about it. We're his eyes more gray or blue?

"Will you agree to be our sponsor, Mrs. Jessup?"

"Oh, please call me Carolina. And, of course, I'd love to."

"Really, Carolina? You've made my day. You are just what we need. And, of course, that's why you're the only one I can think of to help me and Patricia."

"How can I help you and Patricia? C.—" I giggle. Almost called him C.J.

"My parents won't let her move into our house. They feel it might confuse Forrest when he's over there. He spends quite a bit of time with them. Cathy has been really good about that. But the only place, the only one, where I'd feel Patricia would be taken care of properly is with you."

"With me? Why is she moving here already? Maybe you should wait until you get married and you have a home here."

"You're right. That is what we should do, but you know Cathy

121

is here, and Patricia is well, kinda jealous. So can we rent her a room in your B&B?"

"Maybe after the holidays. I'll have to look at the bookings for the first of the year."

"But we want to pay double what you usually charge, and it would be until our wedding in the spring. That's a lot of money to turn down. Patricia wouldn't take any meals there; it would just be a place to sleep. She and my mother get along wonderfully so she'll be spending her free time at Mom and Dad's. Please, Carolina? Just one room?"

Wow, now the quarterback is begging me. "Probably. Let me check with Jackson and also look at our bookings."

"Of course." Stephen stands. I gather my coat and scarf then also stand.

"So I bet you're full all the way until Christmas, he says with a laugh." He helps me put on my coat. He's so tall and sooo polite.

"Mostly with family, but they don't really count do they?"

"I hope not since I had to move in with my family."

"Plus, Ricky should be moved back home by tonight, so that frees up the Chessie room."

I wind my scarf around my neck and stick out a hand to Stephen. He grabs my hand in his right hand and pushes his other hand into his pocket. "Well, since you have that free room, I'd like to reserve it right now for Patricia. Here's three thousand dollars for the month of December, a hundred dollars a night. We'll move her in this week."

Who knew that a wad of money is literally a wad and my hand instinctively closed around it. "Stephen! No. I can't take this much, and I need to talk to Jackson."

"I told you we wanted to pay you well. And if you don't have room after Christmas, well," he shrugs, "we'll figure something else out. You have an empty room and now you have plenty of money for Christmas."

"But, I, this…"

"There's the bell, and I've got to get to class." He leaves the money in my hand and gathers his books and papers. "You've really helped me out." He winks at me again and dashes down the aisle.

Left with a handful of cash, wham. A wink from a handsome man, bam. Seems like someone should be saying, "Thank ya, ma'am."

Chapter 20

My table and I, outside Starbuck's in the mall, look like a commercial for a very Merry Christmas. Bags gather around my legs, fill the seat next to me, and even peek out of the top of my purse. The bags exude waves of warmth and happiness. Shopping doesn't usually fill me with such delight, but then I've never gone shopping with $3,000 cash.

I highly recommend it.

It never dawned on me that one of our rooms, which normally we charge less than $100 a night for, could bring in this much money if rented continually. Running my hands down my arms feels good because my emerald sweater is so warm and it smells new, like it just came off the rack. Which it did. My peppermint-chocolate latte's fragrant steam and mall Christmas music further mellow me.

Decorations of huge blue and purple ornaments hang from golden ribbons. From my vantage point, seven Christmas trees can be seen. They twinkle and glow and are covered with matching blue and purple ornaments. Gold ribbon weaves in and out everywhere my eyes land. It's so easy to forget how Christmas really can, and should be, when Ruby's garish lights and boom box carols have set the mood for your holiday celebration. And that sad tree they were talking about this morning. Those hometown trees on the square are fine at night with their lights, half of which don't work after the first week, but during the day? The limbs droop, birds pull the ribbons off, everything gets rained on and by December 20, it's an eyesore. But try saying that to a local yokel? You'd find yourself swinging from the tallest branch of their beloved hometown Christmas tree.

I take a sip of my latte, feel the softness of my sweater on my shoulders and body, relax into the pop rendition of Little Drummer Boy, and try to forget Chancey.

"Hey, you!"

Should've known. Chancey doesn't go away quite that easily. "Hey, Laney." I peel open my eyes and then close them again. Maybe when I open them back up, she will not be wearing a fur. Nope, no such luck. Guess you can always count on beauty queens to be beauty queens.

"There's hardly room here for me with all your bags." Laney moves the merchandise out of the chair closest to me and settles in. She reaches over, grabs my cup, and takes a drink. "Ooo, that's good. I want one of those. What's it called?" Bags fall around her as she stands back up.

"Peppermint-chocolate latte." I pull my cup back toward me. Only popular girls can take food off your plate or drink from your cup without asking the least bit of permission. And she seriously is wearing a fur jacket. It's not even that cold outside. Of course, it looks unbelievably great on her as she struts, okay, walks to the counter. Jeans, high heeled boots—not the same ones she wore Sunday—and a black and gray fur jacket. Her hair is in a ponytail, and she manages to look like she just threw on something to go shopping. No wonder we unpopular girls never stood a chance.

In a wave of perfume, Laney sits back down. "There, now, isn't this great? I never picked you for a shopper. Is your mother with you?"

Okay, great. It never dawned on me to ask my mom if she wanted to come shopping. I just left the school with the money and drove straight to the mall down in Marietta. "Um, no. This was just an impulse thing. I probably should've asked her, huh?"

Laney is peeking into my bags and then reaches out to lay smooth the arm of my sweater. "No, you seem to have done okay." Perfect, red lipsticked lips frown. "I mean, this sweater is cute, but it is manmade fiber, and you'd probably enjoy cashmere more in the long run." She smiles and pats my arm. "But how would you know that?"

If she says, "Bless your heart…" I roll my eyes and sit up straighter. "Do you know how much cashmere sweaters cost?"

"Of course, but they cost more because they're worth it."

"Is that real fur?"

Laney's big eyes close and she hugs herself. "Of course. Isn't it divine?"

"Where do you get your money?"

Her eyes pop open. "What?"

"You heard me. Why do you have so much money?"

An expression I've never seen on her crosses Laney's face. Guilt. She turns from me and studies while taking the lid off her latte. "I was raised to believe asking about money is rude."

"Well, yeah, me, too. But we are supposedly business partners."

"And the books are always there for you to look at."

"Where? Where are the books?"

"In your office, where the computer is, off the kitchen. In the second drawer."

"Oh." Now my sweater of manmade material feels scratchy and too warm. How could I question my friend, and partner, about money? "I'm sorry. I just…Never mind."

But she did look guilty.

My latte is lukewarm, and the bright red lipstick mark Laney left on the side reminds me of my accusation. I don't want to be like Missus. Rumor and conjecture can ruin someone in a small town.

Should I warn Laney? But I did promise Missus I wouldn't say anything. And if it's true, I don't want to alert her. But it can't be true. No. Shaw has a car dealership in Cartersville. I know from my dad owning one you can make a lot of money in a good dealership. That's it. Laney's too smart to steal from her hometown…and her friends. Right?

I look up to see Laney stroking the sleeve of her jacket. She notices me watching her.

"Here, feel this." She holds her arm out to me. "Nothing like real fur."

"But it came from an animal. Doesn't that bother you?"

"Did my chicken biscuit at Chick-fil-a bother me this morning?" Her ponytail swings as she shakes her head. "Carolina, you sound like the girls last night. I was showing Jenna, Angie, and Savannah my furs, and they turned their noses up like there was something wrong, right up until they tried them on."

"Oh, Laney. For crying out loud, don't try and sway the girls. It's hard enough for them to take a stand without you flaunting it right under their noses."

Laney just grins because my words belie my hand which remains on her sleeve, softly stroking the black softness. I jerk back my hand and my head. "I've got to go."

"No you don't. Sit back and relax a little and tell me what led to your little shopping spree."

She's right. There's no reason for me to leave right now except she's bugging the living daylights out of me, and I'm only one insult away from telling her the town thinks she's embezzling. I slug down my last shot of lukewarm latte and scoot back my chair.

"Did you hear Abby Sue is staying in Chancey?"

Perched on the edge of my chair, I think of Ricky and sigh.

"How long?"

"For good. At least that's what she told Mama yesterday at the chili dinner. She, of course showed up with Scott." Laney shudders. "That reminds me, I need to get my loveseat cleaned."

"Were they always like…like, you know. Like they are?"

Laney places her elbow on the table and cups her chin in her palm. "Scott always was a hound dog, but until Abby Sue got hold of him, he kept his business out of sight. Course, she was the one finally able to get a ring out of him. Susan and I think she only made out with him in public and when they were alone she held him off. Made him crazy. Made half the girls in Chancey crazy, too. Most of 'em had been giving everything they had to Scott for years trying to tie him down. Abby Sue is ten years younger than him, and that might've had something to do with it, too. She was only eighteen when they got married, and you've seen how cute she is."

Laney picks up my empty cup and takes the lid off. "Here's you some of my drink." She pours part of her latte into my cup.

"Thanks. When did they get divorced?"

When Ricky went off to kindergarten and Ronnie was in first grade. Abby Sue started selling real estate and was good at it. She got a job offer from a developer in Atlanta that needed someone to take care of his properties in all the counties north of the city. Things around the city were growing like weeds then. Abby Sue told Scott either they moved closer to Atlanta, or she was leaving. He decided to stay here and so she left."

"She left the kids?"

"Yeah, but you got to remember, she was only twenty-four and Mama took care of Ronnie and Ricky most the time anyway. And then me and Susan were here with our kids the same ages. Nobody really skipped a beat. They divorced, but when Scott wasn't visiting her, she was here living in the house just like before."

"So now she's staying?"

Laney leans back in her chair, opens her coat, and fans herself. "Whew, fur sure is hot. Yeah, she says the market is so slow she's going to settle down and re-evaluate. Mama won the bet."

"The bet?"

"Yeah, we all thought she'd move back, but me and Susan both picked dates after both boys were gone."

I laugh. "So gambling on your relatives is just a fun Troutman family pastime?"

"What?" Laney pounces at my words. Her hands grip the edge of her coat.

My eyes blink and shoulders lift. "Nothing, just actually making bets on them getting back together sounded funny."

"Oh, that. Yeah." Laney looks down the mall aisle and her body visibly relaxes. "So, anyway, she's back."

Laney continues to stare down the sparkly, decorated aisle. I finish my latte, again, and gather my bags. When I stand, Laney looks up at me.

"Oh, you're leaving?" She picks up her cup and takes a sip. "Sorry, guess I was just daydreaming."

"Well, you probably do have a lot to think about with Abby Sue moving back to town. I'll talk to you later. Thanks for sharing your latte."

Laney smiles and then leans back in her chair. I walk away but turn around to wave. Concentration has wiped the smile away and is causing deep furrows in her brow. Laney looks weary and even a little worried. Hopefully, it's about Abby Sue and *not* about the town's money.

Chapter 21

"When Ma found out your name was Trackside Delight she decided she wasn't sure about the B&B Stephen picked out. This is my Ma, and I'm Patty." Those words in a hick accent hit me when I open the front door to two women, but I can't exactly tell where the voice is coming from.

Haloed in late afternoon sunshine, a big woman in a thick gray coat holds the screen door back and steps into my living room. "Now, Patricia, you know I would want to check out any place you'd be living. Especially any place here in Chancey."

Following her is apparently her daughter, Patricia and the first speaker. The daughter isn't much smaller than the mother. Or maybe I should say, "Ma?"

"Which is why I was forced to make this trip and see for myself my daughter's new home. What kind of name *is* Trackside Delight?" The woman's eyebrow straightens into a solid line above her eyes. And she sniffs, literally smells the air as she drops two suitcases at her feet.

"We're glad you could, uh, come." Patricia. Patricia. Stephen. Oh, yeah. Now I'm on solid ground. For a moment, I thought I'd forgotten a reservation. "Patricia, I wasn't sure when you'd be arriving. Here, let me help you with that."

"No, no. I'll get it." Daddy strides in from the kitchen. "Hello,

I'm Jack Butler, not actually a butler, but a man who believes in carrying a woman's bags."

Daddy is tall, six-feet-four easily, but Patty's mom is just as tall and her shoulders are just as broad. Her hair, face, and coat are all iron gray. Daddy's smile isn't returned. "That's good. Not gonna stand here jabbering. Just take us to Pat's room."

With bags in hand, Daddy turns toward the B&B hall with Concrete Woman following. Patricia, shoulders slumped in her emerald green coat, slouches after her mother. I close the front door, lean against it and sigh. No notice or anything, they just show up and barge in. Stephen should've called to warn me they were coming. Although, he did say Patricia would be coming this week, and it is Friday morning.

"Carolina," Daddy shouts.

"Coming." I push away from the door. Did I even tell Jackson about Patricia staying with us? I hate trying to remember late night phone conversations. They get mixed up with my dreams and I'm never sure what's real or not.

Daddy meets me in the kitchen. "That woman is talking about her daughter being here for a long time. Did you know that?"

My smile brightens and I shrug. "Sure. Her fiancé lives here. You've met him. Stephen Cross, Savannah's teacher."

"Well, just be thankful her mother isn't staying. She's not a pleasant woman. But she wants to talk to you."

I shrug again. "Of course, no problem." Smile and shrug. Smile and shrug.

Morning light pours through the door of the Southern Crescent room on my left and fills the hallway. The first door to my right is closed. When I open it, the sunlight pours in and hits Anna seated at the desk computer. "Good morning, Anna."

"Good morning. Is it okay I'm in here? Do you need any help, Mrs. Jessup?"

"Not right now and you're fine." The drawer where the B&B's books supposedly reside mocks me. I still haven't taken a look. "But you might want to meet our newest guest, Patricia, when you get a chance."

"Okay. Are you still leaving around noon?"

A genuine smile slides in place, "Yes, Jackson will be here soon and then we'll pack up for our night at the resort. I can't wait."

"Mrs. Jessup?" Patricia's mom steps out of the Chessie room.

"Yes, I'm right here. Just had to check on something."

"Did I hear you say you're going away?"

"Yes, my husband and I, just for tonight. He has a work conference."

"And who will be overseeing this place? This Trackside Delight?"

Oh my, it sounds worse than imagined coming from her. Stepping closer to the door, I try to maneuver around her and into the room. "My parents are here, and so they'd be available if Patricia needs anything."

"And meals?"

"Meals?" Forget trying to get inside. "Stephen said Patricia would be eating at his parents' home."

"So I paid $3,000 for a bed and miniscule room for a month?"

"You paid? I thought it was Stephen's money."

"Hardly." Ice coats the word. "What kind of place is this? Are you thinking you can rip us off 'cause we're from a small town."

Is she kidding? Like Chancey is the big city full of shysters and swindlers. "No, maybe we misunderstood each other, but we don't provide meals. Do you have any other questions?" She moves a little, and I push into the room. "Patricia, is there anything you need?"

The girl is plopped on the edge of the bed. "Everything is fine. Really, Ma, Stephen explained to you that I would be at his house most of the time."

Her raw accent is jarring. In her mother's mouth it sounded harsh and demanding, but in Patricia's, it's so backward it sounds made up. Her coat is buttoned up to her neck and hides what looks to be a rather lumpy body. Limp brown hair hangs long down her back with a center part emphasizing a rather homely face. Immediately, one thought sets up house in my brain. There is no way Stephen Cross asked this girl to marry him. No way on God's green earth.

"You ready to go?" Patricia's mother still stands in the doorway. Her hair is cut short and molded into a gray helmet. It doesn't move a bit when she bends to look in her pocket book. "We're having lunch with Stephen's folks out at their place." She pulls out a lipstick from her digging and steps to the mirror on the wall, hung between the door and the Chessie cat calendar. Six inches from the mirror she stretches her lips and then colors her lips a garish pinky orchid color. She mashes her lips together to smooth the lipstick out and then reaches into her purse again. This time she comes up with a store receipt tape. Lifting it to her lips she blots her lipstick, leaving a bright purple-pink lip imprint behind.

Patricia stands up. "I'm ready."

"Well, Patricia, welcome." I step back to let her pass. "If you need anything just let me know, and y'all have a good lunch. That's great Stephen can get off early for a family lunch."

Purple-pink lips on level with my forehead twist and then expel an honest-to-goodness "Pshaw." She closes her purse and places it on her arm. "Why would Stevie be there? We don't need that peckerwood at lunch."

My eyes bulge, but they're bulging at the backs of a gray coat and an emerald green coat schlumping out the door and down the hall.

I'm not sure $3,000 was enough.

Chapter 22

"Three thousand dollars cash?" Jackson asks. Again

"Quit saying that every time I take a breath. I'm going to turn the heat down, okay?" We're on the road to the Lodge at Blue Mountain and I'm filling Jackson in on the week as we meander through the North Georgia Mountains toward the North Carolina border. The colors of autumn are gone, now it's time for Southern winter colors of rust brown and dove gray. Even here in the mountains, winter is full of softness.

Leaves gather where they fell, in drifts of warm brown. Tree bark and limbs remain supple, and small twigs make a full silhouette against mother of pearl skies. Punctuations of green are thick and dark. Pines appear specially placed just to fill an empty spot. Magnolias tower with shiny emerald and bronze leaves like they've waited all year for center stage. Crisp is a word used to define northern winters, not ours.

"You probably won't get to meet Patricia's mother, lucky you. But I'm telling you, there is no way this Patricia and Stephen Cross go together."

"Sure doesn't sound like it. Think about it. If we get $3,000 every month she stays with us? When do you think they'll get married?" He looks at me with lifted eyebrows. "I'm hoping for a loooong engagement."

"We can't take them for that much money. They don't look to have it. We'll have to come up with a rate for long-term people. Wonder what they talked about over lunch?" Now I'm anxious to meet Stephen's parents so I can picture them all together. Of course, without the proclaimed "peckerwood."

"Speaking of lunch, you said Susan packed us a picnic?"

I turn to check on the basket in the backseat. "Yeah, she said since we were going past Carter's Lake we should stop and eat outside. She invited Mama and Daddy and the kids, including Anna, down to their house for dinner tonight."

"What did she pack?"

"Sandwiches and chips and Oreos. You know how she is about eating cheap." Can't help it, a grumble escapes. "I was kind of looking forward to lunch at a restaurant."

"Well here's where we turn for the lake."

Wonder if Jackson heard my grumble and ignored it, or didn't hear it at all. What's the use in grumbling if you don't know it was heard?

In my dream, I'm back at the picnic table and the lake still mirrors the blue sky and green pines. Red clay banks edge the water, and the sun warms my chilled nose.

"Hey, sleepyhead, wake up. We're here."

With a deep breath and then a yawn, I look around. "You know, I was dreaming about the lake, and it's hard to believe, but it was just as beautiful in real life as it was in my dream. I'm so glad Susan packed the picnic."

Jackson grins as he slows down then pulls into the resort entrance. "Even though you were looking forward to lunch in a restaurant?"

"You did hear me. I wasn't sure." I sit up straighter. "So, where is this lodge? I just see road and fence all the way up the mountain." Weaving in and out we start to get glimpses of wood and glass above us. Around a loop, we finally arrive at the front doors of the lodge. White lights and burgundy ribbons around bundles of fresh evergreens provide a mountain Christmas welcome, not only at the entrance, but inside as well.

A stone fireplace, several stories high fills the center of the room. As Jackson registers, I wander toward the wall of windows looking over the valley. Leather chairs provide seating between the roaring fire and the magnificent view. At the edge of the window, I rest my hands on the back of a dark green couch.

"Isn't this something?" Jackson comes behind me and wraps his arms around my shoulders.

Wood smoke mingles with the smell of him and tears prick my eyes. "It's perfect. It's been way too long since we've gone away, just us." I turn in his arms. "Thank you for bringing me."

His blue eyes crinkle at the corners. "When Bob asked if I could take his place at the conference tonight, all I could think about was you being able to come. Did I tell you how very glad I am your folks are visiting?"

Wrapped in his arms and kisses, I start feeling just how warm the fireplace can be. At least I guess it's the fireplace causing the heat. "So, did you get our room?"

"Absolutely and I think we should check it out."

"And that, Mr. Jessup, is why you are my favorite husband. You always have a plan. And a room."

An empty elevator is a wonderful place to find yourself with an attractive man who can't keep his hands off you. But my cream sweater is way too heavy and hot to still be wearing. I whisper into Jackson's hair, "When we get to the room, this sweater has to go."

He laughs. "I was thinking the same thing."

We make it down the hall and when we enter the room our

mouths drop. The valley lies outside the window, and there's a fireplace in our room. We dump our suitcase and bags down, figure out how to turn on the fireplace, and then meet in front of the window.

After a minute, Jackson pulls back and looks at me. "Now what were you saying about this sweater?"

CHAPTER 23

Railroaders are just like NFL players and NASCAR drivers. Really, any person who is paid to do what they loved doing as a kid. And just like you'd expect the talk at the dinner leading up to the Major League Baseball All-Star game to revolve around baseball, the talk at a railroad conference is about trains.

And just like NFL wives know about the sport providing their groceries, railroad wives know about railroads. Railroads do have more women playing the game than the NFL or NASCAR or MLB, however, not that many more. It's very much still an overwhelmingly male profession, and I truly believe it has something to do with how many little boys enjoy the best morning of their lives when they open that box under the Christmas tree and see their first model train set. And then somewhere along the way they realize they can be paid to play with trains, after all someone has to do it. So at a railroad conference, the women you see are very likely to be wives who are along for the night and those are usually few.

The hallway outside the conference room is wide and painted golden beige. Small groups of people along the walls eat hors d'oeuvres and talk. Everyone has an eye out for the client they hope to talk to, so there are lots of wandering gazes and nodding. Reports and presentations will be made at the conference, but making contacts is the real goal for many.

Jackson stops at a shrimp platter and picks up two plates. "I don't know what we're having for dinner, but I'm not passing up this shrimp." He hands me a plate. "Besides I worked up an appetite this afternoon."

"Hush," I say and then giggle. I'm more relaxed than I have been in months. After the sweater business was taken care of, Jackson went off to the first session of the conference while I enjoyed the private fireplace and a book. Then a long bath and no one to interrupt me while I dressed and primped. My teal blouse, from my shopping trip, is blousy and see-through. Of course, there's a cami underneath it, but it feels sexy and brings my old black skirt and boots up to snuff. Top it all off with a couple glasses of wine, and I'm feeling really good.

Floating through dinner in my haze of happiness, I finally realize the evening is winding down.

"That was the best pecan pie I've ever eaten." I tell the gentleman on my right. He's from South Georgia, and his wife is a teacher. She couldn't make the trip, but since he also has teenagers, we've shared stories all evening.

Jackson leans toward me. "I need to talk to the guys from Pierson about that project in Alabama. We're going to just grab a place in the corner over there for a while. Shouldn't be more than fifteen minutes."

"I'm good. Maybe I'll go up to the room."

"Or you could get a glass of wine and find a chair out in the lobby. The fireplace looked inviting when we came through."

"Oh, it did. That's where I'll be."

"Good-bye" and "Nice to meet you" is passed around the table and with a quick kiss, Jackson and I go our separate ways.

The long hallway is empty now. Isn't it great when you leave a mess and someone whisks it away while you're dining? The hall empties out into another, shorter hall with several other doorways. Through one, I see the lodge's main dining room.

Another door opens as a woman leaves and a glimpse is granted of a party in full swing.

I spot the chair I want while the bartender fills my glass. With my purse arranged on my shoulder, wine in hand, my path is direct toward a chair beside the window but facing the fireplace and the main hall. All the different events going on here remind me of looking at book covers while selecting something to read. Lots of stories and lots of people.

Settled in place, my attention wanders from group to group. Young people gathered on one side of the hearth are on retreat, maybe? Two older couples sharing coffee and soft laughs over a low table. Men in a group, talking serious business from the looks on their faces. Some women who could be sisters, dressed in jeans and slippers drinking wine and giggling.

When a door off the main hall opens and a couple spills out, the woman's high heels clicking across the stone floor catches my attention. The man's arm is around the woman, and he steers her to the bar. He is leaning over her and talking in her ear so that I can't see her face, but her silky dress and high heels are high class. She sits on a chair at the bar and the way the man stays so close to her makes me itchy until I remember how Jackson and I were earlier this afternoon, right here in this very room.

A smile and warmth slide over me, and I take a sip of wine. So we're not the only couple enjoying a romantic evening at Blue Mountain. The man has to lean away to pull out his wallet and pay for their drinks. When he does the woman's face comes into view.

It's Laney.

But that's not Shaw. The man is older than Shaw and has silver hair. Maybe it's just a friend. Then he leans in on her again, and his lips are on her ear. I'm sure of it. But maybe she just looks like Laney. Then she laughs, and he pulls away to laugh himself. And it is Laney. No doubt about it. Her deep purple dress hugs every curve and cuts low in the front. The diamond heart necklace she got for Christmas, which mother says is Tiffany, settles in her cleavage. The man reaches down, plucks the heart up and kisses it then settles it back with a caress. She looks up through lowered lashes, and he once again leans over her, and I can't see their faces.

Then, with their drinks in hand, he helps her off the stool, puts his free arm around her waist to pull her to him, and they go back toward the door of the party they left only minutes ago.

As the door is closing behind them, Laney's laughter floats out again. Then nothing. The door is closed, and they are gone. No purple dress. No diamond heart necklace. No good-looking, silver-haired man. No cheating friend.

Laney is here…and I wish I weren't.

CHAPTER 24

"So how did you get out of being Mrs. Claus?" Peter's warm voice breaks what hopefully appears to be concentration on the kids climbing on top of the red clad couple in the high back chairs in Chancey Park. Crowded around the still dark cedar tree is the "riff raff" as Missus so delicately categorized us. On one side, are two large wooden chairs, which I think usually reside at the front of the Presbyterian church for the pastors. Lamps and tables have also been set up to look like Mr. and Mrs. Claus's living room is now outside. But the scene pales compared to the scene from the lobby last night, which keeps playing over and over in my mind.

"Oh, hey, Peter. Just lucky I guess. Who are they?"

Peter leans back with his arms crossed on the chest of his worn, brown leather jacket. "Let's see, the man is Mack Davies. He's a farmer out near the highway, and he's played Santa ever since I was a kid. The woman..." He shakes his head. "Don't know her. Or at least don't recognize her."

"That's Vickie Cross, you know, Stephen's mama." Laney pops up from nowhere.

"Laney! Hey." I look down so I don't meet her eyes, and laying on the front of her red jacket is the heart necklace. Last time I saw that necklace...

"Okay, that's right, I do know her," Peter interjects. "But her hair wasn't gray like that last time I saw her. How ya doing, Laney? Keeping Shaw jumping?"

"That's how I keep him interested. Right, Carolina? Gotta keep our men guessing?" Laney nudges me, and I almost fall over.

Peter grabs me. "Hey, you okay?"

"Yeah, just a little shaky, I guess." However, straightening up, I shuffle a little so I'm not right beside Laney, and I turn away from her to face the Santa setup. How can she act so normal? My stomach is lurching and sweat is rolling down my back at just seeing her. And here she stands all happy and smiling and talking to *me* about husbands and keeping them jumping. I ought to tell her…tell her…I don't know, but something.

Who am I kidding? I couldn't even tell Jackson what I saw last night.

Laney examines the Santa setup, too. "That's not her hair. No way Vickie would go gray. That woman is vain with a capital V. Even ran against me for the county Mrs. Title a few years ago." Laney tips her head back while still watching Mrs. Claus. "Gotta admit, though, she looks good, but then you'd have to, to keep ol' Stevie Senior in line." Rolling her big eyes at me and Peter, she nods. "Yep, that man don't know how to keep his business at home."

"What?" Oops, did that shriek come from me? "I, uh, forgot to, um. Gotta go." Shoulders twisting through the dark crowd, I bump right into FM.

"Hey there. Where you going in such a hurry?"

"Nowhere. Where's Missus?"

"She'll be here in a minute. First said she wasn't coming. But she ain't going to let no party like this go on in Chancey without her being here. So, I came on ahead, and she said she'd be here in a bit. Don't ya just love this?"

His black eyes shine in the darkness, and his grin is easy

to see. Taking in his surroundings bit by bit his head moves to and fro, up and down. And it's obvious he enjoys what he sees.

My chest releases the breath it's been holding since last night, and I lift my head.

Bushes along the gravel path behind us wear jewelry of tiny white lights on their bare arms. A fire pit has been made on the other side of where the gazebo once stood. In its light, a Boy Scout stands with water hose in hand, ready to earn his fire safety badge. A few folks linger around the fire to ward off the chill, but most are gathered in the crowd watching Santa and Mrs. Claus. And whether it's from the twinkle of the white lights, the warmth of the fire, or the soft lamps in the Claus' outdoor living room, I suddenly notice the shining faces full of light all around me. Wrinkles, glasses, beards, makeup, all of it enhanced and shining, whether most of the light comes from within or without, I can't say.

Wool, smoke, damp grass, and fresh cut cedar fill the night air, and the moment comes alive. Another lung full of the scented air and the cords stretched and aching in my neck begin to release. My forehead relaxes, and is that a smile I feel creeping over me?

FM's grin stretches even farther. "There now, that's better. Shouldn't be no eyebrow creases on a night like this. Look at them kids."

I tuck my hand in FM's elbow and let the low talking and laughter wash over me. It is a good night, and Laney will not ruin it for me. She ruined last night, but she can't have this one.

"Carolina Butler Jessup, are you trying to steal my husband?" Missus says from behind us.

Only my head moves as I look over at FM, "We better behave. I think your wife is here."

"Awww, shucks. She never lets me have any fun."

"Okay, Missus." I pull my arm away from FM. "You win. He's all yours."

"Not sure it's exactly a win." She sniffs and then smiles. "How was your trip to Blue Mountain?"

"It was good. Sure is a beautiful place."

"Such a shame you had to be out of town and couldn't help your committee set up for tonight."

"Yeah, I hated to not be here. What can I do to help clean up?"

Missus waves her hand at me. "Oh, how would I know that? Cathy was put in charge of this, this *thing*, since certain people insisted it go on. I am handling the Christmas Ball."

FM rolls his eyes, "Crying out loud, I keep telling you it's just a party."

"The Christmas Ball will be at the old mayor's mansion."

"She means our house," FM says.

"On the twentieth. Formal invitations will be going out soon."

"Sounds lovely, but maybe I should find Cathy and see if I can help. Honestly, I forgot I was even on this committee." My laugh dies in my throat at the look of horror on Missus face. "Hey, I'm just joking…"

"What is she doing here?" Missus has her coat clutched under her chin and is staring beyond me.

"Well, I'll be switched. It's Gertie Samson." FM says as he shakes his head. "She's as tall as she ever was."

Turning, I realize they are staring at Patricia's mother. She's standing with her daughter crouched behind her, and they're both watching Stephen's mom play Mrs. Claus. I turn to Missus and FM. "Do y'all know her?"

"Trash. I do not care what they say. She is trash." Missus pulls her shoulders up. "Wonder what in the world brought her to Chancey?"

And that would be my exit line. "Well, I need to find Jackson. See you later." Both of them are still staring at the interloper and don't even notice I left. Good.

Chapter 25

"Missus was right. This apple cider is not good." My mumble precedes my taking another sip. Missus said it would basically be watered down, lukewarm apple juice, and she nailed that one. But it gives me something to do while I stare into the bonfire. The crowd has moved closer to the dark tree as the time for the lighting draws near. Voices and laughter behind me come from the teenagers sitting in the beds of a couple pick-ups parked on this side of the tracks. They want to be here, but not really. Their voices carry, and I can hear the girls wanting to come closer to the tree and the boys convincing them to stay where they are. I'm betting on the girls.

Across the fire, Jackson is talking to Laney's husband, Shaw. Shaw Connor is so good looking and apparently makes lots of money. I mean, Laney isn't buying all those boots and clothes on her part-time treasurer salary. Why would she cheat on him? And the girls, Jenna and Angie, are crazy about their daddy. Disappointment floods over my anger and brings a wave of sadness. But maybe he doesn't make a lot of money, maybe… No. I will not think that. Missus does have a way of getting into your head.

Jackson lifts his chin toward me, "Hey, you ready to go over to the tree? It's five 'til eight."

"Sure."

"Hey, Mrs. Jessup."

"Love your coat, Mrs. J."

"Hey, Mom." Yep, there they are, right on cue. I'm overtaken by the gaggle of girls and as I turn to say hello. I notice the gaggle of shiny hair, cute pea coats, suede boots and tight jeans is followed by a group of boys with shaggy hair, hands stuck in pockets and a wide assortment of baseball caps.

Jackson holds his arm out for me to loop my arm through and we fall in behind the teens.

With a smile, I lean into him. "Things never change do they? Boys talk big, but a smart girl can make a guy follow her wherever she wants."

Jackson laughs. "Nope, things never change. Have you seen Anna?"

"Oooh, I completely forgot she rode down with us. I don't think I've seen her all night." I scan the crowd for a moment, then snuggle closer. "We'll find Anna when people start leaving. Patricia's mom is still here. FM and Missus both know her. Was there a note or anything at the house saying if she's staying the night? Can't imagine she's driving back south tonight. Maybe Mrs. Samson has friends here to stay with."

"I didn't see anything, but I didn't listen to the phone messages."

"Well, all I had time to do was get changed. But wasn't the drive home wonderful? I loved the shops in Blue Ridge and lunch was delicious."

"And we even got to see the train come in." He looks down at me. "Thanks for waiting around for it to come back. We're going to ride that one day."

"Yes, we are. Maybe the kids would even want to go. Sounds like a neat day, up to the state line, have lunch, and back to Blue Ridge."

"Let's try standing over by the Santa place, looks like you

can see the tree from there." Jackson maneuvers us around to the side of the Claus living room setup. Over the crowd of maybe a hundred, the air is filled with puffs of breath vapor. The mayor is talking about the loss of the gazebo and how construction on the new one will start soon. His words cause a stir in the crowd, and the words money and insurance float around. A man beside us says, "Don't know who's paying for it, since we ain't got no insurance on it."

Jackson looks down at me and his scrunched face asks me if I know what's going on.

"Yeah, I'll tell you later," I whisper. A quick search finds Laney standing closer to the tree, and she doesn't appear to have heard a thing. Her red jacket stands out and her smile is as wide as ever.

The mayor speaks up and finishes his remarks by introducing the little girl who's going to flip the switch. She walks past the mayor and then puts her purple, mitten-covered hand up and flips on the lights. Awwws and ooohs replace any remaining grumbling, and bright red, blue, orange, green, yellow bulbs light the twenty foot tree from trunk to tip top. Timothy steps to the front and begins leading Christmas carols. We sing about Rudolph, Santa coming to town, Frosty, and since we're in a little mountain town in North Georgia, Joy to the World and Away in a Manger round out the songfest. Then the crowd falls quiet. I'm not sure what's happening, but the folks who start their Christmas off this way every year seem to be waiting on something.

We're suddenly plunged into darkness. The white lights on the bushes go dark. The just lit Christmas tree is turned off. The store fronts are dark and even the street lights go out. Silence fills the air around us, and I know this is what everyone was waiting for because no one panics or seems upset. And then in the darkness, only punctuated by the wavering flames from the distant fire, stars fill up the black sky.

Like diamonds scattered on folds of black velvet, stars twinkle at us through the bare tree limbs. Cold air sweeps over us and our eyes continue to open wider and wider in wonder at the night sky. Tears gathering in my eyes make the stars twinkle and grow even more. Then Timothy begins to sing "Silent Night," and we join in. Reverently, in awe, we sing to the heavens. I can't see through my tears, and in the choked up voices around me I realize I'm not the only one moved.

We finish singing and the hush remains. Little by little the lights reappear. Street lights, store fronts, the tiny white lights on the bushes and finally the big, happy bulbs on the tree. I look up and the stars are dim and few. But I know, I know how they really look.

I know.

CHAPTER 26

"Mother had to leave with Santa to keep the illusion going," Stephen explains as he stands beside his future mother-in-law. "Patricia and her mother say everything is set with y'all?"

Patricia and Anna huddle on the other side of the big woman. No connection between Stephen and his bride-to-be is evident. His broad smile above his royal blue scarf is relaxed and genuine, just as genuine as his fiancé's face full of anxiety. Between the young people, Mrs. Samson stands, hands on hip, gray coat opened and scowl in place.

"Think everything is good. Mrs. Samson, are you staying the night in Chancey?" I ask.

"No. Just stayed to make sure everything is arranged. We'll be back for the wedding." She whips her attention to Stephen. "Get that date set and let me know. Sooner the better."

Stephen's grin widens. "Of course, Mrs. Samson. Of course."

Jamming her fists into her coat pockets, Patricia's mother looks around her. "Things never change up here in the mountains. Patricia will like that. She's not fond of change. Okay, time for me to go." She nods at us then turns to her daughter. "Behave and don't mess anything up. Just let Stephen and his mom handle everything. Oh…" she looks over her shoulder at me. "You'll get a check beginning of each month."

"Okay," I look up at Jackson. "Mrs. Samson this is…" But she's gone. No hug for her daughter or even a good-bye."

Stephen laughs. "She's not one for standing on any ceremony. Guess I better go find mother. She'll be ready to go home." He turns and leaves. Again, Patricia isn't spoken to or even acknowledged.

Jackson and I are left, wordless and a little stunned, with Patricia and Anna. "You girls ready to go, uh, home?" Their eyes focus on the ground in front of them as they walk beside us. Both girls are wrapped in hurt, and they shuffle past the tree, the fire, and the folks laughing and talking. None of it penetrates their shells. And they don't share their space of misery, either. Each of them hunkers down inside themselves. Alone.

"Want to walk out on the bridge?" I ask Jackson as we start into the house.

"Sure, Here girls, let me unlock the door, and you can go on in." Patty (as we've noticed Anna calls her) and Anna wait on the porch until Jackson pushes the front door open. "There you go. Guess we need to get you both a key. We'll be in in a little bit."

With my arm tucked tightly in my husbands, I pull my black scarf up around my ears and nose. "That was a fun ride home, wasn't it?"

"What a pair. How did we get two sad sacks to live with? At least when Savannah's not talking she's mad, so she's flouncing around, sighing, and generally letting us know we've displeased her. Those girls are like blocks of stone."

"And Patty's mother. What's with her? There's something not right here."

"Yep," Jackson agrees. "Something's just not right."

The railroad tracks, which run in front of our house, cross a long bridge over the river right next to our property. The old railroad bridge turned to a walking bridge is the attraction. Pavement fills in the space where the rails resided, wrought-iron railings line the edges and old fashioned lampposts illuminate the walkway. Folks come out, park in front of our house and walk back and forth on the bridge. The cold night, however, means we have it to ourselves. When we stop walking to lean on the railing out in the middle, the silence is profound. And the stars are back.

"So where did you go?

Jackson's question startles me. "What? Where did I go?"

"Last night. At dinner you were relaxed and easy going. By the time I caught up with you in the lobby, that relaxed lady was gone. I don't think you said more than two words the rest of the evening. Plus, you went from not being able to keep your hands off me to jumping when I even got near you." He leans into me. "I missed you."

"Sorry, but…I don't know why I didn't tell you but…I saw someone in the lobby."

"Who?"

"Laney and a man." Her purple dress, the necklace, his hand on her shoulder—all of it washes over me, and I shudder."

"Like *a man*? She was with *a man*?"

"Yeah, *a man*. Not Shaw and they were together. They came out of one of the other meeting rooms off the lobby and into the bar. She sat down, they ordered drinks, and he, well, he touched her. You know. She was laughing and talking to him. When they got their drinks, they went back into the party where they came from."

"She didn't see you?"

"No. Thank goodness. But then seeing her tonight…" I lay my forehead onto my gloved hands resting on the railing. "How could she do that to Shaw and the girls?"

"Wow. And you're sure it was her?"

"Absolutely. She had on that diamond necklace, same one she had on tonight."

"So Laney has a sugar daddy."

I snap my head up. "What?"

Jackson shrugs. "Griffin told me about the council looking into the town's money, and he said he and Susan can't figure out where Laney gets all her money. They both know Shaw's dealership isn't doing too well. You know, it stands to reason she'd find someone who wants to, um, take care of her. Laney likes expensive things, and she's an attractive woman."

"But for money? Have an affair because he has money? That can't be it." Horror fills me as the bad situation becomes worse. "That's no better than a…"

Jackson's eyebrows spike, "Yeah, you're right." He leans down on his elbows. "Wow, who'd have thought, right here in little ol' Chancey."

Chapter 27

The ringing phone interrupted breakfast with my parents.

"You're not going to like it, but I can't get out of it." Jackson says as I answer.

"Well, good morning to you, too."

The kids are already at school so it's just us three. But with a smile I excuse myself from the table. With my free hand, I twist the doorknob on the glass door leading onto the deck. It's cold but less crowded out here. "What is it?"

"I'm going to be in Alabama the rest of this week and then most of next week. They want to get started before the holidays."

"Your folks get here on Thursday. When will you get here?"

"It'll be late Friday night. And then I'll have to leave Sunday night 'cause work will start at 7:00 a.m. Monday."

Heat rises in my throat and tears gather behind my eyes. Just last night he told me he'd be around until Christmas. "Explain to me how this happens. All those years you were home every night, we never had company. Now, all our parents, a paying customer and one of Will's lost souls are mine to deal with. Mine, all mine. Not to mention, you know who." A quick glance inside tells me Mother and Daddy are watching me but can't hear me.

"They moved up the schedule, something about money they

need to spend before year's end." Jackson joins me with a bit of a whine "It's my project; there's no choice. I have to be here."

"Quit whining," I snap. I prefer center stage when I whine. "I know there's no choice. But…but, this just isn't fair!" Gritting my teeth keeps me from shouting into the phone.

"Seriously? Did you just tell me to 'quit whining'?"

Did I? Doesn't sound like me, but I do remember thinking it. So, obviously, I said it. "I'm sorry. It's just…Shelby?" The name grinds out in a painful whisper. "You won't be here to, to, ah—introduce her. What am I supposed to say?"

"I don't know. We did decide not to say anything and not worry about it."

"But that's what I say about everything!" Now I'm shouting. "Does that *ever* work?"

"Calm down. It's only Tuesday. We'll think about it and talk tonight. Okay?"

A sigh releases a huff of warm breath but also some of the tension in my shoulders. "Okay. I'm freezing anyway and want to go back inside. You'll be home for dinner tonight, right?"

"Absolutely. Dinner and then you and I can talk about all this."

We hang up. Rubbing my hands, a step takes me into the dining room where Mom and Dad are eating bowls of cereal. And waiting.

The twins greet my arrival with a chorus of yips and the urge to kick them away from my feet threatens to overtake me for a moment. Just for a moment. Ashley, legs splayed around him, lifts his head in compassion as if he understands my evil thoughts. Guilt makes me smile down and squeak out a "good morning" and assurances that I wish them no harm. Even though that yipping makes me want to…

"Who was on the phone? You looked a little upset." Mother's eyes convey the same compassion I saw in Ashley's. Daddy steps away from the coffeepot and hands me a fresh cup of coffee. My legs collapse me onto the first chair I reach, and it all comes out.

"When Jackson's parents come this week, they're bringing a woman with them. Her name is Shelby and she's...she's...a long time ago she was married to..." I close my eyes. "Jackson."

"Your Jackson? Our Jackson?" Mother asks and hits the problem square on the head.

My chin lifts. "Yeah, that's right. He's our Jackson. She doesn't have any claim on him, right?"

Daddy speaks up, "Wait a minute. You're saying Jackson was married before and nobody knew? He didn't tell you?"

"*I* knew, but, well yeah, no one else."

"So that's why she's with his parents? They don't know they were married?"

Wow, I am so not doing a good job explaining this. "No, they knew. But that's all. Jackson and Shelby were married less than a year."

"Like secretly married?" Mother asks. "Like in a soap opera?"

"No, it wasn't a secret, exactly. It was kind of a big deal in his hometown."

Daddy gets up and walks around the kitchen, slow and heavy footsteps telegraph he's trying to put things together.

Mother reaches out and lays her beautifully manicured fingers on my hand. "Jackson didn't want us to know? Was he afraid we'd be upset?"

Daddy's pacing stops. "Jackson? C'mon, Goldie. This is right out of Carolina's playbook. Don't say anything. Just keep everything quiet, and it will be fine." He sits back down and stares at me. "Right, Carolina?"

"Well, he agreed."

"Of course he did. That boy's crazy about you. You say jump, and he looks around for a ledge."

Ouch! "We just didn't think it was important. Who knew his

parents would move her practically into their house."

"So she lives in Kentucky? She's close to Mr. and Mrs. Jessup?" Mother asks. "What's she like?"

"I don't know. We always manage to..." This doesn't sound good. "...to not go visit his folks when Shelby was in town."

Daddy pushes up from the table. "So, it's not just a mistake no one knows about this woman. Shelly, did you say?"

"Shelby."

Mother pulls her hands into her lap and sits up straight. Her yellow sweatshirt is soft and warm and looks so clean. The white turtle neck under it is perfectly white, not like mine with the makeup marks all around the top. "So, let me get this straight. The Jessup's are bringing Jackson's ex-wife, Shelby, here for the holidays with your family?"

"Yes."

"What about her family?"

"She doesn't have any, really. And now she works for Jackson's dad with his books, you know the Hillbilly Hank books. They're in Florida at a conference and are coming here on their way home. That's why she's with them. But, well, she's kind of like part of their family now."

"If she's so much a part of their family, why does no one know about her?" Daddy asks from where he's leaning behind me against the kitchen counter.

A shrug and a goofy smile are all I can come up with, but their silence indicates they want more of an answer. So one blurts out. "You'd be amazed at how people don't ask if you don't offer."

"Do the Jessups know your kids don't know about her?" Mother asks.

"Good question. Jackson should ask them. I'll suggest it to him when we talk tonight."

"Honey." Mother's lays her hands flat on the table. "You tell us what you want us to do. Although I think you should just tell the kids. Make it simple and straightforward. Not a big deal."

Daddy sits his coffee cup down in the sink. "I agree. Simple and straightforward."

"Okay. I'll see what Jackson thinks."

Mother smiles. "At least Jackson will be around until Christmas like he said last night. That will help things."

With a groan, I remember why he called. "No, he won't. He'll be here tonight and then part of the weekend. But mostly, we get to entertain Hillbilly Hank and his entourage."

Mother and Daddy exchange looks, and I drop my head onto my arms crossed on the table.

Big family holidays are stupid.

Chapter 28

"Savannah! What is this?" Clutching the slip of bright green paper, I march into the living room, but it's empty. So I head up the stairs. Where is she? I catch my breath a moment in the hallway leading to the stairs to her tower. I'd been outside hanging sheets on the line when the kids came home from school. Just now, moving Savannah's stack of books off the kitchen table, this piece of green paper fell on the floor. Wonder when I would've found out if I hadn't moved her stuff? She not only isn't helping me get ready for dinner tonight and company this weekend, she's making *more* work for me.

The door at the bottom of the stairs opens with my pull, and I clump up her stairs. Her futon is lumpy with the comforter from her bed and four heads stick out above it. Savannah, Angie, Susie Mae, and Jenna are huddled together and staring at the TV screen. Well, they're actually staring at me now.

"I didn't know you were all up here. What are you watching?"

"Spongebob," Savannah answers.

Sure enough, the cartoon character fills the tiny screen. Something feels wrong, but a look around doesn't give me any clues. "When did you girls get here?"

The three cousins look at each other and answer together and not at all.

"Earlier."

"After school."

"Before."

"What do you want, Mom?"

Oh yeah. "This." The green piece of paper waves in my hand. "What is this?"

"It's the fundraiser for Saturday night. Stephen, I mean Mr. Cross, told you about it, right?"

Jenna speaks up, "No, he told you to ask your mom and you said it was fine."

Savannah doesn't even blink. "Whatever. You agreed to be our sponsor for parties and stuff, right?"

"Right. But this weekend? We have company coming and… this weekend?"

Susie Mae's pixie face, framed in jet black wisps, beams. "Oh, Mrs. J, it's going to be awesome. Everyone knows about your bonfires, and we're going to make a ton of money."

"Besides, Grandpa said he'd help."

Oh, Daddy knows about the Chancey High Theater Group Bonfire Fundraiser, but I don't. "It's cold up here. Why don't you turn on the heater? Want me to turn it on?" I reach down toward the little gray box heater. "Aren't you all cold?"

Susie Mae shakes her head and scrunches further down into the comforter, "It's cozy."

"Mom, we're good, and we're watching this." Savannah's blue eyes widen at me and remind me so much of my mother's eyes earlier today when I told her about Jackson's Shelby.

Why does everyone keep looking at me like I should know what I'm doing?

Jackson and the kid's favorite Chicken casserole is on the menu tonight. Melting the butter to add the crackers to, I lean against the counter and wait for the microwave to ping. Orange light pushes across the backyard as the sun goes down behind the mountains across the river. Anna and Patty meander up the hill. The two look like an odd couple, one tiny and one large. Seems in only a few days they've become best friends. They make absolutely no waves about anything and constantly have their heads bent toward each other in whispery conversations. Patty stayed here all weekend as Stephen had his son, Forrest, and they didn't want to confuse him. Everyone's worried about confusing the poor boy, but what about me? This whole thing completely confuses me.

The microwave pings, and I remove the bowl and set it on the counter. Handfuls of crushed Ritz crackers get dropped into the butter, and behind me, I hear the girls come in from the backyard.

"Hi, Mrs. Jessup. We want to ask you something?"

"Okay, ask."

Anna and Patty come stand beside me. Anna's tiny face is flushed, and her cheeks are a rose pink. Her fine hair cups her face and acts like a frame for her delicate features. Patty's skin is rough and doughy white. There's no pink in her cheeks, only patches of acne lend color to her face. Her hair is thick and course and the color of wood. It seems to want to hide her face, and she helps it by always having her head at a forward tilt. Bangs droop from either side, seeking to meet in the middle. She's wearing the emerald coat, and although it's beautiful, and looks expensive, she has it all bunched around her.

Anna wears an old flannel shirt coat, but it drapes and falls like a cape. One is all grace and the other is all—not.

"You want to ask me something?"

Neither has said a word since they moved closer to me.

Patty pulls her hand out of her coat pocket and swipes at her bangs. Her eyes dart to Anna.

Anna lifts her chin. "We want to know how much it would cost for Patty to eat meals here."

"Excuse me. Let me get to the faucet." My buttery, crumb-covered hands lead my way to the sink. Under the warm water the crumbs fall away. "Patty, your mother paid us very well for you to stay here. We were actually going to reduce the amount because it's too much. However…" I grab a towel to dry my hands and turn to face them. "…we could just let it be if you want to eat here. But I thought the idea was for you spend time with the Crosses."

"Ma'am, I really don't want to do that." Pain pulls at her face the same way she pulls at her coat.

Concern for her friend leaps into Anna's green eyes, and she lays a hand on Patty's arm. Anna switches her eyes to meet mine and pleads with them.

"Sure. Whatever makes you happy, Patty. Is there anything else?"

"Can I help you around here? Anna says she's doin' that. I sure would like to have something to do. On the farm there's always stuff to do."

"On the farm? I thought you were in college? Didn't you and Stephen meet at Georgia Southern?"

"No, ma'am. Our folks known each other forever. That's how we, uh, met. But I could be a right good help."

"Of course, that's fine with me. Anna can tell you, I'm not the best housekeeper by far. Any help is appreciated."

"Thanks so much, ma'am. I really do thank you. Gonna set the table as soon as I get this coat off. C'mon, Anna." Patty turns toward the B&B wing and moves faster than I've seen her move since she got here, but she still lumbers.

Anna looks at me with gratitude and there are tears in her eyes.

"What's going on?"

Anna shrugs and smiles then turns to follow her friend.

Spreading the cracker topping on the casserole, thoughts of the group that will surround the table fill my mind. Me and Jackson, Savannah and Bryan— nope, Bryan's eating at Grant's tonight— Mother and Daddy, Anna and now Patty.

Good thing I doubled the casserole. Hope I have an extra-family-sized bag of frozen broccoli.

"We may have to start paying *her*," Jackson says with a laugh.

We're seated in the car and headed to the depot to pick up Bryan and Grant. My arms wrap around myself for warmth. "Seriously, Patty's gardening ideas alone already make me feel guilty. But tonight's the first time I've seen her animated at all. She didn't look like a lump. So, now about Shelby and your folks. We don't need to pick up the boys for another half hour. Where do you want to go to talk?"

"Anywhere is good. It's just hard to think in that house. Wasn't it bigger when we moved in?"

"Sure seemed like it. How about up at the top of the hill overlooking the river? There's that little gravel pull-in near Susan and Griffin's house."

"Sounds good." Jackson rocks across the crossing, both of us looking for train headlights. At the end of the drive, we turn right and head up a little incline. At the top, the road curves, but we pull straight ahead onto the gravel. Between two houses, both with unobstructed views of the river, the pull-in provides a place for folks to stop and see the river, without blocking the road. However, it's not secluded enough for teenage parking, so it's rarely used.

"Dinner was great. Thanks." Jackson says as he puts the car

in park. "You want me to leave the heater on?"

"Yeah, if it gets too hot, we'll turn it off."

Below us the river is dark, there's no moon tonight to make the water shine, so it's just darkness. Above us the sky is gray-black and cold looking. The dashboard lights provide an intimate setting and warmth relaxes my arms and legs. "I told Daddy and Mother about Shelby."

"Really?" Jackson leans up and his tongue starts worrying his bottom lip. "What did they say?"

"Not much really. Just kind of shocked we hadn't told anyone." Daddy's comments about that being my fault isn't a necessary part of this conversation, I decide. "They think we should just tell the kids. Make it simple and straightforward."

"What do you think?"

I chance a look at Jackson. He's so sincere. So trusting. So willing to do what I think is best. But... "Why is this all my decision?"

Eyebrows lifted and his mouth working without producing words, Jackson shakes his head. "It's not your decision, alone. But I want to know what you think. You're the one that's going to be here with them all the most."

The truth of that weighs me back against my seat. Dealing with all this during the first whole family holiday we've shared is impossible.

Jackson echoes my thoughts. "We should've dealt with this a long time ago. When we had more control of the situation."

Silence and stillness in the car makes the heater louder. My eyes are fixated on the dashboard clock as the minutes tick off. I press my lips together. This is Jackson's decision.

"When do we need to pick up Bryan?" he asks.

"Eight thirty. We should be heading that way soon."

"Okay." He pauses and then whispers, "This sure would be easier if everyone wasn't going to be here."

"Maybe it would be better if we told the kids in January.

They'll be able to deal with everything without her right in their face." What did I just say? He threw me off with the talk about what time to pick up Bryan, and while my mouth was open my thoughts came out! "But, honey. Honey, it's *your* decision." I gaze at him with open, innocent eyes to let him know I'm fine with whatever he decides.

He nods. "You might be right. January when things have slowed down again. I like that idea." He reaches over and pulls me to him. Our lips barely meet over the middle console. With our foreheads pressed against each other, he says, "We make a great team."

I bite my tongue. Not to keep from saying anything, because I've already done that. I bite it as punishment for betraying myself.

Jackson releases me and sits back. "Glad that's decided. I feel so much better, don't you?"

Luckily, he's not really looking for an answer.

CHAPTER 29

Laney's diamond heart catches the firelight and looks like a small blaze sitting on her chest. Black curls push out from beneath her cream-colored toboggan hat. Her gloved hand grips my upper arm from the underneath, and there's no escape from standing next to her. "Law, I always hated Melanie in *Gone with the Wind*, didn't you?" Laney's eyes are pinned across the fire. "That Shelby girl is just another Melanie, so sweet she makes your teeth hurt."

"That's it! That's who she is. Couldn't figure it out for the life of me." My head bends toward Laney, relief loosening my tongue. "Several times a day I just want to slap her, and I can't think what for? I mean, I know she was married—" Whoa, pull it back! "Melanie, yep."

"So, is it an act? Married to whom?"

I shake my head slowly side to side but it's hard to talk over my heart stuck in my throat, "I don't think it's an act."

"Ya'll staring at the Virgin Mary?" Savannah leans in front of me.

"Savannah Jessup!" I hiss.

But Laney laughs and offers my daughter a high five. "Your mother was just saying how she wants to slap her ever so often for no reason at all."

"Laney, you're not helping."

"So, what do you think, Savannah, is it real or an act?"

"If it's an act, she's a better actress than me."

"Quit staring at her. Someone's going to notice."

Laney turns her back to the fire and gazes at us. Her bright eyes shine. "So, do you think there's anything going on between Saint Shelby and Hillbilly Hank?"

"Pawpaw?" Savannah yelps.

"What?" My shriek is controlled in volume only. "No. No way." And yet, over Laney's shoulder he stands behind Shelby massaging her shoulders. He does seem to always be wherever she is. Could there...? "No."

"You girls circled up to stay warm?"

"Meemaw!" Savannah exclaims as Jackson's mother steps between me and my daughter and into a conversation she shouldn't hear.

"Etta, are you warm enough out here. We have extra coats in the house if you want one." My voice squeaks, so I cough to cover it up.

"Oh, I'm toasty in my snowman set." Etta has on a bright blue sweatshirt with snowmen and large snowflakes appliquéd all over it.

"Mrs. Jessup, did you make that? It's adorable." Syrup and long vowels dripping out of Laney's mouth makes me want to kick her.

"Lands, no. Got it off TV. One of those shopping channels. I have sets for pretty much every season and holiday. Savannah, I'm going to get a refill on my coffee, and then I want you introduce me to your friends. Everyone seems so nice."

Savannah has to bend down to hug her Meemaw, but I'm pleased to see her hug is sincere. Jackson's mother is sweet and as innocent as a lamb. "Okay, Meemaw."

"Snowflakes on your rear end don't help when you already look like you're made of snowballs. Plump, little thing, isn't she?"

"Laney, you are awful. Etta's a sweet lady. Savannah, don't listen to Laney."

My business partner's eyebrows shoot up and her eyes dart at Shelby across the fire. "Yeah, she might just be too sweet to see what's going on right under her own roof."

"You don't know what you're talking about." Under my breath and away from my daughter, I murmur at Laney, "And what about your own roof?"

"What? Shaw? Shaw cheat on me? Not hardly." Laney doesn't seem to care who hears her. She laughs and reaches out to hug me. "You are just so cute. Okay, I'll lay off that interesting trio from the hollers of Kentucky and go count up how much money we raised tonight."

"You're treasurer of the theater group, too?"

"Sure am." She holds up hands covered in red leather gloves, shows them to me, and winks at Savannah. "Most the money in Chancey goes right through these hands."

She walks away, dark jeans, black sweater coat edged with fur, red leather gloves, and boots. She looks like a million bucks and from what Mother tells me about her wardrobe, that number might be a tad low.

Savannah puts her arm through mine and lays her head on my shoulder. Cuddling? Her highness? My head nuzzles hers, and I stuff my cynicism down somewhere deep, like where my good sense wanders dazed and confused. We sigh together.

Another sigh slips out my mouth, along with words. "Incredible, isn't it? Kind of like a dream, where folks from all areas of your life end up together and you keep saying, 'But wait. You don't know each other.'"

Savannah pats my arm. "Boy, Mom, you sure have lame dreams." She lifts her head and focuses across the yard. "I'm just wondering why I keep letting Ricky hang around. He's cute and popular but kind of a redneck. The truck, boots, and 'yes, ma'am' thing is getting old."

Piled high on the wagon we used for the hay ride, teenagers laugh and flirt and fight. When they finished the last ride, the adults jumped off and hurried to the fire and hot chocolate. The kids found more warmth in sitting closer and laughing louder. Wait a minute. "Are they drinking?"

Savannah barely lifts her shoulders. "Where would they get alcohol? I'm going inside to get some gloves."

She doesn't get far because my arm doesn't let her go so easily. "Savannah, tell me what's going on?"

Her head tilts to the side and her ponytail swings. "There's nothing going on. You're always suspicious, but there's nothing going on. Nothing at all." She gives me that, "you're-so-out-of-it" look teenagers perfect when we think they're watching TV. Cause, c'mon, that look can't just happen, right? Then right at the end there's that look of sympathy which says, "Poor Mom, it's so sad how the world has just passed you by." Then they walk off shaking their heads. I know when they turn away they smile. I just know it.

'Cause I always did.

Jackson sits down on the bed while I mill about our bedroom, thinking over the evening.

"So I told Savannah it was like in a dream where folks from all parts of your life are talking to each other and you keep thinking, 'But you don't know each other.' She then told me how lame my dreams are and how she's thinking of dumping Ricky 'cause he's a redneck."

Jackson nods. "Wow, that's so true."

"Ricky's a redneck?"

"Well, yeah, I guess he is. But I meant the dream thing. That is what it's like. My dad talking to FM. Your mother talking to Shelby. Savannah talking to Shelby. Shoot, anyone talking to Shelby makes me think I'm in a dream."

I kick him as I walk by to the bathroom. "Dream?"

He looks up. "No, you're right. A nightmare."

At the bathroom sink, I lather up my hands with soap and water. The mirror isn't kind. My eyes are dark and circled. Worry lines between my eyebrows are deep enough to grow potatoes. To smooth them out requires stretching my forehead high and wide. Now I look like those Real Housewives on the reality shows who do Botox the way I do Snickers bars, routinely and secretly. "Laney calls her, Melanie. Like from *Gone with the Wind*."

"Who?"

It's hard to maintain a smooth forehead and roll your eyes at the same time.

"Shelby. You remember, Shelby?"

"Of course, I remember Shelby. How could I forget her?"

Beep! Wrong Answer. "Excuse me?"

Jackson lifts his foot up and jerks a tennis shoe off. "Give me a break. I got in from work last night after eight. This morning you had me running all over kingdom come looking for heaters and extension cords so we'd be warm outside at the bonfire. And a bonfire? Why would we be doing a bonfire for half the high school the weekend my folks and," his voice drops to a whisper, "ex-wife are coming." The shoe leaves his hand and hits the closet door.

"This wasn't my idea."

"Then whose was it? You act like all this happens, and you have no control. But you met with Stephen and agreed to sponsor the theater group. You took the money to have Patty stay here. You're the one that talked to Will and agreed for Anna to stay. I don't remember telling your folks they could park their motor home in our driveway for a couple months. And seems it was you who guilted me into inviting my parents for a *wonderful family holiday*." His other shoe comes off in his hand and he lifts it to pitch it where its mate lies. "Seems if we want to pin this on someone, you're the one to look at." And the shoe flies.

"You have lost your mind. This is…is not my fault." Staring him down isn't working because my eyes belie the confused state of my mind. He's right. All this *is* my fault. What is wrong with me? Tears rush to clog my throat, but I will not let him see me cry. He'll think I think he's right. I do, but…but…"Whatever. I'm going to bed." My robe drops to the floor, at the same time I yank the covers on my side of the bed, then I bury myself under them. My back faces his side of the bed and covers hide my face. I feel him standing over me now, unsure what to do. Without moving the covers, I growl, "Jackson, we're both tired and tomorrow's another long day before you have to leave again. We'll talk about all this sometime when you happen to come back to town. It's all my fault *and* all my worry. Good night."

He stands there for a minute. Then he grumbles under his breath before turning away. He turns off the lights and crawls into his side of the bed. "I don't know how everything got so out of control, hon. Next weekend we'll deal with it, okay." He flops over and lies still, but then he moves around like he's thinking.

I lay still, waiting to see if he'll apologize.

"Carolina? Do you want to go to church with me in the morning?"

Church? What a hypocrite. "No. I don't want to go to church with you in the morning. I'm tired and besides, someone has to stay here and take care of all these problems *I've* created."

"Just thought I'd ask. Good night."

This time he settles in and goes right off to sleep. How dare he just climb into bed and go to sleep? How dare he!

Chapter 30

Around 2:00 a.m., pancakes seemed like a good idea. Pancakes for everyone. Then I started counting. Grandma, Grandpa, Pawpaw, Meemaw, Shelby, Patty, Anna, Savannah, Bryan, me, and Jackson. Guess the counting made me sleepy, cause its morning and I'm alone in bed.

Wonder who all went to church?

My feet strain against the covers, and my arms stretch toward the headboard. Sunshine pours in the sliding door in our room and I know it's late. Jackson woke me a little when he got up and left. But sleep found me again. Pancakes when they get home. Sausage or Bacon? Both?

My robe is at my feet, just where it was flung last night. What were me and Jackson even fighting about? The sunshine helps everything seem brighter and syrup will make all my problems disappear. Syrup on a buttery stack of pancakes. Bryan loves pancakes, and sausage, to roll around in the syrup.

The house hasn't been this quiet in forever. Down the stairs, the upstairs silence becomes even deeper with the big, sunshiny spaces just waiting, empty. Did everyone go to church?

"Thank you, whoever left coffee." The red light says it's still warm so with a cup of hot coffee, I step onto the back deck for a breath of fresh air. The smell of wood smoke from the bonfire still hangs in the blue morning air. Through bare trees the river shines at me. Not sparkly, but a dull shine, like light on pewter. Gauzy clouds give the sun something to stay veiled behind so as to not wake everything up too quickly. My nose freezes with cold, inhaled air but my mind clears. This. This is what I imagined as a family holiday. The well-being of loved ones gathered together. Going to church, eating meals together. Lazy mornings to cook and plan and relax. Jackson was right. This *is* all my fault. So, all the credit is mine, too. All of us seated around the table, passing plates of pancakes and talking about the morning. It's all my fault. One more deep breath of chilled air, then on to making breakfast for my family.

"I smell bacon."

With voices in the living room, I switch on the electric griddle and brush it with oil. "Yep, you smell bacon *and* sausage, Dad."

"Look at this." Daddy and mother appear first in the kitchen. "Everything smells and looks delicious. What can we do to help?"

Patty rushes into the room, "Not a thing in that beautiful dress, Mrs. Butler. I'll help, Mrs. Jessup." She takes an apron off the hook in the pantry closet and ties it around her girth. She has on black polyester pants and a shapeless blue sweater. She shoves the arms of the sweater up and looks at me. "What do you need me to do?"

"You can set out the orange juice and apple juice. The bacon and sausage are staying warm in the oven. The first batch of pancakes are about ready to flip so folks can start eating."

"Whoa, Mom. Pancakes!" Bryan barrels into the kitchen from the back deck. He slides into the chair next to his grandpa.

"Dad is looking at Pawpaw's car window. It won't stay up. They'll be in in a minute."

Etta admonishes her granddaughter as they come into the kitchen. "Savannah, your car is a mess. How do you ride in it like that all the time?"

"Well, Meemaw, at least the windows stay up." Savannah comes to lean on the counter next to where I'm working. She has her hair piled in a messy way on top of her head, but with her snowy white turtle neck and dark jeans, she looks like a model ready for the runway. Her nonchalance makes the rest of us look amateurish and lumpy.

Jackson's mother comes to where I stand pouring more batter onto the griddle. "Carolina, what a feast you've made. I should've stayed home and helped you."

"No, Etta. I'm glad you got to go to church. I really needed to sleep in. Just this once."

Savannah's big eyes open wider, so I can't miss them rolling. My tongue sticking out is pure involuntary response.

"Here," I say to Etta, "you can put these on the table. Another batch is almost ready. So, I take it you and Shelby rode with Savannah since Hank's window is stuck open?"

Taking the warm plate from me, Etta turns to the table. "I rode with Savannah. Shelby rode with Hank. Those two thought the cold ride would be invigorating. They are a mess, aren't they?"

Both my daughter and I go still. I will not look at Savannah. I will not look at Savannah. Making eye contact would imply we are sharing a thought. So, I will not look at Savannah.

"Mom, can you put chocolate chips in some?" Bryan asks with his mouth full.

"Oooh, chocolate chip pancakes. That sounds divine. Oh my, this is just perfect, Carolina. Perfect." Melanie's here. Oops, Shelby.

"Well, grab a seat. I'm taking up another batch right now."

A warm hand on my arm makes me look up. And there she

is. Doe eyes, petal pink lips and cheeks. Honey brown hair cut in an adorable bob around her cute little face. It's like she fell right out of a Disney movie and if birds start flying around the kitchen it will be because they want to carry her plate to the table and unfold her napkin to place in her lap. "Morning, Shelby."

Tears shine in her eyes, and she whispers, "You are so good to me. Just so good."

My smile doesn't let any teeth show and I hand her the plate. "Oh, it's nothing. Just put this on the table."

She squeezes my arm again and takes the plate.

I'd throw up in the bowl of batter, but I don't have enough eggs to make another batch.

"Patty, your future in-laws seem real nice," Mother says. "Vickie and SC, right?"

The young woman's jaw shifts to and fro, "Yes, ma'am."

Mother continues, but looking at me, "They stopped us on our way out of church to see if Patty wanted to have dinner with them."

Patty's whole upper body moves with a shrug. "I'm going to start cleaning up the kitchen." She stands and picks up her half-full plate.

"Well, Vickie and SC said you told them you had work to get back here to. What kind of work?"

Already headed away from us, Patty stops and then answers without turning around, "Paperwork for Mama. And the farm."

"I didn't care for your preacher much, Jackson." Hank says as he stabs at the pancake and sausage pieces swimming in syrup on his plate. "Didn't hold my attention much. I like a preacher to preach like he's earning his money. Put some umpff into it." With a forkful of food he points at Jackson. "Know what I mean, son?"

Jackson nods. "Sure do, Dad, but we're good with Don. Um, there anymore of those chocolate chip pancakes left?"

Bryan groans and then lifts the plate toward Jackson. "They're all yours. I can't eat another one." Then my son falls out of his chair onto the floor, moaning and cradling his stomach. "I'm so full."

"Bryan, cut it out." I place his empty plate onto mine. "Get up and take these dishes to Patty."

Shelby folds her yellow paper napkin like its fine linen and lays it across her plate. "What a wonderful breakfast, Carolina. Now for a nap in that luxurious room you gave me." Her big brown eyes look sleepy, and she stretches her arms out in front of her and then rises. She's wearing a soft green sweater dress, cream tights, and, I'd swear, Loves Baby Soft perfume. Same perfume I wore in, let's see, junior high.

Walking around the table she lets her hand float across each person's shoulder, at Jackson's Dad, she stops. "Can I get you to take a look at that lock on my suitcase?" It just doesn't seem to want to open, and that's where my robe is packed away. Can't lay down for a nap in my dress."

A dark cloud crosses Hank's face. "That's what you get for buying cheap luggage and then packing it so plum full." He shoves in a mouthful before he pushes away from the table, mumbling, "Carolina, thanks for the breakfast. It hit the spot." He then turns to Daddy. "Let me help Shelby out, and then I'll be out to take a look at that window with you." He hitches his pants up, "If it's not one thing, it's another." Hank is wiry and short. For church today he wore a dark brown suit, beige shirt, and a classy orange, brown and gray tie. Where Etta is soft and easy, he's tough and headstrong. Jackson is a good mix of the two. Jackson's two brothers each take after one of the parents, Emerson is like their mother, and Colt is just like his dad.

Emerson is in healthcare in Virginia. He and his wife have three daughters. Colt is like their dad and is a high school coach up in Kentucky. He's never married, and I always thought maybe he and Shelby could get together.

Etta stands and moves to pick up Shelby and Hank's dishes. "That suitcase has given her fits this entire trip, poor thing."

This time I forget and Savannah eyes lock on to mine. We look away as soon as we each see the suspicion reflected between us. I'm bolted to my seat as Etta cleans up after her husband and Shelby. Savannah slips out of her seat, picks up her dishes, and goes into the kitchen.

"Mom, you want to come see what we've done down at the depot today?" Bryan asks as he pulls himself up from the floor. "Dad's coming."

Hearing that Jackson will be at the depot stops the "sure" from jumping out of my mouth, and a look at my husband shows me that he knows he's the reason for my hesitation. "Probably. Let me see what Grandma and Meemaw want to do today, okay?"

Mother leans toward Daddy, "Jack, let's go to the depot today. The other times we've been there Bryan's been at school."

"You've already been to the museum at the depot?" Jackson and I ask in unison.

"Of course. That Peter is on the ball." Daddy lifts an eyebrow toward his son-in-law. "You're going to love his ideas for the railroad exhibit."

"Cool," Bryan says as he begins piling dirty dishes high. "Can Meemaw and Pawpaw come, too?"

Etta hollers from the kitchen sink, "Count me in. Hank, too. Oh, and Shelby. She always likes to join in. Her naps aren't usually that long."

Naps? Plural?

Daddy pushes back from the table and plants his big hands on his knees, "Sounds like a plan. I'm going to go put on some jeans, though, and get my toolbox for a look at that window. Let's say we go in about an hour? Does that work?"

"Sure." I answer, push my chair in, and grab the juice containers. When I enter the kitchen, Patty opens the refrigerator for me to put the orange and apple juice away.

"Hey, Mrs. Jessup, can me and Anna come, too?"

The pleading in her face makes her even more unattractive. She wrings the folds in the front of her sweater. Just the slight nod of my head, makes her face relax, and her hands stop their worrying motion. She looks over at Anna, who just smiles at both of us before turning back to loading the dishwasher.

With the table clear of dishes and food, Savannah pulls her cell phone out of her pocket and steps out on the deck. She wraps her arms around her for warmth, but she isn't out there long enough to get cold. Closing the phone, she strides over to me and says close to my ear. "Me and Ricky are going for a ride. Okay?"

"Okay. What's up?"

"We just need to talk. This might not all be working for me anymore."

"This? As in dating Ricky?"

She pulls her sleeves down over her hands and bends her head forward. Speaking into her covered hands, which are balled up near her mouth, she mumbles, "Yeah, and, other stuff." Her eyes lift suddenly and dart around the room. They rest quickly on her grandmother, her meemaw, Anna and Patty. "I'll talk to you later. Kinda crowded in here." She walks off, but I follow. And catch up when she's on the first stair.

"We can talk now."

The vulnerability from the kitchen has melted away. Her eyes roll. "Mom, it's nothing big. Just, yeah, like you said, I'm thinking of breaking up with Ricky. That's all. He'll be here in a minute. So later, okay?"

"Sure. Later." Talking and laughter comes from the kitchen.

It *is* kinda crowded in there. They won't miss me, so I walk across the room. Through the front window, there's Bryan, his grandpa, and Jackson. Afternoon sunshine reflects off the gray, blond, and golden brown heads. Hank isn't out there. Wonder if he's still with Shelby?

Ricky's red truck pulls in the driveway, and he jumps out to talk to the guys. His dark hair is shaggy, but not long. His shoulders are broad, and his black letter jacket with the gold letter and gold trim looks like it was made for him. That big smile on his face makes me sigh. How hurt will he be if Savannah breaks up with him?

"Don't worry. He won't be that upset." Savannah says behind me.

"Why do you think I'm worried about him?"

She pauses at the bottom of the stairs to put on her jacket. Not a letter jacket. She didn't want one, even though we offered at Christmas. "I heard you sigh. Mom, you really shouldn't worry. He'll be fine." Then reaching back to push her arm in the sleeve she mumbles something.

"What?"

"Nothing. I'm going now." She opens the door and then pushes open the screen door. As she does *she* sighs and her shoulders drop. Then she closes the door behind her.

Again, something doesn't feel right. And I did hear what she mumbled. She said, "He'll be *more* than fine."

What does that mean?

Chapter 31

Lemons. First thing that comes to mind as we cross the threshold of the depot. Lemons, and soap, and polishing oil. In front of me Bryan, Jackson, and the two grandfathers peel off to the right where the train display is. Sunlight streams in through the sparkling windows that line the top of the walls. Last time I was in here for the October's Women's Historical Society meeting was a month ago and the change is remarkable. Dust no longer floats in the air and cobwebs no longer drape from window sill to display case and back again. The walls sport fresh cream paint and the dark woodwork gleams. Lights spotlight the exhibits, and the old wood floor is clean and enhanced with old braided rugs which are old and faded, but clean.

"Peter, you've done a lot of work." My feet are still rooted in place and I'm sure my apparent astonishment causes my friend's smile to widen.

"Glad you like it." Peter walks toward me and holds out a hand.

I place my hand in his, and he bows with a wave of his other arm to the room behind him, "Welcome to the Chancey Depot Museum." He tucks my hand into his arm and we walk to the middle of the room.

"What you've done is amazing. You did all the cleaning and

painting? That took a lot of time."

"You forget where I live. Being here is a treat." He leans toward me, and his ponytail falls across his shoulder. His deep brown beard, makes his gray eyes darker and a smile precedes his rich laugh. "Mother hates this place. She says it has swallowed her husband *and* son. Honestly, I think it eats at her because she doesn't have a bit of say so how things are done here. Dad, of course, loves it. Gives us both a place to hide."

"You can say that again." FM comes up on my other side. "Especially now she's got that Christmas Ball coming up she's always harping on." FM hangs his thumbs in the waist of his work pants and expands his chest. "Peter did a right good job, didn't he?"

"He did a marvelous job." I turn to smile at Peter and find his face closer than before. I jump a little and Peter apologizes, drops my arm, and steps back. A prickly heat races down my back, and I spin around to FM. "Show me what you're working on."

"Over here." FM leads me to a stack of boxes, all full of old magazines. "Flora and Fauna, you know them, right?"

I nod my head.

"Well, them girls donated about forty-five years of *Good Housekeeping* magazines—every copy from 1915 to 1960," FM says. "Their mother started her subscription when she got married and moved into the house. They won't donate the ones from 1960 to now because, and I quote, 'They might need to look up something.' Peter wants one for every year put out on this stand and then the rest will go on this book case for folks to look at. We're going to put a chair here and a reading lamp."

"Oh my," just looking at the covers of the couple on top make me want to sit down and start going through them. "It'd be easy to get lost in them, wouldn't it?" I look over to where Patty stands, seemingly not interested in any of the exhibits, in the center of the room. "Patty, did you see these?"

She steps closer and looks over mine and FM's shoulders for a moment as we flip through some from the 1920s. Then she comes around my side, takes one out of the box, and slumps down in the floor. Sitting cross legged, she's reverently turns the pages of the one she chose.

FM clears his throat, "Um, Patty, I saw your mother here for the Christmas Tree lighting. How is Gertie?"

"She's fine. She was only here for the day, just getting me settled." Patty's voice is calm. She doesn't look up, just keeps flipping pages.

FM chews on the ragged ends of his mustache for a minute. "So, you're going to marry Stephen Cross?"

"Uh huh."

More chewing and now he's rocking a little on the balls of his feet. I'm standing perfectly still, practically holding my breath to not miss a word.

"So, how do you know Stephen?"

Pages fall one after the other and finally, "We met down south."

This time there's hardly a pause as FM seems determined to keep going. "Did you know he was from Chancey?"

"I'd never heard of Chancey."

"But your mother, surely she talked about her hometown."

"Nope." The bent head never sways or turns or lifts.

"So it's all just a coincidence?"

"I guess."

FM's eyebrows dive toward his nose, "Now see here, young lady, that just don't make good sense. Not at all. What is going…"

Anna dashes up, darting right in front of FM, and then kneels down beside Patty, "What's that? Oh, I want to look at one." She grabs another magazine and starts pointing and jabbering with her head next to Patty's.

FM shakes his head and looks at me. He jerks his chin toward the back wall. "Let me show you something over here."

At the coffeepot, FM pours us each a Styrofoam cup full. Before taking a sip, we turn back toward the girls and the magazines. Both of their heads are still bent together.

"So, Carolina, what the story with that Patty girl being here?"

"All I know is what was said just now. She's engaged to Stephen…"

FM sounded his disbelief with a forced "pshaw" through his mustache at the same time he shook his head.

Nodding, I continue, "I totally agree. There's no way they're a match and despite what Stephen told me the plan was, they've not spent one minute together since she got here. Patty doesn't seem to like him or his family."

"But there's a wedding date set?"

"Apparently. It's in the spring. And now that I'm thinking about it. He told me Patty wanted to move here because she was jealous of Cathy. There's no way Patty is jealous. No way."

FM worried his moustache a bit then downed a big gulp of coffee. "If I was you, I'd keep an eye on all this. Gertie Samson is not someone to trifle with. Her folks lived back up in the woods here and they were mean. Don't think there's any of 'em left back in there now, but her Pa—Albott Samson caused a sight of trouble when Gertie was little and then into her teen years. She's Missus' age so makes me a bit older. Albott ran moonshine and talk was he killed some of his competition. Things got hot up in the woods about that time and they sent Gertie into town to live with some distant relative and go to high school. Then one day in her and Missus' senior year, Gertie just up and left. Sherriff said her folks left, too. Nobody really cared. It was more like good riddance, if you know what I mean."

"Sure, makes sense."

FM looks around and then finds the trashcan. "We heard they bought some mansion down in the southern part of the state. Big old farm with hired hands and everything. Her daddy even ran for the legislature and won a couple times fore he died. Albott about ran that part of the state, and they put on the big dawg. Gertie went from being dirt poor trash to the daughter of a mover and shaker. Don't know who she married. Patty talk about her dad?"

"No, not at all. But her name is Patty Samson, so maybe there wasn't a marriage."

FM claps his hands once and then puts them in his pockets, "Well, I sure don't know, but that Patty doesn't seem anything like Gertie, thank the good Lord! Here comes Bryan, looks like it's time for your tour."

"Well, I stole some of your help." Peter helps me put on my coat by the front door. "Patty and Anna are going to come over a couple afternoons a week and work on some of the displays. They're fascinated with those old magazines."

"Good, they need to interact with some other folks and maybe you can figure out what's going on with Patty marrying Stephen."

"I saw you and Dad talking and looking at them. Is that what you were talking about?"

"Yeah. It just doesn't seem to add up." Fitting my gloves over my fingers, my head dips and I mumble, "But whatever does?"

"Huh? What is it?" Peter leans on the glass case I stand beside and suddenly he's close.

"Nothing." I turn. "Jackson? You're staying and bringing Bryan home?"

In only a couple quick strides, Jackson is with us. "Yep. Everyone else going back with you?"

"Think so. I've got to get back and get laundry done so you

can pack tonight." And I can't keep my mouth shut so I add, "so you stay here and have fun."

Jackson's chin hardens and without turning his head, he announces. "Bryan, let's go. We need to help your mom."

Oops. A little guilt was all I was going for. "No, y'all stay. Bryan is having fun."

"No. We're coming home. It's not fair to leave you with everything." Then he adds, "Don't want you feeling burdened by my family and my schedule." He yanks his coat off the coat rack, "Bryan, let's go!"

Bryan slides past with cutting eyes making me feel about two inches tall.

All the chatter is gone, and it's downright chilly in the depot now. Must be everyone opening and shutting the door. Don't ya think that's it?

Deep red-orange fills the sky outside the depot. Everyone has walked to the side of the building where the black mountains provide a foundation for a blazing sky. When I step up, I see Savannah.

"Ricky drop you off here?"

"Yeah."

"How did it go?"

She presses her lips together and tightens her arms around herself, but only shakes her head. Then she walks away. Ahead of me stands a huddled mass of my family all gazing up at the sky through a spider web of black branches, like an ink drawing on a watercolor background. I watch them and my eyes roam over each one and yet I can't seem to walk the few yards to join them. Then feeling a pull of someone behind me, I turn around. There stands Peter, back at the corner.

I'm not sure what he's watching.

Chapter 32

"I noticed Pawpaw and Shelby weren't at the museum with y'all." Savannah says on her way down the basement stairs.

"Shhh," I hiss with a look past her and up the stairs. "Here, give me that."

She hands me her dirty clothes basket. "Don't worry. I closed the door. Oh, and Patty and Anna wanted me to tell you they'll be down here in a minute to do the ironing."

Our basement is old and not used for much of anything but storage and laundry. It's chopped up into a bunch of little rooms and some of them I don't think have been opened since we moved here. Which is how Peter, playing the ghost all fall and summer, was able to slide down the old, no longer used coal chute on the front porch into one of the little rooms, and then walk right out the back door and into the woods.

However, there's lots of good lighting down here. So even with all the corners and closed doors, it's not really a creepy basement.

Savannah looks around her as she sits down on the lower steps. "I think those two like being down here. That way they can talk and whisper and no one can hear them."

"What do you think they have to talk about so much? They didn't even know each other until a couple weeks ago."

She reaches up and pulls her hair out of the messy bun she's worn all day. Running her fingers through the long, dark waves, she shrugs. "Don't know. Guess I don't really care. But now, about Pawpaw and Shelby. They were here, alone, all afternoon? Who is this chick?"

"Shelby? Well, she's Pawpaw's secretary. You know, for his Hillbilly Hank books."

"Have you looked at those books? Full of old junk. How many has he done?"

"The last one was his eighth. Yeah, they're not my cup of tea, but all the senior citizens love them."

"And that's why he needs a secretary? Like I said, 'Who is this chick?'"

Her blue eyes stare at me and are such a stark reminder of how much she's a perfect combination of my parents. Mother's blue eyes and Daddy's glare. With a shake of my head and a mumble about fabric softener, I turn to the washer.

"Guess I'll just ask Daddy." She waits for a minute and then stands up and turns to walk up the stairs.

Jackson? Naw, she won't. "Wait, what, uh, what about Ricky? Did you break up with him?"

Over her shoulder she spits, "No. He may be a redneck, but with the noise and crowd and the *secrets* here at home he doesn't seem that bad." Near the top she pauses. "Never thought I'd say my family is weirder than Ricky's, but it's at that point." Then she's through the door, and it's closed behind her.

Ouch! But, she's so overly dramatic. There aren't *that* many secrets. Are there?

"Here's your shirts, fresh from the ironing board. I'll just put them here in the front of the closet. Patty and Anna are great help. They did all the ironing."

On his side of the bed, Jackson has his suitcase laid out, so I sit on my side and recline on the pillows piled there. "You about packed?"

He grunts. "Thanks for the laundry and shirts."

Several trips between the bathroom cabinet, the closet, and his suitcase are done in silence. He's still mad. It's evident by the way he's manhandling everything he's packing. Surely there's something for me to say that can ease the tension. But everything that waits to jump out of my mouth won't help. Don't know what he has to be so ticked off about. He's at least escaping all this. All this, as Savannah put it, noise and crowd and secrecy. What's he got to be mad about? Mad that I'm not making everything smooth for him? Mad that the house is as busy as the Grand Ole Opry on a Saturday night? Well, whose idea was all this anyway? The big house by the railroad tracks? A great big Family Christmas? Marrying some stupid girl when you were barely old enough to vote? And then letting her come right into the house with your family?

The bed bounces when I jump up. "Fine. You want to sulk around and be mad up here. Fine. It's just fine! I'm going downstairs. Have a good trip to...to wherever you're going!"

Good old houses have sturdy, heavy doors. They take a little bit to get going, but when they find their resting spot against the doorjamb—the sound is extremely satisfying.

Chapter 33

My roommate in college used to talk about how it was almost worth fighting with her boyfriend because making up was so great. There's even that term "make-up sex".

Right now, 5:00 am with Jackson slipping down the stairs headed out of town for the week and me, lying here faking sleep, I'd settle for a make-up pat on the head. We haven't spoken since I let the bedroom door do my talking last night.

Up until now, making up with Jackson was easy. We never fought. Boring, uncomplicated lives make for very peaceful living. Few friends, limited access to extended family, well-behaved kids, two time consuming careers, and a couple who'd rather cave than argue, all makes for very little conflict.

Back in the suburbs, our lives were as fenced in as our yard. Nice, self-closing garage doors kept us in, and the world out, in such a clean, concise manner. Our neighborhood association, which I used to think was a cross between the CIA and Martha Stewart, is but a fond, faraway dream, and my parents not being able to park their motor home in my driveway was a magnificent blessing I never fully appreciated. Lack of a guest bedroom was a gift straight from God, for which I never once said "thank you".

Jackson and I got along fine before we moved to Chancey.

You know what else? I want to talk to Susan. That's odd,

for me, to want to talk to someone, but another day with these people is more than I can stand the thought of. These are the kinds of day I miss my job at the library most. To go somewhere orderly and controllable. To come home to a semi-clean house because no one was there all day. To have the kids off in their rooms at night with their computer and TV so I could have peace and quiet to read. When is the last time I lost myself in a book? Forget talking to Susan, a good book is what I need.

Covers fly back and a quick trip down stairs and right back up them results in me back in bed, pulling the covers back over me. This paperback has been calling to me from the kitchen desk for weeks, but my time to read has just disappeared. But now I'm making an effort. Plumped pillows, cozy table lamp, and thick covers. This is just what I need.

"Susan, can you go to Ruby's this morning?" I'm going whether she says yes or not, so I throw my book across the bed and sit up.

"Sure, I guess. Around nine-thirty?"

"Perfect. See you then."

Now I'm just pissed. Excuse my language. I know good Southern girls say "ticked." But I'm really not happy. It is near impossible to get lost in a book when the real people in your life won't stay in their designated places in the far, back recesses of your mind. The main character, a woman with dark hair made me think of Laney and her sugar daddy. And the heroine is only seventeen. I know it's another century, but seventeen? Savannah is almost seventeen, and if she were pregnant with the blacksmith's baby, or anybody's baby, what would I do? And the patriarch of the family has his eye on the girl, too. Some patriarch to have a roaming eye when he has a sweet wife. Who does that? Except you know who? No, absolutely not. Then there's the mystery woman staying at the manor. Why have one when you can have two like I do right here in my own house?

This is why women resort to having friends. Talking to yourself about all this stuff will send you right over the edge.

"Hey," Bryan says when we leave our rooms at the same time.

"Hey, yourself. Did you sleep good?"

"Uh-huh."

"Hey, I'm sorry about not letting you and Daddy stay at the depot yesterday. I just had a lot on my mind." My words just hit his back as I follow him down the stairs. His hair is getting longer than he usually wears it. His feet look huge in his size 10 tennis shoes and make him gangly and out of proportion.

"It's okay."

As we make the landing and only have a few steps to the living room floor, the voices in the kitchen reach us.

Bryan hesitates.

"What is it?" I ask.

He sniffs and shrugs, but his eyes focus on the kitchen table. All four of his grandparents are there, and it sounds like they're all talking at once. Shelby's singing along with the pop song on the radio and Savannah's talking a mile a minute on her phone also float out to us.

Involuntarily, I lean my head one way and then the other, stretching my neck to forestall the tension building there. Bryan is making the same motions with his head. Great, we both feel headaches coming on, and the day isn't even started.

"Carolina. There you are," Daddy announces. "Thought I was going to have to come get you out of bed. Good morning, Bryan."

Mother holds her arms open for a kiss and hug from her youngest grandson. We both move closer to the threshing machine. I mean the table.

"Painting is on the agenda for the week," Daddy says. "Hank and I noticed the kitchen and living room need sprucing up and we haven't got anything to do. Your mother and Etta say they have lots of Christmas things to keep them busy, shopping and baking and such. So, you just let me know what colors you want, and then Hank and I will take a ride out to the Home Depot at the interstate.

"Daddy, I don't think we want to be painting with all our company here and with it being Christmas."

"Nonsense. Right, Hank?"

"Your dad is right. Between the two of us, we'll have it knocked out in no time. Besides, my next book is *Hillbilly Hank Does Home Repair*. This old house will be great research."

Coffee. Breathing in slowly and deeply at the coffeepot, I pour a full cup. Savannah comes to the sink to sit her orange juice glass in it and she leans close to me. "See, Ricky's house looks better all the time."

My eyes cut to her, but the smile I anticipated sharing with her isn't there. She looks miserable. "What's wrong?"

"Nothing." She says with a toss of her hair. "Let's go, Bry."

Grandmother kisses and hugs are distributed again and they leave. My cup is somehow empty, so I turn to the pot for a refill. "Daddy, can you just bring me back some paint chip cards, and then I'll talk to Jackson about it?"

"You're turning down free help? Not wise, honey. You two look to need some help. The B&B rooms look great, out here. Kinda of dingy."

He's right. There are water spots on the kitchen ceiling and the walls are faded blue, really gray now. The living room is fine if you don't look too closely at the old nail holes and marks from the former owners pictures. Lots of pictures. Lots. Our old house in Marietta had just been repainted a year earlier. Every room. Every ceiling. And it was done by professionals because I had a job and a paycheck.

Hank stands and wanders around a minute, his eyes taking in the ceiling. "I bet it would be weight off Jackson's mind to have this taken care of, don't you?"

"Of course, go out of town for a week and come back to all your work done. How convenient," I say, and five pairs of eyes stare at me for just a moment. Then they all drop. Okay, that sounded bad.

Hank just shakes his head a little and looks back at the table.

Shelby glides to my side and puts a hand on my shoulder. "Carolina, I'm sure Jackson misses being here with his family something awful. I know he'd much rather be here with you and Bryan and Savannah, even if he had to paint. Poor thing."

Please, God, let her be saying 'poor thing' about Jackson and not me.

"Fine. Paint. Whatever you want."

Mother leans back and smiles at me. "And if you're worried about the money for the paint, we've all have decided we want it to be our housewarming gift to you."

Yippee, it's a party. "That's awfully sweet. I've got a meeting I need to get to. So, fine. Whatever y'all decide. Just something neutral and tasteful. I've got to go."

Letting them pick out the paint isn't a huge risk. Both of their homes are completely painted in shades of white. The most outrageous my dad ever got was when he painted the upstairs bathroom green, really cream with a hint of mint. Once every eight years, every room at Hank and Etta's gets a coat of off-white, same shade. I don't know how they came up with eight years. Guess I'll have to read *Hillbilly Hank does Home Repair* to discover that little nugget. So, fine. The house will be freshened up, and I'm not involved. Amen. Hallelujah. The end. Over and out.

Chapter 34

"Savannah's acting weird and says our family is crazier than Ricky's. Sorry, I know he's your kin, but…"

Susan laughs and acknowledges the craziness of her brother, Scott's, family with lifted eyebrows, a grin, and a nod.

"Speaking of your family, your sister has given my home and business a horrible name, but I can't nail her down on changing it; and well, she's just hard to figure out sometimes." My gaze drops, and I lift my cup of coffee to my mouth giving Susan time to talk. About Laney, hopefully.

"Yeah, Laney…well, who knows." Susan resumes picking at and eating her muffin. She eats like the birds at the feeder on our deck.

Okay, she's not going to talk. My cup clinks as it hits my saucer. "Then there's the whole family stuff. My dad and Jackson's dad are at this moment buying paint for the living room and kitchen, two weeks before Christmas. Shelby is, well, that sweet as sugar act is just on my last nerve. Will comes home tomorrow, and we still are housing his little mystery friend, Anna. The three dogs are a complete nuisance. Ashley's not so bad, but the twins? They yip and yap all the time. And shed." I settle my elbows on the table, ignoring my untouched bran and raisin muffin. "You know, we're watching *Gone with the*

Wind. Again. Except now Hank keeps arguing with my dad over historical accuracy."

Susan laughs. "My father was just like Hank. Couldn't stand when something wasn't completely accurate and felt he had to tell us all about it. Can drive you crazy."

"Crazy. Exactly. And, then, what's up with Patty Samson and Stephen Cross? I'm not sure they even know each other, but they're engaged?" My voice rises as my litany winds down.

Susan lays her hand on my arm as Stephen's former mother-in-law, Libby Stone, offers a refill of coffee to the table next to ours.

"Do you think she heard me?" I whisper.

Susan's ponytail sways back and forth with her head, "No. Libby doesn't seem to be all here today. Hey, Libby." Susan pushes her cup to the edge of the table.

"Hey, girls. Here ya go." Steam pours from the pot and our cups, carrying dark richness.

Susan pulls her cup toward her, "Libby, you okay?"

Our waitress's sigh is followed by the pot of coffee coming to rest on our table. "No. No, I'm not."

Susan reaches out to hold Libby's forearm. "What's wrong?"

"It's Cathy. Why can't she stay out of trouble? You know I love her, but she's messing up again." Libby lifts the pot and pulls away from Susan's hand. "Honey, I'm sorry. You don't want to hear my troubles."

Susan comes off as straightforward and simple. Straight brown hair, no highlights, no curls or mousse. Faded, clean blue jeans and a red turtleneck. Her jacket is a blue, hooded, zip-up jacket with no writing, she probably got it on the sale rack at Wal-Mart. Her eyes staring up at Libby are bare of makeup and her only jewelry is her wedding ring and a watch. "Libby, if you need to talk…"

Libby's face twitches and her lips draw tight. "No. Not here."

Her eyes flick to me and I gulp, "What? I can leave." My

feet push my chair back.

"No, Carolina, no. It's just, that Patty staying up at your place, well…" Now her whole face works to help her mouth come up with words. Her white hair is cut short and years of yard work in the Georgia sun shows in her skin. She has a sweet smile, but today that smile is gone.

"What about Patty?" I ask.

"Why is she never with Stephen?"

Susan and I lock eyes. She must've overheard us.

Libby's surveys the tables around us, but no one seems to need her. She bends down a little and whispers, "I'm afraid Cathy is seeing Stephen."

Susan and I both lean up from our bent positions. "But… he's engaged." We stammer at the same time.

Libby's wrinkled eyes close. "I know."

"Libby, can I get some help here?" Ruby yells from behind the counter, and Libby hurries off.

"Okay, that explains some things." I pick up my healthy, bran muffin and then sit it back down. "I'll take that one home. I'm getting a double chocolate one. Ruby was taking them out of the oven when we got here, so they're still warm. Want one?"

Susan shakes her head. "No, but I would like another little cup of that whipped cream cheese."

At the counter, I hike one hip up on the red seat of the chrome stool. In the window of the refrigerated case, there's a reflected bush that is actually my hair. I haven't had a haircut since we moved here, and it shows. Tugs at the front and back of my sweater, does nothing to hide my lower half and how tight these jeans are. First order of business back home, throw these jeans into the back of my closet and put on some sweat pants. Besides, with Mother and Savannah and Laney around, no one looks at me anyway.

Last thing I need is a chocolate muffin, but I do need to get that cream cheese for Susan. Might as well get them both. Back in the depths of the kitchen, Ruby and Libby still shove pans around in the bakery racks. When things seem to be back in order, they both come to the counter.

Ruby, wipes her forehead with the back of her hand then plants both fists on her hips. "Mornin', Carolina. Running away from that pack of hyenas up at your house?"

Libby smiles at me and makes apologies with her eyes as she scurries off with a newly filled coffeepot.

"Hyenas, huh? Okay, that could fit. Can I get a double chocolate muffin. One that's still warm and a container of cream cheese?"

Ruby turns and the flashing lights on the front of her Christmas tree sweatshirt no longer assault me. When she comes back to the counter with my dark, rich muffin on a plate and a little tub of cream cheese beside it, she nods behind me toward the door. "Your friend is here."

My eyes hit the door at the same time Missus hits it. With a push my stool swivels back to the counter. "My friend?"

"Sure, she called like she does most mornings wanting to know who's here. So told her you and Susan were hunched over a table. Knew that would get her here."

"I didn't think you liked her?"

Ruby reaches under the counter and comes up with a tube of lipstick. She swipes Christmas Red on her lips, rubs them together and frowns. "Times are hard. Business is business."

"Carolina, Add an apple-cinnamon muffin to your plate. Ruby, I also need a coffee cup since I don't see but two at the table." The commands come from behind me.

My stool swivels around again, "Missus, good morning to you, too. Which table are you referring to?"

"Don't be obtuse, Carolina. It's not attractive." With that she pulls out a chair next to Susan, and I'm forgotten.

Ruby sits another plated muffin on the counter. "Here, Libby'll bring her cup over in a minute." She rests her folded arms on the counter and tilts her head as she looks at me. "Don't know exactly how you do it, but you seem to attract the crazies."

My grimace doesn't put her off, because she just grins. Then just as my back turns, she adds, "Don't understand it, but sure makes for a good show."

Putting both plates on the table, I decide to be nice. "Here you are, Missus. Your coffee will be here in a minute."

She gives me the royal nod of acknowledgement. "That hillbilly, putting lipstick on out in public. She must have Yankee ancestors hiding in her family tree." Her voice raises, chin lifts, eyes focus. "Now, Susan, why is Griffin not returning my phone calls?"

Missus' teased and puffed and sculptured hair still smells of hairspray. She must've just come from Beulah Land Beauty Parlor. It's the only hair styling place in Chancey. A converted garage attached to the owner/operator's home at the end of Main Street. Lots of blue, gold and white stone for outdoor décor. Understand why I haven't gotten a haircut, yet?

Susan waves her hand in front of her nose, probably because the hairspray overtakes the smell of fresh coffee, cinnamon and chocolate. "I don't know anything about who Griffin calls. And if it's city council business, I'd rather not know."

Missus shakes her head in disgust, and the mound of gray cotton candy on her head jiggles. "You better be concerned. Your sister is going to be brought up on embezzlement charges. She can't be allowed to get away with this." Missus chokes off her words and she takes a deep breath. "Down at Beulah Land this morning they are calling for her head and it doesn't look good that the council president is her brother-in-law. Not to mention your standing at the church. She cannot hide behind you anymore."

Muffin bits come flying out of my mouth as I picture Laney ever standing behind Susan, much less trying to hide. Me being nice and talking to Missus don't mix. "Laney? Hide? She had on a leopard print skirt and red leather boots Sunday. And hide behind *Susan*? Her hair alone is bigger than Susan and Scott's families put together."

Missus frowns at me, but I don't rate a comment. Her focus shifts back to the other side of the table. "Will you tell Griffin he cannot ignore me any longer? As a ranking President-emeritus of the Chancey City Council, I'm calling a special hearing. We'll get to the bottom of this."

"I'm sure he's not ignoring you. He probably doesn't have anything to say. Let the council look into things and then at next month's meeting it can be discussed."

Missus swallows the muffin in her mouth. "Next month? I think not." She pivots my way. "And you? This name you've selected for the B&B is a joke, correct?"

Laney so deserves to be thrown under the bus for this, but I've had enough Laney bashing in the past five minutes. "We're working on it. Do you have any suggestions?"

"Yes, now that you mention it I do."

Well, that was stupid, and I walked right into it.

Missus spreads a dollop of soft butter on her muffin, places it back on the plate and then wipes her fingers on her napkin. "Yes, I propose a contest to name the B&B. I've already spoken to the Chamber of Commerce, and they are excited about the promotional aspect. We're putting together a basket of Chancey goods and services as an award."

"What, like a tire change at Walt's?" I lift my muffin up. "A muffin with free cream cheese, twenty-five percent gift certificate for a funeral at Murphey's Funeral Home?"

Missus' chin turns to stone. "I liked you so much better when you were silent and sulking."

"Hey, now, enough with the insults."

"And I've had enough of your insolence. You moved to Chancey, not the other way around."

Ouch! Now that hurt. "Well you—"

"Okay, too far. You both need to settle down." Susan waves a hand between us. "Carolina has a lot going on right now with her family here and Jackson traveling. She just said she doesn't like the new name either."

Missus' shoulders straighten, and she blesses me with one of her Queen Elizabeth smiles. Stiff upper lip, stiff bottom lip and "you're so wrong" in her eyes.

Susan shrugs in my direction. "We have to do something about the name, right?"

"Okay…"

"Then that's handled," Missus closes the subject and sure, what do I care?

Old Cotton Candy Head, picks up her cup and then leans toward Susan and me. "I do need to get your opinion on something. Peter is, well, I'm afraid Peter is getting lured into a difficult situation."

Libby walks up to our table and conversation ceases. She sits a cup down in front of Missus and fills it. She offers to heat up our coffee, but we both say no and she moves on.

"What kind of a difficult situation?" Susan asks.

"I believe he's seeing that, that cheerleader, Cathy Stone."

Again, Susan and I rare back at allegations against Chancey's perkiest young mom.

"No. Really?" Susan asks and then whispers, "Cathy? Are you sure?"

"Well, it's someone. He's moping around and reading those old books he read in high school and college whenever he was in love."

Susan chews on her bottom lip then asks, "But why do you think it's Cathy?"

"Because that's who FM thinks it is. FM says Cathy is over at the depot often, blames it on that boy of hers, but she wouldn't be the first woman to use a child to get to a man."

Books? Did someone mention books? "Okay, but wait, what

kind of books is he reading?"

Susan and Missus both stare at me.

My upraised hands indicate my sincerity, "Seriously, I didn't know guys did that. What is he reading?"

Peter's unromantic mother dismisses me and turns to Susan. "Besides, Cathy is attractive in a cheerleaderly, teen-agey kind of way. There isn't much of an appropriate selection of women for him here in Chancey. Which, of course, is why we sent him off to Harvard." She purses her lips and sighs, "My poor son. Being tracked down and hunted by that girl. And *you know* how she trapped her last husband. Peter has been raised a gentleman, so of course she knows he would do the right thing. Poor Peter, at her mercies."

Susan points a finger at Missus, "For crying out loud! He's not exactly a helpless lad faced with an enchanted siren."

Amen! Thank goodness she said it before I got into it with Missus again.

"However." Susan pauses. "However, he would be a catch, and he is good looking and financially sound. Cathy does need a knight in shining armor right now, but there's nothing we can do, right?"

"Be his friend. Stop in at the Depot. He's just lonely." Missus' face fills with concern, and for the first time, she looks to me like a mother. Do mothers never get a break from the fixing, the thinking, the worrying? Even when their baby is forty-five?

"Carolina, have him up to your house. He seemed fine when he was playing the ghost up there. He likes talking to you and hanging out with you."

Wait, how did I get in the middle of this? "I think I've got enough to handle up there already."

Susan crosses her arms and sits back in her chair. I can't read her face, but for some reason, my face feels hot.

My last bite of muffin gets my full attention, and Missus gazes into her coffee cup. She sits it down with a clank and picks up her purse. She pulls out a little snap-closure change purse and takes out a couple bills. "Here is money for my muffin and coffee." She stands up. "Now, Susan, I have your and Griffin's RSVP for the ball. Carolina, your parents have responded, but what about you and Jackson?"

"My parents are invited?"

"Of course. Decorations for the ball are their area of expertise. *Gone with the Wind* is our theme. Only in décor, of course, not in dress. Oh, and here is an invitation for Jackson's parents and that delightful Shelby." She pulls two of the large, specially printed gold invitations from her purse. "I was going to run them up to your house, but this saves me a trip." Suddenly her face lights up. "I know. Peter can escort Shelby. She's much more appropriate than that cheerleader."

"No," explodes out of my mouth. "I mean, does Shelby *have* to come?"

"Why, Carolina, what could you possibly have against that sweet young woman?" Missus asks.

"First of all, she's not that young. She's practically my age and she, well, she…" There's nothing allowable to say. "Fine. Whatever." I jerk the invitations out of Missus' hand.

"So, you and Jackson will be there?"

"Yes, we'll be there."

"Fine." Missus says with a tip of her head and hair and she leaves.

Susan still sits with her arms crossed staring at me. "So, what's up with all that? Just who is this Shelby? And who do *you* think Peter is pining for?"

And it all comes spilling out, well everything about Shelby and Jackson, and Laney's suspicions about Shelby and Jackson's dad. All of it.

Peter? I don't know anything about that.

"Still can't get over Jackson being married before," Susan says as the door of Ruby's shuts behind us.

"Yeah, I know, and Savannah being so suspicious makes me wonder if she's figured it out." We move a few yards down the sidewalk to stand in front of Chancey Floral's display window, gazing in at the baskets and flowers and ribbon.

Susan pushes my shoulder with her shoulder. "Maybe she doesn't know exactly, but what I learned when we went through all that with Susie Mae and my keeping her fooling around a secret, is that everyone felt *something* was going on and that put us all on edge. Not good for a peaceful life. Did I tell you that Grant finally told Griffin he thought we were getting a divorce? He seemed the most unaffected and now, come to find out, he was worried sick."

"Do you think we should tell Savannah now? We're trying to keep it under wraps until after the holiday."

"I honestly have no earthly idea. Just do what your insides tell you."

Silence fills the sidewalk and the steady breeze causes us to hunch down in our coats further. My eyes lose focus and instead of seeing the display, my bush of a hairdo reflected in the window comes into view. "Don't know what my insides say, but my hair is screaming, 'Do Something.' Have you ever been to Beulah Land?"

Susan grins and rocks back and forth on her new white tennis shoes for a minute. "Of course. Where else would I go?"

"Why are you grinning?"

"Just hearing an outsider say the name. We've all gone there for so long, we don't think of the name anymore. But when you say it, well, it's just funny."

"Maybe I'll stop in and make an appointment."

"Yeah, do that. Good idea." My friend continues rocking and grinning. "I bet Peter would love it."

"Don't you dare. Don't you even go there."

She laughs out loud. Then turning away from the window she adds, "If I were you I wouldn't let Laney know. The best looking guy in town having a crush on you instead of her, will not go over well."

Heat flushes my face and then races down my back. Susan doesn't see my rolling eyes however, because she's staring at the space where the gazebo stood. "Carolina, this money business isn't funny. Griffin is dodging Missus' phone calls because the city accounts are in a real mess, well, the files they can find are in a real mess. Laney's at the middle of it and she's putting them off big time. She won't talk to me or Scott or Mama. Shaw is avoiding us all. He wasn't even there when we went over for the chili dinner."

Now, I bump my shoulder into hers. "Are they doing okay? You know, their marriage?"

"I hope so. I know they went up to Blue Mountain lodge a couple weeks ago for a night away. Laney asked me to keep an eye on the girls 'cause she had a romantic evening planned."

"For her and Shaw?" The words jump out my mouth.

"Of course." She pivots toward me. "Who else?"

And she sees it in my face. I know she sees it. Her eyes widen and her head shakes "no." Her mind goes into overdrive and shows in the sudden wrinkles in her forehead and the biting of her lip.

I stammer, "Nobody…" but my voice fades as she pushes a hand toward me and then backs away.

"If she asked me to watch out for her girls so she could go…" Susan swallows and then waves her hand at me. "I've got to go." She runs across the street, past the yellow tape marking the new building site for the gazebo, straight to her car. She flings open the door and dives inside.

A breeze pushes around me and bells reach me. There, on the branches of the dark green Christmas tree are wreaths of jingle bells. The limbs droop under the weight of the decorations; ribbons swags are damp and heavy; and the bright paper stars put on by the children at the celebration are faded and folded in on themselves.

Merry Christmas and a happy affair to you, too.

CHAPTER 35

Slowly I turn, step by step.

Well, block by block. Twice now, I've driven by Beulah Land Beauty Parlor. Twice now, I've curved up the hill, driven past the elementary school and the kids on the playground, past the woman in front of the rusty trailer running extension cords all over her front yard for her blow up Christmas decorations. Her electric bill will probably double this month, but oh, the beauty and grandeur of lit up snow globes, reindeer, and giant gingerbread men.

And twice I've sat at this stop sign debating on home or Beulah Land. My inability to say no means if I walk in there and they have an open chair, I'm getting my hair cut today. But at home there's Daddy, Hillbilly Hank, Mother, Etta, and paint and lights. Lots and lots of paint and lots and lots of lights according to the latest phone call from Mother. She and Etta went along to Home Depot, and she says the decorations and paint nearly filled up Hank and Etta's whole car. She said, and this is word for word, "Luckily, Etta and I are short, and we could sit our feet on the boxes of lights. We couldn't even see each other over the stack of them on the seat between us."

Beulah Land looks better and better. One more drive-by.

Dark-red, two-story buildings stand in a row on one side of

Main Street while the park shoulders the other side. Once the park and the shops are passed, it becomes just another rural two lane road. Gravel driveways peel off on both sides and speak of days when not much room was needed for parking cars. The houses sit close to the road and while some could be spruced up, most aren't worth the time or effort. They run the spectrum of browns and grays for the walls, but the roofs tend to all be green, except for the black patches where the green shingles have gone missing. The trees and bushes alone might be worth more than the houses. Giant magnolias and oaks, walls of azaleas higher than my head and camellia bushes nearly the size of the Christmas tree downtown hide the houses and junked cars. Must be beautiful in the spring, but now it's all brown, dark green, and gray.

Until you reach Beulah Land.

My favorite crayon was Sky Blue. Beulah Land Beauty Parlor looks like some of those pictures from my second grade year when every house I drew had lots of windows, flowers in the front yard and window boxes, a pony in the side yard and every square inch of the house painted Sky Blue. No pony at Beulah Land, but the yard and window boxes do have flowers. In December. Think they're fake?

White stone fills the entire front yard, or parking lot would be another word for it. Turning off the road, my tires crunch on the rock, and I pull next to a car parked near the shop door. There is a front door and a shop door. The front door is in the middle of the house-front and is a highly varnished wooden door. The shop door is painted gold, not gold color, but gold like a shiny trumpet and over it is a sign saying, "Welcome to Beulah Land." The sign is white and the words are black, written in the script you'd find in an old, old Bible. Gee, wonder why I've never been here before.

But I'm here now.

Beulah was the name of my high school secretary, Beulah

Greenway. And the word possibly is from a song or a hymn, but nothing concrete comes to mind. The wind whips my coat around my legs. There's nothing to block the wind since the yard is bare and across the street is an open field. Bunches of silk daffodils and daisies line the walk and ruffle in the breeze. Feels strange to just open the door of a house and go in, but that's what the little sign over the doorbell says to do. The door opens easily, and suddenly, I'm out of the wind and in a wide open, modern looking shop. Shiny, hardwood floors spread out toward the mirrored wall at the back. A line of black hair-washing sinks and hair drying seats are to my far right. In front of the mirrored wall are plush barber chairs and stainless steel rolling carts with all the hair care items neatly arranged. In the far left back corner, behind a row of what appear to be live, palm trees, four pedicure-massage chairs form a comfortable grouping. This place makes my old hairdresser in Marietta look downright ragged.

The subtle lighting and light jazz music relax my bunched up neck muscles immediately. A deep breath and a minute to appreciate the waterfall running along the front wall is all that's needed for a smile to take over my face.

This place is beautiful, and empty. "Hello?"

From my right, a gauzy curtain pulls back. "Hi. Sorry I didn't get out here sooner, but when you came in I had just taken a big bite of sandwich." She's tall and happy looking, her hair is red and just as curly as mine, except hers looks good. "I'm Beau Bennett, and you're Carolina, right?"

"Right. I'm sorry, have we met?"

Her Hershey-brown eyes smile all on their own. "No, but it's a very small town."

"Looks like I've come at lunch time. Really, I just want to make an appointment."

"I'm taking lunch right now because the book is empty until two. If you've got time, I can take care of you right now. Plus, we'd get to know each other without the crowd."

And suddenly, that sounds like a wonderful idea.

"Here's let's turn you away from the mirror and comb through these curls. Your hair was just crying for conditioning."

When the comb pulls through with barely a tug, I begin to believe in the magic Beau keeps talking about.

"So my aunts love what I've done with the inside of the shop, but they won't allow me to touch the outside." Beau shrugs her wide shoulder and dimples appear in her cheeks, "I can live with that. It is kind of a Chancey Landmark. My nephew manages a stone company over in Marble Hill, so our white gravel comes at the family rate. The blue paint and gold touches keep me humble."

"How long has Beulah Land been here?" Dark curls fall around me to the floor, but Beau's calm, deep voice helps me control my panic.

"Since before I was born. Aunt Bea, yes like in Mayberry, styled hair from her house when my uncle died in an accident in the marble quarry. This was their house. My aunt Pearl joined her when my cousins started school. Mom, her name is Crystal, did their book work. Matter of fact, she still does our book work. Up until three years ago, I owned a shop down in Roswell. About the time I was ready to get away from that Atlanta traffic, a national group offered me a boatload of money to sell. So sell, I did. Moved me and my kids up here to the sticks and used the money to renovate the shop.

"It really is nice. So, your name, is it a nickname?"

"Yep, my name is Beulah, after my aunt, but I came up with something a little more in this century when I was in elementary, thank God, it stuck. Granny named all her girls heavenly names, you know like Beulah means a heavenly place and Pearl is for the Pearly gates and Mom is Crystal like the Crystal Sea." She starts clipping up sections of my hair, "Law, you got a mess of hair here."

"Yeah, I don't know if you can do much with it. I've let it go for so long."

Beau winks at me and her dimples flash. "Oh, honey, you're going to love what I'm going to do. Just relax and let me work my magic. Afternoons are quiet here. The mornings are a show. Me and my aunts plus two cousins work. They all leave at lunch time, come back in shifts after school is out, and the next busy round starts. So we won't be disturbed and transformations like yours, are what I live for."

All afternoon Beau won't let me see the mirror. When she hears my stomach growling, she brings me a plate of crackers and cheese. She asks permission to try some makeup on me and how can I say no? She just fed me. Then she rubs oil on my hands and places them in these awfully nice heated gloves. A quick nap in the dryer chair ends when she moves me back to her station.

"Is that aluminum foil?" I ask when I see the bowl beside her on the steel cart filling with pieces of shiny foil-looking paper she's removing from my hair.

"Just a little highlighting. You'll love it."

"Highlighting? I don't know."

"Trust me. Won't be long now. Your phone's been ringing in your purse, you know."

"Yeah, but I don't want to deal with my family. I'm sure it's nothing important. Besides, before there were cell phones no one could've reached me at the hairdressers, right?"

"Right. It's your time to chill."

"You're cutting more hair?"

"Relax, earlier I had to take off some of the ends before I

could do the highlighting. Now, I'm doing the shaping."

Eyes closed, my focus struggles to shift from the scissors, the foil and my phone to the background music and waterfall. Rippling water and soft saxophone do their magic, as I close my eyes and drift. Beau knows when to be quiet and my shoulders drop, my breathing slows. Time passes, but I'm not aware.

A brush grazing my neck and chin stirs me.

Beau smiles when I open my eyes. "You're going to love it. You really are. Ready?" Beau unpins the draped apron from my neck, brushes my chin and neck with the big, soft brush one more time, and then turns the chair.

Curls, soft smooth curls fall on one side past my ear, just down to my neck. There they taper down to lay against my skin. On the other side the curls are tucked behind my ear and thin, wispy bangs push my hair off my forehead. I haven't worn bangs since I was in junior high and then they looked like a Groucho Marx mustache on my forehead. My face is open to the light, and my eyes actually have little gold flecks in them. Gold flecks which mimic the streaks of gold in my hair. The dull, bark brown shines and the curls look like curls you'd put in your hair on purpose. My neck. It appears I have a neck and it's long. So are my eyelashes, and there's that red lipstick the South runs on. But it looks good. It looks like I put it there on purpose and know its red and like it. Finally my eyes lift to meet Beau's.

"You can close your mouth. It's really you. That mess you had on your head just needed to be whipped into shape and you need some new styling products. Curly hair has to be treated nice or it will get the upper hand. I know. I've waged battle against it my whole life."

"The makeup, it's so not me."

"It's not the old you, the new you is a different matter altogether. It's nothing special, just some good mascara and the perfect shade of red lipstick. And the lipstick is on the house.

Mom sells Mary Kay so I get a good price on it. However, she'll want to come do a makeover on you, just warning you."

We move to the counter, and as she adds up everything, the mirror behind her tells me the other mirror wasn't lying. My fingers keep touching my neck and the pretty little curls lying there.

"You're going to want to get you some scarves so your neck doesn't freeze this winter. But wait until the summer. You're going to be so much cooler." She holds out my coat for me. "Sure was nice to finally meet you, Carolina. Sorry it took so long, but between this and my kids, I'm kept jumping."

"It was wonderful to meet you and thank you so much. I don't know what to say."

At the door, Beau hugs me and sends me on my way. Out on the white stone, I hurry to the car. Wonder if my rearview mirror will agree with the mirrors at Beulah Land?

Chapter 36

"I was coming right home. Why would I have listened to my messages?"

Mother tries again, "Sweetheart, I'm just saying if you'd listened to your messages you wouldn't have been surprised,"

"And how did this happen so fast?"

Savannah's blue eyes burn. "Grandpa put it on Facebook. Painting & Decorating party at Trackside Delight. Free pizza and soda. My life, my entire life, is a joke."

Mother frowns at Savannah. "It's mostly your friends that showed up, so I don't know why you think it's a joke. Look at how much we've gotten done."

White icicle lights hang from every horizontal line of the house. The maple trees are full of young people, all with handfuls of loops of lights. Red ribbon entwines every vertical post of porch railing.

Honking turns our attention to the road where Ricky's truck is backing into the front yard. In the bed of his truck is a full size manger scene. Full-size as in our own holy wax museum display.

"Perfect. Right there."

I know that voice. Missus, should've known. Turning around, the commandant of this loony bin is standing on the front porch. She's wearing crisp tweed pants and jacket with a turquoise scarf around her neck and then she spots me.

"Carolina, it's about time you showed up. You cannot run a successful business lounging at Ruby's with your little friends. And it's not very hospitable for you to leave your parents and in-laws to do your work while you play. Fortunately for you, Jack and Hank don't wait to be asked. They just step in and do what needs to be done."

"A manger scene? Missus, where did that come from?"

"It's the Presbyterian's old one. They bought a new one last year and donated this to you. You'll need to remember to write them a thank you note."

Closer to the house, I can see sheets and drop clothes through the front window and screen door. Forget the yard. It's only for a couple more weeks. "How did the painting go?"

Missus shakes her head at me. "And didn't I tell you to check with me before you painted? Luckily, I'd told your father that I have pictures of some of the original colors of the rooms so your restoration will be accurate."

With a sigh, I lift my head to look up at the queen of Chancey. "Missus, I'm not interested in restoration. It's just a house, for crying out loud. Just. A. House."

"No, it's history, and once again you're fortunate that others stepped in. Jack and Hank knew to consult me."

No. No they didn't. Did they?

I push around Missus and pull open the door. Fresh paint smell greets me first, but a wall of robin's egg blue comes a close second. Blue? Nothing I own is blue, especially not this fresh as spring, little girl color of blue.

"Hey there." Daddy grins from across the room. "How's this for authentic? Same color as Mount Vernon's main dining room when Washington built it."

"But, Daddy, I told you something neutral and tasteful."

"I know. Isn't it a great color?"

"But every room in your house and in Hank and Etta's house

is off-white."

Etta shouts from the kitchen, "Not after we get home. These colors make all the difference in the world. Come look in here."

Careful steps avoiding drop clothes and paint cans, delays my arrival in the kitchen. That and a dread building in my stomach.

"Sunshower, isn't that an adorable name?" My mother-in-law, paint brush in hand and yellow paint swiped on her cheek, beams. Or maybe it's just the smile-'til-you-throw-up color of my kitchen wall just makes her look like she's beaming. Or on fire.

"Yellow?"

"Missus told us how much you loved the sunflowers at the pageant tea, so we thought with the black countertops the yellow would be perfect. Wait, not yellow, Sunshower. And these girls are just the biggest help." She waves her brush toward the girls on ladders painting above the tall kitchen cabinets.

"Hi, Mrs. Jessup. Mr. Cross sent the stage crew over as soon as he heard y'all needed help. I'm Cut, that's Jen, and the guy on the floor over there is Jimmy."

Both girls look kind of familiar, but they're not in the group who usually hang around. These aren't the cheerleaders, the actors, the front people. The girls are chunky, wear baggy jeans, black tee shirts and no makeup. The boy sprawled on the floor painting around the baseboards is long and thin. His sideburns and his wristbands are thick and dark. And smooth complexions are not the order of the day in the kitchen crew.

Finally, teenagers I can identify with.

"Well, we appreciate your help. I guess." Everything in me wants to rant and rave and throw a fit. But, well, Jackson's right. It's my fault we now live in Candy Land. No reason for me to yell at anyone else.

Daddy steps into the kitchen. "So, isn't this right pretty? At first Missus had to sell me on yellow, but gotta admit, she was right. Brightens it up a good bit. That Patty and Anna need to be picked up down at the depot. Hank and Shelby dropped them off on their way to buy the ceiling paint. We didn't realize how dingy the new wall paint would make the ceilings. You want to go get 'em?"

My eyes blink as my mind tries to catch up. "Who? Shelby and Jackson's dad?"

"Naw, they're already back. Or should be. That Patty and Anna. At the depot. Seeing as everyone else is busy…"

My hand clutches my car keys in my pocket. "Sure." My purse is still on my shoulder so with head lowered, I make my way back through the living room and out the front door. The baby Jesus is being worshiped in my front yard by six foot tall shepherds and wise men. And thank goodness they're setting up a flood light. Wouldn't want to miss out on the night crowds. Missus is barking orders at Mother and Ricky and Ricky's dad, Scott, and probably the shepherds and wise men. Not getting involved there, so I head straight for my van. As I get closer, I see Ricky's on again, off again mother, Abby Sue in her hooker/realtor get up talking with Savannah, whose back faces me. The conversation appears tense, so I march right on up.

Abby Sue's orange tinted legs, face and cleavage speak to the effectiveness of tanning beds in creating Oompa Lumpas. Her perfectly tailored black suit would be conservative on someone built like Susan, or a fourth grader. However, being a couple sizes too small, it looks like the first thing to be flung at the base of the pole down at a place called, "Pink Pony."

Abby Sue's eyes slide to me and then back to my daughter. "Savannah, you're playing with fire."

Savannah spits, "You're just jealous."

"Hey, Carolina," Abby Sue throws over Savannah's shoulder.

My daughter swirls. "Mom." She gathers herself, "Mom, have you seen that thing they are putting up on the lawn. It's huge."

"What are you and Abby Sue talking about?"

"Nothing. Where are you going? I'll go with you."

Abby Sue stands posed with one hip jutted out, her hand placed on it, and her jaw set while she glares at the back of Savannah's head.

"Abby Sue, what 'fire' is Savannah playing with."

"Mom, you don't need to ask her. I'll tell you in the car. Let's go. I'll drive."

Abby Sue just shrugs at me and walks toward the manger scene. "Guess I'll go help Missus and the boys."

Savannah jogs to the van and has it started by the time I get there.

"Okay, what's going on?" I ask.

"Abby Sue's just bothered by Stephen. I mean, Mr. Cross." She backs out and then maneuvers turning around before crossing the tracks. "She can't believe I'd break up with Ricky unless I'm interested in another guy."

"Wait, she thinks you're interested in Mr. Cross? Are you?"

"No way. But I do want to be his favorite. I have to get the lead in the spring play. I have to."

"You're only a junior. There's time to get another leading role. You just started this acting thing."

"Where are we going?"

"To the depot to get Anna and Patty."

Yeah, he's ancient to her, I'm sure. "So you *are* breaking up with Ricky?"

"Probably. He's going to freak out when play practice starts. He wants to be with me all the time now that football is over. He's so clingy."

At the bottom of the hill she turns toward Main Street.

"How are things at his house, with Abby Sue and Scott?"

"I guess she's back for good. Mr. Troutman is sooooo happy. You saw him hauling that manger scene around with Ricky. He does anything she wants. She wants to be Chancey Society. That's what she calls it. So she's jumping through Missus' hoops to get an invite for the Christmas Ball Saturday night."

"But there's nothing going on with Mr. Cross and you, right?"

"Mom, I told you. Be serious."

"I am being serious, and Abby Sue seemed serious, too. Maybe she knows Mr. Cross better than you."

"Okay, okay. It's all good. It's all under control, but you know, I think Miss Laney's right about Pawpaw and Shelby. They're together all the time. Plus, I heard Daddy and Pawpaw arguing about it last night when I came up from the basement."

"Your Daddy and Pawpaw were talking about Shelby? And you overhead them?"

"They were in the kitchen practically shouting."

"What were they saying?"

She tosses her hair off her shoulder with her hand. "Oh, I'm not sure. But her name definitely came up a couple times."

I chew on my lip as we turn into the depot parking lot. "I'll go in and get 'em." Gravel crunches under my feet and puts sound effects to my lip chewing. So Jackson fought with his dad and then fought with me. He was batting a thousand last night, wasn't he?

Inside the depot, Patty and Anna are waiting in a couple chairs beside the stack of old magazines across the room. "Hey, girls." They both stand as Peter comes out of his office and heads my way. My face flushes, so I take a deep breath and say, "Hello."

"Hello, You! Look at your hair. And your makeup."

My hair? Makeup?

Startled, I jerk my head up and lift my hand to check out the curls lying on my neck. I'd completely forgotten. And no one else had even mentioned it! "Oh, thanks."

Peter reaches out to touch my hair and his thumb falls across my cheek.

"Love your hair!" the girls say together as they advance toward us, and Peter steps back.

Both stroke their dirty-blonde and brown, unsculpted, running to wild, hair as they point out details of my makeover. Peter won't stop staring at me, and my smile won't behave.

"Savannah's waiting in the car, and there's a crew of kids working up at the house. So we need to go." We all, Peter included, walk out to the van.

The girls climb in, and Peter comes to close my door on the passenger's side. "You really do look great," he whispers while he tucks my coat away from the door. Then as he backs away, he waves to us.

Patty leans forward. "Where did you get your hair done?"

Savannah studies me for a moment. "Hey, yeah. That looks good."

"Thanks, um, I went to Beulah Land." At Savannah's rolling eyes, I add, "The inside looks nothing like the outside." I give them a rundown of the shop, every detail. But my mind fills with fog. Peter does have a crush on me. That should not cause a shiver in my center.

But it does.

Chapter 37

Savannah makes the last turn to our house and slams on the brakes just before we cross the railroad tracks. And not because there's a train. White lights by the thousands make our mouths drop and eyes widen. Until the glare forces us to squint.

And do I hear music? A touch of my window button reveals that, in fact, I do hear music. Little Drummer Boy is playing now. Across the tracks we bounce until we come to a rest in the driveway.

"Y'all have been busy today," Anna opines.

"Not me." Savannah and I say at the same time.

"And wait until you see the inside. We're living in technicolor," I add.

"Ooo, a manger scene," Patty says as she exits her side of the van.

All the lights, including the flood light for the manger scene, grow brighter by the minute. The sun still stood above the tree line when we left the house, but now as the sky grows darker, our house and yard shine. Through the front windows the robin egg blue walls shine out at me. What an odd color they chose. Nothing is going to go with that. Nothing at all.

Missus meets us on the front porch. "Carolina, where are the invitations for the ball I gave you this morning for Hank and Etta and Shelby?"

"Oh," I glance back at the van. "In the car."

She marches past the four of us. "Must I do everything myself?"

I hand my keys to Anna, "Here, take these to her. It's locked."

Patty grabs the keys. "I'll do it." Then she lumbers off. Anna looks down at the ground. Oh yeah, Missus and her don't get along.

The living room is chilly because the windows are cracked to lessen the paint smell. Voices from the kitchen draw us there.

Daddy stands at the stove, stirring a something in a big pot. Mother, Etta, and Shelby sit at the table. Hank is out on the deck talking on his cell phone. Pounding down the stairs, tells me Bryan is headed this way.

"We're back. What's up?" I ask as Savannah goes to the stove.

"Umm, chili," she says. "Can Ricky come over for dinner?"

That stops me. "What? I thought..."

Daddy looks over his shoulder at me. "Sure, we've got plenty. Only a few days here and we found that making extra never goes to waste. Carolina, y'all sure do like to have people over."

"But they're all so nice." Shelby purrs. "You and Jackson just have the sweetest friends. And all these wonderful teenagers are so helpful."

Hank lets out an expletive loud enough for us to hear through the French doors, and Mother jumps. "Wonder what has Hank so upset?"

Etta lifts her hands in confusion, but Shelby answers. "He's been on the phone all day. There's a problem with some publicity for the next event back up in Tennessee or something."

Mother's blue eyes find my brown ones, and they are filled with suspicion. Suddenly, though, the suspicion flees. "Honey, your hair. Why, it's beautiful."

Everyone turns to stare at me and looks of astonishment

jump from face to face.

Bryan comes up and examines the back. "There's blond parts. Cool."

"You have on makeup, too." Savannah shakes her head. "I didn't notice in the car, but here in the light, I can see it. Your lips are even like red."

"You should've seen me when I left Beulah Land. They were real red. And not one of you noticed a thing when I got here this afternoon."

"But, Peter noticed. Right?" Anna says from behind my shoulder.

Missus, invitations in hand, was striding across the kitchen, but at Peter's name she turns toward me. "What did Peter notice? Oh, your hair." But she's staring into my eyes and despite my frantic attempt to stay cool, my cheeks heat up.

Savannah squints at me and laughs. "Give me a break. You're blushing because we're saying how good you look. Okay, forget we said anything." But Daddy gives me a thumbs-up.

"God al...Gosh sakes!" Hank changes his words but his slamming of the door behind him lets us know how upset he is. Etta pushes up from the table. "Hank? What's wrong?"

Intensity in his eyes dampens as he puts his hand on Etta's shoulder, "Just business stuff. That's all. Chili smells awful good, Jack." His gaze roams the room, and the heat from him fills the room. His anger is palatable. "Shel, we've got to do something about this. I need you to, uh, to get on the phone and talk to these people. Sorry folks, but we've got some work to do."

Savannah doesn't turn around, but she speaks loudly. "It's night time. Who can you call at night?"

Hank stops and rapid blinking looks like a counter of the thoughts racing in his mind. "E-mails, we need to send some e-mails so they'll be there first thing in the morning."

The room stills.

Finally, Shelby stands up. "I'll get the laptop hooked up." She softly walks toward her room. Despite Shelby's movement, the silence and stillness in the room grows, except where Hank rocks back and forth one foot to the other.

Etta sighs and shame washes her face. "Well, work can't wait." She lowers her heavy self back to her seat. Staring at her hands placed one on top of the other, she says, "Hank, honey, we'll save you and Shelby some chili." The bubble of quiet tension doesn't burst, it just leeks out all its air with Etta's simple words.

Hank releases some of his pent-up energy with a fast nodding motion. Then he hurries to follow his ex-daughter-in-law.

Making room for Hank to pass by, I step out of the kitchen and into the living room and Anna steps out with me. We avoid making eye contact. "So how do you like this color?" I ask.

She tips her head, looks around and nods, but before she can answer Missus flies into the room and has her head pushed into our space.

"What is going on with that, that girl and your father-in-law? How dare he, well, how dare he do whatever it is he's doing to his family. What about honor and trust and fidelity? I took him to be a man of the South, a true gentleman. And her, Carolina, how could you allow someone like *her* to be under your roof?"

My eyes close under her assault and under the glare of the truth being spoken. She's right. I can't allow this to go on. "Missus, you're—"

"You're a hypocrite!" When my eyes fly open there's a red faced Anna shouting at Missus. "Honor? Trust? Fidelity? You don't know what any of those things mean."

Missus loses her footing for a second, but then her eyes turn to steel and her chin lifts. "Young lady, you don't know who you're talking to. You're a wimpy little trouble maker who has gotten on my nerves since you got here. Mealy mouthing around like you wouldn't harm a flea, and then you dare accuse me?

Like I said, you don't know who you're talking to."

"Yes I do." Anna's thin shoulders square and she shouts, "I'm talking to my grandmother."

And in that moment, it's obvious. The lifted chin, bright cheeks, steel gray eyes belong to them both. Even their builds, as they stand face to face, echo each other.

"Impossible," Missus says, but there's no fire in the word. "Impossible."

The front door swings open and Will and his suitcases fall into the room, "Hey, y'all. It's lit up like the Atlanta airport out there! Merry Christmas!"

His merriment turns to confusion when no one moves toward him. The people in the kitchen stay where they were as they listened to the fight in the living room. The three of us in the living room are like statues, until Missus sees the break.

"Will, welcome home. I have to go." She ignores his open arms and pats him on his shoulder as she shoves past him.

Anna's eyes are no longer narrowed and mad, they are large and fearful. She opens her mouth, but nothing comes out and she rushes toward Will. Once again his open arms are ignored as she weaves around him and his baggage then escapes upstairs. Patty darts after her, and breaks the spell bound on the rest of us.

After I hug my son, my wobbly legs take me to the sofa covered with an old blue flowered sheet from our early days of marriage, which now serves as a drop cloth. Missus had said, "Impossible," but Anna seemed so sure.

Mother sits down beside me.

"Sweetie, didn't you suspect this?"

"What? You knew?"

"Suspected. They look so much alike, and you know how Anna always disappears when Missus is around. Plus Missus just couldn't stand her, and while Missus can be judgmental and hard to like, there seemed to be something off. Haven't you notice the child who is most like you is the very one you have the most trouble with? Look at you and Savannah."

"But Anna and Missus are nothing alike."

"Why, of course they are. Surely you've seen how Anna's practically taken over your house. She's rearranged your cabinets, has you on a cleaning schedule, and then look at her and Patty. Big ol' grown Patty follows around little seventeen-year-old Anna like a dog on a leash. Or like FM and Missus."

"Oh, FM. Poor FM."

"Miss Carolina?" Patty stands at the top stair. "Anna wants to talk to you if that's okay."

Mother pats my hand. "It's so good she has you to talk to."

"Me? I didn't have a clue. You're the one she should talk to. Would you?"

The perfect pink lips stretch and mother laughs. "You just don't see yourself. You truly don't. You make people feel safe, and yet you give them all the space they need, and you have no idea what a gift that is." Mother leans to me with open arms and then holds me as we sway a little. "Go talk to Anna. She needs you."

"Okay." A mumble is all that works up. "I'll go, but I don't want to." I reach midway on the stairs when Mother's words hit me. "Me and Savannah are alike?" Now, there's absolutely no room for that in my head.

At least not now.

CHAPTER 38

Savannah's shower is running. Bryan has his stereo going. Sunshine peeks through the bedroom blinds. Someone's made coffee, and the twins are yapping to go for a walk. Everything is as it should be from the vantage point of my bed. Except the sleep fairy didn't put any umpf in her job last night. That is, when I finally left Anna and Patty's room and crawled here, into my bed, which technically was no longer night.

Laney? Laney's laugh gets my head off the pillow. Why would Laney be here this early?

I'm staying right here. Who cares what she wants? She doesn't always get her way. I'm not related to her or beholden to her. "She's not the boss of me," I say out loud as I roll over and snuggle deeper in the covers. Mother and Daddy will take care of everything because they know I was up late with Anna last night.

And I'm not thinking about that either.

"Rise and Shine!" The bedroom door flings open, and Laney crosses the floor in two skips and jumps on my bed.

"You don't sleep naked, do you? Well, if you do, cover up, 'cause I'm here!"

"What is wrong with you? I'm trying to sleep."

"Nope. C'mon. I'm going to start walking in the mornings,

and I want you to come with me."

"No."

"They're already opening paint cans downstairs. If you stay here you have to paint."

"Mother knows I was up late and need to sleep in."

"But your Daddy says you're to come down right now. They've got some questions about painting the dining room."

"Not the dining room, too." Now my eyes are open. I push up to sit against the headboard.

"It's looking good down there. Love the new colors. Oh, and look at your new haircut."

"Oh, yeah. I forgot." My hand searches around my neck which feels very bare. "I met Beau at Beulah Land. She seems really nice."

Laney nods and moves off the bed. "That she is. So c'mon. I told your mom and dad we'd take the dogs for a walk."

"We're really going for a walk?" Did that sound too much like a whine? I pull my flannel night shirt in place as I wriggle off the bed and search for my slippers. "You walk every morning?"

"Sometimes I just walk on the treadmill at home, but this morning I wanted some company. We can go down to the track at the elementary, but we have to be done by 10:00 a.m. when the kids start recess." She opens the door to the hall as I move into the bathroom. "See you downstairs pronto."

How does my hair look this morning? Not bad, not bad at all, is my assessment in the bathroom mirror. Still smooth, no frizz, and it is sooo cute. My black gym pants and Georgia hoodie will keep me warm. Thick socks feel good and lacing up my tennis shoes so early in the morning seems to give me energy. The white turtle neck is to keep my newly bare neck warm. What a great idea!

My feet pounding down the stairs sounds like Bryan. Mother even calls out for him from the kitchen.

"Nope, it's me." Turning the corner of the stairs, I stop as the morning light reflects on the blue walls, which now have a tinge of green. Water and dawn comes to mind and a feeling of calm sweeps over me. I notice how my brown and beige furniture look like faded driftwood or a secluded beach and work beautifully with the wall color. My things do match. Matter of fact, they look new, different.

But that yellow in the kitchen? Preparing as my steps lead there next, I expect to be jarred by the sudden happy onslaught. But even swimming in sunshine, the color is gentle and while enlivening the dark cabinets and black counters it pulls the room together. "Wow, this is nice. This does work."

Mother looks around. "Yes, it does. Do you know if Bryan prefers scrambled or over easy eggs?"

"You're making breakfast?"

"Sure, I told him I would today and then next week when he has midterms. Do you want an egg?"

"No, thanks, and Bryan likes his scrambled. Where's Laney?"

Mother waves the spatula, "Down the B&B hall, I think. Your daddy is in the basement, but he'll be up in a minute. He wanted to run something by you for the dining room."

From a basket in a bottom cabinet, I grab a granola bar. "We're going for a quick walk. Is that okay?"

"Sure." She looks around the kitchen and whispers, "Come here. What did Anna say last night? Is she all right?"

I lean on the counter next to the stove. "I can't tell if she knows what she's talking about. Her mother and grandparents are dead. She has no one else who knows her history. I'll tell you about it later," I whisper as Shelby comes into the kitchen.

"Carolina, I do love your hair. Maybe I should go down to that Beulah place while we're here." She sits in a kitchen table chair and tucks one leg beneath her. She has soft blue pajamas on and her hair bounces around her face. Her big brown eyes survey the kitchen. "This room just feels different, don't you think? This yellow is like butter."

Mother turns from the stove, "Can I make you some eggs, Shelby?"

"Oh, no," she says and then she giggles.

"What's funny?" I ask.

She stretches her arms above her head, "Oh, nothing."

While keeping my eyes from rolling, I turn toward the living room just as Savannah walks in the door way. Her eyes cut to Shelby as she tosses her hair that direction and walks to her grandmother, still at the stove. "Morning, Grandma. I want to put that on a piece of toast."

Maybe I should get up and make them eggs in the mornings. I honestly never thought of it. I lean against the refrigerator side. "Savannah, what have you got going on today? How late was Ricky here last night?"

"Oh, he left early, right Savannah?" Shelby smiles and encourages Savannah with several little bobs of her perky hair.

With a scowl and another toss of *her* hair, Savannah turns her back on both of us. "He was here late, sorry. We got to watching a movie with Will and Shelby and Pawpaw."

Now I scowl at Shelby. "Why did you say he left early?"

She giggles and wraps her arms around her waist. "Just taking care of my girlfriend, right Savannah?" She unfolds from the chair and prances over to the stove to give quick hugs to Mother and Savannah. "I better get dressed. This is so fun, all being under one roof like this."

I hurry to the sink to wash my hands, so I won't get a hug when she dances back by and then down the hall.

"I am not her girlfriend." Savannah growls. "We didn't know what to do. She and Pawpaw were like waiting us out, and Will said we couldn't leave him alone with them and that we couldn't leave them alone either. So we just sat there."

Mother bends closer. "This is awful. They can't really be fooling around right under Etta's nose, can they?"

Reaching for a paper towel moves me closer to them. "What

did Will say? He must've thought something was going on to not want to be alone with them."

Savannah's dark hair drapes almost to the counter as she leans forward. "He, well, he asked me who she is, that he remembered the name but didn't think he'd ever met her. He said he thought there was some secret about her…" Mother's and my eyes meet. "But I told him what the secret is, that they're *together*. Poor Meemaw."

Could we be wrong about them? Could it just be that everyone feels there's a secret, so they're grasping at straws? Maybe that's what's happening.

"Okay, let's get this show on the road." Laney's command comes from the hallway.

The three of us scatter when Laney marches into the kitchen. Her deep rose exercise outfit fits her like a glove and the black side panels make her look even trimmer than usual. Her hair is in a high ponytail of glossy black and her thick, fuzzy head band/ear warmer is the same shade of dark pink as her outfit.

"Savannah, honey. You look adorable. Do you know yet what you're wearing for the ball on Saturday?"

"Wait, I thought invitations were hard to come by. Why is my eleventh grade daughter invited?"

"She's not, but I've enlisted her and Jenna to run the door prizes and to oversee the entries in the 'Name the B&B' contest. That's what beautiful girls in the South do, encourage people to spend money and give away prizes. Haven't you been to a boat show or watched NASCAR? Anyway, find something really pretty to wear, from somebody." With a nod to Savannah, she loops her arm through mind. "Okay, I've done all the damage here I can do. We're going for a walk. Jack is getting the puppies' leashes and putting everything, including the dogs, in the car. Let's go."

"So, what have you done this time?"

We are barely across the railroad tracks when I'm accosted. "What?"

"Missus has, and these are FM's exact words. 'Missus has taken to her bed.' Now, I've heard those words about Southern women, but mostly in movies or books. I think Aunt Pitty Pat in *Gone with the Wind* took to her bed on a regular basis. But these days? It's a first, and she took to her bed after coming from your house. So, what have you done this time?"

"Are we even going walking or is this just an excuse to find out the latest gossip?

"Of course we'll go walking, but isn't the best part of walking with a friend, talking?"

"Well, we're going to have to talk about something else because what happened last night involves confidences that aren't mine to reveal. Just aren't. So that's it on that subject."

Down the hill and through town we drive in silence. At a stop sign, I point at Beulah Land sitting caddy corner from our car. "So, you know Beau and her family? She said she has kids. Are they close to our kid's ages?"

"Not really. They're all in elementary. She has four, and none of them have the same daddy, bless their hearts."

"Laney, how would you know that?"

"Beau doesn't have a problem with it." She'll tell you about each one, and their daddy, if you ask. She's not got a shy bone in her body." Laney pulls into the back parking lot of the elementary school. "Beau and I were good friends in high school. You saw how beautiful she is. We were both on the beauty queen circuit and cheerleaders and all that. But then, when she and Miss Fountain Lake got caught in nothing much but their sashes and crowns, well, things got a little rough for her here. So just before graduation she moved to Atlanta and got a modeling contract."

"No way."

Laney pops open her door, but I motion for her to close it.

"Wait, let me grab the leashes before you open your door." Twisting around, I push the white dust mops back and pat sweet, patient Ashley on the head. "Okay, got them."

The yapping ascends several decibels when Laney opens her door. Then she pulls open her back door and takes the leashes from my hand. "Here, now you can get out."

I pull my gloves on, swipe Chap Stick on and then get out of the car and walk around to the track entrance where Laney waits.

"So, Beau? Was she ever married?"

"Not that I know of. She says men are a nuisance, but she always wanted a bunch of children."

"Does she have a, well, a partner, or a *friend*, here?"

"Not that I know, but believe me, there are eyes peeled. For that and for the next daddy-to-be."

"You've got to be kidding?"

"Personally? I think she'll go back down in the city for both like she has in the past. The pool for either isn't too deep here. Eligible guys who won't brag about their fathering ability or girlfriends."

Pitty Pat and Prissy pull me, Laney, and Ashley around the track. Why on earth would Beau move back to a small town with all this baggage? "She's got to feel like she lives in a fish bowl here? I bet she hates it."

Laney shrugs. "Naw, her family belongs, and she really just doesn't care what people think. I'll invite you over next time we get together for margaritas. She's really a hoot."

From up on the little rise where the low, red brick school sits, we hear bells. Patches of winter browned grass checkerboard the ground around the building. Sun reflecting off the car windshields and mirrors in the black top parking lot winks at us. There's not the slightest breeze to put the swings hanging on long, gray chains into action. Blue sky is endless, but not bright like in the fall. There's a haze of white and even though we walk in sunshine, my nose is cold.

Laney breaks the quiet. "Okay, we can't talk about Missus. So tell me why your dad is so angry at Jackson's dad? He was muttering under his breath this morning and was pretty hot."

"Did Susan tell you about Jackson and Shelby and well... did she tell you?"

She wrinkles her nose and bends her head to look at me. "Would you be mad if she did?"

"No, figured she would."

"Okay, then, yes. She told me."

"Well, I finally told my mom and dad about it, so that's a start. But then this whole thing going on, or not going on, between Hank and Shelby is getting worse. Last night they left the rest of us in the middle of getting dinner to go off and do some *work*, and Etta practically gave them permission. Even Missus picked up on what was going on, then that started, well, started everything else. But, anyway, yeah. That's what's going on."

"I'd say, 'hate to say I told you so,' but I love to be right. Remember I called this at the bonfire?" She looks at me from under arched, well-manicured eyebrows. "However, could it just be work?"

My free hand on my nose to warm it doesn't keep me from talking. "Just this morning I was wondering if the secret of Jackson and Shelby being married isn't where the weirdness is coming from. There's just no way Hank would do that to Etta. No way. Susan told me how weird their house got when she was keeping all the secrets about Susie Mae."

Laney looks at her watch then starts walking faster. "We've got time to make one more loop before recess time, and we need to get the dogs put away before the kids are out. Now, speaking of Susie Mae, her and Angie are teamed up against Jenna and Savannah on this theater thing, you know."

"No, I don't know. Savannah won't say what's going on."

"Well, this is what Susan and I have pieced together. Susie Mae and Angie both really dislike Stephen Cross, but Jenna and Savannah think he's Mr. Magnificent. From what I remember about him when he was growing up here, he was the most stuck up thing to walk the halls of Chancey High. He probably treats Jenna and Savannah like princesses 'cause they're so pretty and so popular."

"Abby Sue and Savannah were fighting about him yesterday in the driveway. Abby Sue said Savannah was 'playing with fire.'"

"Abby Sue, huh?" Laney steps off the track and into the gravel path leading to the car.

Ashley perks up when he sees we're done. The mops don't have a clue. We get them, and us, into the car, their yapping forestalling conversation.

Laney turns the key in the ignition. "Abby Sue sure knows about playing with fire. Wonder what's really going on?"

"Don't know."

Before putting the car in gear, she looks at me. "However, let me once again make an observation. If Abby Sue is warning someone about fire, it ain't good."

CHAPTER 39

"You in any hurry to go home?" Laney asks at the stop sign at the Beulah Land corner.

"Not really. Why?"

She wrenches the wheel to the left and we head down Main Street. "Let's check out the flower shop. See what Shannon's doing for the ball. What are you wearing Saturday?"

"Wearing? I haven't even decided if I'm going."

"Silly goose, of course you and Jackson are going." Laney swerves into a parking place by the park and turns off the car. Pulling the rearview mirror toward her, she swipes on dusty rose lipstick to match her exercise outfit.

Looking closer, I realize she has on full makeup. Eye liner, shadow, and even blush. What time does she get up to do all that? "Do you always wear full makeup?"

Startled blue eyes dart at me, "Of course. Why?"

"No reason, just wondering."

We're in the middle of the street crossing when her phone rings. She answers and then at the door, motions for me to go on in. The small, brass bell above the glass shop door jingles when I cross the threshold. The space inside is huge, with half of the room sitting empty behind shelves set up in the middle of the area to block off some of the space.

"Hello, Carolina."

"Hi, Shannon."

Shannon never pushes her flowers or crafts, she stays behind the counter and other than saying "hello or good-bye" she only answers direct questions. My kind of shop owner.

As I wander along looking at the shelves, wall hangings, and cooler fronts, one thing fills my senses—Cardinals. The red birds with the dark orange beak are everywhere. Arranged in flowers, both silk and real. They're perched on lamps, cages, feeders, and statues. It's Hitchcock's movie come to life, but instead of menacing black winged villains, the menace is perky and bright and stuffed.

"Wow, there are a lot of cardinals."

Shannon nods but continues with the taping of flower stems.

Oh, yeah, I forgot about the direct question thing. "What are all the cardinals for?"

"For the Cardinal Ball, Missus' theme for Saturday night."

"Oh, yeah. She did talk about something like that. They're beautiful." And they really are. One grapevine wreath entangled with frosted grape leaves, and emerald green pine catches my fancy with the cardinal couple, dad in bright red and mama in her muted brown and gray, tucked behind the leaves. As I imagine how it would look on our front door, the little bell tinkles, and Laney swooshes in.

"Missus is out of the bed, hey, Shannon, and it's not good news for me. While we were out getting healthy, that woman worked the phones, and there's a town council meeting scheduled tomorrow night about the town's finances."

Bopping around the shop, Laney talks about the town council and Missus, but doesn't mention what she's going to do about it all. In between those comments, she spouts a running commentary on the arrangements. All with me floating behind her murmuring yeses and nodding my head. With our tour complete, back at the counter Shannon is punching away at her adding machine. Laney leans her backside against the counter and crosses her arms. "You want to come?"

I automatically nod. Then I realize what she asked. "Come where?"

"To the council meeting."

"Why would I go?"

Laney shrugs and turns around. "So what's the damage, Shannon?"

"Four hundred and eighty-seven dollars."

"Woo hoo, under $500. Shaw told me $500 was my limit."

I so missed something. "Limit for what?"

"Christmas flowers and wreaths." Laney pulls her debit card from the side pocket of her pants and runs it through the machine.

"You mean you were buying all those things you said you liked?"

Laney and Shannon both look at me, but only Laney answers. "Of course. Did you think I was just talking to hear myself?" She shakes her head as if to imply I'm the one with problem thinking. "Deliver them this afternoon?"

"Sure thing. Carolina, did you see anything you wanted," Shannon asks.

"Yes, now that you mention it, I did." I lift the grapevine wreath off its hook and step around Laney to lay it on the counter.

"Beautiful. For your front door?" Laney asks.

"Yep. Oh, wait. I don't have any money."

Shannon smiles and flutters my ticket after she tears it off her pad. "No problem, I'll stick it in the drawer and you can run in and pay it when you get the chance."

"I'll be back here as soon as we get home."

"No hurry. Seriously, no hurry at all." She scrawls my name on the ticket and slides it under the money drawer on her cash register.

We turn toward the door and intense eyes stare at us from the other side of the window. FM, both hands buried in his pants pockets, waits for us. Or is it just me he's waiting for? Oh no.

"Morning, FM."

"Carolina. Laney."

We all stare at each other, waiting for someone to start.

"So, I hear Missus is stirring things up?"

Should've known Laney wouldn't let that much silence go untested.

"She wants to talk to you, Carolina."

"Why does everyone want to talk to me? I don't want to be involved."

FM shuffles back and forth a little. He sniffles and wrinkles up his nose. "She's real mad, talking about court. For both of you."

"Court?" Laney and I both ask.

"Laney, you know you don't have good answers for this money situation with the town, so it'd be best if you'd come clean and let the council help you out. We shouldn't have given you free rein, but well, we all know your daddy did the town books for three decades, and we never had a worry since you were a Troutman. We want to help you, but you've got to let us in on what's going on."

Laney's jewel-blue eyes narrow as does her dusty rose lips. She crosses her arms and there's no question that she and FM don't see eye to eye on things. So FM shifts his focus to me.

"And Carolina, she says you're messing with our good name. She won't say what's going on, but you've got to figure this out, or she'll take you to court. I can't hardly believe you'd do anything like that, but she is my wife, and I gotta stand by her. She was real hurt last night, real hurt."

Tiredness weighs FM's face and body down. His gray hair, gray pants, and gray work shirt are covered partly by his brown Carhartt jacket. For all the fighting and fussing him and Missus do, here's the real FM. A man in love with a difficult woman, standing by her side for decades. Anna can't be right, mostly because of what it would do to this man standing in front of me. She just can't be right. "Okay, FM. I'll take care of it. You tell Missus. It's all okay."

Laney's stance and face have relaxed, and she pulls her car keys from her pocket. "We need to go. I've got to be at the high school to volunteer in the office in an hour." She puts her arm around my arm and pulls me toward the car.

We cross the road but don't open our mouths. Matter of fact, not another word is spoken on our entire ride home.

CHAPTER 40

"Anna and Patty went out to tour some college. They said you told them about it?" Etta is in the kitchen washing paint brushes and rollers. "Your daddy and Hank only have a second coat to put on the dining room, and the painting is all done. Ceilings are done and we're going to start putting everything back in place."

Anna's not here, and I'm all worked up and ready for a confrontation. My breathing slows, and I remember Laney saying Daddy wanted to ask me about the color for the dining room. Wonder what he decided? Then I see the paint Etta is washing out of the brushes—lavender. Great.

Just a couple steps and, sure enough, the dining room is lavender.

"Isn't this such a pretty color?" Shelby sits on the top step of the ladder, touching up the corner. "There, all through. Hank and your dad will do another coat after lunch. Can you believe how much painting we got done? Jackson is going to be so surprised, isn't he?"

Maybe it's because my nerves were set to deal with Anna, or maybe just the fact that my dining room is lavender, but whatever the reason. Shelby hit a chord and I jump. "Why are you here?"

Shelby's head tips to the side like a dog does when you try and talk to it. "Pardon?"

"Pardon, my foot. Why are you here? Here in Jackson's home with his kids and his wife? Do you honestly think I want to spend Christmas with my husband's ex-wife? Do you?"

Shelby steps down the ladder. Her innocent mouth forming an "o" at my shoulder, she lifts those brown eyes. "But this is my family. There's no one else. Hank and Etta and Jackson, well, and you and the kids." Her head drops and her shoulders shake. "This is like a dream come true for me to be here, with all of you for the holidays. But maybe I can get a bus ticket home."

"Ex-wife?" Will comes out of the B&B office. "Mom?"

Shoot, I forgot Will was home. "Will, I, uh…"

"You were married to my dad?"

Shelby nods and then steps to my son. He's so tall compared to her tiny stature. "You look so much like he did then. So strong and sweet, and I'm sure you would've done the same thing he did."

"Don't you dare. My son wouldn't have been fooled by you and this puppy dog act. No."

"You think I fooled Jackson?" Her tiny heart shaped face is pale. "He knew everything."

"Everything except who the father was. Were you even really pregnant?"

Shelby's eyes well up, and she begins to shake. Will steps to her and puts his arm around her. "Mom, cool it." The distrust and anger in his eyes takes my breath.

"No, Will. It's not like she's making it seem."

"Forget it, Mom. You haven't wanted to talk about it before. Why talk about it now? Here, Shelby, let's go sit down." My tall son leads the sobbing woman into the living room and I'm left alone, staring out the back window.

This is a disaster. Jackson is going to be so mad.

CHAPTER 41

"No," Laney responds to the council's request. Just as she's responded to pretty much every question put to her so far.

"Take her to court," Missus screeches before Peter yanks on her arm to pull her back in her seat.

"Missus, you gotta sit there quietly or we'll have you removed." Griffin scowls at her from behind the table the council sits at. We're gathered in the depot, which looks different at night with its dark corners and shadowed ceiling.

"Council President being related to the accused is ridiculous," Missus mutters for everyone to hear. She turns to the row behind her. "Can we force him to recues himself?"

"Mother," Peter hisses.

From my perch at the back of the room, the camps are laid out. There's Missus and Peter in front of the Women's Historical Society folks, including Flora and Fauna and Cathy Stone and other movers and shakers who move and shake on Missus' schedule. Then on the front row to the far side, near Laney's end seat at the table is the Troutman contingency, Susan, her and Laney's brother Scott with Abby Sue, and their mother. They have some friends with them, but I don't know them, well, except for the preacher. Shaw is conspicuously absent.

Then there's the onlookers like me who have nothing better

to do than hang out at a city council inquiry meeting. After last night and today spent in a house where half the people aren't talking to me and the half that are just keep asking, "How could you do that?" a city council meeting sounded delightful.

Will, my easy going, always happy, first-born isn't speaking to me. He's grouchy and mad and snaps at everyone. That has his brother and sister on edge, and they've figured out it has something to do with something I did. So, they're wary around me. When Shelby sees me her bottom lip starts trembling and those big brown eyes fill with tears. Then Hank or Etta pat her on the arm and help the poor thing out of the room and away from the mean lady. Daddy is so proud of his paint job, he can't see past that except to say wise things like, "You know, putting everything off, like the truth, is what got Scarlett in trouble, too." Mother says I need to call Jackson and tell him what's happened before he gets home, but well, maybe I'll do that tomorrow. Anna was talking to me until I asked her for more details about her grandmother claim and maybe said something like, "How could you do this to Missus and FM?" Now, apparently, she and Will have banded together to protect each other from me. They've taken to sitting down at the river underneath *my* willow tree.

Griffin and the mayor end their private discussion and Griffin looks to his wife on the front row with pleading eyes. But Susan shrugs and shakes her head just once. So his eyes swing to his sister-in-law, the town treasurer, and he's reduced to begging. "Laney, please? We need to see the books. You can't just not let us see them."

Laney's hair is pageant big, she has on a white wool suit and a jewel blue blouse which makes her eyes look like blue diamonds, even from the back of the room. She smiles wide, but says only one word, "No."

The men on the council are stumped, their mouths move up, down, side to side and their eyes search for answers in the audience but there are no answers. Laney is one of their own. They went to elementary school with her. Laney's mother taught them in Sunday school. Her father served on the town council for thirty-five years. They all trusted her with the town's money. They played little league baseball with her husband, Shaw, and raised their children alongside her daughters. Two of them were pall bearers at her daddy's funeral and three of them are directly related to her. I know all this history, because it has all been laid out tonight in their pleas for this to end with Laney handing over the town's books, nice and sweet-like. The two women on the council spit and argued and threatened, and the men were glad to have them because they could not accost a woman like that, not being good Southern gentlemen. But nothing moved Laney.

Another private conversation between Griffin and the mayor results in Griffin announcing the council would be going into executive session, which means no audience. "Under the rules about discussion of legal matters we're able to do this. Any decision made will be announced afterwards in open session." After another minute or two Griffin announces they'd go over to the police station for their discussion.

While everyone listened to Griffin, I slipped out the door of the depot museum. Around the side of the building, several clumps of Camilla bushes provide cover for some privacy. What's going to happen when they all find out what this is really all about? That Laney is having an affair, probably taking money from the town to afford her lifestyle and stonewalling them all? What's going to happen when I have to face those same facts about my friend? What will Susan think? She's learning to deal with her daughter not being who she thought she was, but what about her sister, a grown woman? And then Laney's mother and brother and there's her girls, Jenna and Angie. There's that saying about giving someone enough rope to hang themselves? Well, that's exactly what happens in a small town. You get rope because of your family, oh, and here's some more rope because we know your husband and your kids. And well, we did date back in high school, so how about a little more rope for old times' sake.

Leaves rattle high in an old oak tree. Most of the leaves have fallen and are now dressing the flower beds around the depot and park, but high pushed up in the dark sky a few leaves hang on. I lean back against the trunk and let my head rest on the thick bark. My eyes lift up and through the branches stars twinkle in the dark, mountain sky. The moon is almost full and rests in a circle of milky white. Clouds push past the moon on hurried breezes, which make the remaining leaves shake and tremble. Cold seeps beneath my coat. With a push away from the tree, I turn back to the depot building. It's Thursday. Jackson will be home tomorrow, and he's going to walk into a mess at home. He knows things aren't good here, but I haven't told him his son knows he was married before and that it was me who let him know. Weaving through the Camilla bushes, I run right into a thick brown coat.

"Carolina. Oh…" Peter turns and steps toward me but whoever he was with darts the other direction behind another clump of bushes. The person looks small and has on pink.

"What are you doing? Who was that?"

Peter doesn't even look back. "No one. What are you doing out here?"

"Just getting some fresh air."

"It's a mess in there, isn't it?"

"Yeah, so they'll probably get a court to make her give them the books, right?"

He runs his hand across his neat beard, "Unless she comes to her senses. Do you know what Laney's hiding?"

"Me? No." However, my eyes drop too quickly and my words are too loud.

"You do know something, don't you?"

"Where's Shaw?"

Peter waits to answer. "Shaw? I don't know. Why?"

"Just wondering. I'm cold. I'm going back inside. You?"

Now it's his turn to look guilty. "Not right now," he says after a quick sideways glance at the clump of bushes behind us to the left.

"Okay. See you later." He's out here with Cathy Stone, I bet. She had on a pink sweater tonight. So Missus and FM were right about that. Peter's with Cathy. But wait, the person's hair wasn't dark, like Cathy's, it was blond and long. Kicking at the leaves on the path around the building, my minds wander through the other people in the meeting. Blond wearing a pink... blond wearing a pin—oh no. Abby Sue. Yep, that's who he was sneaking around in the bushes with. Wow, if Missus didn't like him with Cathy, wait until she finds this out. Oh, wait until Abby Sue's besotted husband, Scott finds out. Question is, why do I keep finding out these things?

And isn't he supposed to have a crush on me?

With my hand on the doorknob, I decide to wait until tomorrow to hear what happened in the executive session. "Yep, tomorrow's good enough," I say out loud and Daddy's words about Scarlett O'Hara comes to mind. My hand drops and my voice lilts, "Well, if it's good enough for Scarlett, it's good enough for me."

Chapter 42

"It really is a dead day at school, just reviews for mid-terms next week. Nobody's going to be there. Please let me go," Savannah pleas at the breakfast table.

"I think it'll be fine. Let her go with you." Daddy spreads strawberry jam on his toast and lays the piece of toast on his plate. "Where all you going anyway?"

Mother sets a bowl of scrambled eggs on the table and hands the spoon to Bryan. "Down to the perimeter, right?"

While I take a sip of coffee, my head bobs. "Wherever you want to go. It's your dress. I'm just along for the ride, well, actually along to drive."

Daddy stops with a scoop of eggs mid-air, "But, Goldie, I thought you said you're buying Carolina and Savannah dresses."

"Jack! It was supposed to be a surprise."

"Oh, I'm not even sure I'm going to the ball. Jackson doesn't like these..."

"But how can he say no if you have a beautiful new dress?" Mother's honey blond hair picks up golden threads in her brown sweater and her rust lipstick is the perfect shade. She looks so happy to go shopping, and I know from experience it will be a full day.

Savannah exclaims, "So I have to go if I'm also getting a

new dress."

Mother shrugs. "Guess so. Just us three girls."

"Okay, but I'm not trying on anything, and you two are not to badger me, okay?"

So innocent, so pretty—but I know how these two are in a mall.

"How come you're not complaining about having to go to school?" I ask Bryan.

He doesn't look up from his plate, just lifts his shoulders, and shoves his last corner of toast in his mouth. "Gotta go. Grant and Susie Mae are picking me up." He dashes off without once having met my eyes this morning. He feels the distance between me and Will more than the rest of them. And that distance is the one and only reason I'm going on this shopping trip. Jackson will be home tonight, and Will can get some of the answers he wants so badly.

And maybe I can start breathing again.

"I love my dress," Savannah says again as we put our bags ahead of us into the restaurant's booth. "And it will be perfect for the Senior Formal."

"But you're not a senior. Why do you think you're going?" I question as I sit down and let my body melt into the cushioned seat. "You keep talking about breaking up with Ricky. Maybe he'll want to take someone that wants to be with him."

Savannah tucks her hair behind her ear and leans toward me. "Maybe I'm not talking about going with Ricky."

"Not go with Ricky?" Mother stops arranging her silverware and glasses and stares at her granddaughter beside her in the booth. "But I thought…" Mother's eyes slide to me, but then she fixes her gaze back on Savannah. "Not go with Ricky?"

"Hey, what was that look for? What's going on?" I ask.

"Can I get you ladies something to drink?" Our waiter is an older gentleman, and he stands at the end of our booth, waiting.

With our waters and iced teas ordered, my question is repeated. "Really, what was that look for?"

Savannah sighs. "It's just that last fall, well, I told Grandma I think I love Ricky, but now…" She turns to her grandmother, "Now, I'm not sure. He seems so young, so immature."

"Is this about Stephen Cross?"

"Mom. You don't understand. It's not like I like, like him. But he's so different from the boys at school. So different from Ricky."

Mother and I both exclaim, "Of course he is. He's a man."

Mother puts her hand on Savannah's arm. "He hasn't led you on, has he?"

Savannah smiles and pats her Grandma's hand. "Of course not. He just has made me realize that these high school boys need to grow up. Ricky is so childish."

Thank goodness Mother is here, because my mouth won't work. All this sounds so familiar. So familiar to me, my freshman year of college, and my literature teacher, Mr. Walters. How he made every other boy, even Jackson, seem so foolish. Only Mr. Walters—Aaron—understood me. "You have to stay away from him," blurts out of my numb lips.

Two pairs of light blue eyes stare at me and Savannah asks, "Mom, are you okay?"

"No, I, uh, just remembered something. My freshman year of college and this professor, who—who made me feel just like you're saying Stephen makes you feel."

"Mom, he's not done anything inappropriate. Nothing, I promise. But do you think Ricky could ever finish college? Not likely. And all he wants to do is make out. Sorry Grandma, but that's the truth."

Mother pulls her attention from me and smiles at her granddaughter. "Honey, you're not telling me anything I don't already know. But you do know, if this teacher crosses the line, you have to let your mother know, right?"

Savannah peers into her grandma's face. "Absolutely."

"So, honey, you were telling us how much you like your dress." Mother keeps Savannah talking after she glances at me and sees I'm not here. My mind goes back. Now, from this vantage point I can see what he did. He took advantage of me. None of that was my idea. He had a wife and two kids he never had any intention of leaving. I was a sheltered, backward girl, that's all. He was a man who knew exactly what to say. My stomach swirls, and I excuse myself from the table. In the bathroom, I throw up and then splash water on my face. All this time I thought of that as a sweet first romance, which went a little too far, but…hearing Savannah talk about Stephen, my rose-colored glasses fell off.

Peering into the mirror and breathing deeply I remember my obsession with Aaron, no with Mr. Walters, is why I refused to date Jackson that summer.

The summer he went home and married Shelby.

"I'm going to check out the salad bar. Can I get out, Grandma?" Savannah slides out of the booth while she checks me out. Concern in her eyes lets me know she's giving me some time with Mother. Obviously I look like I feel: like I'm going to burst.

"Mother, that teacher of mine. He seduced me, played me. I was just a kid. Younger than Will and not nearly as savvy as Savannah. Oh my God, it's like having a curtain pulled up all at once, and the whole thing is laid out in front of me." A laugh bursts out and it feels so good.

Seriousness tightens and pales Mother's face. My hand quickly covers hers. "Don't worry. I'm not having a breakdown. But I always saw myself as the instigator, the one who started it all until just now. I was a kid and he was a pro."

"Did he force you, or…?"

"No, it was definitely what I wanted, but I see now how he knew what to say and do. How he compared to Jackson and the other boys. But everything with Jackson and Shelby I've carried as my burden, that if I hadn't been running after Aaron, no, not Aaron. Mr. Walters, Jackson wouldn't have gone home, felt sorry for Shelby when she thought she was pregnant, and married her. But now I see. It wasn't me running after Mr. Walters as much as it was him chasing me. I'm not innocent, but I wasn't in control." Another laugh bubbles up. "Mother, do you hear that? I wasn't in control."

My mind races round and round and every time ends at the same thought: *I wasn't in control.* Then a wave of anger washes over me. "Mr. Walters was, probably still is, a jerk. A manipulator. A real jerk. Do you know that's the first time I've been mad at *him*? I actually felt sorry for him and his awful marriage and mean wife and hard job." Laughter from even deeper spills out.

This time Mother pats my hand and makes me look at her, where her eyes are warm and deep. "You've forgiven yourself. That's what this is all about. It's a hard thing to do. I had to after I married your father and started realizing just what I'd been doing with all those boys. It horrified me and threatened to suffocate my very soul, but your Daddy was so good to me and helped me see I had to forgive myself and move on, free of all that guilt."

We clutch hands and share another smile. "Savannah," I say in the direction of the salad bar.

She pops out the other side.

"How does it look? Anything good?"

"Yeah, that's what I'm getting," she says as she slips back in her seat.

"Well, me, too. It will be fast, and I'm suddenly in a hurry to find the perfect dress for the ball."

Mother's eyes light up. "Well, then make it three salad bars. We have a lot of shopping to do."

My hand lifts to wave for the waiter. "Plus we need to get home before too late, because Jackson will be home tonight, and it will be so good to see him."

Then there on my daughter's face is the smile of a little girl who loves being Daddy's princess, but knows she's Daddy's second love.

And that's what makes her world right.

CHAPTER 43

"What do you mean they went camping?" My smile, heart, and bags all drop at Daddy's greeting.

"Here, give me those." Daddy grabs several of the bags and steps back so we can all get in the living room. "Just that. He got here a little after lunch, said they'd cut out early. He and Will took a walk out on the bridge, and then they messed around in the basement. Gathering gear, I suppose. Hank and Etta and Shelby have been gone all day, doing some Hillbilly Hank stuff up near Chattanooga. He's speaking up there next week, isn't he?"

"I think so. But Daddy, Jackson and the boys are camping?"

"Well, when Bryan came home they headed out. Said to tell you they'd be back tomorrow or Sunday, but not to worry."

"Not worry? I turn to the window. It's starting to sleet out there."

Savannah stomps her foot, "They went without me? Not that I'd go camping in this weather. But did they say anything about me?"

Daddy wrinkles up his mouth, "Did y'all bring any supper home?"

Mother walks to the couch, puts down her bags, then unbuttons her green wool coat. "Let's get out of these coats and get our bags put away. Carolina, Jackson and Will are smart. They'll be fine for a night. Let's see to supper. How does chili and sandwiches sound in front of the fireplace?"

Savannah, heads up the stairs, and I watch her go. When her door slams, my shoulders relax. "Did Will tell Jackson he knows about Shelby?"

Daddy stuffs his hands in his back pockets and his upper body sways forward a little. "Yep."

"Was he very mad?"

"Yep."

"At me."

Daddy's head cocks, "Well, he weren't mad at me."

"Shoot, I really wanted to talk to him tonight."

Mother comes up behind me. "Go get comfortable and put away your stuff. This time with the boys will be good for all of them. You'll get to talk to him soon enough."

Arms loaded, my steps up the stairs are slow. Halfway up I stop. "Wait, did he say he'd be back in time for the ball tomorrow night?"

Daddy just shakes his head at me and lifts his shoulders again.

"But I got a new dress…"

Daddy and Mother turn into the kitchen. Nothing left for me to do but trudge up the rest of the stairs and into our room. The bed is huge and bare. Another night of sleeping alone.

"I want my big toe. I want my big tooooeeee," Hank's menacing voice, slow and deep has us all on the edge of our seats. Firelight licks at our faces in the dark, sleet pings against the window and our hearts beat somewhere in the vicinity of our throats. Then he leaps forward and yells, "Got it!"

Screams and laughter are followed by applause. For the first time, my father-in-law's appeal to his Hillbilly Hank followers reveals itself to me.

"Pawpaw! You scared me to death," Savannah exhales in a rush. "My heart is beating so fast."

Shelby says, "That one sounds crazy. A ghost wanting his big toe that got chopped off in the potato patch, but it scares me every time. Now, tell the one about the headless man fishing. Tell it." Shelby's eyes are deep and full in the dark. She beams at Hank, and I can't help but steal a look at Etta. In the rocking chair, her face hides in the shadows. Her deep purple robe moves slightly as she gently rocks. She's not said much of anything since they all arrived home.

"Don't y'all think it's time for someone else to tell a tale?" Hank's eyes glitter in the light from the fireplace he sits beside. We started out with some of the stories he planned to tell up at the seniors' center in Chattanooga, but then he flipped out the lights and started with the ghost stories. We've been jumping and screaming ever since.

Mother clutches her robe up under her chin. "Hank, you're as good as those storytellers we saw last year over at that Storyteller's Festival in Jonesborough. You should go over there this year and enter."

Shelby nods and stands. "See, haven't I been telling you that same thing? Being in Tennessee, it's not far from home at all." Can I get anybody anything? More popcorn?"

"No, thanks." Mother says, as she cuddles closer to Daddy on the couch. "So, Savannah have you been to this cabin of Ricky's dad where Jackson and the boys are holed up at?"

That the three were at Scott's cabin was learned from a text message Savannah received right after we got home. However, since then all calls to their phones have gone straight to voicemail. Either they're out of range, or they've turned off their phones.

Savannah doesn't look toward Mother as Anna has her hands wrapped around tails of her hair, plaiting a braid down Savannah's back. "I've been out there a couple times. It's pretty rustic and the fireplace is the only heat. Its way back in the mountains. You have to drive through a creek to get up to it."

"When were you up there? I don't remember you asking permission to go out to any cabin."

Savannah rolls her head on her shoulders and the silence lengthens. "I'll ask next time. Guess I forgot."

Behind her Anna says, "Hold still so I can finish this braid." Anna's back is against the side of the couch, and Patty lies in the floor beside the two girls.

Patty rises up on her elbows. "Stephen's folks have a cabin up in the mountains. That's where we're going to honeymoon."

Okay, I'll ask. "So the wedding is still on?"

She takes a deep breath and lets it out slowly. "Of course."

"Ouch!" Savannah yelps.

"Sorry," Anna says, but in the soft light her face appears hard and set, not sorry at all.

Patty shoots a worried look at Anna's stormy countenance and chews on her lip, but looking away a smile begins to play on her face. "I saw a ghost once."

"Well, tell us, girl." Hank leans back beside the fireplace, and Shelby sits a bottle of water down on the hearth and settles in on the other side of the fire opening.

Patty pulls back on her knees and then settles into a crossed leg position. Her navy sweat shirt and pants cover her in darkness. She looks around the room as if to ask each of us if she should start and the quiet becomes deep, with only the fire sizzle and the sleet for background sound. "Well, our house down in Polktown is big and old with these balconies all around the second story. Mama's bedroom is on a corner, and so she has these glass doors on both outside walls. Her bed is in the corner so that from the bottom of the bed you can see out both doors."

"The house is one of the old plantation houses, and there's nothing around but out buildings, some of them half torn down and some of them still in use. But at night there's only one yard light out by the end of the driveway and a front porch light and a back porch light. But both porch lights are ground level and don't shine much light at all up on the second floor balconies."

She scrunches her face. "Did I tell you Mama's room is on the back of the house?"

We shake our heads, and she nods. "Okay. Well it is, so no light from the yard shines in her windows."

Hank clears his throat. "So what you're sayin' is it's dark back near your mama's room, right?"

"Yes, sir. Dark. Real dark." Well, I liked to lay in Mama's bed and wait for her to come home at night when she worked late, and I didn't want to mess up all her pillows and dolls so I always laid down at the foot of the bed. When she came in, she'd put me on a pallet on the floor or sometimes I'd wake up in my own bed. Ya know, I don't think I ever was awake when she got home." After a moment of thinking, she agrees with herself. "Yeah, that's right. Never was awake."

But I'd lay there real still so I wouldn't mess up her bedspread. It was shiny and slippery and the color of a ripe peach. One night I was laying there, wrapped up in my night gown with my feet tucked up underneath when there was a light out the glass door. It wasn't bright, but it wasn't just moonlight. It was like a floating light. Then the light got dimmer, but at the same time it got a shape. It was a woman, and she was standing at the door like she was going to come in. My heart beat so fast and I wondered if I was dreaming so I swallowed real big and opened and shut my eyes a couple times. But she was still there. She seemed to not understand the door knob, and she turned to walk away from the door. She walked toward the corner. Laying there holding my breath I could hear her footsteps creaking on the old boards of the porch. I listened, following the steps to the corner then around the corner, and I rolled over to watch the next set of glass doors. As she came near them the dark picked up her glow. Then there she was. She walked to the door, turned, reached for the door handle but then looked straight at me. My heart just stopped. She backed away from the door, back toward the balustrade, and the light went out."

Goosebumps covered my arms, and I couldn't move. No one else moved or seemed to breathe either.

"Did you ever see her again?" Etta finally spoke.

Patty shook her head, "No, ma'am, but I heard her footsteps lots of times. She walked that balcony a lot."

"Do you know who she was?" Savannah asks.

"Well, I did look in the library and found some old ghost stories of South Georgia. They say a young woman who lived in our house killed herself in the 1920s because her brother and sister-in-law took away her baby. Said she was unfit to care for it. The brother lived in our house. I've always wondered if it might be her. Looking for her baby."

"How sad, a young mama searching for a baby," Savannah laments. Her lament is followed by a shout when the phone rings. "Okay, enough scary stories and all this jumping."

"I'll get it," I say and pry myself out of the easy chair. In the kitchen, the cordless phone rings again from the kitchen counter. "Hello?"

Laney's whispering, "Why did Jackson run off to Ricky's cabin?"

My voice matches hers. "He found out I told Will about Shelby."

"Thought so. Can I help with anything? I'm really good at fixing things like this."

My hand holding the phone pulls away from my ear and staring at the receiver, my eyebrows raise. My voice isn't quite as low when the receiver comes back closer to my mouth. "You're real good at fixing things? Laney, have you forgotten the council meeting? Your hometown is getting ready to take you to court. Just saying, 'No' isn't fixing things."

"Oh, that. I mean I'm good at fixing things in relationships. With other people."

My whisper comes back, a little on the tense side. "Laney, are you having an affair?"

Laughter bounces through the receiver and against my ear, causing me to once again pull the phone away. Even at a little distance, I can hear Laney hollering at Shaw, "Shaw, honey, Carolina thinks I'm having an affair." Now Shaw's laughter comes through the phone.

Forget whispering. "If I'd known it would give you two such a big laugh, I would've called up weeks ago. I'm hanging up now."

"Wait, don't hang up. So you're the one that's got Susan's panties in a wad. She came at me like a duck eating day old bread and wanted to know who I was messing around with. Wouldn't tell me who put that in her head. Didn't even think of you."

Whispering is back. "Well, I saw you up at Blue Mountain Lodge. You were with a man."

"Now, Carolina, well, hmmm. Let me think. Okay. I'll talk to you about this later. But it's not what you think." She continues to hem and haw without saying anything. Finally she goes quiet.

There's nothing for me to say, so I wait.

"So, listen. I'll talk to you tomorrow. You're going over to Missus' to decorate, right? But an affair, you know, that might just work. I've got to talk to Shaw. Bye, now."

And she hangs up the phone. Can you believe that? All the worry I've done about her marriage, and first she laughs and then acts like it was a suggestion. From nowhere, a laugh leaps up in my throat. And she wants to help me!

CHAPTER 44

My hair, spread out on my pillow, smells like wood smoke. We sat around the fire until late, everyone drowsy and relaxed, and when we finally put out the fire and made our ways to our rooms, I just fell into bed. Sleep came quickly and hard. Around six, I woke up and went to the bathroom. Since then, I've laid in bed half awake, half dreaming. My feet stretch out across the bed. Wonder if I'll still be sleeping alone tomorrow morning?

Jackson. Maybe it's good for him to have some time with just the boys. Apparently, he promised to make up the weekend with Savannah sometime, just the two of them. All that in another text.

He's not sent me a text. Or called. Or anything.

Kicking my feet, I push the covers off me and down to the bottom of the bed. My night gown over my head and then thrown onto the bed. The pinging of the pipes and the water spray hitting the shower walls are the first sounds in my quiet house. With only my panties left on, I lean on the counter and look closely into the mirror. Yesterday at the mall, after talking to Mother about that scumbag teacher of mine, Mister Walters, I felt so good. So clear about how to move forward, but it never occurred to me Jackson wouldn't be here waiting, ready to share my good news. Ready to understand how all this wasn't my fault. Instead he's acting like a spoiled little boy who gets mad and runs away. He sets up these impossible scenarios he doesn't want to deal with and then gets mad when I attempt to deal with them. Like moving here. This was all his idea, and I follow through, making it work. And like running home and marrying Shelby because I was kid being taken advantage of by my teacher. Yeah, I made a mistake, but then he made a bigger mess of everything. A mess which is now sleeping downstairs. And how about him inviting his parents here, then going off not only to work but now on a camping trip.

Steam from the shower clouds up my view of the mirror. With my back stiff, I pull back the shower curtain and step in. "Well, buddy, I've had enough. You're going to have to stand up and take responsibility for your actions. I've not been perfect, but you're not going to get away with running out on things anymore."

Beau was right. My hair is easy to style.

With only a second's hesitation, I reach for the mascara. Sure, I can get used to this. Mascara, some eye shadow, foundation, and blush. My lipstick in in my purse downstairs. *Maybe I should buy an extra tube to keep up here.* My jeans are still tight so we're not talking high fashion here, but instead of my old tennis shoes, I reach farther back in the closet for some short suede boots Laney gave me last summer. She said they were too big for her. The boots slouch, but cover the bottom of my pant legs. Then, on top, a caramel colored, long sweater. Mother gave it to me for an early Christmas gift. It's soft and hugs my figure. But instead of looking like there's too much of me around the middle, it calls attention to my chest, which the sweater definitely improves, and my face—my made up face.

Even with as long as it took for me to get ready, no one else is up when I tiptoe down the stairs. The light aqua living room walls give an early morning sheen to the room. Low, thick gray clouds wrap around the house and hide the train tracks in front and the river out back. Silvery light testifies that the sun is rising above the tree-lined river, but that's the only evidence of the sun. Careful to not clank the spoon against the coffee canister—four large scoops makes a strong pot of coffee—and shortly after pouring in the water, my Bunn coffeemaker emits delicious smells and delightful gurgles. Through the back doors, I step onto the deck. Cold air caresses me, and I wrap my arms around myself. Last night was really fun. Bryan would've enjoyed hearing his pawpaw tell the ghost stories, but Jackson had to run away. Run away and leave me with this house full of people, including *his* family and all their weirdness.

At first I thought it would be easier dealing with our families rather than the Chancey folk. Missus, Laney, FM, Cathy Stone, and her mom, Libby, Susan and then add in the teenagers who are so difficult to figure out. But turns out, family comes with the same problems as all those strangers. And since they're family, they act like they can do what they want. Paint two weeks before Christmas, ground your kids, stock the refrigerator with stuff you'd never buy and then there's all the advice. Well-meaning, but advice all the same.

"See how this wood breaks off? Dry rot. Better fix it."

"Do you think it's wise to let Savannah eat Moon Pies for breakfast?"

"Don't the shirts get wrinkled when you fold them like that?"

"If you leave that wood piled up there, you'll get termites."

"A coat of paint or a good layer of mulch or a box of baking soda or a touch of vinegar or, or, or whatever, would fix that right up."

My body jerks as a shiver rolls over me. It's really gotten

colder since yesterday. The sleet from last night isn't still covering the deck and grass, so it must not be freezing. But it feels so damp and, well, cold. When I turn to the door, Ashley stands looking at me with big black eyes. I pull the door open, and he trots out, across the deck and down the four steps to the yard. He doesn't take long, and we both hurry inside.

"Good, you're up." Daddy says with coffeepot in one hand and cup in the other. "Your Mother and I want to get to Missus' early. We're in charge of the decorating, you know."

With coffee cup extended, I nod. "That's right, someone did tell me that. So all the cardinals down at the floral shop were your idea?"

Daddy fills my cup while a look of disgust contorts his face. "No, that's all Missus' idea." He puts the pot back then turns to lean on the counter. "That woman is not easy to work with."

Coffee burbles out of my mouth, and I lean over the sink to keep it from falling on my sweater. "Really? You think so?" I swipe my hand across my mouth and take my coffee to the kitchen table and sit down. "You're supposed to just feel honored she's allowed you to participate."

"And we do. We do. And we all loved the idea of following the decorating described in *Gone with the Wind* at the big war bond rally. You remember when Rhett buys a dance with Scarlett, but she's in mourning for her first husband and can't dance. 'Course, she does dance, but anyway, when we found out how much the flowers like they had in the book cost this time of year…" he frowns, "…something else had to be worked out."

He sits down across from me, ready to explain about the cardinals, but with a quick look around, I lay my hand on the table between us. "Dad, what do you think about Hank? I'm sure Mother had told you what we suspect."

His eyebrows bunch up, and his mouth follows suit, but he nods just a bit.

"So? What do you think?"

His still frowning mouth loosens up and moves. "Nothing. At least nothing for you to be all concerned with. Folks have different ways, and until Etta acts like she wants your nose in her business it should stay out. Way out." Then his face relaxes. "Besides, don't you have enough to worry with getting your own husband home?"

"Okay, I hear you. Keep my nose out of it. And Jackson will be home today...or tomorrow." I stand and take my cup of coffee over to look out the glass doors. "This move has not been good for us in a lot of ways. He's never here, and there are so many things to get bogged down in. I know you like being in the center of everything, but I don't, and I think Jackson's figuring out he doesn't either." A sigh escapes and with a slow turn, I walk to the sink and set my still half-full cup in it. "What if this isn't what either of us want? Maybe one day, when the kids aren't around or when Jackson retires, but what if it was the wrong thing to do?"

"Maybe you're just tired from having all this company. You go from never having company to non-stop company. That'd wear anyone out."

"Not you. Not Mother. You two would eat this up."

Daddy laughs and then drains a last gulp from his cup. "Honey, you've got to realize what makes us happy isn't what will make you happy. But be honest. Were you really happy back in Marietta? You and Jackson both so bogged down in your jobs you didn't have time for friends or family or even each other? Could the problem be you two are actually having to get to know each other all over again? Not to mention getting to know your own selves?"

"I know. I know."

"Do you realize we've not spent more than two nights in your house since you've been married? Even after we got the motor home, it couldn't be parked in your old neighborhood. You never slowed down enough for us to come visit, and here you open up your house to not only me and your mother and your in-laws, but also these other people you hardly know. That is not the Carolina you've always seemed to be. It would be shocking if you and Jackson weren't off-kilter some.

Daddy said all this standing a few feet behind me. When I look up, our reflections are in the door glass. Our eyes meet, and we both smile.

He steps up closer, lays one hand on my shoulder, and reaches for the doorknob with the other. "Those low clouds look like snow clouds. Are you supposed to get any snow today?"

"I don't know. We didn't really have the TV on last night. I'll go check it out." I turn and look up into Daddy's face. "Thanks."

He just pats my shoulder, and we turn as Shelby comes into the room. "Did I hear you say it might snow?"

She never looks her age, but fresh out of bed in those flannel pajamas and her hair all tousled, she looks as more like a contemporary of Will's instead of mine. And the way she can pull her legs right up onto the chair seat—unnatural. She leans back, "Etta, did you hear it might snow?"

"Oh, is Etta up?" I ask.

"Um hum, she's just sitting in the dining room doing her devotional. She likes to have a table to sit at. But I prefer to do my daily devotions while I'm still all warm and cozy in bed."

Golly gee, that's just peachy! There's a term I remember from high school. Let me see if I can remember it: Gag me with a spoon. Yeah, that pretty much sums it up.

Etta lumbers down the hall, her purple fluffy robe like a tent. "Good morning. Why Jack, you and Carolina are already dressed." She comes to me and gives me a hug and kiss on the cheek. "Darling you look so adorable in that sweater. It's a wonderful color on you. You should always take your mother's shopping advice."

Daddy leans against the counter, "Speaking of shopping, did you find a dress you like for tonight? You had enough bags with you to have bought a half-dozen dresses."

"Oh, yes. I did find one, but I don't know. I was in a strange mood when I bought it. I'm not sure it's appropriate now that I think about it."

Shelby lifts to tuck her feet underneath her bottom. "Oh, Carolina you're always appropriate. So stately and composed and with your new haircut. Oh, and we can all do each other's makeup!"

She actually claps her hands several times. And what does she mean–stately? Composed? Like the old Queen of England, I guess. I gotta get out of here. That urge to smack her grows with every smile, clap, and nose wrinkle. "Well, I want to check the TV for today's weather and then get on the road." I turn my back on Shelby. "Etta, you're welcome to come help with the decorating."

Etta reaches up and scratches at her iron gray haircut, barbershop short on the back of her neck. "Naw, honey. I told Hank I'd go down to your library and do some research on that train engine down in Marietta. He thinks it might make a good Hillbilly Hank story. Did you know your library's going to be closed all next week right up to Christmas and then through New Year's?"

"No, I didn't. But if there's this grouchy old woman working there, don't tell her you're related to me, okay?"

Shelby, never to be left out, pipes up, "Oh, you silly goose, everybody loves you, Carolina."

Okay. Gotta go.

CHAPTER 45

"All four of these crates cannot be full of those stupid cardinals." I say, tapping my cute little boot on the sidewalk outside the florist shop.

"Oh, but they are. Missus ordered them special." Susan pushes the arms of her sweatshirt up and bends down to lift one of the plastic storage crates. "She has a grand vision of white lights, magnolia leaves and cardinals—everywhere."

How heavy can several dozen stuffed cardinals be? I bend to lift one of the other crates, find it lifts easily, and place it next to the one Susan just loaded in the back of my van. "What else are we supposed to pick up?

"Shannon has it all separated in the back room. Why don't you go check with her so we'll know how much room we need?"

"Okay." I push open the front door, but when I don't hear the bell ring I look up and see it's been pulled out of the way, probably for the loading of the van. Shannon isn't in sight but I hear someone. Out of the office she strides while she almost yells at the person on the phone. "You can't keep doing this. You can't just keep making it like everything is fine. People are going to find out and, Laney, I just hope they find out before you're sitting in jail." She turns, our eyes meet, widen, and she pushes a button on her phone, then drops it on the counter.

"What do you want?"

"Shannon, what's going on with Laney? Do you really think she could go to jail?" Shannon's eyes dart to the front sidewalk where Susan is arranging things in the back of my van.

The florist is very short with long brown hair and shaggy bangs. Her eyes start blinking rapidly, and she moves toward me. "Maybe you can talk some sense into her. She has to come clean. She has to let everyone know what's going on. It's her only hope. And if she speaks up now it can all be fixed. I just know it." She jumps back. "Here comes Susan."

Susan pushes through the door, holding her arm out. "Look, snowflakes. Look before they melt."

And sure enough her sleeve is dotted in tiny crystals, which vanish before our eyes. We look at each other like we're getting out of school early. Some years there's hardly any snow to speak of; other years there might be more. But either way, the first snow—especially the week before Christmas is magical. We rush to the door.

Outside, the large, fluffy flakes have brought quiet to the square. A hush settles in and around us, and the others now standing in doorways, with hands on car doors or stopped on the sidewalks. Our chins point upward and our mouths part in wonder at the beauty.

"Not supposed to stick," FM says from outside Ruby's Café. "Ground's too warm. But it sure is pretty, isn't it?" He pulls his coat to and walks toward us. Y'all working on the decorations for the ball?"

Susan nods. "Yeah, we are." She turns to Shannon. "So what else do we need?"

Shannon takes one more wistful look at the heavy snow and then steps back into the shop. "The magnolia leaves were delivered directly to Missus, and the table arrangements I'll bring over at three when I close. 'Bout the only thing left are these bolts of ribbon. Here, Susan." She hands the three huge bolts of red velvet ribbon to Susan. "Carolina, you come back here with me to check real quick-like."

"Here, let me get the door." And with a skip, I get to the door before Susan and say, "I'll meet you in the van, okay?"

"Sure."

Back through the store and the half door, and I'm in Shannon's work space. The table is old and scarred, and cutters and knives lie all around. Buckets of flowers give a heady scent to the small area. Shannon is waiting for me.

"There's nothing else for you to take, but you've got to talk to Laney, okay. She's worried about what it's going to do to her family when everything comes out."

"Yeah, the girls being only in high school, it's hard—"

"Not on them, on her Mama more than anyone. You don't know how it is in a place like this. Everything you do reflects on your family, and if you've got a sweet, church-going Mama like Laney does you've got to keep your nose clean. That's all there is to it." Shannon points a tiny finger at me. "So you've got to help Laney settle this 'cause you and me are the only ones who know what's going on. Well, and Shaw but he's no help as his family's reputation weighs on him as much as on Laney."

"But I don't know what's going on."

Shannon pushes me around and toward the swinging doors. "You know enough. Go talk to her. You promised."

Stepping away from her strong hands, I turn to face her. "I didn't promise anything. Why me? Like you said, she has lots of family here. Shoot, her whole life is here."

With one hand on her hip, Shannon sticks her chin out at me. "You aren't from here. You don't remind Laney of all the family tangles. So, promise or not, you're the one that has to do this."

My hands fly up in the air, "Whatever. I'll see what I can do."

"Good."

All that velvet ribbon we carried to Missus's? It's for the front porch. Where it's freezing. My fingers are so numb, the ribbon so stiff, and my nose so cold, but every time I try to go back inside to help, Missus catches me. She called me "good-for-nothin'" last time.

"So here you are, Outer Mongolia and just the weather for it." Peter says as the screen door pivots past him. "I brought you some hot chocolate, but even better, leather gloves."

Pushing up off my knees, I almost tear up at someone being kind to me. "I love hot chocolate."

"Here, sit on this bench. It's a little out of the wind, and the cushion will be warmer than the bare wood."

The bench is painted dove gray and has peach and gray, paisley-patterned cushions. I sit down, and he hands me a thermos cup, steam rising out of the little drinking hole. Not only does the steam smell wonderful, but it begins to thaw my nose. Peter settles onto the bench with me, and he's so warm I don't think about the fact that he's not my husband and he's sitting really close. Matter of fact, I distinctly am not thinking about that.

"And here. Give me those worthless kid gloves."

I sit my cup down on the little table in front of us and yank off my cheap, red knit gloves, which I buy by the dozen for the whole family. Everyone gets the same color, red, so we can interchange them and spot them wherever they try to hide. Peter pulls from his pocket a pair of real leather, navy blue gloves and gives them to me. They slide on like butter and immediately mold to my hands. Flexing my fingers, I marvel at how they fit. "These are your mother's, aren't they?"

"Yep."

"I'm probably stretching them out because her hands are not nearly as big as mine, aren't I?"

"Yep."

"Good." I pick up my hot chocolate and settle back to take a sip.

"Now, seeing as I'm such a good Samaritan, tell me something. Why is she so mad at you? What happened the other night up at your house when she came home and took to her bed then roared out of it the next morning threatening to sue you for defamation?"

"Ummm, this is real hot chocolate. I can taste the cream." Both hands clutch my tall cup and my face is buried near the opening.

"Yes it is, and remember who thought of you and brought it to you."

His voice is so tender, so low. My shoulders begin relaxing, and I look out at the snow. It's so much prettier when you're warm. The flurry of flakes provides a see through screen when looking at the square and the Christmas tree. The water-logged, bedraggled handmaid ornaments look whole and shiny, the lights twinkle behind the wall of snow. The red mud, is now muted under a see-through sheet of fallen snow. Whether they're leaving Ruby's full of coffee and muffins, or leaving the florist with a decorated wreath or headed into the library for a stack of books, everyone seems happier. "Merry Christmas" is said over and over with laughter being the sound track.

Cuddled up like this—wait—the word "cuddle" is a poor choice. Sitting here with my warm gloves, hot chocolate, and a friend to block the wind from around that corner and watching the snow, brings Christmas to me. Next to me, a look assures me Peter feels the same way. His dark beard is trimmed and his hair, still flops down on his forehead, but his sideburns are trimmed. "Hey, you got a haircut. Getting fancied up for the big ball?"

"I'm not some twenty-year-old who has to be told when to

get a haircut." His voice is still low and smooth, but a flush rises over his cheeks. Then he breaks into a grin, "Plus Mother made me an appointment at Beulah Land, and I couldn't resist chatting with Beau. She and I are those prodigals that couldn't wait to get out of Chancey, and now look at us."

"Well, it looks nice. I visited Beau also this week."

"Yep, that's what she said. Your hairstyle looks really nice." He lifts up a hand and touches the side of my hair near him. "And I guess these are the highlights she put in. Beau said they brought out the gold in your eyes."

Now it's my turn to blush as our eyes meet. He stares as if he's panning for the gold Beau told him was there. Then he jerks his hand away from my hair and leans forward. He takes a deep breath and it causes him to cough. "So, why is Mother so mad at you?"

"Just something that was said to her. I don't even know if it's true."

He tilts his head toward me. "But you think it is, don't you?"

Going over my attempts to get Anna to talk and Missus' over-the-top reaction has made me thing Anna might know something. But I'm not ready to accept what she said as the whole truth. "Peter, I'm just not sure. Why, what have you heard?"

He looks down at his hands clasped in front of him, forearms resting on his knees. "Well, Abby Sue has some interesting stories to tell."

"Oh, that's right. You and Abby Sue in the bushes the night of the city council meeting. She probably did have some *interesting* things to *talk* about."

His low laugh agrees. "It's awfully hard to keep Abby Sue's mind on talking when she's got other things in mind."

"But I thought she was getting back together with Scott?"

"Oh, she is. She'll always be with Scott, but well, she likes to have other interests. She believes in diversification of her portfolio. Always has. And you know I have been out of pocket recently. So, she's just checking in to see what investment potential I might have."

Any lingering chill vanishes with a wash of anger. "So? Do you?"

Peter goes still. "Potential for Abby Sue? No. Absolutely not. She just told me what I wanted, and then I told her to close my account."

I will not ask. I will not ask. I will not... "Why?"

He stands up and turns to look down at me. His dark eyes go from soft to hard as he jams his hands in his coat pockets. "I've grown up, and I don't want what Abby Sue has to offer anymore. I'll leave you to get your work out here done." He bends to gather our cups and then takes them back inside.

Jackson needs to come home now.

CHAPTER 46

"Jackson is still not home." My words to Susan on the phone are short and taut. "I'm so mad I could strangle him right here."

"Are you worried if they're safe?"

"No, and that *would* make it easier. He keeps texting Savannah but won't answer my calls or texts. So I know they're safe. But…" trying to shut down thoughts of Peter gets harder and harder the madder I get at Jackson. "But he needs to be home now!"

"Calm down, Carolina. He's upset and like I learned with Griffin and how I betrayed his trust with not telling him about Susie Mae, the only thing that will fix things is time. So give Jackson this time. We'll have a great evening anyway."

Susan would die if she knew what I'm really worried about is having too much of a great time. Dancing with Peter won't stay out of my head. "Okay. But, uh, don't leave me alone, okay?"

"Sure, honey, me and Laney and Peter, we'll all make sure you don't end up sitting in the corner alone."

She laughs, and I'm glad because it covered my groan. "Fine. Fine. We'll see you soon."

Out in the upstairs hallway, the noise from the living room jumps at me. We're leaving an empty house tonight. Mother and Daddy, Hank and Etta, me and Shelby are all going to the ball. Savannah is also going to the ball but to sell raffle tickets on naming the B&B. Anna and Patty were hired this afternoon when I overheard the caterer down at Missus' say she needed some more kitchen help. They were promised they wouldn't have to leave the kitchen, so Anna finally agreed. Plus, both girls have been looking for ways to make some extra money. They rode to the party with Savannah earlier.

A peek over the railing from the top stair, says everyone is there, but me. Daddy and Hank both have on rented tuxes, Mother has on a long olive green dress with three-quarter length tight sleeves, a wide sash around her tiny waist and the full skirt even has hidden pockets. Etta has on a brown velvet jacket and long skirt. Underneath the jacket she's wearing a soft ivory blouse and strings of colored jewels, obviously costume jewelry, but they add to her coloring and catch the light in an amazing way. Shelby is wearing a knee-length white sweater dress with long sleeves. Her breasts are clearly outlined in the dress, well the part of her breasts which are in the dress. About half of each of them isn't covered and if she drops a napkins and leans to pick it up tonight, there might just be a "wardrobe malfunction." Hank, sitting across from her in the rocking chair, looks like he's on alert. That napkin could be dropped at any moment.

Okay, here goes.

Mother is watching for me, and she catches my eye when I step down to the landing. Encouragement travels from her to me. I've never even owned a red dress before. But this dress is perfect. Off the shoulder, it covers my upper arms with a swath of red layers. The push-up bra recommended by the sales woman at Saks gives all that red something to swath once it leaves my arms and the way the waist is gathered, actually gives me one. A waist, that is. Then the skirt flares out to just below my knees. The black heels are a little awkward, but not too bad.

Daddy struts to the bottom of the stairs. "Well, Hank, you

might be giving me a good run for my money tonight in who gets to escort the most beautiful women to the ball, but I still think I got you beat."

Hank laughs as he rises, and gives his arm first to Etta. I'm heartened to see him squeeze her arm and wink at her. I don't even watch as they approach Shelby. But then Shelby calls my name.

"Carolina, you're just beautiful."

Oh my goodness, she has tears in her eyes. There's nothing going on between Hank and this girl child—she's just insane. "Thanks, Shelby. That's a beautiful dress you're wearing."

"Really? Do you think so? Hank picked it out for me." And then she practically lays her boobs on Hanks offered arm.

Mother and I both turn quickly toward the door. "Everyone got their wraps or jackets?"

We're taking two cars, so we pile in and head down the hill to town. The roads are warm and so are only wet from the all-day snow fall. However, the grass, bushes, and trees are covered in white. Flakes continue to fall and are caught in the car's headlights. However, an approaching warm front is assured to turn all this to water by early morning. But for right now, all dressed up and on the way to a Christmas Ball, it's perfect.

We park on the square and then walk through it on the brick walkways. Lack of any work being done and the caution tape flapping in the breeze around the gazebo foundation speaks to the impasse with the city council. It also reminds me what Shannon thinks I promised her about speaking to Laney. Okay, that will help keep my mind off other stuff. Talk to Laney.

On the other side of the park, we pause as the full Bedwell house comes into view. "Oh, it looks like a Christmas Card," Shelby breathes. And for once, she's actually not being over the top.

Snow covers the yard and bushes, and luminaries along the sidewalk and path cause wide circles of golden lights in the whiteness. Along the banisters are candles in hurricane globes, which look like a layer of candles on a decorated birthday cake. Red ribbon weaves in and out of the porch posts and looks like it was draped by fairies and not a cold, grumpy bed & breakfast owner. The front door is wreathed in a foot wide border of layered magnolia leaves. Our skirts rustle and our eyes grow wider as we cross the street. It looks too pretty to walk into, and yet we do. We walk right into a fairytale setting. Inside, the candle glow continues, the velvet ribbon continues, the magnolia bowers continue—and there's obviously a taping for an Alfred Hitchcock Christmas edition of "The Birds." Cardinals are everywhere. If I squint my eyes they become just little red blobs and not nearly so creepy. But squinting wastes all that time spent applying my eye makeup.

Shelby, Etta, and Hank all do a double take but recover and take their cue from those of us who knew the cardinals were attacking tonight. Kind of like the swallows returning to Capistrano, in a much more sinister way. A young man dressed in a black pants and a white tuxedo shirt takes our coats and wraps. The hall opens with double door sized entries to either side, and we can see that most of the furniture has been removed. There are white chairs along the walls and some of the couches have been placed along the ends of the rooms.

Several groups of people gather around, and we are greeted as just whom everyone was waiting for. Missus can be heard from around the corner, so I turn in the opposite direction and enter what is normally the formal dining room.

"Wonder where they put all the furniture?" I ask Abby Sue and Scott who are standing near the entrance.

Abby Sue turns and gives me a hug. "I heard the rental company just puts it all in one of their trucks for the night."

Scott nods and sticks out a damp hand for me to shake. "Hey, Carolina. Where's Jackson?"

"Oh, he's still out at your cabin, right?"

"Sure, yeah, that's right. This to-do has my brain shot. Sure wish I'd hightailed it out of town this weekend. This ain't nowhere near my idea of fun."

Abby Sue's shoulders square, and she stiffens up, "You going to start belly aching already you piece of…of…well, you know."

Scott twists up his red face, so newly shaved his white skin attests to where his normal three day growth usually resides. "I put on this monkey suit, didn't I? Paid for it, rented shoes, and everything, didn't I?"

Suddenly Abby Sue falls forward, up against her husband. She's so small that when she wraps her arms around his neck she has to stand on tiptoe. And then one leg, curiously tanned for December, snakes out the slit in her black, slinky dress and curves between Scott's legs and then twists around his right leg. She moves on him, and he grabs her with both arms. She starts whispering to him, but it's loud enough to hear, so I move away and bump right into Susan.

"So, you and Abby Sue were through talking, I see."

I shake my head and lean toward Susan. "From what I heard, Missus and FM might want to keep a close eye on closed closet and bedroom doors. Some kind of bet was being alluded to in all that whispering."

Susan shudders. "If he wasn't my brother, I'd be shocked and ashamed. Since he is, I just have to hope he wins the bet."

"Yeah, this family thing is overrated, isn't it? How did I ever think it would be good to get everyone together for Christmas? Now, here I am with all the family I managed to avoid all these years and yet the family I really want is across the state in some godforsaken cabin."

Susan snaps a rubber band on her wrist, "I so know what you're talking about. See this? I usually have one there so if the one holding my ponytail breaks, I'll still have one. But tonight it's to remind me to stay close to Griffin and to not let the conversation get on the council and Laney's troubles. Have you seen her yet?"

"Nope. You?"

"No, but you *know* she's coming. She probably thinks this whole thing is *for* her. But forget all these other people. Look at you! You are stunning tonight. I know this is going to sound bad, but you don't look anything like you. I mean, makeup *and* boobs? Jackson doesn't know what he's missing."

Blushing from the compliments, there has to be something to say back. Susan has on the black skirt she wears to church most every Sunday in the winter. It's straight and falls mid-calf. She's wearing black boots and a black turtle neck. She does have on a silver necklace with big shiny loops, which I know is Laney's. "And you look great, too."

"I look the same as always, except Laney forced me to wear this necklace, and for mother, I'm wearing my hair down. But back to you and your red dress. You seem so confident and, well, radiant. And if Jackson is missing it, there's someone here who isn't. Here comes, Peter. We need to fix him up with someone so he can move his infatuation along. Good thing you and Jackson are so tight."

"Susan…" I growl under my breath.

"Look here, the two most beautiful women at the ball. How are you ladies?"

Peter places a hand on each of our backs, but Susan doesn't look like his touch burnt her. I step away from his hand and blurt, "Oh, there's Savannah. Maybe I should go check on how the raffle is going."

Hurrying across the room, the spot on my back still burns, and I feel like it's glowing for everyone to see. It's just the dress, probably. Its makes me feel beautiful and sexy, so it's the dress. Gotta be the dress. Has to be.

"Mrs. Jessup, nice dress." Jenna is seated on a chair behind the table and raffle box and next to Savannah.

"Thanks. How's it going?"

279

Savannah leans forward to look at my feet. "You're wearing heels? And makeup and…" her eyes narrow. "You've got on a push-up bra, don't you?"

"Savannah, shush. You don't have to tell everyone."

Jenna smirks and nods her head in time with her shoe hanging mid-air due to her crossed legs. "I bet if Mr. Jessup knew, he wouldn't still be hiding out in that smelly old cabin."

Savannah slaps Jenna's leg. "Shut up."

"So how's the raffle going?"

"Mom, you are so not going to choose the name for our house out of these, right? Some of them make Jenna's mom's name of Trackside Delight look good. Flower Bower, Railroad Rooms, Bate's Motel. Seriously, someone gave five dollars to put in Bate's Motel. How weird is that?"

"Are you supposed to be reading them?" Then I lean closer, "There are some decent ones, right?"

"A couple," Jenna opines with a shrug. "We've already raised $175 in the past week. Tonight is going kind of slow, but we're glad we get to be here."

"Mom, when is Daddy coming home?"

"What did he text you?"

She pauses and then asks, "What did he text *you*?"

Tears jump to my eyes, and Savannah's eyebrows go flat and her lips thin across her mouth.

Jenna watches us then sighs. "I'm sure it will be okay. My mom and dad used to fight a lot, but they don't much now. But, well, I don't know that's a good thing."

Savannah twists her head to look at Jenna, who just shrugs and frowns at her. "Sorry, but that's the truth."

My daughter stands and comes around the table. "Let's go get some punch."

Peter still stands with Susan, but his back is to the center of the room. We walk that way and then back out into the main hall. Just as we do, Stephen Cross and his parents come in the front door.

They are busy with the young man taking coats, so we both watch. Vickie doesn't look anything like Mrs. Claus, and I wonder how she got the role. Her hair is dyed, almost platinum blond. It is big and full with large curls all sprayed in unnatural stances. She's tan like the tennis matrons back in the suburbs and, even though they are tan, wrinkles attest to years in the sun. She has on a brightly blocked jacket and underneath a royal blue satin sheath. She sees us first, and her attention darts between me and my daughter.

"So, why wouldn't you allow Patty to come to the ball?" Vickie demands of me.

"What? I don't have any control over Patty. She's your son's fiancé. Ask *him* why she's not on his arm tonight."

Stephen stammers as he looks between me and his mother, but moves closer to Savannah. I reach out and pull Savannah toward me.

In a flash, he regains his footing in the situation and smiles that deadly smile. There are some people just too good looking for their own good.

"Mom," Stephen explains, "Patty didn't want to come to something fancy like this. I pleaded with her and then suggested that she and I just have another quiet night at the Jessups, but she didn't want to disappoint you and Dad. She insisted I join you."

"But you told me she wasn't allowed to come." Vickie's large, jewel green eyes are opened wide in astonishment that her son didn't tell her the truth. "You always choose to spend time with her instead of me, I mean, us."

He bows his head and lifts her brown, weathered, store-bought manicured hand to his lips. "Please forgive me. You know I do everything to keep you happy, Mother. Please don't be sad tonight."

Sincerity flows from him, and it's so thick we're standing in it. I look over at Savannah to share the joke, but she's enthralled.

She's looking at him like he's, like he's Mr. Walters. Oh, no. There is something between them. He turns and barely lifts his head, but I see him wink at Savannah. Oh, he is so fired. And killed.

My hand tightens on Savannah's upper arm, and I propel us both across the hallway and into the back corner bathroom. Behind us I shut the door and then lean against it.

"What is going on? You're looking at him like you want to eat him up. And I saw him wink at you. You know he doesn't spend time with Patty. He's never been to our house once. I want the truth right now."

She turns away from me and leans on the sink, staring into the mirror. "Mom, they're making him marry Patty. It's some agreement his parents have with her mother. Stephen needs someone more like him." She twirls toward me. "You know he and Patty should not get married, right?"

"Of course, but not because...not because he should be with you."

"But you just don't know how, how sensitive he is. How much he cares. He needs someone more like him." Suddenly, she turns to close the lid on the toilet. She pulls her full skirt of her dress out of the way and sits down. Then I can see she's laughing.

"What is so funny?"

"You, Mom. Of course, I don't like Mr. Cross. I'm acting."

"But why?"

She tilts her head and wrinkles her nose. "He's such a flirt at school and he started zeroing in on some of the, well, the younger girls. Like Susie Mae. They believed everything he said, and he started putting them on committees where they had to stay after school. So, Jenna and I started messing with him."

"Not, messing with him messing with him, right?"

"No way. He's scum. But the younger girls kind of faded away when Jenna and I threw around that *we* were his girlfriends."

"You told people you were his girlfriend?" Now it's my turn to lean on the sink.

"But, Mom, the people who matter know we're not, and the younger girls are safe. Plus, Patty cannot marry him. He's so full of himself and smarmy. She's got to figure a way out of this mess."

My stomach is still roiling from the thought of her being in love with him, so this is better. But not by much. She just sounds so logical and so in control that I can't get my thoughts to come up with reasons for her to stop. "So when are you going to stop?"

"After the spring play. He really is a phenom teacher and director so we want him around through that and then afterwards we'll see what happens. But you can't tell anyone, okay?"

"So no other adults know about this?"

Savannah stands up and starts playing with the flower arrangement on the wall. "Well. Maybe one."

"Who?" Although there's no doubt who she's going to say. Only one parent I know would think this was a good idea."

"Jenna's mom."

I knew it. "Okay, I'll talk to Laney but I want you to pull back on this. You understand you are playing with fire, right? Wait, playing with fire. That's what Abby Sue said to you. Does she know?"

"She doesn't really *know*. She suspects. She overheard me and Ricky fighting about it one night."

Savannah squeezes past me and opens the door. "So we're cool? You won't say anything? Right, Mom?"

"For now." I nod and straighten my dress. "But we'll talk more."

She turns, but I think of something.

"Hey, so what were you and Ricky fighting about?"

She shakes her head. "Nothing really. He just thinks Mr. Cross could get mad and get physical with one of us when we're alone. But there's no way. We've got this totally under control."

And with that she slips out the door.

My relief she doesn't like him made me feel better, but that good feeling is gone now. Completely gone.

CHAPTER 47

So this is supposedly invitation only?

Out of the bathroom, and purposely not following my daughter back to the more crowded room where she is stationed, my pinched feet take me first to the punch bowl for a refill and then across the front parlor. A burgundy and dark wood sofa is set against the front window and calls to me. Now, from this perch by the front window, a scan of the room causes me to doubt the invitation only barricade. Not that I think anyone has crashed the party, but I think in a town the size of Chancey there's no one you can afford to *not* invite.

Sipping the sweet, orange sherbet laced punch, I scan the room. Even sitting, my shoes hurt, so I slip them off, careful to sit them close where I can get them on in a hurry if Missus spots me. Somehow, I think she'd frown on me bopping around in stocking feet. Bopping around. That's funny.

Libby Stone, waitress at Ruby's, is here along with her daughter Cathy, who is the unpaid assistant cheerleading coach at the high school. She's also the ex-wife of scumbag Stephen Cross. Maybe she has some insight into him. Of course, he dated, impregnated, and married her when she was only a high school student, but then, so was he. Ida Faye is here. Granted she's Chancey's head librarian, but she and Missus are mortal enemies. But then, who hasn't got a shot at that title? Maybe we should have a contest, and there could be a crown, but if there's a crown then Laney would make sure she won. Bopping around wearing a crown. Now, that's funny, and it rhymes.

It's so great just sitting here watching everyone, and this couch is so soft, and right behind me is the porch where I sat with Peter this morning. Where is Peter? Where is he bopping around? I laugh and lay my head back.

Do you know what happens when you wear a low cut dress, a push-up bra and sit down? Yep, boob city. And here comes our illustrious newspaper editor, Charles Spoon, well-known observer of fine cleavages everywhere.

"Is that for me? Thanks." I take the cup of punch from his hand and take a long sip. I mean, mine was empty and a view like this isn't free.

"Uh, yeah, but well…" He wipes the back of his neck with his empty hand and then shrugs. "So, you know, haven't seen much of you lately, Carolina."

"Well, take a long look now." A giggle pops out and something in my brain says there's a problem. I struggle to sit up a little straighter. "Hmmm, yeah. I have a lot of family in for the holidays and they've kept me busy."

Charles motions at the empty seat on the couch. "May I?"

"Of course." I pull my skirt closer to me and kick my feet around to make sure my offensive heels are not in the way of his feet.

"You know, I hear the B&B is done up right pretty for the holidays. Can I come up and get some pictures? And maybe, you know, interview Hillbilly Hank."

Another giggle bubbles out at his well-known overuse of 'you know'. "Of course, you know, you might even want to interview Sassy Shelby—she's Hillbilly Hank's sidekick."

"Really? Doesn't she have a white dress on tonight?"

"You know, that's right, and she has a pair you don't want to miss, you know." I emphasize it when I repeat it this time, but he doesn't seem to quite get it. "But, yeah, come on over. You know what Missus says about PR. Never too much, you know. And maybe we'll even have a name by then. Well, a new name. Trackside Delight, well, that's just a little too suggestive, don't you think? Unless we want to, you know, get some side action going, you know." This time the giggle is more like a full out laugh and I pop my hand across my mouth.

Charles joins me in laughing and leans a little closer, "Well, I don't know about that, you know, but uh, you…" he reaches for my cup, but I pull back and drain it.

He chuckles and lifts his hands. "Never mind."

I plop the empty cup in my other hand. "I'm sorry, Charles, but my cup is empty. It must be nerves because I'm so thirsty. Would you refill my cup, or your cup? Or both!" I motion him closer. "I can't get up because I took my shoes off and one kind of got pushed too far back." I lift my skirt and look down. "See? I can't find my shoe under there at all."

We watch my feet for a minute and then Charles stands up, takes both cups, and heads off, hopefully in the direction of the punch bowl. Good. Now I can rest a minute and just enjoy the show. People seem to be having a great time. There's a lot of laughter, and the lights are so pretty. And with my head laid back against the couch, when I tilt my head down I see I have these amazing boobs and this beautiful red gown. But I have to find my shoes so I'll be ready when the dancing starts. Has the music started? My eyes close, and I try to hear the music over the talking and laughing.

"Carolina, are you asleep? You're snoring."

With a jerk of my head, my eyes pop open, and Laney's in my face. "What? Asleep? No, no, well…" I swallow and shake my head. "Well, maybe. Oh mygosh, I fell asleep in the middle of the party." Sadness wells up and tears pool in my eyes.

Laney takes my hand and sits down beside me. "How much

punch did you have?"

I can't remember. Oh, how incredibly sad is that? My bottom lip trembles, and I look helplessly at Laney. "I don't know." With a deep breath though, comes the thought, "and just why would that be sad?" Something is not right.

Laney grins and stands in front of me. She leans down and whispers, "The punch is spiked. I told Abby Sue to let you know so you wouldn't drink too much. You are such a light weight."

My shoeless feet splayed out in front of me, both my hands lifted in mid-air by Laney's hands and confusion all over my face, but finally my mouth works, "What?"

"Come on. You'll be fine. Surely, you didn't have that much, and you slept it off some."

She pulls me up.

"Wait. My shoes are under the couch. Wait." I stand there a minute and my head starts clearing a little.

Laney bends down, but there's no way she's bending far in that dress. The navy halter dress isn't short, but it's tight. She rights herself and looks around the room. "Stephen? Could you help us out a bit?"

Stephen excuses himself from his conversation and strides his cocky quarterback strut across the room to us. "How can I help you, beautiful ladies?"

My eyes narrow as he joins us. I think a growl came from me, and Laney slaps my arm. "Behave." Then she holds that same hand out for the ex-jock, answer to all woman kind, smiling slime ball.

Laney tilts her head and smiles at him. "Silly Carolina let her shoe fall off, and it somehow got kicked back too far for us to reach. Would you mind seeing if you can get it?"

Yeah, bend down so I can kick you.

Stephen kneels down and retrieves my shoe. "Here you go." The way he holds Laney's arm and leans toward her, he must've also had some punch.

I'd like to punch him.

Laney leans into him and at the same time pushes him away. "Thank you so much. We are so appreciative." She turns her back on him and hands me my shoe. "Put this on. Now, I know you like the punch, but how's the rest of the party going?"

"Earlier I was surprised by all the laughter, but now that I know about the punch. Wait, *you* spiked it, didn't you? But you weren't here yet, were you? Were you?"

Wide, sparkly blue eyes attest her innocence, but her smile is pure evil. "Come on, let's mingle."

Walking a party with Laney Troutman Conner should be a commodity you can buy. She talks to every person and makes them smile before she leaves. People with their noses in the air at first glimpse of her are hugged and complimented into a cozy coma. Council members who are threatening to put her in jail greet her with regret and fear but are left relaxed and calm. She holds the room in the palm of her hand by the time we step out into the center hall.

With my hand on her shoulder, I turn down the hall. "Wait, I need to go to the restroom and look at my hair. No telling what my little nap did to it."

"Good, I'll join you."

Another thing skinny, popular girls do—go to the restroom together. They think that's normal, and I'm here to tell you, it's not. But since they're skinny and popular, who's going to tell them that. "Okay."

While I peer in the mirror, she does her business. Shannon's words this afternoon in the florist come to me. "Laney, Shannon wants me to tell you to come clean. To fess up and make everything fine. She seems to think you can do this just by talking and after seeing you work that room out there, I tend to agree with her."

"Blast that girl and her mouth. So she told you about the poker, huh?"

Another layer of lipstick covers the one I just laid and my eyes never leave the mirror. My punch fog lifts as I lie. "Uh-huh."

"Well, now you know about that guy at the lodge you thought I was having an affair with. Those card guys are suckers for a Southern belle." She pulls and shimmies her dress into place. "They'd never make it on the pageant circuit." She nudges me to share the mirror. "Can I borrow your lipstick? Not a great color, but my purse is out there and unlike in your full skirt, there's no room for a pocket on my dress." She lines her lips and then steps back. "And they even fall for it when we're online. But, oh honey…" She pulls her top around and lifts her breasts to form more cleavage, "…when we play in person and these things are on the table? Well, let's just say I'm really, really good."

"So that's where the money went? Poker?" My voice cracks because my friend is going to jail. J-A-I-L "Laney, this is bad. Really, really bad. Do you have a lawyer? You can't smile and talk and flash your way out of this. Poker? What about your girls? Your mother?"

Suddenly the bathroom door flies open and Missus stands there in full rage. "Poker? You've lost all our money playing poker?"

Laney looks from me to Missus then walks right past us both. Loud enough for us to hear behind her she says, "So, Missus, you eavesdrop on your guests? Even when they are in the restroom?"

Years on the pageant stage taught Laney how to command an audience. She silences the center hall with her question. Then a series of "shhh, something's happening" rush through the two rooms and the entire party is hushed. Laney turns when she is at the wide openings into the rooms. When she turns, her eyes lock in on Missus and everyone can read the dare.

Missus pulls the ruffled neck of her cornflower blue evening gown together as if she were a man straightening his tie. And she steps to within a couple feet of Laney. "You owe us an explanation and, no, I wasn't eavesdropping. Anyone here can tell you I just left the raffle table and was coming to look for you and Carolina. When I passed the bathroom door, I heard what Carolina said."

With my head bowed, I come up behind her. Unlike the two women at odds, being heard by everyone is not my desire. "Eavesdropping or not, it *was* a private conversation."

Missus turns to me. "But it is a serious charge, is it not?"

My hesitation speaks louder than my words. As a buzz flies around the room, I lower my head and step to the side. My parents are waiting there, along with Hank, Etta and the ever-present, Shelby. Savannah weaves her way through the crowd and pushes Shelby out of the way to stand beside me.

"So, Laney, do you have anything to say?" Missus asks.

Laney smiles and lifts her arms. "Have at it. Ask what you want."

"Have you been playing poker? Both online and participating in actual games? For money?"

Just as Savannah had made her way to me, the crowd forms and reforms as Shaw, Jenna, Susan, Griffin, Scott, and Abby Sue come to stand near Laney. FM comes through the crowd like a little bull to lean against the staircase beside his bride. Peter walks in from the other room, working his way behind me and Savannah. I know he's coming to stand beside his mother, but having him near reassures me. I'm not analyzing it or fearing it, but very much enjoying having him there.

Laney reaches over and grabs Susan's hand but never lowers her head. The she lifts her chin and speaks loud and clear, "Yes."

She holds firm to Susan's hand, even as Susan jerks and swallows hard several times. Abby Sue and Scott work to hide their surprise, but the darted look between them makes it obvious this is news to them. Griffin just falls back against the wall and lowers his head.

Peter's eyes are on me, so I look at him. With a tiny shake of my head his questioning look is answered. Soon, it's obvious the only person not surprised by the revelation is Shaw. He stands behind his wife with a hand on her shoulder—and a smile. A smile?

"Yes, everyone. I play poker. About seven years ago, I tried it and, low and behold, I'm good." Laney smiles and then looks over her shoulder at Shaw. "Aren't I, honey?"

"Best I've ever seen. All natural."

"Thanks, Sweetie. But, anyway, about the town's money. At first it was just a little thing, and I knew it would balance back out at some point. But, then well, it just never did."

Griffin steps into the only open space in the hall, the middle area between the two women. "Everyone, I knew nothing about this, but I will type up my resignation as soon as I return home tonight. A professional auditor will be called in and," his face contorts to hold in his emotion as he turns to Susan, "and the broken laws will be addressed by the criminal system."

Missus' face is white and she looks shaken. "I think that's best."

"But wait." Laney steps forward and puts a hand on Griffin's upper arm. "I don't want the money back or anything."

Where before the silence still held the undercurrent of whispered words or inhaled breaths being released, or tongues clicking against teeth, now the silence is complete.

Laney pulls Shaw forward, "Right, Shaw? We don't want the money back. We love Chancey, and we'd have given the money outright, but then that would've seemed like charity and we know how folks can be about that." Her smile is wide and then she laughs. "Like I said, at first it was just money to pay for extra road grading when we had a bad summer storm. Or when the library requested more books than the budget allowed." She waves a hand at Ida Faye. "Right, Miss Ida Faye? Who can say no to more books? Or it was a safety issue, remember when that man from over at Cleveland was hanging around at the high school at night, and we all wanted Deputy Lawson's patrol extended? Well, the money had to come from somewhere."

Susan grabs her sister's shoulder and turns her to her. "Are you saying you didn't take money from the town but gave it?"

"Of course. Y'all know me. I'm a liar, but I'm not a thief. Like I said, I'm really, really good at poker, and at first, it was just little things, but then two years ago when the property values took that hit, the towns budget wouldn't balance so, well, I just made sure it would."

"I need to sit down," Missus says as she moves past FM and sits on the second stair. With a sigh, she asks, "You're saying Chancey has been the in black, unlike every other town in the area, because you've been supplementing our budget with your gambling gains?"

"Yeah, I have all the records and what I hoped was that we'd get that tourism grant last fall and then we could balance the books once and for all and then I'd step down as treasurer and, well, no one would ever have to know."

Around the room, smiles begin to appear and the whole house takes a deep breath. Okay, this isn't so bad. No one goes to jail for giving away money, right?

Then Missus stands up, with a hand on Griffins chest pushes him to the side, and comes into Laney's space. "You. You, all on your own, without the sense God gave a goose, decided to involve our town, my town, in gambling? A town founded on truth and morals and which prides itself in not caving in to the lower elements of human nature. A town you have chosen, quite happily, to drag through the mud and filth of gambling." Missus pulls back and then shaking her head and closing her eyes, expresses her disgust. "But what can anyone expect from a Troutman. Your family has tried to pull this town down in so many ways. Your father, God rest his soul, and his shady businesses, Scott and Laney sleeping their way through Chancey

High. Letting this one," she points to Abby Sue, "cavort all over Atlanta then come back to the bosom of your family whenever she feels like it. Yet, through it all you hold your heads up and teach Sunday school, run for city council, keep the town's books. Well, now we know what comes of letting people like you be in charge." She shakes her head and looks around the room encouraging others to agree with her. "We cannot accept this immorality. We cannot or we just become another town with a crumbled foundation."

Murmurs of agreement skitter through the room and suddenly a tiny figure in a tight, black, strapless gown steps up to Missus. There's a good foot and half height difference and when Missus pulls herself up in disdain, it might be two feet.

Abby Sue flips back her mane of sprayed, teased, and streaked hair. "Wait a minute, there, Shermania. That is your name, right?"

"Of course, it's my name. Everyone here knows my family history and the inheritance of that abominable name. I do not like to use it due to the pain that awful man imposed upon the South, but yes, it is my name and despite the horror you may think you've filled me with, it is just a name. Now, everyone, the staff has put out dessert and coffee in the front parlor and the music for dancing will be starting momentarily. Please enjoy the rest of your evening."

"Hold on, you stuck up piece of dried manure. So, you don't use Shermania here in Chancey, but on a legal document? Say like a birth certificate you'd use it, wouldn't you?"

Those that had begun moving around, or heading for dessert, stop, including Missus. Peter pushes past me. "Abby Sue, not now…"

Missus meets her son's advance. "Son, she's trash. No one listens to trash and their tales. No one."

Susan steps up to Missus, and I see in all the tension she's pulled her hair back in that familiar ponytail. It swishes as she plants herself right up in Missus' face. "I've had about enough of you calling my family trash. We are not perfect, but we are not trash. You might be a founding family of Chancey, and you might have this big house right on the square, but it doesn't make you better than us. You're not stupid. Surely you have to see that."

"Susan, dear," Missus smiles at Susan and shakes her head. "You are a well-meaning woman, and you try. But blood and family will out. That's just how it is."

"Like the blood and family in that baby you adopted out in 1970 at St. Mary's Hospital in Athens?" The gleam in Abby Sue's eyes fades when Missus laughs and waves a hand at her.

"Young lady, and I use that term loosely, you do not know what you're talking about. Please leave my house. Peter, see that she leaves so we can continue the party."

Abby Sue steps to Peter's other side. "Peter, tell her that you know."

Missus turns to her son. "What does this woman think you know?"

Suddenly we can hear fighting in the kitchen, loud voices and then glass breaking. Peter pushes away from both women holding to him and hurries past all of us down the hall to the kitchen. He's only in the kitchen for a moment when Patty comes out. She stays close to the wall and comes to me.

"Miss Carolina, Anna heard all this. Her own Grandma don't want her, so she was going to run away, but I tried to stop her. That's what you heard, us fighting. We've got to stop her."

So it's true. Of course, I knew it was true but when both she and Missus swore it wasn't—well, that was just easier to go with. "Okay, I'll—"

But before I get to the kitchen door, it opens and Peter comes through with Anna tucked beneath his arm, close to his side.

Patty and Savannah both clutch at me. What is he doing? I step in front of him. "Peter, she's not ready for this. Not here, not like this."

"Carolina, Mother has to face the truth, and the truth is Anna." He looks down, and Anna meets his look. They have the same eyes and it dawns on me. They are both alone, unless this is true.

"Okay. But now?" I ask.

He smiles at me. "Sweetheart, you are so surrounded by people who love you and belong to you that you have no idea what this means. Anna and I have to know."

Sweetheart? Of course, it's something we say in the South to total strangers, but, well, we're not total strangers. I step back, nod, and smile my blessing.

Peter and Anna walk through the parting crowd to stand in front of Missus and FM. But one look at Missus' face demolishes the potential for a storybook ending. Her words are cold and hard. "What is she doing here?"

"I was working in the kitchen. Hi, Mr. FM."

FM nods at Anna and then looks down at the floor.

Missus ignores the girl. "Peter?"

"Mother, she was working in the kitchen, and she heard you say you never had a child, a daughter, her *mother* at St. Mary's in 1970. Is that true?"

"I did not have any other child than you, Peter. Is that all?"

Peter lifts his chin and his arm around Anna tightens. "Yes, Mother, that's all." With his free arm he leans to his mother and hugs her, never letting go of Anna. He talks into his mother's ear, and her eyes widen and fill with tears.

Peter steps away from Missus and with his head down walks back to the kitchen with Anna.

Missus watches him but when the door closes she shuts her eyes, draws in a deep breath and says under her breath. "He doesn't mean it."

Everyone waits for her.

"Are the musicians set?" she asks as she turns and steps into the room set for dancing. She then reaches back to my father. "Jack, as our honored guest, would you please dance this first dance with me? FM and Goldie, I bet would be happy to join us. Hank and Etta, you also."

Those of us left in the hall after the three couples head to the dance floor look around and our mouths are still gaping. Laney, steps to the middle. "Okay, who has the bottle of hooch for the punch?"

CHAPTER 48

"So Peter spent the night here?" Mother asks mid-yawn as she sits beside me at the kitchen table.

"Yeah." With minimal movement, I grab the coffeepot, put a cup in front of Mother, and fill her cup.

"Did you know they were coming here?"

"No. It never occurred to me. Really, when they left the hall and returned to the kitchen I thought....well, I don't know what I thought."

Rain pelts the deck outside the back door. It's a steady rain that makes staying in sound like a great idea.

Mother looks around the kitchen. "I take it Jackson and the boys didn't get home last night."

"Nope."

"Shame he had to miss such a good party."

"Yeah."

We listen to the rain, and then our gazes meet and with baggy eyes still rimmed from last night's makeup, hair still stiff from last night's hairspray, and throats still hoarse from last night's talking we begin laughing. And laughing. Wiping the tears away with the sleeve of my robe takes care of some of my mascara.

"Oh my." Both of my hands plow through my stiff, sleep-skewed hair. "And the strangest thing about the whole night, with everything that happened is that the party just went on. We didn't leave there until one thirty."

"Shouldn't it have ended when we found out the town treasurer is financing the town with poker winnings? Or maybe when the hostess was confronted with her unknown granddaughter?" Mother croaks all this out in half whisper, half gasp.

"Shhhh," I try to admonish when I can draw breath between laughing. Then I remember. "What about Missus and Laney teaching everyone how to walk a pageant runway. Oh, and Abby Sue explaining the finer tips of the strip tease, and Scott just getting up, grabbing her hand and leaving."

Tears are running down mother's face and she grabs my arm, "Then Griffin taking bets from everyone how far they got before they got to it."

"And FM said he bet they were out on the front porch, so he turned off the lights!"

We wipe our eyes again and try drinking some coffee. "And I saw how much liquor went in the punch. There was only about half a cup in the bottom of the bottle that Scott put in the big punch bowl."

Mother shakes her head, "I know those people weren't drunk. Most of them were drinking coffee. Shoot, I know I only had coffee, but that was the most fun I've had in I don't know how long. They just kept telling stories, and when FM started telling about growing up with seven older sisters, he had me doubled over."

"But to be so mad and to call each other such names and then be singing together by night's end. It just doesn't make good sense."

"Oh, but it does. Good morning, Ladies." Peter has on a pair of jeans and his dress shirt from last night, buttoned with the tail hanging out. "There is no greater sin for a Southern hostess than to let an argument, or a gun fight, ruin her party. In golf they talk about "playing through." Here it's "party through." Today they may all be talking about each other and plotting revenge, but last night was different. The party must be preserved. Judging by the time y'all came in, and your laughter this morning, Mother's Ball was a success."

"I'm sorry, Peter." My gaze drops to the table. "How are you?"

"No, don't be sorry. There's nothing to be sorry for, especially since you provided me shelter on a rainy night. Anna left you a note that Patty gave me her room?"

"Yes, and I am sorry for how things went last night. Such a disaster. How's Anna?"

He puts both elbows on the table and holds his coffee cup in both hands. "She's great. Really she is. And last night was just what we needed to happen. We were both afraid to say what we thought about who her mother was. Then last night the flood gates opened. And you didn't wake us up because we scurried off to our beds when we heard y'all pull in. We sat out there in the living room stuffing ourselves on that tin of fudge, drinking huge glasses of milk and talking." As he remembers his eyes shine and his color rises. "She's remarkable."

"But what about your mother?"

"Carolina, I left there last night determined to never speak to her again. Never. I really was through. That's what I told her when I hugged her." He shrugs, "Of course she didn't believe me. But then talking to Anna last night and hearing how her mother, my half-sister died, and how alone Anna's been, I realize there's been too much pain in her young life, and I'm going to focus on giving her a safe, wonderful life. Focus on my niece." A chuckle erupts and he sits down his cup and rests his face in his hands. "My niece."

Mother leans forward. "You don't have to tell us, but I've been wondering what Abby Sue thought you knew last night."

"She's made several allusions to my mother having a secret.

I wasn't sure it was true or just an, well, an excuse for she and I to, uh, be friends."

"Don't worry, hon. Everybody knows about Abby Sue." Mother pats his hand, and Peter blushes, even under his beard.

"Okay, well, she had what seemed like hard facts. By some fluke, when she was in real estate down in Atlanta there was a buyer in her office who had a client who had found a house, sitting empty in Athens that he wanted to buy. However, the title was tied up with some trust fund in of all places, Chancey. So she did some research and found out it was owned by Mother's Aunt T, short for Tecumseh. But Abby Sue knew my Aunt T had never lived in the house because she'd been handicapped all of her life. She was Mother's youngest sister and lived with Mother and Daddy all her life. She died about seven years ago."

Mother stands. "But only someone familiar with Chancey, like Abby Sue, would've caught that. Can I put some toast in for anyone else? I'm starving."

Peter and I nod, "Sure."

"So, yeah, Abby Sue starts looking into it and now with so many records online, and then being Abby Sue, privacy laws didn't seem to slow her down much. She found out Mother and I lived there the year I was five. And I remembered not living in Chancey, but Mother always said it was a vacation we went on when I'd ask about it."

"How about some jam and butter?" I ask as I unfold from my chair. "So where was FM?"

"He'd signed up with Veterans Affairs to oversee the end of the Vietnam War. He was gone for almost three years with just a couple short furloughs home."

Mother and I meet eyes but busy ourselves getting plates and knives and napkins. Who did Missus have an affair with? Someone in Chancey? Did FM know before now?

Peter sighs. "All the information Anna had was that her grandmother's name had something to do with General

Sherman, and she was from Chancey and that she was over thirty when she had the baby. So, it didn't take long to figure out who was her grandmother."

Mother brings the basket of toast to the table and we all take a piece. Mother puts butter and strawberry jam on hers. Mine gets butter and cinnamon-sugar, and Peter opens a jar of apple butter. We smooth and sprinkle and then eat in silence.

Peter chews and swallows. "And you know what? Anna and I decided last night we just don't care about all that. We're family. I'm buying a house in the next week or two, and if she wants to move in with me, then that's exactly what she can do. I told her last night I'm paying for her college and as soon as the holidays are over we're going to get her a driver's license and a car. Anna and I are staying in Chancey, and my parents can do with that what they want."

Mother swipes up crumbs from around her plate and brushes them onto her empty plate. "Good for you. But the real question is, what are we going to do with this horrible rainy day? Christmas is only six days away and my shopping is nowhere near done, but I'm not going out in this."

"Baking? There's a list of things I wanted to try this year." My chest expands and then falls. "So many things I wanted to do this year but look at this place. With all the painting and company and junk, we don't even have a tree up yet. And if Jackson goes back on the road tomorrow, he might just have to miss it." My voice wavers, and I cough to try and cover it.

In the awkward stillness the front screen door screeches open.

Mother looks toward it. "Must be Jack. I left the door unlocked when I came in from the motor home this morning. Then we all jump when the front door pushes open and a bellow rocks the house.

"Patty! Patty Samson! Patricia Gertrude Samson get down here right this minute!" Then she spots me. "There you are. What kind of caretaker are you?" Stomping toward us is Gertie

Samson. She's huge, she's wet, and she's mad.

"Now wait a minute. What's wrong?" Peter stands up to slow down her progress and takes her focus off me.

She stops and looks at him. "Oh, Lord. You're a Bedwell, aren't you?"

Peter stammers, "Yes, Peter Bedwell."

Gertie stares at him harder and thinks. "That's okay." She turns back toward the living room. "Patty!"

And this time the house comes alive. Down the stairs comes Patty with Anna right behind her and Savannah right behind her.

Daddy flies in the front door still trying to buckle his belt. He pushes through the girls and comes to me and Mother. "Where is that woman? She tore into the driveway and then stormed right in the house."

Hank comes roaring in from the B&B rooms. "What in the Sam Hill is going on out here?"

Etta and Shelby clutch each other in their pajamas and peek out from behind him.

Gertie spots Patty and yells, "Get dressed and packed. You've screwed up everything here, and it's time you get home and learn how to do something right."

Patty keeps shoving back her hair away from her face, but it won't stay put. "What are you doing here, Ma? What about the wedding?"

"Wedding happened last night from what I hear. That peckerwood got drunk at some party, and he and that ex-wife of his ran off to some town down near Savannah and got married again."

Gertie walks to the cabinet, opens it, and pulls down a coffee cup. She sits it down and takes off her damp, shapeless, brown-tweed coat. She turns around and then steps past Peter to hand it to Hank. "Here, do something with this." Then she goes back to fixing her coffee.

Hank stands holding her coat with his mouth hanging open.

He turns around and shoves it at Etta. She backs away, but Shelby takes it.

Gertie looks around and then reaches for the basket with the one piece of cold toast in it. She holds it up and grimaces. "This what you're having for breakfast?"

"Uh, no. But you're welcome to it."

"I'm sure I am. It's a dried up piece of toast." She then opens the refrigerator. "Y'all want biscuits and gravy? I've been thinking of biscuits and gravy since the sun came up." She pulls open one of the refrigerator drawers. "Here we go. Sausage, not the brand I use, but it'll do. Hope you got Crisco, and I'll make you folks the best biscuits you ever put in your mouth. Patty, you go pack and one of you others come help me find everything."

Nobody moves. Probably they're all waiting for me to do something about this woman I apparently know who is taking over *my* kitchen. Gertie turns around, sharp knife pointing at us. "Y'all do like biscuits and gravy and sausage, right? And y'all were going to have some breakfast, right? Well, it's a bit rude for you to not offer to help me out, don't you think?"

Then we're all apologizing and underway. Daddy gets a cup of coffee and says he's going to go finish getting dressed and Hank, Etta, and Shelby all tiptoe back down the hall saying they'll be out to set the table in a bit. Peter follows them to his room, and Mother starts pulling out frying pans.

"Crisco, buttermilk, and flour are the first things I need. You get them, and I'll get this sausage started."

"Here's you a skillet for the sausage," Mother says as she slides by Gertie.

"And what's your name, little bit?"

"Goldie, I'm Carolina's mom. Think we should just make a big bunch of scrambled eggs?"

"Sure," then I venture more. "So Stephen and Cathy eloped? How did you hear?"

"Stevie's folks called in the middle of the night last night. Wanted to know if he and Patty might be down at the farm. They said there was some big to do up here, and he hadn't come home when they expected him. You got a lid so this sausage don't splatter everywhere?"

"I'll get it. How many eggs y'all think?"

Gertie shrugs. "No tellin' I never seen so many people come a runnin'. Here I thought Patty was your only paying guest over the holidays."

I scrunch my nose and try to laugh. "She is."

Gertie laughs. "Then you like your family a whole lot better than I like mine. But anyway, about the time I was up and dressed, Vicki and SC called back wailing and crying."

Mother pauses with a container of orange juice in one hand and apple juice in the other, "Really? Seems like they'd be happy their grandson's parents are back together. To be honest, Gertie, uh, Patty and Stephen do not match. She's much too nice for him."

"Ya don't say. She's such a big ol' lump, and I thought he might liven her up some. Besides, it never had much to do with the two young'uns. Grab me a cookie sheet and rub a handful of Crisco on it, won't you?"

With both hands she blends the white ingredients and grunts approval when I place the greased pan beside the bowl. Washing the Crisco off my hand, I ask, "If the marriage wasn't about Patty and Stephen, what was it about?"

She breaks off a lump of the biscuit dough, mashes it in her hand a bit and then puts it down on the greased pan. Then she pats it down with her knuckles and the back of her fingers. A heavy sigh implies the biscuits aren't going as desired, but I think her sigh is really about her daughter. "Me and my folks were run outta here back in '58 due to Pa's shinin'. Moonshine. Some boys got themselves killed up at our place. Folks always thought we was poor. Shoot, I thought we was poor, but come to find out, 'bout near every person round here owed Pa for something. You can take up that sausage and then put a cup or so of flour in the grease, and we'll get the gravy going. So, one thing we owned, still do, that folks didn't know was the Dawson family farm and homestead where Stevie and his folks live."

"Really?" the towel in my hands has my hands dry, but I keep rubbing. "Everyone says they live on her family's land. But you say they don't own it?"

Gertie doesn't pause a second in making biscuits. "Nope. Pa held the deed all these years and called 'em 'sharecroppers.' When Pa died old SC and Vicki called me to arrange a buyout, but shoot I don't need their money. But I sure did hanker after a husband for Patty and a respectable name for my grandkids. Win-win for everyone. Oven's on, right?"

"Right," I murmur and pull the door open for her. "Is Patty your only child?"

She wipes her hands on a dishtowel and stares at me. "Now why would you ask that?"

"No reason. Just curious."

"Let's put it this way. She was my last, okay?"

"Okay. Um, you want me to stir that flour?"

"No, you get the eggs on." She rears back, and Mother and I both jump when she hollers, "Breakfast in ten minutes!"

When the flour has soaked up the sausage grease, Gertie salts and pepper the thick paste and then begins pouring milk, straight from the jug into the pan. She stirs and then lets it sit and bubble up, threatening to boil over the sides. But then she lifts the pan and stirs some more.

"Sure smells good down here," is heard more than once as everyone comes to the table.

By the time the two loaded baskets of hot biscuits are placed at each end of the table, the chairs are full, and we can hardly wait to dig in. I'm the last one to sit down, and just as I do my hand is grabbed by Gertie.

"I'll say the blessing. After all it is the Lord's Day. Y'all join hands round there." She watches until every hand is joined and then bows her head. "Thank You, Father, for this meal and take care of us that will be on the road today. And Lord You've blessed us with such wonderful new friendships here in this room and we thank You. Amen."

Wonderful friendships? Now I really do feel like I need to pray.

Chapter 49

"Anna, you think we should go get the tree now?" I ask hoping to take her attention off the loss of her friend. Patty and her mother were shortly on the road after breakfast.

"I guess. You want me to start clearing a space."

"No, you've worked around here hard enough. Come sit down and help me make out this grocery list for Christmas Eve and Christmas Day."

She's always looked small, but now she seems diminished. Peter left right after breakfast not saying where he was going. Patty and her mother left at the same time. Now, the rest have scattered and the house is quiet.

Jackson texted Savannah that they'd be home around three.

Anna folds into the couch cushion and huddles against the arm. She has on blue pajama pants and a fuzzy light blue top. How can I feel sorry for myself with this poor lonely girl in front of me?

She mumbles, "Mama hated Christmas."

"Really? Do you know why?"

She presses her lips together, and her head barely moves side to side. "She wasn't a happy person most of the time. She never felt good. All the drugs, I guess."

My throat closes, and I try to think what to do. She stares at her hands in her lap and then clears her throat. "Sorry for being here. I know there're already too many people."

"Oh, no. No, you're no problem at all. No problem."

And then I realize it. Who wants to just be a no problem? She wants to be wanted. She just wants to be wanted somewhere.

My list drops to the floor, and I go to sit beside her and stroke her hair. "Anna, you are so welcome to stay here. You are a delight, and you make this place much more of a home. You make me a better person. Please stay?"

Hard swallows jerk her thin body and she squeaks, "Okay."

Tears run down my face and fall when I bend to look at her. "Can I have a hug?"

Tentatively she nods, lifts her head, and turns ever so slightly toward me. Then I grab her and hug her like she's needed.

Because she is.

"I'll be back in a little," Savannah yells as she runs down the stairs.

"Where are you going?" isn't answered, and by time I look into the living room from the kitchen where I'm melting butter, she's out the front door, but passing her, coming the door is Bryan.

"Mom!"

"Hey, you!" We embrace and he smells like a happy little boy. Camp smoke and bacon and good old dirt mix in his tangled hair. "Where's Will? Where's your Dad?"

"Will's coming. Dad and Savannah are going for a drive. He called and told her, right?"

"Ah, sure. So did you have fun?"

"The best. It snowed! Did it snow here?"

"Sure did." His coat is stuck on his elbows so we work to get it off and then Will comes piling in the door.

"Here I am, home from the wilds of North Georgia." He drops all the gear in his hands and then steps over several piles and grabs me. "Mom, it's so good to see you." Then he whispers, just for me, "I'm so sorry. So very sorry. You forgive me?"

"Of course. Do you forgive me?"

He pulls back and smiles at me with his mouth and his eyes, pure and genuine. "Always. Always." The room fills up as we continue to hug. All the grandparents gather to give and get hugs and stories.

Will jerks off his knitted hat, "Dad wanted to see Savannah for a little bit. He felt like he ran out on her. So they'll be back soon, and then we're going to get the tree, right?"

"Right." I say. "Y'all hungry?"

Will wrinkles his nose. "All I want is a shower." He takes a swipe at his little brother. "How about you, buddy?"

"Naw, I don't think I need a shower. Not for just getting a tree."

But his grandmothers on either side of him disagree and start pushing him up the stairs.

Daddy stands watching both his grandsons trudge up the stairs and when they turn off toward their rooms, he laughs. "Those are good boys, you got there. Good ones. Now, do we have directions for getting this tree? Some farm or something? A real country adventure?"

"Oh, I don't think so. We always just go to the Home Depot."

Disappointment fills all four grandparents' faces. "Home Depot?"

Daddy shrugs. "Well, I guess you can take the girl out of the suburbs, but you can't the suburbs out of the girl."

Chapter 50

Savannah holds on to Jackson's arm as they walk ahead of me down the wide aisle of the Home Depot Garden center. There's no roof, and so the black sky presses down on us, despite the fluorescent lights around the edges of the area. Spicy, raw pine cuts through the crisp, chilly night air. This is all so not right, and yet it's so very familiar. Bryan and Will and Anna chase each other around the bins of trees, all varieties and sizes. Savannah pushes her daddy toward the taller trees whenever he stops at the shorter, and cheaper, ones. Except, I should be tucked arm and arm with Jackson, and Savannah should be convincing *both* of us. But there are two sets of grandparents between me and my husband. I'd like to say Jackson is the only one comfortable with that, but I've avoided him as much as he has avoided me on this little outing.

Shelby is at my elbow, and the little jingle bell earrings she's wearing are about to get yanked out of her earlobes and crushed beneath my heel, right between the five foot and six foot Scotch Pines.

"Carolina, what size tree do you think is best?" Jingle, jingle. "You have such great taste in just everything." Jingle, jingle. "Do you like the long needles or the short ones?" Jingle, jingle.

All I hear is "blah, blah, blah, jingle, jingle." If "Grandma

Got Ran Over by a Reindeer" can make it, just imagine how high on the charts, "Ex-wife Jingle Bell Earring Stomp" can go. Sky's the limit.

"What's everyone think?" Jackson has pulled out an eight foot Fraser Fir. He turns it and tries to step out from the branches so we can imagine it in the living room.

"It won't be too tall when it's in the stand?"

"How does the trunk look for fitting in the stand?"

"Those lower branches will have to be cut."

"It's kind of bare on this side, but that can go against the wall."

Opinions and questions shoot around like bottle rockets until the tree is deemed perfect.

Bryan grabs the trunk to lift and carry, but Will pushes him to the side. "Let me get the bottom, you get the top. Savannah, make sure there's a tag on here somewhere."

Jackson finds himself without a job and I find myself standing next to my husband.

"My hands are sticky, now," he says as he pushes his palms together and then pulls them apart. The tree procession begins moving down the aisle away from us, but the two of us don't move.

"You're tan. All those hours outside on the job, I guess."

He looks at the back his hands, "Must be. Used to, this time of year, I wouldn't even see the sun. I'd leave the house before dark and get home after sunset and spend all day in the middle of the office away from any windows."

Really? My eyes narrow as I think about it. Why did I never realize that before? "And you went into civil engineering so you could be outside."

"Yeah," he says as he tips his head to the side and stares at me. His blond hair needs to be cut, and so it looks a little untidy, but makes him look younger and less sure of himself. The collar of his flannel shirt is twisted around in the back, so it's not even and the jacket he has on is one he's had since college. Its brown corduroy lined with orange nylon and awful. He looks like the Jackson I know.

A smile works its way to my mouth. I'm such a drama queen. There's nothing wrong in my marriage. This is Jackson. This is me. It's having all this family around. We just need to get through the holidays, and we'll be fine. I reach up and tighten my red and white knitted scarf around my neck. I love how my new haircut bares my neck.

"Do you like my haircut?"

Jackson looks at my hair and nods, "Sure. It's nice. But Carolina, I'm just not sure…"

"Oh, it takes some getting used to, I know." I turn to show him the back. "But see how it is in layers. Isn't that cute?"

"No, your hair's fine. But this isn't working."

"What's not working? The family all being here? You're right, but they'll be gone soon." Why does he look so serious? So distant?

"No, this. Living here. My job. I mean, my job works, but well, us."

Air comes in my mouth and my chest lifts, falls, air comes out of my mouth. That's all. Breathe. Breathe. Breathe. "I don't understand."

"This isn't working for me. I mean, I don't think I want a divorce or anything, but you're so wrapped up in everything happening at the house and town and the kids school. And I'm so not a part of any of that."

Divorce! "Because you're on the road all the time," I hiss. "Remember why I never wanted you to work for the railroad again?"

"But you don't leave any room in your life or the kid's lives for when I am home. I'm like a visitor. A guest at the B&B. You're always running on about what Laney's doing or Susan and her kids or Savannah's friends and all their goings on. And your rants about Missus, oh my God."

"Me? You're upset with me? I moved here for you and made us a life and now you don't feel like you fit into that life? You've lost your mind."

"Well, do I? Do I fit into your life? I don't even know who you are since we moved here. Throwing parties, volunteering at school, having gossip sessions with your girlfriends, and look at your hair. You're wearing makeup, too. Then you have Peter mooning around after you, and I think you like it."

"At least he's here."

"You do like him."

"No, not like that." But my face heats up, and I remember wanting to see Peter last night. How nervous I was. How much he liked my dress. A dress my husband hasn't seen because he ran off on a stupid camping trip. I swallow any guilt trying to work its way to the surface. "Well, you could've been with me last night at the ball, but you ran away."

"Because you told me not to tell anyone about Shelby and then you went and told our son."

Through gritted teeth, I spit, "It was an accident."

"But you betrayed our trust." Jackson straightens up and takes a step back. "Like I said, I don't know you. This is just not working out. We should've never left Marietta."

"But we're stuck. There's nothing we can do about it now, is there?"

He turns away, "Forget it. I guess we'll just be like my mom and dad. Stuck with each other, forever. Let's go."

He walks away and I realize he's right. He doesn't know me. And I don't know him.

Chapter 51

And don't we come home and crawl into the same bed? Don't we laugh and joke, drink hot chocolate with everyone? Don't we say "good night" to everyone, turn off the lights together, walk up the stairs together, and enter our bedroom together? Don't we deserve an Academy Award?

However, lying here in the dark on the very edge of my side of the bed, the truth can be admitted. No one was fooled. Even Bryan kept shooting me and his daddy dark, questioning looks.

Etta's mouth got tighter as the evening wore on, and my mother's eyes got sadder. Shelby cooed and jingled, while Savannah and Will took center stage in a desperate, but appreciated, effort to keep the focus off us.

Jackson is off work this whole week of Christmas. Christmas day is Wednesday, three days from now. Tomorrow we're having pancakes for breakfast and then decorating the tree. The rest of the week is full of activities, but I've got to take them one at a time. Fighting with Jackson feels like relearning to breath. And think. And exist.

Divorce. Divorce. Divorce. My head pounds with that word. In one horrible moment it leapt to life—fully animated, 3D, Techno-color and Dolby Sound (whatever that is).

But that will never happen. I won't let it. I can go back to being like I used to be. Why does my heart fall and my stomach turn over when I think that? No. I can go back. I will go back. I will.

Now to remember how.

Pulling on my robe, I tiptoe out our bedroom door. Making myself lay there and wait until at least 6:00 a.m. was excruciating. Jackson is left sprawled across the bed snoring softly. At the top of the stairs, I peek down. Waves of brewing coffee-scented air meet me, but no lights are on. The house has that soft illumination from multiple electronic devices charging lights or clock faces. The sky is still dark, but when I reach the living room floor, through the kitchen French doors a gray strip of sky above the tree lines promises the sun is somewhere and headed here.

"Good morning," Etta whispers from her seat at the kitchen table.

"Good morning. I'm sorry. Am I disturbing you? Are you doing your devotionals?"

"No, honey. Just waiting on the coffee. I couldn't sleep. Why are you up so early?"

I wrap my arms tighter around me to keep the shivers at bay and take up a position beside the brewing coffeepot. "I couldn't sleep either."

Only the coffeepot disturbs the silence. When it finishes, Etta begins to stand.

"No, I've got it. You stay there."

She and I both take our coffee black. We're the easy ones. "Here you go. Can I sit with you?"

"Please do."

We sip and breathe and think. The furnace kicks on and the smell of fuel oil seeps into the room on a tide of warmth.

"Reminds me of my grandmother's house." We can't see each other well, but I can hear a smile in Etta's voice. "Her furnace used fuel oil, too. Such an old-fashioned smell." Etta sits her cup down, "Did you know my grandparents were divorced?"

"Really? I thought back then no one got divorced." There's that word again.

"Folks didn't. It was quite the scandal, according to my mother." Etta shifts her bulk. "Matter of fact, I don't think mama ever got over it. She said people would point at her and her sisters, shake their heads and cluck their tongues. Not just children, adults, too."

"How awful."

"Yeah, but not as awful as living with my grandfather, at least that's what my grandmother always said. Mama determined she'd never be divorced, and she badgered my father into an early grave making sure he didn't get out of line. My aunts said dying was the only way he could get away." The kitchen is slowly filling with gray light, and I can see, not just hear, Etta's smile this time.

"Must've been hard for you."

"I sure loved my daddy and always thought Mama made him miserable. But he told me one time that he knew Mama just needed to make sure he stayed right where he was, and he didn't mind."

"Sounds like a wise man."

"Puh. Sounds like a stupid man to me. Well at least now he does."

"Etta! Why would you say that?"

"Because I've come to see lately that I did just as he did. Keep the peace, just keep the peace."

Pictures run through my mind of last night when Shelby sat on a footstool near Hank's chair and how he kept touching her back and how she kept leaning back toward him. Even leaning against his knees for a while.

My mother-in-law bends her head and focuses on the cup captured under her fingers on the table. "Hank and Shelby are having an affair and have been for over a year."

My breath catches and my hand darts out to touch her arm. "No, no. They wouldn't do that to you. No."

"Yes, at first they snuck around, but then I found out. Caught 'em out in the field behind our house on a quilt. A quilt my grandmother made." She lifts her head and in the soft light, her face is surprisingly calm. "And you know, I was more upset about the quilt. Upset that I didn't at least tell them to get up and give me my quilt. But I didn't. I didn't say a word. Still haven't."

"Oh, Etta. I'm so sorry."

"But you knew, didn't you?"

"Oh, well, I don't think it…"

She smiles at me. "No, don't feel bad. It's obvious to everyone. When Hank told me we were coming here and bringing her with us, I should've put my foot down then, but no. Just wanted everyone to be happy, to get along." She sighs and shrugs, "So, here we are."

So badly the words, "what are you going to do?" desire to jump out of my mouth. But do I really want to know?

Etta reaches out and pats my hand, which lies out in front of me. "Maybe that's some of what's bothering Jackson."

"Could be. But I think I have more to do with that." I pull my hand back and cross my arms around me. "This move hasn't been good for us. We've changed too much here. Things are too different now. I have to figure out some way to get back to how things were."

Etta stands up and moves behind the chair. "Sorry, didn't mean to interrupt, but I need to get up and stretch out my back a little." She twists a bit to each side. "Carolina, what you were just saying? Honey, there is no going back. It looks attractive, but it's not possible. Don't waste your time attempting to move backward. You can only go forward. Jackson and you as a couple can only go forward. God's truth? You're already going forward. It's a new day; it's not last year. It's not even yesterday." She pushes her chair under the table. "I'm going to go get in the shower."

"Wait, so, well, what are you going to do?"

Jackson's mother turns to me just as the winter sun, all white and blue peeks over the trees and lights up our backyard and kitchen. "Honey, I'm going to move forward. Don't have no other choice." She looks toward the beams of light pushing through the glass doors in front of her. "It's a new day, and yesterday is in the books."

She lumbers down the hall, and my heart breaks for her sadness. But she's got to be wrong. I have to figure out a way to go back, back to how things were before.

Chapter 52

Anna bounces into the kitchen where the breakfast cleanup is underway. "That was Peter. He's picking me up. Says he has something to show me." Her little face shines. She's wearing a gray sweater that matches her eyes. She loosely wraps a dark green scarf around her neck. "Can you believe I have someone like Peter Bedwell for an uncle? He's just wonderful. Saturday night after that awful ball we came back here, and we talked and talked. About everything. He really listened to me. "She pulls on her navy coat. "Wonder what he wants to show me?"

"You are positively glowing," I say as I dry my hands on a dish towel. "And Peter's as lucky to have you for a niece as you are to have him for an uncle."

Mother crosses the kitchen with a wet dishrag to wipe the table, "Now, when you're done, you be sure and bring Peter back with you for some of those cookies we made yesterday, and maybe you'll be in time to help us finish decorating the tree."

With a toss, the towel lands on the counter. My eyes follow it and then stay glued on it. Peter coming here is not a good idea, but how do I un-invite him now?

Etta puts away the left over pancakes in the freezer and from behind its door she says, "Maybe we should invite folks over tonight. Lord knows we made enough cookies."

"Um, ah…" is the only warning I get out before Bryan swoops in.

"Can we? I'll go call Grant now. Me and him want to talk to Peter about a new idea for the museum."

Savannah comes from the living room, "Hey, Anna, Peter's here. Angie says her mom think's they'll be here tonight. Just let them know what time. Angie says she's got to get out of that house 'cause the phone is ringing off the hook with either folks calling and reading the Bible to her mom about the sin of gambling or calling to invite her to their poker games. Apparently, the underground poker society of Chancey feels they can come out into the open now. I'll check with Ricky's folks about tonight."

Anna says good-bye to us and piles out the door. Savannah and Bryan follow her to the door but then turn to go upstairs. Probably to put tonight's festivities up on Facebook. Maybe we should call WJTM, the local radio station.

Okay, I'll try one more time. Loudly, from the center of the kitchen where everyone can hear me I say, "Wait, Jackson just got home. Shouldn't we try and not make it another big to-do?"

Daddy and Hank are in the living room checking strands of lights for burnt-out bulbs. Daddy yells, "Why not? We've got all week to be cooped up here with just us. It'll be good to see everyone again before we leave. Right, Jackson?"

I'd heard the front door open and close, but because I had turned around facing the back of the house, I wasn't sure who it was until Daddy addressed him. In only three steps I'm at the door between the kitchen and living room.

Jackson sighs, steps to the back of the couch, and rests both hands on the back of it while he looks over at my dad in the rocking chair, his lap full of multi-colored lights. "What?"

But my voice jumps in first as I hurry to Jackson's side. "I was just saying we do not want to have a bunch of people over tonight. You just got home, and it should be just us."

When my hand reaches out to touch my husband's arm he pulls back. "But from what Anna was saying to Peter outside just now, you've already invited him to come over tonight. Wouldn't it be rude to un-invite him?" Jackson's green eyes are hard as he looks at me and between us is the knowledge learned only last night that we don't know each other anymore.

"But *I* didn't invite him," I whisper at Jackson when I walk past him and open the front door. "Come here." Out on the porch, with my arms wrapped around my middle, I move to the railing away from the living room window.

Jackson pulls the door closed behind him and lets the screen door fall shut. "What? You going to tell me this isn't your fault either? It just happened?"

Now, what am I going to say? He knew my line before I did. We stand facing each other, jean clad statues staring at each other like strangers, and I don't even know what we're fighting about. My mind swirls with questions and one pops out. "Do you *really* hate all this? Me and the kids having friends and wanting to get together with them?"

He lowers his head and walks to the railing beside me. He faces the railroad tracks, not me.

I lean back on the railing and sigh. "And you're right, I *was* going to say this just happened, but maybe that's not right. Maybe I want it to happen." He stiffens and out of the corner of my eye, I see his jaw tighten. My voice softens and I try to keep the whine out of it. "You know the old me, but the kids apparently have forgotten who I used to be. The folks here in Chancey think this is the real me. Our folks are tickled to death and, well, as much as I'd like to go back, it may not be possible."

"But you have to keep inviting Peter over?"

"Well, he's...it's a small town, and he is Anna's uncle, Missus' son. I mean..."

"Did he spend the night here Saturday night?"

Who told him that? "Yes, he and Anna were talking. They were asleep by the time we got home."

"Yeah, right."

A wave of heat pulsing through me pushes the cold away. "You think there's something going on with me and Peter?"

He turns to face me. "Is there?"

"No," I exclaim. But what about us sitting on the front porch at Missus' yesterday? Him bringing me out gloves and hot chocolate? I jerk my eyelids shut, and it's the wrong thing to do. My evasive action belies my words of innocence—even to myself. The wash of heat is gone and shivering sets in, chattering teeth and all.

Jackson is stone cold hard and unreachable, *even if I tried to reach him.* "It's cold out here. You're shivering, and we have a tree to decorate and the kids are waiting." He opens both arms toward me, not to hold me but in a gesture of futility. "And here we are, just where I promised myself I'd never be. Make-believing family fun time is fun just for the kids' sake, while we can hardly speak civilly to each other. This is how I grew up, and I swore it wouldn't be like this for my kids."

Ignoring his hard stance, I reach out and smooth his sleeve. "You never told me Etta and Hank fought. I thought..." My brain searches for some knowledge of this part of Jackson's memory, but he never told me this, I'm sure of it. "We can talk, Jackson. We don't have to fight."

"Whatever." He shrugs off my hand and steps to the door. He stares at his hand on the screen door handle, takes a deep breath. "Your little party tonight will be fine. If it gets to be too much, I'll just leave quietly and not make a scene in front of your friends."

He pulls open the door but stops when he hears me laughing.

"Are you serious? You sound so melodramatic. So your parents fought. We're fighting. Things aren't perfect. We'll fix it all. We're fine, do you hear me? We're fine."

Jackson nods but doesn't look back at me. "Sure." Then he leaves me alone on the porch.

Cold and alone.

Chapter 53

"Your tree is beautiful." Laney stands next to me, gazing up at the tree with a cup of eggnog perched in her palm.

Susan comes up behind us and yanks at her ponytail as she steps close to both of us and then leans her head toward us. "Jackson wanted me to tell you he's going for a walk out on the old train bridge. What's going on?"

My hand voluntarily runs through my hair, rearranging the layers I'd so carefully arranged earlier. "I don't want to talk about it, but we're fighting. He came home all tired and unhappy from work last week when he found out I'd told Will about Shelby, and he thinks things here at home move on without him because he's gone so much. And, well, me. He says I've changed." My hand holding my egg nog pushes forward. "And you know what? I have."

Laney tsks. "Well watching his daddy mess around with his ex-wife has to be screwing up his mind, too."

"Oh, yeah, that." They both lean even closer and as one we turn our heads to watch Shelby standing behind Hank, massaging his shoulders.

"What about that?" Laney asks.

"They are having an affair. Etta told me. She actually caught them out on her grandmother's quilt in the backyard over a year ago."

"What?" is said in horrified unison. "She caught them?" And now we all look to find Etta, standing near the stairs, in a brown velour top and pants, with a couple long loops of pearls.

Laney shakes her head and mummers, "First that jeweled necklace at the ball and now those pearls. I didn't think Jackson's folks had money?"

"They don't. He's making some extra with these books, but barely enough to pay their travel expenses. Why?"

Laney squints. "Honey, those are real, just like the jewels at the ball. Those ropes around her neck right now are worth an easy ten grand. Look how long they are and how perfectly matched."

Susan and I just stare. Then Laney laughs. "Of course my keen eye came in handy at poker. Did I tell you it's all wrapped up, and I'm out of the treasurer's job?"

Susan nods. "Griffin told me. I hope you've learned your lesson."

"Yep, never try to do a good deed for a stingy, stuck in the dark ages, unappreciative, bunch of jerks. Present company excluded."

Her sister frowns, "I meant about gambling."

"Oh, yeah, the lesson about not telling anyone what you're doing? Yep, got that lesson, too."

"Never mind," Susan sighs. "So what does Anna think of Peter's house?"

"She's over the moon. But can you believe he bought the one only two doors down from Missus and FM?"

Laney wrinkles her nose and pushes up the sleeves of her navy and red sweater. "He's got a mess on his hands. The Wickham house is practically falling down. Wonder where he'll stay until its ready?" Her hip juts out and shoves me. "Got any extra room up here at the Trackside Delight?"

"No!" comes out a little more forceful than I meant, and both

Laney and Susan stare at me.

"Wait just a gosh darn minute, is that what's got Jackson's panties in a wad?" Laney's eyes widened. "He thinks there's something going on with you and Peter?"

My face flames and my eyes fly back and forth making sure no can over hear her. As my glance races past the front door the person coming in causes my eyes to fly back there and stay. "Look, FM is here."

We watch him greet folks and make straight for Peter and Anna. FM shakes Peter's hand and then talks quietly with him. Then with a slight turn he faces Anna and opens his arms. She falls into his arms, and they hug for quite a while. Peter's eyes look damp and that wetness seems to spread across the room. In the midst of the tenderness, my attention is called back to the front door. This time by a shout.

"Mom, we're going to get something we'll be right back, okay?" Savannah, Angie, Jenna, and Susie Mae are in a tight knot squeezing out the door together.

"Where are you going?" is met with the closing of the door.

Susan, Laney, and I all shrug our shoulders at each other, then separate to talk to other people. In addition to mine and Jackson's families, there's only Susan and Griffin, Laney and Shaw, and Peter and FM. The college kids are mostly upstairs. I step to be half hidden by the Christmas tree so I can survey the room. Quickly, I skip over Hank and Shelby. Etta is no longer by the stairs. Matter of fact, she's no longer in the room. My parents are sitting on the couch and visiting with Griffin and Shaw. Susan went over to sit on the floor beside Griffin, but he pulled her onto his lap in the rocking chair. They share a look of gratitude and appreciation for still being together after an awful year for them.

Watching Griffin and Susan makes me miss my husband. I'm going to go find Jackson, but as I step away from the tree he comes in the kitchen door, so I turn that direction, however,

Etta beats me there, coming from the B&B hall. Not wanting to intrude, but not wanting to let him get away, I pause in the doorway.

"Here, Carolina, you come here, too." Etta holds a hand out for me. Her other hand is laced with Jackson's. Her whisper is intense, and there's something like excitement in her voice. "Son, I told Carolina this morning what I told you Friday when you came home—"

"You told him about, about, well, you know?" I stammer.

"Yes, about his father and Shelby, which helps explain why he ran off on the camping trip, doesn't it? He didn't tell you because I asked him not to." Her eyebrows straighten and press down. "How stupid of me, but I've lived with knowing what's going on for so long I forgot how upsetting the news would be." She raises one eyebrow at me. "Like I said this morning, always just trying to keep the peace at all costs. Completely ignoring how I *should* feel or *do* feel. Stupid, stupid."

Jackson's eyes are no longer cold or hard or distant. Pain fills them as he watches his mother. He reaches to hug her, but she steps back.

"No, no sympathy or pity. I'm sick to death of feeling sorry for myself and just going along."

"But what are you going to do?" I ask, like I did this morning. Then suddenly her eyes no longer match our mournful ones. Hers turn merry and twinkling.

"Darlings, I'm moving to the beach!" she squeals. "My grandfather, you know the one that was divorced from my grandmother?"

Both Jackson and I nod. All I knew about that was what I'd been told this morning. Between that revelation and Jackson telling me Hank and Etta fought all of his growing up tells me how very little I've settled for knowing about my husband's family. Have I just not heard it, or just not cared enough to wonder? Either way, it's not right.

"Well, apparently after he left Grandmother, he made a lot of money and actually left a trust for my mother and her sisters. However, when Grandmother changed their names to her maiden name, everything got confused. A lawyer contacted me in October to tell me of my inheritance since Mother is gone and I'm an only child."

"Oh, that explains the jewelry."

Etta lifts the pearls toward me, "You noticed?"

"Well, Laney did. They're beautiful, but what about you moving to the beach?"

Etta looks around as if making sure we're still alone in the kitchen. Then she whispers, "I'm tired of playing the long-suffering wife. Hank and Shelby can have the house in Kentucky and the whole Hillbilly Hank universe with my blessing. Here, look at this." Out of her pocket she pulls a sheet of paper, a realtor's page from a website. A white and gray, raised house sits on sand and at its back is the ocean. A full description of the house is listed below the picture.

Jackson finally says something, "So, uh, what's this?"

His mother beams, "My new home. And look, the basement apartment has doors leading right onto the beach. That's where y'all will stay when you visit."

"You bought it, already?" I ask.

"The realtor called me just a little while ago to tell me the owners accepted my offer."

"But have you even seen it?" Jackson's face is pale and his voice is raspy.

"Of course, silly, when Hillbilly Hank did the South Carolina tour. It's near Beaufort, not far from the B&B we stayed in. It was for sale, and while Hank and Shelby were, well, busy one day, I got a tour of it. I dreamed of that house and escaping, but never thought it could come true. Even after I got the money, I didn't think I could, but being here with you and seeing how you've changed your lives, well, son, you gave me the courage to make my life more." She drops my hand and reaches up to gather her tall, blond, stunned son to her wide chest.

While they hug, my hands find the back of the kitchen table chair nearest me to lean on. My feelings are so jumbled. What must Jackson be thinking? His parents are splitting up and his mother is thrilled. Ecstatic. Overjoyed. And does this mean his ex-wife will become his stepmother? Yikes.

Etta lets go of him and folds up her paper to slide back in her pocket. "Now, I'm not telling everyone until after Christmas Day. On the day after Christmas, Will is driving me home, I've already checked with him, and I've lined up a moving company to pack up the things I want at the house in Kentucky. Mostly pictures and plants and clothes. Hank and Shelby can have the rest of it. And before they even get home from here, I'll be gone. That is, if they can stay here for the rest of the week? Would that be all right with you two?"

"Mom, I need some time to process all this. Don't you think you're moving a little fast?"

"Honey, no. I've not moved at all in so many years that it would take a couple decades of light speed to even catch up with where I should be." She tips her head forward but looks up through her eyelashes at me. "Change is much easier to take when it happens slow and steady. However, some of us have no idea we need to change until things are almost unchangeable. Right, Carolina?"

I nod and Jackson clears his throat. "I'm sure all this somehow applies to things here, but right now my head's too screwed up to figure it out. So, whatever makes you happy, Mom, makes me happy." He clears his throat again, "When are you going to tell Dad?"

Etta frowns. "Soon." Then she grins and hesitates. "Maybe I shouldn't tell you this, but just now while everyone's been visiting and eating cookies, I moved all his stuff out of our room and into Shelby's. All that sneaking back and forth must get old. Besides why should I have to put up with his snoring if I don't get any of the benefits of sharing a bed with the man?"

Both Jackson and I groan and turn away. Way, *way* too much information.

CHAPTER 54

My reflection in the back door glass is all I can see once Jackson leaves the deck. Etta is smack dab in the middle of the party in the living room. Her laughter reaches me here. She returned to the party, and Jackson returned to the cold, dark yard. Me? Not sure where I want to return to. As much as I long for a magic wand with the power to make all this disappear, that life back in Marietta in the subdivision house, barricaded from life, no longer attracts me. But where did that feeling go that wherever Jackson is, is where I belong? He always seemed like more than enough and now, well, he's right. My life doesn't revolve around him. Heck, it barely includes him.

Earlier today Mother and Daddy had on *Gone with the Wind* and it was near the end, where Scarlett has married Rhett, and she's loving the freedom she has. Not only the monetary freedom, but the freedom to be herself—smart, savvy, business-like. But it's sad to me, because I know she doesn't know how to hold on to that. I know how the movie ends.

So how do I hold on to what I'm discovering about me? How do I hold on to it all: the B&B, Chancey, and Jackson? There seems to be a gaping hole opening up inside me full of fear about what to do next. Which direction to move, what to want more?

"Hey, girlie," FM says quietly, walking up behind me. His

reflection joins mine in the dark glass.

"Hey, FM." When I turn, his smile makes me smile. "That sure was sweet with you and Anna out there."

"Yeah, I like her. Really do. Missus just ain't enough anymore."

"What?" Was he reading my mind?

"Don't go getting me wrong, I love her. Always have, always will. But she's not enough anymore to make me turn away from my son. I always let her have the lead about how to treat Peter or about having more kids or..." he shrugs "or just everything. Now this is just for you, but I knew she'd had a baby when I was overseas. Knew it was a girl. That was why we never had no more babies. Missus said she'd lose her mind if she had another girl, knowing she'd given one up." He pulls out a kitchen chair and drops into it. I leave the door and my questions about Jackson to sit down beside him.

"That's another place I let her have her way. We should've found that baby and gotten her back, but no. Too unsettling, too many sins to face. Even now, she swears she's never coming out of the house again. Says she can't face Peter or Anna or the town. Can't face the questions about the man, the father."

"It's mighty tempting to just hide away and not have to face stuff, isn't it?"

FM nods for a while. "Shoot, everyone knows I was gone a long time, and she was, *is*, a passionate woman. She made a mistake. A mistake made a long, long time ago." He lifts his head and winks at me. "But it ain't a mistake no more. Peter has a niece. An honest-to-goodness niece. That's something, ain't it?"

"Yes, it is and, FM, she's a doll and, well, she is so much like Missus. Savannah says we should've figured it out a long time ago. Mother actually did. She says we all think of Anna as quiet, but that in all the quiet she's running all our lives."

"And I got me a granddaughter. That's right; she's my wife's granddaughter, so she's mine, too. Wanted me a girl to spoil my whole life, and she's not getting away. Missus can sit in that house and rot. If I have to, I'll move in with Peter and Anna 'cause I don't think that hardhearted, hardheaded woman I'm married to is going to bend. But, like I said, I'm through playing her games."

He stands up and offers me his hand to also stand. "Carolina, we're going to have some fun here in Chancey, now. Aren't you glad y'all moved here?"

And I let it fall into that gaping hole inside me, the gratitude which swells and lifts inside me. It's doesn't fill the hole, but it's a start. However, my eyes drift to the dark glass doors through which Jackson left only minutes ago. There is no going back; there's just walking forward, even if it's dark. "Yes, I am glad."

FM stares into the dark with me and then squeezes my hand. "You're wise, Carolina, but you don't know it. Folks need you to share that wisdom, you hear me? Now, what I really want is some decaf coffee, but the carafe out there is empty. Can we get a new pot started?

"Sure." Turning from the dark windows, the light from the living room reaches out for me and the room, framed by the doorway opening, looks like a painting of a Southern Christmas party. Old and young, red sweaters and red lipstick, magnolia leaf garlands, punchbowl of eggnog, a fire in the fireplace and Mother and Daddy right in the middle of it all. Sorry, but the dark just can't hold a candle to it. And as soon as I get this coffee started, I can return to the midst of the party.

Rummaging through the cabinet takes a moment. "Let me see, the decaf should be right here, yep."

FM measures water into the pot while I scoop the coffee in. Coffee grounds from the third scoop scatter across the counter when I jump at a sudden, loud commotion in the living room. Shouts of "Merry Christmas" reach us, even in the kitchen.

"What in the Sam Hill is going on out there?" We both leave our duties and step to the living room doorway.

Susie Mae and Angie are first in the door and are blocking us from seeing what's behind them.

FM laughs. "I bet we got us some carolers." We both step forward. Then the girls dart to the side and Missus' gray eyes pierce us with lava or magma or something really hot and dangerous. It's hard for her to maintain eye contact as she's bouncing around a lot, and she's not screaming about the bouncing because there's a folded bandana over her mouth. And she's bouncing because she's tied into a wheel chair with bungee cords. However, the bungee cords aren't cutting into her or anything since she's wearing a full-length fur coat.

And my daughter is pushing the wheel chair. Well, Savannah *and* Jenna, which might also explain the bouncing. The girls are arguing about how to get the wheel chair in the door, but more than arguing, they're laughing.

"Get out of the way," Jackson demands as he takes over the handles of the chair and pushes Missus on into the living room. Susie Mae and Angie keep saying, "Ho Ho Ho, Merry Christmas!" and Savannah and Jenna are doubled up laughing, but other than that there is stunned silence.

Peter has come to stand beside his father and he looks at Jackson then asks, "What's going on?"

Jackson pulls his hands off the chair handles and steps back. "I have no idea. I just saw the girls wheel someone up the walk and then lift them up the stairs, so I came running to help."

"Untie her, somebody!" Mother yelps from where she stands beside the couch.

Peter reaches for the bungee cords, and Jackson starts to work on the bandana muzzle, but Peter catches his eye and shakes his head. Missus throws more lava at her son, but he ignores her. "Okay, girls, what's going on? It will take me a little bit to get these untangled, so talk fast while her hands are still bound."

Susie Mae says, "It's a Christmas gift for Anna."

"What?" Anna exclaims. "I didn't have anything to do with

this."

"Of course not. It's *for* you," Jeanna says. "Tell them, Savannah. It was all your idea."

Great, of course it was.

Savannah steps up and lays a hand on Missus shoulder. Funny, you'd think my daughter would've burst into flames by now with the looks she's getting from her hostage. Savannah's stage voice carries, and she's so tall and forceful. Only now do I notice the girls are all wearing dark blue hoodies, so they'd planned their little kidnapping. Great.

"Missus has been so good to us girls since we moved here. She helped me discover my passion for acting. She lets us hang out in her cool attic and look at all that old stuff. She's bought us pizza and soda and lets us try on her furs. In her spare bathroom she's bought ever color of nail polish there is, and she lets us use it all, anytime." Savannah tilts her head and looks down at Missus. "She even bought us black nail polish which was 'against her better judgment'." The dead-on imitation brings forth a few chuckles. "Missus holds tea parties for us and is teaching us how to set a table, really set a table. Not that we'll ever need to know, but her china and silver is so beautiful."

Jenna steps up and links arms with Savannah, "So when we found out she actually had a granddaughter and that the granddaughter was Anna, we were thrilled. How wonderful for everyone."

"Except Missus got all stubborn and mean…"

"Savannah," Daddy says. "Show a little respect for your elders."

Hank laughs. "Think it's a little late for that. She's got her elder tied up and gagged."

"Not for long," Peter tell us. "I'm going to take this last one off, and then she'll get rid of that gag." He moves over to be face to face with his mother. "Mother, I want to hear your side of this, okay? But first just let the girls finish and just sit here, okay?"

I don't know what kind of sign he wanted, but she didn't look like she agreed to anything he said.

"Anyway, like Savannah said," Jenna continues, "Missus wouldn't even talk to Anna. We begged her and tried to explain how great Anna is and how she'd now have her own granddaughter and not have to borrow us. But she said, 'Never' and swore to stay in that house for the rest of her life."

Susie Mae pipes up, "And you know, Missus, she'd do it, too."

Griffin leans toward his daughter from beside the couch, grabs her arm, and pulls her to stand between him and Susan. "This might be better when she gets loose," he murmurs.

Peter stays crouched beside his mother and then reaches up to take off the bandana. "Could someone get her a glass of water?"

Laney just lifts her hand into the air as a sign of willingness and heads through the dining room door toward the kitchen.

Missus squares her shoulders and gives a queenly nod to Peter. "Thank you. Water would be divine. Being kidnapped by young hooligans whom you've taken in and cared for is hard on an old, well a woman or anyone."

Laney bustles through the door behind me, and FM, squeezes through us and broaches Missus. "Here you are." She hand the glass to the hostage and then steps to the side, right near Peter.

Oh, that's why she was so quick to the get the water—an upgrade to a better viewing seat.

Susan prods her niece. "So, how did you come up with this idea?"

Jenna beams. "This is an old wheel chair FM used one time when he had hip surgery and we'd ridden around in it at Missus' house. So we just went to her house, put her in it, tied her up, and brought her here. She doesn't weigh much more than a large dog, so we knew we could handle her."

"A large dog? Take me home right now, Peter. Right this

minute."

Peter stands up and bites his lower lip then he shakes his head. "No."

Missus lifts her elbows to rest on the arms of the chair and rubs her wrists. "Oh, that's right. You decided to leave your family and take up with, with her. I do not know where you think you will get the money to restore the Wickham house. *I* am not paying for it."

FM steps closer to his wife and son, "Well, since it looks like I'll be living at the Wickham house, too, guess I'll be helping them with the bills."

"Don't be ridiculous, FM. You're not moving out. Now, drive me home."

He wiggles his mustache for a moment then crosses his arms. "No."

The fire in Missus' eyes dims and her lips part, but nothing comes out.

FM addresses the room. "Does anyone here think Anna is not Missus' granddaughter?"

Multiple shakes of heads around the room answers him. "Good. Does anyone care how this all came about, you know, all the gory details?" Heads shake a little slower this time, but there is consensus until...

"Well, I do." Laney says. "The child not only has a grandmother, but she has a grandfather somewhere, too. She has a right to know who he is, and well, I am curious, but I can live with that." She sighs. "If I have to."

FM rolls his eyes, "Laney, let us deal with one thing at a time, okay? We'll cross that bridge later."

Missus clears her throat, and the room goes silent. "He was a soldier who was visiting my Aunt Nan, his old teacher, for," her voice weakens, "for an afternoon. It just happened and that should've been my sin to deal with alone, but then I found out my sin would also rest on others, mainly my baby. Everyone knew FM had been gone a year. There didn't seem to be any other choice for me, or for the baby. And FM knew what I'd done. I confessed to him as soon as I knew I was, well…he tried to talk me into staying here and facing the music, but…I couldn't. Just couldn't. So, Peter and I moved to Athens to take care of my supposed aunt for almost a year and then returned to Chancey."

She said all this looking down at her lap. When she looks up, the likeness to Anna is shocking. Gone is the defiance and bitterness, instead out shines Anna's pain and doubt and sadness. Missus lays her hands on the arms of the chair, and she stands. She even walks differently as she brushes past us and finds her way to where Anna stands half-hidden behind the Christmas tree—the same spot I hid in earlier.

"Anna. Please forgive me. I am your grandmother. Your mother was my daughter." Missus opens her arms and reaches for Anna's shoulders. Anna leans into her grandmother and tears stream down her face. Her tiny voice threads its way around the room, "I forgive you. I love you." Over and over.

Then the party really begins.

Chapter 55

Christmas day dawned while we sat piled in the living room in various degree of dress. Bryan woke us up at four, and since we all know our days of seeing Christmas day dawn are dwindling as our littlest one ages, we trudged out of bed. Coffee and reheated cinnamon buns gave us the oomph to open gifts and welcome the sun. But that oomph is gone, and we all stare at the TV screen at our first, of dozen, viewings today of "The Christmas Story" movie set back in the fifties and focused on the obsession a boy has about getting a BB gun for Christmas.

"Hey," Will raises up his head from the unnatural slant it had fallen earlier when he was dozing. "You ever notice in this movie there's no extra family, just the four of them?"

Everyone else, like me, must assume it's a rhetorical question because no one answers. Will continues, "That's how we used to be. Every Christmas, of course there were five of us and not just four. But it was just us five all calm and simple. Now look at us!"

Jackson has Bryan tucked up next to him on one end of the couch. I'm sitting in the floor with my back against the big chair where Mom and Dad are cuddled. Hank rocks in the rocking chair, alone. Since Etta moved him in with Shelby, he's been fairly shell-shocked and not as quick to rub Shelby's back.

Savannah and Will have both figured out what's going on. Shelby has taken to staying in her room (bout time for a little discretion to raise its head) but this morning she's sitting in a dining room chair across the room from both Hank and Etta. Etta holds down the other end of the couch with Savannah snuggled up close to her. Will, is lying on pillows sprawled across the floor. He's rolled onto his back, is looking around the room, and repeats, "Look at us."

As my gaze wanders the room, warmth fills me and a feeling of rightness settles deep inside my hollow place. But the gnawing even deeper inside acknowledges that I'm avoiding meeting Jackson's eyes. What if I can't handle what I find there? We've avoided each other and the busyness of the holiday has easily afforded, and hopefully masked, our distance.

Finally, I let my eyes find Jackson's face, but his eyes focus down on Bryan's head underneath his arm. Jackson strokes Bryan's hair and won't look up, but I find myself unable to look away. What is he thinking?

Bryan moves a little, just shifting a bit, but it breaks his daddy's concentration and Jackson looks up. His eyes meet mine, and we both smile. Sure, there's sadness still there, but he knows this is right. He knows it. Surely, that's what his smile means. Right?

Jackson clears his throat and breaks my gaze to look at his oldest son. "Yeah, Will, just look at us. It's good to be us, isn't it?"

And I wait. Wait for my husband's words to fill that empty space inside me, but they don't. We have to be fine, here. Just have to.

Will looks around at our family a minute more, nods, and then flips back onto his stomach. "But you know, this movie's going to be on all day. Do you think we can watch *Gone with the Wind*? It kinda reminds me of our family now."

Somebody hand me a pillow to throw at him.

Author's Note

Kay is enjoying the publishing glow from her first book, *Next Stop, Chancey*, being so warmly received and, even better, so warmly enjoyed. With the publication of this second book in the Chancey Series, she is settling into the writing and publishing life and finding it better than she ever imagined.

While currently working on the fourth book in the Chancey series, Kay looks forward to the release of the third book in the series in 2016. Kay writes from her home in Fernandina Beach, Florida where she lives with her husband, Mike.

Don't miss...

Next Stop, Chancey
Book One in the Chancey Series

Looking in your teenage daughter's purse is never a good idea.

After all, it ended up with Carolina opening a B&B for railroad buffs in a tiny Georgia mountain town. Carolina knows all about, and hates, small towns. How did she end up leaving her wonderful Atlanta suburbs behind while making her husband's dreams come true?

Unlike back home in the suburbs with privacy fences and automatic garage doors, everybody in Chancey thinks your business is their business and they all love the newest Chancey business. The B&B hosts a senate candidate, a tea for the County Fair beauty contestants, and railroad nuts who sit out by the tracks and record the sound of a train going by. Yet, nobody believes Carolina prefers the 'burbs.

Oh, yeah, and if you just ignore a ghost, will it go away?

Next Stop, Chancey is available in both print and ebook on Amazon.com

You can find out more about Kay and her books on her web-site, kaydewshostak.com

CPSIA information can be obtained
at www.ICGtesting.com
Printed in the USA
LVOW11s0146031116
511448LV00003B/227/P